THE ADVENTURES OF TOM SWIFT

VOLUME 5

Tom Swift and His Photo Telephone

Tom Swift and His Aerial Warship

Tom Swift and His Big Tunnel

Tom Swift In the Land of Wonders

THE ADVENTURES OF TOM SWIFT

VOLUME 5

VICTOR APPLETON

BROWNSTONE BOOKS

CONTENTS

TOM SWIFT AND HIS PHOTO TELEPHONE

Or, THE PICTURE THAT SAVED A FORTUNE

CHAPTER I

A MAN ON THE ROOF

"Tom, I don't believe it can be done!"

"But, Dad, I'm sure it can!"

Tom Swift looked over at his father, who was seated in an easy chair in the library. The elderly gentleman—his hair was quite white now—slowly shook his head, as he murmured again:

"It can't be done, Tom! It can't be done! I admit that you've made a lot of wonderful things—things I never dreamed of—but this is too much. To transmit pictures over a telephone wire, so that persons cannot only see to whom they are talking, as well as hear them—well, to be frank with you, Tom, I should be sorry to see you waste your time trying to invent such a thing."

"I don't agree with you. Not only do I think it can be done, but I'm going to do it. In fact, I've already started on it. As for wasting my time, well, I haven't anything in particular to do, now that my giant cannon has been perfected, so I might as well be working on my new photo telephone instead of sitting around idle."

"Yes, Tom, I agree with you there," said Mr. Swift. "Sitting around idle isn't good for anyone—man or boy, young or old. So don't think I'm finding fault because you're busy."

"It's only that I don't want to see you throw away your efforts, only to be disappointed in the end. It can't be done, Tom, it can't be done," and the aged inventor shook his head in pitying doubt.

Tom only smiled confidently, and went on:

"Well, Dad, all you'll have to do will be to wait and see. It isn't going to be easy—I grant that. In fact, I've run up against more snags, the little way I've gone so far, than I like to admit. But I'm going to stick at it, and before this year is out I'll guarantee, Father, that you can be at one end of the telephone wire, talking to me, at the other, and I'll see you and you'll see me—if not as plainly as we see each other now, at least plainly enough to make sure of each other."

Mr. Swift chuckled silently, gradually breaking into a louder laugh. Instead of being angry, Tom only regarded his father with an indulgent smile, and continued:

"All right, Dad. Go ahead, laugh!"

"Well, Tom, I'm not exactly laughing at *you*—it's more at the idea than anything else. The idea of talking over a wire and, at the same time, having light waves, as well as electrical waves passing on the same conductor!"

"All right, Dad, go ahead and laugh. I don't mind," said Tom, good-naturedly. "Folks laughed at Bell, when he said he could send a human voice over a copper spring; but Bell went ahead and today we can talk over a thousand miles by wire. That was the telephone."

"Folks laughed at Morse when he said he could send a message over the wire. He let 'em laugh, but we have the telegraph. Folks laughed at Edison, when he said he could take the human voice—or any other sound—and fix it on a wax cylinder or a hard-rubber plate—but he did it, and we have the phonograph. And folks laughed at Santos Dumont, at the Wrights, and at all the other fellows, who said they could take a heavier-than-air machine, and skim above the clouds like a bird; but we do it—I've done it—you've done it."

"Hold on, Tom!" protested Mr. Swift. "I give up! Don't rub it in on your old dad. I admit that folks did laugh at those inventors, with their seemingly impossible schemes, but they made good. And you've made good lots of times where I thought you wouldn't. But just stop to consider for a moment. This thing of sending a picture over a telephone wire is totally out of the question, and entirely opposed to all the principles of science."

"What do I care for principles of science?" cried Tom, and he strode about the room so rapidly that Eradicate, the old colored servant, who came in with the mail, skipped out of the library with the remark:

"Deed, an' Massa Tom must be pow'fully preragitated dis mawnin'!"

"Some of the scientists said it was totally opposed to all natural laws when I planned my electric rifle," went on Tom. "But I made it, and it shot. They said my air glider would never stay up, but she did."

"But, Tom, this is different. You are talking of sending light waves—one of the most delicate forms of motion in the world—over a material wire. It can't be done!"

"Look here, Dad!" exclaimed Tom, coming to a halt in front of his parent. "What is light, anyhow? Merely another form of motion; isn't it?"

"Well, yes, Tom, I suppose it is."

"Of course it is," said Tom. "With vibrations of a certain length and rapidity we get sound—the faster the vibration per second the higher the sound note. Now, then, we have sound waves, or vibrations, traveling at the rate of a mile in a little less than five seconds; that is, with the air at a temperature of sixty degrees. With each increase of a degree of temperature we get an increase of about a foot per second in the rapidity with which sound travels."

"Now, then, light shoots along at the rate of 186,000,000 miles a second. That is more than many times around the earth in a second of time. So we have sound, one kind of wave motion, or energy; we have light, a higher degree of vibration or wave motion, and then we come to electricity—and nobody has ever yet exactly measured the intensity or speed of the electric vibrations."

"But what I'm getting at is this—that electricity must travel pretty nearly as fast as light—if not faster. So I believe that electricity and light have about the same kind of vibrations, or wave motion."

"Now, then, if they do have—and I admit it's up to me to prove it," went on Tom, earnestly—"why can't I send light-waves over a wire, as well as electrical waves?"

Mr. Swift was silent for a moment. Then he said, slowly:

"Well, Tom, I never heard it argued just that way before. Maybe there's something in your photo telephone after all. But it never has been done. You can't deny that!"

He looked at his son triumphantly. It was not because he wanted to get the better of him in argument, that Mr. Swift held to his own views; but he wanted to bring out the best that was in his offspring. Tom accepted the challenge instantly.

"Yes, Dad, it has been done, in a way!" he said, earnestly. "No one has sent a picture over a telephone wire, as far as I know, but during the recent hydroplane tests at Monte Carlo, photographs taken of some of the events in the morning, and afternoon, were developed in the evening, and transmitted over five hundred miles of wire to Paris, and those same photographs were published in the Paris newspapers the next morning."

"Is that right, Tom?"

"It certainly is. The photographs weren't so very clear, but you could make out what they were. Of course that is a different system than the one I'm thinking of. In that case they took a photograph, and made a copper plate of it, as they would for a half-tone illustration. This gave them a picture with ridges and depressions in copper, little hills and valleys, so to speak, according to whether there were light or dark tints in the picture. The dark places meant that the copper lines stood up higher there than where there were light colors."

"Now, by putting this copper plate on a wooden drum, and revolving this drum, with an electrical needle pressing lightly on the ridges of copper, they got a varying degree of electrical current. Where the needle touched a high place in the copper plate the contact was good, and there was a strong current. When the needle got to a light place in the copper—a depression, so to speak—the contact was not so good, and there was only a weak current."

"At the receiving end of the apparatus there was a sensitized film placed on a similar wooden drum. This was to receive the image that came over the five hundred miles of wire. Now then, as the electrical needle, moving across the copper plate, made electrical contacts of different degrees of strength, it worked a delicate galvanometer on the receiving end. The galvanometer caused a beam of light to vary—to grow brighter or dimmer, according as the electrical current was stronger or weaker. And this light, falling on the sensitive plate, made a picture, just like the one on the copper plate in Monte Carlo."

"In other words, where the copper plate was black, showing that considerable printing ink was needed, the negative on the other end was made light. Then when that negative was printed it would come out black, because more light comes through the light places on a photograph negative than through the dark places. And so, with the galvanometer making light flashes on the sensitive plate, the galvanometer being governed by the electrical contacts five hundred miles away, they transmitted a photograph by wire."

"But not a telephone wire, Tom."

"That doesn't make any difference, Dad. It was a wire just the same. But I'm not going into that just now, though later I may want to send photographs by wire. What I'm aiming at is to make an apparatus so that when you go into a telephone booth to talk to a friend, you can see him and he can see you, on a specially prepared plate that will be attached to the telephone."

"You mean see him as in a looking-glass, Tom?"

"Somewhat, yes. Though I shall probably use a metal plate instead of glass. It will be just as if you were talking over a telephone in an open field, where you could see the other party and he could see you."

"But how are you going to do it, Tom?"

"Well, I haven't quite decided. I shall probably have to use the metal called selenium, which is very sensitive to light, and which makes a good or a poor electrical conductor according as more or less light falls on it.

After all, a photograph is only lights and shadows, fixed on sensitive paper or films."

"Well, Tom, maybe you can do it, and maybe you can't. I admit you've used some good arguments," said Mr. Swift. "But then, it all comes down to this: What good will it be if you can succeed in sending a picture over a telephone wire?"

"What good, Dad? Why, lots of good. Just think how important it will be in business, if you can make sure that you are talking to the party you think you are. As it is now, unless you know the person's voice, you can't tell that the man on the other end of the wire is the person he says he is. And even a voice can be imitated."

"But if you know the person yourself, he can't be imitated. If you see him, as well as hear his voice, you are sure of what you are doing. Why, think of the big business deals that could be made over the telephone if the two parties could not only hear but see each other. It would be a dead sure thing then. And Mr. Brown wouldn't have to take Mr. Smith's word that it was he who was talking. He could even get witnesses to look at the wire-image if he wanted to, and so clinch the thing. It will prevent a lot of frauds."

"Well, Tom, maybe you're right. Go ahead. I'll say no more against your plans. I wish you all success, and if I can help you, call on me."

"Thanks, Dad. I knew you'd feel that way when you understood. Now I'm going—"

But what Tom Swift was going to do he did not say just then, for above the heads of father and son sounded a rattling, crashing noise, and the whole house seemed to shake Then the voice of Eradicate was heard yelling:

"Good land! Good land ob massy! Come out yeah, Massa Tom! Come right out yeah! Dere's a man on de roof an' he am all tangled up suthin' scandalous! Come right out yeah befo' he falls and translocates his neck! Come on!"

CHAPTER II

BAD NEWS

With startled glances at each other, Tom and his father rushed from the library to the side of the house, whence came the cries of Eradicate.

"What is it, Rad! What is it?" questioned Tom.

"Is someone hurt?" Mr. Swift wanted to know.

"He mighty soon will be!" exclaimed the colored man. "Look where he am holdin' on! Lucky fo' him he grabbed dat chimbley!"

Tom and his father looked to where Eradicate pointed, and saw a strange sight. A small biplane-airship had become entangled in some of the aerials of Tom's wireless apparatus, and the craft had turned turtle, being held from falling by some of the wire braces.

The birdman had fallen out, but had managed to cling to the chimney, so that he had not reached the ground, and there he clung, while the motor of his airship was banging away, and revolving the propeller blades dangerously close to his head.

"Are you hurt?" cried Tom, to the unknown birdman.

"No, but I'm likely to be unless I get out of here!" was the gasped-out answer.

"Hold fast!" cried Tom. "We'll have you down in a jiffy. Here, Rad, you get the long ladder. Where's Koku? That giant is never around when he's wanted. Find Koku, Rad, and send him here."

"Yas, sah, Massa Tom; directly, sah!" and the colored man hastened off as fast as his aged legs would take him.

And while preparations are thus under way to rescue the birdman from the roof, I will take just a few minutes to tell you a little something more about Tom Swift and his numerous inventions, as set forth in the previous books of this series.

"Tom Swift and His Motor Cycle" was the first book, and in that I related how Tom made the acquaintance of a Mr. Wakefield Damon, of the neighboring town of Waterford, and how Tom bought that gentleman's motor cycle, after it had tried to climb a tree with its rider in the saddle. Mr. Wakefield Damon was an odd man, whose favorite expression was "Bless my shoelaces!" or something equally absurd. Waterford was not far from Shopton, where Tom and his father made their home.

Mr. Swift was also an inventor of note, and Tom soon followed in his father's footsteps. They lived in a large house, with many shops about it, for their work at times required much machinery.

Mrs. Baggert was the housekeeper who looked after Tom and his father, and got their meals, when they consented to take enough time from their inventive work to eat. Another member of the household was Eradicate Sampson, a genial old colored man, who said he was named Eradicate because he used to eradicate the dirt about the place.

Koku, just referred to by Tom, was an immense man, a veritable giant, whom Tom had brought back with him from one of his trips, after escaping from captivity. The young inventor really brought two giants, brothers they were, but one had gone to a museum, and the other took service with our hero, making himself very useful when it came to lifting heavy machinery.

Tom had a close friend in Ned Newton, who was employed in the Shopton bank. Another friend was Miss Mary Nestor, a young lady whose life Tom had once saved. He had many other friends, and some enemies, whom you will meet from time to time in this story.

After Tom had had many adventures on his motor cycle he acquired a motor boat, and in that he and Ned went through some strenuous times on Lake Carlopa, near Tom's home. Then followed an airship, for Tom got that craze, and in the book concerning that machine I related some of the things that happened to him. He had even more wonderful adventures in his submarine, and with his electric runabout our hero was instrumental in saving a bank from ruin by making a trip in the speediest car on the road.

After Tom Swift had sent his wireless message, and saved the castaways of Earthquake Island, he thought he would give up his inventive work for a time, and settle down to a life of ease and quiet.

But the call of the spirit of adventure was still too strong for him to resist. That was why he sought out the diamond makers, and learned the secret of Phantom Mountain. And when he went to the Caves of Ice, and there saw his airship wrecked, Tom was well-nigh discouraged, But he managed to get back to civilization, and later undertook a journey to elephant land, with his powerful electric rifle.

Marvelous adventures underground did Tom Swift have when he went to the City of Gold, and I have set down some of them in the book bearing the latter title. Later on he sought the platinum treasure in his air glider. And when Tom was taken captive, in giant land, only his speedy airship saved him from a hard fate.

By this time moving pictures were beginning to occupy a large place in the scientific, as well as the amusement world, and Tom invented a Wizard Camera which did excellent work. Then came the need of a powerful light, to enable Uncle Sam's custom officers on the border to detect the smugglers, and Tom was successful in making his apparatus.

He thought he would take a rest after that, but with the opening of the Panama Canal came the need of powerful guns to protect that important waterway, and Tom made a Giant Cannon, which enabled the longest shots on record to be fired.

Now, some months had passed, after the successful trial of the big weapon, and Tom longed for new activities. He found them in the idea of a photo telephone, and he and his father were just talking of this when interrupted by the accident to the birdman on the roof of the Swift home.

"Have you got that ladder, Rad?" cried the young inventor, anxiously, as he saw the dangerous position of the man from the airship.

"Yas, sah, Massa Tom! I'se a-camin' wif it!"

"And where's Koku? We'll need him!"

"He's a-camin', too!"

"Here Koku!" exclaimed a deep voice, and a big man came running around the corner of the house. "What is it, Master?"

"We must get him down, Koku!" said Tom, simply. "I will go up on the roof. You had better come, too. Rad, go in the house and get a mattress from the bed. Put it down on the ground where he's likely to fall. Lively now!"

"Yas, sah, Massa Tom!"

"Me git my own ladder—dat one not strong 'nuff!" grunted Koku, who did not speak very good English. He had a very strong ladder, of his own make, built to hold his enormous bulk, and this he soon brought and placed against the side of the house.

Meanwhile Tom and his father had raised the one Eradicate had brought, though Tom did most of the lifting, for his father was elderly, and had once suffered from heart trouble.

"We're coming for you!" cried the young inventor as he began to ascend the ladder, at the same time observing that the giant was coming with his. "Can you hold on a little longer?"

"Yes, I guess so. But I dare not move for fear the propellers will strike me."

"I see. I'll soon shut off the motor," said Tom. "What happened, anyhow?"

"Well, I was flying over your house. I was on my way to pay you a visit, but I didn't intend to do it in just this way," and the birdman smiled grimly. "I didn't see your wireless aerials until I was plumb into them, and then it was too late. I hope I haven't damaged them any."

"Oh, they are easily fixed," said Tom. "I hope you and your biplane are not damaged. This way, Koku!" he called to the giant.

"Say, is—is he real, or am I seeing things?" asked the aviator, as he looked at the big man.

"Oh, he's real, all right," laughed Tom. "Now, then, I'm going to shut off your motor, and then you can quit hugging that chimney, and come down."

"I'll be real glad to," said the birdman.

Making his way cautiously along the gutters of the roof, Tom managed to reach the motor controls. He pulled out the electrical switch, and with a sort of cough and groan the motor stopped. The big propellers ceased revolving, and the aviator could leave his perch in safety.

This he did, edging along until he could climb down and meet Tom, who stood near the ladder.

"Much obliged," said the birdman, as he shook hands with Tom. "My name is Grant Halling. I'm a newcomer in Mansburg," he added, naming a town not far from Shopton. "I know you by reputation, so you don't need to introduce yourself."

"Glad to meet you," said the young inventor, cordially. "Rather a queer place to meet a friend," he went on with a laugh and a glance down to the ground. "Can you climb?"

"Oh, yes, I'm used to that. The next thing will be to get my machine down."

"Oh, we can manage that with Koku's help," spoke Tom. "Koku, get some ropes, and see what you and Rad can do toward getting the aeroplane down," he added to the giant. "Let me know if you need any help."

"Me can do!" exclaimed the big man. "Me fix him!"

Tom and Mr. Halling made their way down the ladder, while the giant proceeded to study out a plan for getting the airship off the roof.

"You say you were coming over to see me, when you ran into my wireless aerials?" asked Tom, curiously, when he had introduced his father to the birdman.

"Yes," went on Mr. Halling. "I have been having some trouble with my motor, and I thought perhaps you could tell me what was wrong. My friend, Mr. Wakefield Damon, sent me to you."

"What! Do you know Mr. Damon?" cried Tom.

"I've known' him for some years. I met him in the West, but I hadn't seen him lately, until I came East. He sent me to see you, and said you would help me."

"Well, any friend of Mr. Damon's is a friend of mine!" exclaimed Tom, genially. "I'll have a look at your machine as soon as Koku gets it down. How is Mr. Damon, anyhow? I haven't seen him in over two weeks."

"I'm sorry to say he isn't very well, Mr. Swift."

"Is he ill? What is the trouble?"

"He isn't exactly ill," went on Mr. Halling, "but he is fretting himself into a sickness, worrying over his lost fortune."

"His lost fortune!" cried Tom, in surprise at the bad news concerning his friend. "I didn't know he had lost his money!"

"He hasn't yet, but he's in a fair way to, he says. It's something about bad investments, and he did speak of the trickery of one man, I didn't get the particulars. But he certainly feels very badly over it."

"I should think he would," put in Mr. Swift. "Tom, we must look into this. If we can help Mr. Damon—"

"We certainly will," interrupted Tom. "Now come in the house, Mr. Halling. I'm sure you must be quite shaken up by your upset."

"I am, to tell you the truth, though it isn't the first accident I've had in my airship."

They were proceeding toward the house, when there came a cry from Koku, who had fastened a rope about the airship to lower it.

"Master! Master!" cried the giant. "The rope am slippin'. Grab the end of it!"

CHAPTER III

TOM'S FAILURE

"Come on!" cried Tom, quickly, as, turning', he saw the accident about to happen. "Your craft will surely be smashed if she slips to the ground, Mr. Halling!"

"You're right! This seems to be my unlucky day!" The birdman, limping slightly from his fall, hurried with Tom to where a rope trailed on the ground. Koku had fastened one end to the airship, and had taken a turn of the cable about the chimney. He had been lowering the biplane to the ground, but he had not allowed for its great weight, and the rope had slipped from his big hands.

But Tom and Mr. Halling were just in time. They grabbed the slipping hempen strands, and thus checked the falling craft until Koku could get a better grip.

"All right now," said the giant, when he had made fast the rope. "Me fix now. Master can go."

"Think he can lower it?" asked Mr. Halling, doubtfully.

"Oh, surely," said Tom. "Koku's as strong as a horse. You needn't worry. He'll get it down all right. But you are limping."

"Yes, I jammed my leg a little."

"Don't you want a doctor?"

"Oh, no, not for a little thing like that."

But Tom insisted on looking at his new friend's wound, and found quite a cut on the thigh, which the young inventor insisted on binding up.

"That feels better," said the birdman, as he stretched out on a couch. "Now if you can look my machine over, and tell me what's the matter with it, I'll be much obliged to you, and I'll get on my way."

"Not quite so fast as that!" laughed Tom. "I wouldn't want to see you start off with your lame leg, and certainly I would not want to see you use your aircraft after what she's gone through, until we've given her a test. You can't tell what part you might have strained."

"Well, I suppose you are right. But I think I'd better go to a hotel, or send for an auto and go home."

"Now you needn't do anything of the kind," spoke Tom, hospitably. "We've got lots of room here, and for that matter we have plenty of autos and airships, too, as well as a motor boat. You just rest yourself here. Later we'll look over your craft."

After dinner, when Mr. Halling said he felt much better, Tom agreed to go out with him and look at the airship. As he feared, he found several things the matter with it, in addition to the motor trouble which had been the cause for Mr. Halling's call on the young inventor.

"Can she be fixed?" asked the birdman, who explained that, as yet, he was only an amateur in the practice of flying.

"Oh, yes, we can fix her up for you," said Tom. "But it will take several days. You'll have to leave it here."

"Well, I'll be glad to do that, for I know she will be all the better when you get through with her. But I think I am able to go on home now, and I really ought to. There is some business I must attend to."

"Speaking of business," remarked Tom, "can you tell me anything more of Mr. Damon's financial troubles?"

"No, not much. All I know is that when I called on him the other day I found him with his check book out, and he was doing a lot of figuring. He looked pretty blue and downcast, I can tell you."

"I'm sorry about that," spoke Tom, musingly. "Mr. Damon is a very good friend of mine, and I'd do anything to help him. I certainly wouldn't like to see him lose his fortune. Bad investments, you say it was?"

"Partly so, and yet I'm inclined to think if he does lose his money it will be due to some trickery. Mr. Damon is not the man to make bad investments by himself."

"Indeed he is not," agreed Tom. "You say he spoke of some man?"

"Yes, but not definitely. He did not mention any name. But Mr. Damon was certainly quite blue."

"That's unlike him," remarked Tom. "He is usually very jolly. He must be feeling quite badly. I'll go over and have a talk with him, as soon as I can."

"Do. I think he would appreciate it. And now I must see about getting home."

"I'll take you in one of my cars," said Tom, who had several automobiles. "I don't want to see you strain that injured leg of yours."

"You're very good—especially after I tangled up your wireless aerials; but I didn't see them until I was right into them," apologized Mr. Halling.

"They're a new kind of wire," said Tom, "and are not very plain to see. I must put up some warning signs. But don't worry about damaging them. They were only up temporarily anyhow, and I was going to take them down to arrange for my photo telephone."

"Photo telephone, eh? Is that something new?"

"It will be—if I can get it working," said Tom, with a smile.

A little later Tom had taken Mr. Halling home, and then he set about making arrangements for repairing the damaged airship. This took him the better part of a week, but he did not regret the time, for while he was working he was busy making plans for his newest invention—the photo telephone.

One afternoon, when Tom had completed the repairs to the airship, and had spent some time setting up an experimental telephone line, the young inventor received a call from his chum, Ned Newton.

"Well, well, what are you up to now?" asked Ned, as he saw his chum seated in a booth, with a telephone receiver to his ear, meanwhile looking steadily at a polished metal plate in front of him. "Trying to hypnotize yourself, Tom?"

"Not exactly. Quiet, Ned, please. I'm trying to listen."

Ned was too familiar with his chum's work to take offense at this. The young banker took a seat on a box, and silently watched Tom. The inventor shifted several switches, pressed one button after another, and tilted the polished metal plate at different angles. Then he closed the door of the little telephone booth, and Ned, through the ground glass door, saw a light shining.

"I wonder what new game Tom is up to?" Ned mused.

Presently the door opened, and Tom stuck out his head.

"Ned, come here," he invited. "Look at that metal plate and see if you can notice anything on it. I've been staring at it so steadily that my eyes are full of sticks. See what you can make out."

"What is this?" asked Ned. "No trick; is it? I won't be blown up, or get my eyes full of pepper; will I?"

"Nonsense! Of course not. I'm trying to make a photo telephone. I have the telephone part down pat, but I can't see anything of the photo image. See if you can."

Ned stared at the polished plate, while Tom did things to it, making electrical connections, and tilting it at various angles.

"See anything, Ned?" asked Tom.

The other shook his head.

"Whom am I supposed to see?" he asked.

"Why, Koku is at the other end of the wire. I'm having him help me."

Ned gazed from the polished plate out of a side window of the shop, into the yard.

"Well, that Koku is certainly a wonderful giant," said Ned, with a laugh.

"How so?" asked Tom.

"Why he can not be in two places at once. You say he ought to be at the other end of this wire, and there he is out there, spading up the garden."

Tom stared for a second and then exclaimed:

"Well, if that isn't the limit! I put him in the telephone booth in the machine shop, and told him to stay there until I was through. What in the world is he doing out there?"

"Koku!" he called to the giant, "why didn't you stay at the telephone where I put you? Why did you run away?"

"Ha!" exclaimed the giant, who, for all his great size was a simple chap, "little thing go 'tick-tick' and then 'clap-clap!' Koku no like— Koku t'ink bad spirit in telumfoam—Koku come out!"

"Well, no wonder I couldn't see any image on the plate!" exclaimed Tom. "There was nobody there. Now, Ned, you try it; will you, please?"

"Sure. Anything to oblige!"

"Then go in the other telephone booth. You can talk to me on the wire. Say anything you like—the telephone part is all right. Then you just stand so that the light in the booth shines on your face. The machine will do the rest—if it works."

Ned hurried off and was soon talking to his chum over the wire from the branch telephone in the machine shop. Ned stood in the glare of an electric light, and looked at a polished plate similar to the one in the other booth.

"Are you there, Ned?" asked Tom.

"Yes, I'm here."

"Is the light on?"

"Yes."

"And you're looking at the plate?"

"Sure. Can you see any reflection in your plate?"

"No, not a thing," answered Tom, and there was great discouragement in his voice. "The thing is a failure, Ned. Come on back," and the young banker could hear his chum hang up the telephone receiver at the other end.

"That's too bad," murmured Ned, knowing how Tom must feel. "I'll have to cheer him up a bit."

CHAPTER IV

RUN DOWN

When Ned Newton got back to where Tom sat in the small telephone booth, the young banker found his chum staring rather moodily at the polished metal plate on the shelf that held the talking instrument.

"So it was no go; eh, Tom?"

"No go at all, Ned, and I thought sure I had it right this time."

"Then this isn't your first experiment?"

"Land no! I've been at it, off and on, for over a month, and I can't seem to get any farther. I'm up against a snag now, good and hard."

"Then there wasn't any image on your plate?"

"Not a thing, Ned. I don't suppose you caught any glimpse of me in your plate?" asked Tom, half hopefully.

"No. I couldn't see a thing. So you are going to try and make this thing work both ways, are you?"

"That's my intention, But I can fix it so that a person can control the apparatus at his end, and only see the person he is talking to, not being seen himself, unless he wishes it. That is, I hope to do that. Just now nobody can see anybody," and Tom sighed.

"Give it up," advised Ned. "It's too hard a nut to crack, Tom!"

"Indeed, I'll not give it up, Ned! I'm going to work along a new line. I must try a different solution of selenium on the metal plate. Perhaps I may have to try using a sensitized plate, and develop it later, though I do want to get the machine down so you can see a perfect image without the need of developing. And I will, too!" cried Tom. "I'll get some new selenium."

Eradicate, who came into the shop just then, heard the end of Tom's remarks. A strange look came over his honest black face, and he exclaimed:

"What all am dat, Massa Tom? Yo'ah gwine t' bring de new millenium heah? Dat's de end of de world, ain't it-dat millenium? Golly! Dish yeah coon neber 'spected t' lib t' see dat. De millenium! Oh mah landy!"

"No, Rad!" laughed Tom. "I was speaking about selenium, a sort of metallic combination that is a peculiar conductor of electricity. The more light that shines on it the better conductor it is, and the less light, the poorer."

"It must be queer stuff," said Ned.

"It is," declared Tom. "I think it is the only thing to use in this photo telephone experiment, though I might try the metal plate method, as they did between Monte Carlo and Paris. But I am not trying to make newspaper pictures."

"What is selenium, anyhow?" asked Ned. "Remember, Tom, I'm not up on this scientific stuff as you are."

"Selenium," went on Tom, "was discovered in 1817, by J. J. Berzelius, and he gave it that name from the Greek word for moon, on account of selenium being so similar, in some ways, to tellurium. That last is named after the Latin word tellus, the earth."

"Do they dig it?" Ned wanted to know.

"Well, sometimes selenium is found in combination with metals, in the form of selenides, the more important minerals of that kind being eucharite, crooksite, clausthalite, naumannite and zorgite—"

"Good night!" interrupted Ned, with a laugh, holding up his hands. "Stop it, Tom!" he pleaded. "You'll give me a headache with all those big words."

"Oh, they're easy, once you get used to them," said the young inventor, with a smile. "Perhaps it will be easier if I say that sometimes selenium is found in native sulphur. Selenium is usually obtained from the flue-dust or chamber deposits of some factory where sulphuric acid is made. They take this dust and treat it with acids until they get the pure selenium. Sometimes selenium comes in crystal forms, and again it is combined with various metals for different uses."

"There's one good thing about it. There are several varieties, and I'll try them all before I give up."

"That's the way to talk!" cried Ned. "Never say die! Don't give up the ship, and all that. But, Tom, what you need now is a little fun. You've been poking away at this too long. Come on out on the lake, and have a ride in the motor boat. It will do you good. It will do me good. I'm a bit rusty myself—been working hard lately. Come on—let's go out on the lake."

"I believe I will!" exclaimed Tom, after thinking it over for a moment. "I need a little fresh air. Sitting in that telephone booth, trying to get an image on a plate, and not succeeding, has gotten on my nerves. I want to write out an order for Koku to take to town, though. I want to get some fresh selenium, and then I'm going to make new plates."

Tom made some memoranda, and then, giving Koku the order for the chemist, the young inventor closed up his shop, and went with Ned down to Lake Carlopa, where the motor boat was moored.

This was not the same boat Tom had first purchased, some years ago, but a comparatively new and powerful craft.

"It sure is one grand little day for a ride," remarked Ned, as he got in the craft, while Tom looked over the engine.

"Yes, I'm glad you came over, and routed me out," said the young inventor. "When I get going on a thing I don't know enough to stop. Oh, I forgot something!"

"What?" asked Ned.

"I forgot to leave word about Mr. Railing's airship. It's all fixed and ready for him, but I put on a new control, and I wanted to explain to him about it. He might not know how to work it. I left word with father, though, that if he came for it he must not try it until he had seen me. I guess it will be all right. I don't want to go back to the house now."

"No, it's too far," agreed Ned.

"I have it!" exclaimed Tom. "I'll telephone to dad from here, not to let Halling go up until I come back. He may not come for his machine; but, if he does, it's best to be on the safe side Ned."

"Oh, sure."

Accordingly, Tom 'phoned from his boat-house, and Mr. Swift promised to see the bird-man if he called. Then Ned and Tom gave themselves up to the delights of a trip on the water.

The *Kilo*, which name Tom had selected for his new craft, was a powerful boat, and comfortable. It swept on down the lake, and many other persons, in their pleasure craft, turned to look at Tom's fine one.

"Lots of folks out today," observed Ned, as they went around a point of the shore.

"Yes, quite a number," agreed Tom, leaning forward to adjust the motor. "I wonder what's got into her?" he said, in some annoyance, as he made various adjustments. "One of the cylinders is missing."

"Maybe it needs a new spark plug," suggested Ned.

"Maybe. Guess I'll stop and put one in."

Tom slowed down the motor, and headed his boat over toward shore, intending to tie up there for a while.

As he shifted the wheel he heard a cry behind him, and at the same time a hoarse, domineering voice called out:

"Here, what do you mean, changing your course that way? Look out, or I'll run you down! Get out of my way, you land-lubber, you!"

Startled, Ned and Tom turned. They saw, rushing up on them from astern, a powerful red motor boat, at the wheel of which sat a stout man, with a very florid face and a commanding air.

"Get out of my way!" he cried. "I can't stop so short! Look out, or I'll run you down!"

Tom, with a fierce feeling of resentment at the fellow, was about to shift the course of the *Kilo*, but he was too late.

A moment later there came a smashing blow on the stern port quarter and the *Kilo* heeled over at a dangerous angle, while, with a rending, splintering sound of wood, the big red motorboat swept on past Tom and Ned, her rubstreak grinding along the side of the *Kilo*.

CHAPTER V

SHARP WORDS

"Great Scott, Tom! What happened?"

"I know as much as you, Ned. That fellow ran us down, that's all."

"Are we leaking?" and with this question Ned sprang from his place near the bow, and looked toward the stern, where the heaviest blow had been struck.

The *Kilo* had swung back to an even keel again, but was still bobbing about on the water.

"Any hole there?" cried Tom, as he swung the wheel over to point his craft toward shore, in case she showed a tendency to sink.

"I can't see any hole," answered Ned. "But water is coming in here."

"Then there's a leak all right! Probably some of the seams are opened, or it may be coming in around the shaft stuffing-box. Here, Ned, take the wheel, and I'll start up the engine again," for with the blow the motor had stopped.

"What are you going to do?" asked Ned, as he again made his way forward.

"Take her to shore, of course. It's deep out here and I don't want her to go down at this point."

"Say, what do you think of that fellow, anyhow, Tom?"

"I wouldn't like to tell you. Look, he's coming back."

This was so, for, as the boys watched, the big red motor boat had swung about in a circle and was headed for them.

"I'll tell him what I think of him, at any rate," murmured Tom, as he bent over his motor. "And, later on, I'll let the lawyers talk to him."

"You mean you'll sue him, Tom?"

"Well, I'm certainly not going to let him run into me and spring a leak, for nothing. That won't go with me!"

By this time Tom had the motor started, but he throttled it down so that it just turned the propeller. With it running at full speed there was considerable vibration, and this would further open the leaking seams. So much water might thus be let in that the craft could not be gotten ashore.

"Head her over, Ned," cried Tom, when he found he had sufficient headway. "Steer for Ramsey's dock. There's a marine railway next to him, and I can haul her out for repairs."

"That's the talk, Tom!" cried his chum.

By this time the big, red motor boat was close beside Tom's craft.

The man at the wheel, a stout-bodied and stout-faced man, with a complexion nearly the color of his boat, glared at the two young men.

"What do you fellows mean?" called out the man, in deep booming tones—tones that he tried to make imposing, but which, to the trained ears of Tom and Ned, sounded only like the enraged bellow of some bully. "What do you mean, I say? Getting on my course like that!"

Ned could see Tom biting his lips, and clenching his hands to keep down his temper. But it was too much. To be run into, and then insulted, was more than Tom could stand.

"Look here!" he cried, standing up and facing the red-faced man, "I don't know who you are, and I don't care. But I'll tell you one thing— you'll pay for the damage you did to my boat!"

"I'll pay for it? Come, that's pretty good! Ha! Ha!" laughed the self-important man. "Why, I was thinking of making a complaint against you for crossing my course that way. If I find my boat is damaged I shall certainly do so anyhow. Have we suffered any damage, Snuffin?" and he looked back at a grimy-faced mechinician who was oiling the big, throbbing motor, which was now running with the clutch out.

"No, sir, I don't think we're damaged, sir," answered the man, deferentially.

"Well, it's a lucky thing for these land-lubbers that we aren't. I should certainly sue them. The idea of crossing my course the way they did. Weren't they in the wrong, Snuffin?"

The man hesitated for a moment, and glanced at Tom and Ned, as though asking their indulgence.

"Well, I asked you a question, Snuffin!" exclaimed the red-faced man sharply.

"Yes—yes, sir, they shouldn't have turned the way they did," answered the man, in a low voice.

"Well, of all the nerve!" murmured Tom, and stopped his motor. Then, stepping to the side of his disabled and leaking boat, he exclaimed:

"Look here! Either you folks don't know anything about navigation rules, or you aren't heeding them. I had a perfect right to turn and go ashore when I did, for I found my engine was out of order, and I wanted to fix it. I blew the usual signal on the whistle, showing my intention to turn off my course, and if you had been listening you would have heard it."

"If you had even been watching you would have seen me shift, and then, coming on at the speed you did, it was your place to warn me by a whistle, so that I could keep straight on until you had passed me."

"But you did not. You kept right on and ran into me, and the only wonder is that you didn't sink me. Talk about me getting in your way! Why, you deliberately ran me down after I had given the right signal. I'll make a complaint against you, that's what I will."

If possible the red-faced man got even more rosy than usual. He fairly puffed up, he was so angry.

"Listen to that, will you, Snuffin!" he cried. "Listen to that! He says he blew his whistle to tell us he was going to turn in."

"That's what I did!" said Tom, calmly.

"Preposterous! Did you hear it, Snuffin?" puffed the important man.

"Yes—yes, I think I did, sir," answered the machinist, in a hesitating voice.

"You did? What! You mean to tell me you heard their whistle?"

"Yes—yes, sir!"

"Why—why—er—I—" the big man puffed and blew, but seemed to find no words in which to express himself. "Snuffin, I'll have a talk with you when we get home," he finally said, most significantly. "The idea of saying you heard a whistle blown! There was nothing of the kind! I shall make a complaint against these land-lubbers myself. Do you know who they are, Snuffin?"

"Yes—yes, sir," was the answer, as the man glanced at Tom. "At least I know one of them, sir."

"Very good. Give me his name. I'll attend to the rest."

Tom looked at the big man sharply. He had never seen him before, as far as he could recall. As for the machinist, the young inventor had a dim recollection that once the man might have worked in his shop.

"Go ahead, Snuffin!" said the big man, mopping his face with a large silk handkerchief, which, even at that distance, gave out a powerful perfume. "Go ahead, Snuffin, and we will settle this matter later," and, adjusting a large rose in his buttonhole, the self-important individual took his place on the cushioned seat at the wheel, while the big red motor boat drew off down the river.

"Well, of all the nerve!" gasped Ned. "Isn't he the limit?"

"Never mind," spoke Tom, with a little laugh. "I'm sorry I lost my temper, and even bothered to answer him. We'll let the lawyers do the rest of the talking. Take the wheel, Ned."

"But are you going to let him get away like this, Tom? Without asking him to pay for the damage to your boat, when he was clearly in the wrong?"

"Oh, I'll ask him to pay all right; but I'll do it the proper way. Now come on. If we stay here chinning much longer the *Kilo* will go down. I must find out who he is. I think I know Snuffin—he used to work for me, I now recall."

"Don't you know who that big man is?" asked Ned, as he took the wheel, while Tom again started the motor. The water was now almost up to the lower rim of the fly wheel.

"No; who is he?" asked Tom.

"Shallock Peters."

"Well, I know as much as I did before," laughed Tom. "That doesn't tell me anything."

"Why, I thought everybody in the town knew Shallock Peters," went on Ned. "He tried to do some business with our bank, but was turned down. I hear he's gone to the other one, though. He's what we call a get-rich-quick schemer, Tom—a promoter."

"I thought he acted like that sort of a character."

"Well, that's what he is. He's got half a dozen schemes under way, and he hasn't been in town over a month. I wonder you haven't seen or heard of him."

"I've been too busy over my photo telephone."

"I suppose so. Well, this fellow Peters struck Shopton about a month ago. He bought the old Wardell homestead, and began to show off at once. He's got two autos, and this big motor boat. He always goes around with a silk hat and a flower in his buttonhole. A big bluff—that's what he is."

"He acted so to me," was Tom's comment. "Well, he isn't going to scare me. The idea! Why, he seemed to think we were in the wrong; whereas he was, and his man knew it, too."

"Yes, but the poor fellow was afraid to say so. I felt sorry for him."

"So did I," added Tom. "Well, *Kilo* is out of commission for the present. Guess we'll have to finish our outing by walking, Ned."

"Oh, I don't mind. But it makes me mad to have a fellow act the way he did."

"Well, there's no good in getting mad," was Tom's smiling rejoinder. "We'll take it out of him legally. That's the best way in the end. But I can't help saying I don't like Mr. Shallock Peters."

"And I don't either," added Ned.

CHAPTER VI

A WARNING

"There, she's about right now, Ned. Hold her there!"

"Aye, aye, Captain Tom!"

"Jove, she's leaking like a sieve! We only got her here just in time!"

"That's right," agreed Ned.

Tom and his chum had managed to get the *Kilo* to Ramsey's dock, and over the ways of the inclined marine railway that led from the shop on shore down into the river. Then, poling the craft along, until she was in the "cradle," Ned held her there while Tom went on shore to wind up the windlass that pulled the car, containing the boat, up the incline.

"I'll give you a hand, as soon as I find she sets level," called Ned, from his place in the boat.

"All right—don't worry. There are good gears on this windlass, and she works easy," replied Tom.

In a short time the boat was out of the water, but, as Tom grimly remarked, "the water was not out of her," for a stream poured from the stuffing-box, through which the propeller shaft entered, and water also ran out through the seams that had been opened by the collision.

"Quite a smash, Tom," observed the boat repairer, when he had come out to look over the *Kilo*. "How'd it happen?"

"Oh, Shallock Peters, with his big red boat, ran into us!" said Ned, sharply.

"Ha, Peters; eh?" exclaimed the boatman. "That's the second craft he's damaged inside a week with his speed mania. There's Bert Johnson's little speeder over there," and he pointed to one over which some men were working. "Had to put a whole new stern in her, and what do you think that man Peters did?"

"What?" asked Tom, as he bent down to see how much damage his craft had sustained.

"He wouldn't pay young Johnson a cent of money for the repairs," went on Mr. Houston, the boatman. "It was all Peters's fault, too."

"Couldn't he make him pay?" asked Tom.

"Well, young Johnson asked for it—no more than right, too; but Peters only sneered and laughed at him."

"Why didn't he sue?" asked Ned.

"Costs too much money to hire lawyers, I reckon. So he played you the same trick; eh. Tom?"

"Pretty much, yes. But he won't get off so easily, I can tell you that!" and there was a grim and determined look on the face of the young inventor. "How long will it take to fix my boat, Mr. Houston?"

"Nigh onto two weeks, Tom. I'm terrible rushed now."

Tom whistled ruefully.

"I could do it myself quicker, if I could get her back to my shop," he said. "But she'd sink on the home trip. All right, do the best you can, Mr. Houston."

"I will that, Tom."

The two chums walked out of the boat-repair place.

"What are you going to do, Tom?" asked Ned, as they strolled along.

"Well, since we can't go motor boating, I guess I may as well go back and see if that new supply of selenium has come. I do want to get my photo telephone working, Ned."

"And that's all the outing you're going to take—less than an hour!" exclaimed Ned, reproachfully.

"Oh, well, all you wanted to do was to get me out of a rut, as you called it," laughed Tom. "And you've done it—you and Mr. Peters together. It jolted up my brain, and I guess I can think better now. Come on back and watch me tinker away, Ned."

"Not much! I'm going to stay out and get some fresh air while I can. You'd better, too."

"I will, later."

So Tom turned back to his workshop, and Ned strolled on into the country, for his day's work at the bank was over. And for some time after that—until far into the night—Tom Swift worked at the knotty problem of the photo telephone.

But the young inventor was baffled. Try as he might, he could not get the image to show on the metal plate, nor could he get any results by using a regular photographic plate, and developing it afterward.

"There is something wrong with the transmission of the light waves over the wire," Tom confessed to his father.

"You'll never do it, Tom," said the aged inventor. "You are only wasting a whole lot of time."

"Well, as I haven't anything else to do now, it isn't much loss," spoke Tom, ruefully. "But I'm going to make this work, Dad!"

"All right, son. It's up to you. Only I tell you it can't be done."

Tom, himself, was almost ready to admit this, when, a week later, he seemed to be no nearer a solution of the problem than he was at first. He had tried everything he could think of, and he had Eradicate and Koku, the giant, almost distracted, by making them stay in small telephone booths for hours at a time, while the young inventor tried to get some reflection of one face or the other to come over the wire.

Koku finally got so nervous over the matter, that he flatly refused to "pose" any longer, so Tom was forced to use Eradicate. As for that elderly man of all work, after many trials, all unsuccessful, he remarked:

"Massa Tom, I reckon I knows what's wrong."

"Yes, Rad? Well, what is it?"

"Mah face am too black—dat's de trouble. You done want a white-complected gen'man to stand in dat booth an' look at dat lookin' glass plate. I'se too black! I suah is!"

"No, that isn't it, Rad," laughed Tom, hopelessly. "If the thing works at all it will send a black man's face over the wire as well as a white man's. I guess the truth of it is that you're like Koku. You're getting tired. I don't know as I blame you. I'm getting a bit weary myself. I'm going to take a rest. I'll send for another kind of selenium crystals I've heard of, and we'll try them. In the meanwhile—I'll take a little vacation."

"Get out my small airship, Rad, and I'll take a little flight."

"Dat's de way to talk, Massa Tom," was the glad rejoinder.

"I'm going over to see Mr. Damon, Father," announced Tom to Mr. Swift a little later, when his speedy monoplane was waiting for him. "I haven't seen him in some time, and I'd like to get at the truth of what Mr. Halling said about Mr. Damon's fortune being in danger. I'll be back soon."

"All right, Tom. And say—"

"Yes, Dad, what is it?" asked Tom, as he paused in the act of getting in the seat.

"If he wants any ready cash, you know we've got plenty."

"Oh, sure. I was going to tell him we'd help him out."

Then, as Koku spun the propeller blades, Tom grasped the steering wheel, and, tilting the elevating rudder, he was soon soaring into the air, he and his craft becoming smaller and smaller as they were lost to sight in the distance, while the rattle and roar of the powerful motor became fainter.

In a comparatively short time Tom had made a successful landing in the big yard in front of Mr. Damon's house, and, walking up the path, kept a lookout for his friend.

"I wonder why he didn't come out to meet me?" mused Tom, for usually when the eccentric man heard the throbbing of Tom's motor, he was out waiting for the young inventor. But this time it was not the case.

"Is Mr. Damon in?" Tom asked of the maid who answered his ring.

"Yes, Mr. Swift. You'll find him in the library," and she ushered him in.

"Oh, hello, Tom," greeted Mr. Damon, but the tone was so listless, and his friend's manner so gloomy that the young inventor was quite embarrassed.

"Have a chair," went on Mr. Damon. "I'll talk to you in a minute, Tom. I've got to finish this letter, and it's a hard one to write, let me tell you."

Now Tom was more astonished than ever. Not once had Mr. Damon "blessed," anything, and when this did not happen Tom was sure something was wrong. He waited until his friend had sealed the letter, and turned to him with a sigh. Then Tom said boldly:

"Mr. Damon, is it true that you're having hard luck—in money matters?"

"Why, yes, Tom, I'm afraid I am," was the quick answer. "But who told you?"

"Grant Halling. He was over to get me to fix his airship," and Tom briefly related what had happened.

"Oh, yes, I did mention the matter to him," went on Mr. Damon, and his tone was still listless. "So he told you; did he? Well, matters aren't any better, Tom. In fact, they're worse. I just had to write to a man who was asking for help, and I had to refuse him, though he needs it very much. The truth is I hadn't the money. Tom, I'm afraid I'm going to be a very poor man soon."

"Impossible, Mr. Damon! Why, I thought your investments—"

"I've made some bad ones of late, Tom. I've been pretty foolish, I'm afraid. I drew out some money I had in government bonds, and invested in certain stocks sold by a Mr. Shallock Peters."

"Shallock Peters!" cried Tom, almost jumping out of his chair. "Why, I know him—I mean I've met him."

"Have you, Tom? Well, then, all I've got to say is to steer clear of him, my boy. Don't have anything to do with him," and, with something of a return of his usual energy Mr. Damon banged his fist down on his desk. "Give him a wide berth, Tom, and if you see him coming, turn your back. He'd talk a miser into giving him his last cent. Keep away from

Shallock Peters, Tom. Bless my necktie, he's a scoundrel, that's what he is!" and again Mr. Damon banged his desk forcibly.

CHAPTER VII

SOFT WORDS

"Well, I'm glad of one thing!" exclaimed Tom, when the ink bottle and the paper cutter on Mr. Damon's desk had ceased rattling, because of the violence of the blow. "I'm glad of one thing."

"What's that, Tom?" asked his friend.

"I heard you bless something at last—the first time since I came in."

"Oh!" and Mr. Damon laughed. "Well, Tom, I haven't been blessing things lately—that's a fact. I haven't had the heart for it. There are too many business complications. I wish I'd never met this Peters."

"So do I," said Tom. "My motor boat would not have been damaged then."

"Did he do that, Tom?"

"He certainly did, and then he accused me of being at fault."

"That would be just like him. Tell me about it, Tom."

When the young inventor finished the story of the collision Mr. Damon sat silent for a moment. Then he remarked slowly:

"That's just like Peters. A big bluff—that's what he is. I wish I'd discovered that fact sooner—I'd be money in pocket. But I allowed myself to be deceived by his talk about big profits. At first he seemed like a smart business man, and he certainly had fine recommendations. But I am inclined to believe, now, that the recommendations were forged."

"What did he do to you, Mr. Damon?" asked Tom, with ready sympathy.

"It's too complicated to go into details over, Tom, but to make a long story short, he got me to invest nearly all my fortune in some enterprises that, I fear, are doomed to failure. And if they do fail, I'll be a ruined man."

"No, you won't!" exclaimed Tom. "That's one reason why I came here today. Father told me to offer you all the ready money you needed to get out of your trouble. How much do you need, Mr. Damon?"

"Bless my collar button! That's like your father, Tom," and now Mr. Damon seemed more like his old self. "Bless my shoes, a man never knows who his real friends are until trouble comes. I can't say how I thank you and your father, Tom. But I'm not going to take advantage of him."

"It wouldn't be taking any advantage of him, Mr. Damon. He has money lying idle, and he'd like to have you use it."

"Well, Tom, I might use it, if I had only myself to think about. But there's no use in throwing good money after bad. If I took yours now this fellow Peters would only get it, and that would be the last of it."

"No, Tom, thank you and your father just the same, but I'll try to weather the storm a bit longer myself. Then, if I do go down I won't drag anybody else with me. I'll hang on to the wreck a bit longer. The storm may blow over, or—or something may happen to this fellow Peters."

"Has he really got you in his grip, Mr. Damon?"

"He has, and, to a certain extent, it's my own fault. I should have been suspicious of him. And now, Tom, let me give you a further word of warning. You heard me say to steer clear of this Peters?"

"Yes, and I'm going to. But I'm going to make him pay for damaging my boat, if I possibly can."

"Maybe it would be wiser not to try that, Tom. I tell you he's a tricky man. And one thing more. I have heard that this man Peters makes a specialty of organizing companies to take up new inventions."

"Is that so?" asked Tom, interestedly.

"Yes, but that's as far as it goes. Peters gets the invention, and the man, out of whose brain it came, gets nothing."

"In other words, he swindles them?"

"That's it, Tom. If not in one way, then in another. He cheats them out of the profits of their inventions. So I want to warn you to be on the lookout."

"Don't worry," said Tom. "Peters will get nothing from my father or me. We'll be on our guard. Not that I think he will try it, but it's just as well to be warned. I didn't like him from the moment he ran into me, and, now that I know what he has done to you, I like him still less. He won't get anything from me!"

"I'm glad to hear you say so, Tom. I wish he'd gotten nothing out of me."

"Are you sure you won't let my father help you, financially, Mr. Damon?"

"No, Tom, at least not for the present. I'm going to make another fight to hold on to my fortune. If I find I can't do it alone, then I'll call on you. I'm real glad you called. Bless my shoestring! I feel better now."

"I'm glad of it," laughed Tom, and he saw that his friend was in a better state of mind, as his "blessings" showed.

Tom remained for a little longer, talking to Mr. Damon, and then took his leave, flying back home in the airship.

"Gen'man t' see yo', Massa Tom," announced Eradicate, as he helped Tom wheel the monoplane back into the shed.

"Is that so, Rad? Where is he?"

"Settin' in th' library. Yo' father am out, so I asted him in dere."

"That's right, Rad. Who is he, do you know?"

"No, sah, Massa Tom, I doan't. He shore does use a pow'ful nice perfume on his pocket hanky, though. Yum-yum!"

"Perfume!" exclaimed Tom, his mind going back to the day he had had the trouble with Mr. Peters. "Is he a big, red-faced man, Rad?"

"No, sah, Massa Tom. He's a white-faced, skinny man."

"Then it can't be Peters," mused Tom. "I guess perhaps it's that lawyer I wrote to about bringing suit to get back what it cost me to have the *Kilo* fixed. I'll see him at once. Oh, by the way, it isn't Mr. Grant Halling; is it? The gentleman who got tangled up in our aerials with his airship? Is it he?"

"No, sah, Massa Tom. 'Tain't him."

"I thought perhaps he had gotten into more trouble," mused Tom, as he took off his airship "togs," and started for the house. For Mr. Halling had called for his repaired airship some time ago, and had promised to pay Tom another and more conventional visit, some future day.

Tom did not know the visitor whom he greeted in the library a little later. The man, as Eradicate had said, was rather pale of face, and certainly he was not very fleshy.

"Mr. Tom Swift, I think?" said the man, rising and holding out his hand.

"That's my name. I don't believe I know you, though."

"No, I haven't your reputation," said the man, with a laugh that Tom did not like. "We can't all be great inventors like you," and, somehow, Tom liked the man less than before, for he detected an undertone of sneering patronage in the words. Tom disliked praise, and he felt that this was not sincere.

"I have called on a little matter of business," went on the man. "My name is Harrison Boylan, and I represent Mr. Shallock Peters."

Instinctively Tom stiffened. Receiving a call from a representative of the man against whom Mr. Damon had warned him only a short time before was a strange coincidence, Tom thought.

"You had some little accident, when your motor boat and that of Mr. Peters collided, a brief time ago; did you not?" went on Mr. Boylan.

"I did," said Tom, and, as he motioned the caller to be seated Tom saw, with a start, that some of the drawings of his photo telephone were lying on a desk in plain sight. They were within easy reach of the man, and Tom thought the sheets looked as though they had been recently handled. They were not in the orderly array Tom had made of them before going out.

"If he is a spy, and has been looking at them," mused Tom, "he may steal my invention." Then he calmed himself, as he realized that he, himself, had not yet perfected his latest idea. "I guess he couldn't make much of the drawings," Tom thought.

"Yes, the collision was most unfortunate," went on Mr. Boylan, "and Mr. Peters has instructed me to say—"

"If he's told you to say that it was my fault, you may as well save your time," cut in Tom. "I don't want to be impolite, but I have my own opinion of the affair. And I might add that I have instructed a lawyer to begin a suit against Mr. Peters—"

"No necessity for that at all!" interrupted the man, in soft accents. "No necessity at all. I am sorry you did that, for there was no need. Mr. Peters has instructed me to say that he realizes the accident was entirely his own fault, and he is very willing—nay, anxious, to pay all damages. In fact, that is why I am here, and I am empowered, my dear Mr. Swift, to offer you five hundred dollars, to pay for the repairs to your motor boat. If that is not enough—"

The man paused, and drew a thick wallet from his pocket. Tom felt a little embarrassed over what he had said.

"Oh," spoke the young inventor, "the repair bill is only about three hundred dollars. I'm sorry—"

"Now that's all right, Mr. Swift! It's all right," and the man, with his soft words, raised a white, restraining hand. "Not another word. Mr. Peters did not know who you were that day he so unfortunately ran into you. If he had, he would not have spoken as he did. He supposed you were some amateur motor-boatist, and he was—well, he admits it—he was provoked."

"Since then he has made inquiries, and, learning who you were, he at once authorized me to make a settlement in full. So if five hundred dollars—"

"The repair bill," said Tom, and his voice was not very cordial, in spite of the other's persuasive smile, "the bill came to three hundred forty-seven dollars. Here is the receipted bill. I paid it, and, to be frank with you, I intended bringing suit against Mr. Peters for that sum."

"No need, no need at all, I assure you!" interrupted Mr. Boylan, as he counted off some bills. "There you are, and I regret that you and Mr. Peters had such a misunderstanding. It was all his fault, and he wants to apologize to you."

"The apology is accepted," said Tom, and he smiled a trifle. "Also the money. I take it merely as a matter of justice, for I assure you that Mr. Peters's own machinist will say the accident was his employer's fault."

"No doubt of it, not the least in the world," said the caller. "And now that I have this disagreeable business over, let me speak of something more pleasant."

Instinctively Tom felt that now the real object of the man's call would be made plain—that the matter of paying the damages was only a blind. Tom steeled himself for what was to come.

"You know, I suppose," went on Mr. Boylan, smiling at Tom, "that Mr. Peters is a man of many and large interests."

"I have heard something like that," said Tom, cautiously.

"Yes. Well, he is an organizer—a promoter, if you like. He supplies the money for large enterprises, and is, therefore, a benefactor of the human race. Where persons have no cash with which to exploit their—well, say their inventions. Mr. Peters takes them, and makes money out of them."

"No doubt," thought Tom, grimly.

"In other cases, where an inventor is working at a handicap, say with too many interests, Mr. Peters takes hold of one of his ideas, and makes it pay much better than the inventor has been able to do."

"Now, Mr. Peters has heard of you, and he would like to do you good."

"Yes, I guess he would," thought Tom. "He would like to do me—and do me good and brown. Here's where I've got to play a game myself."

"And so," went on Mr. Boylan, "Mr. Peters has sent me to you to ask you to allow him to exploit one, or several, of your inventions. He will form a large stock company, put one of your inventions on the market, and make you a rich man. Now what do you say?" and he looked at Tom and smiled—smiled, the young inventor could not help thinking, like a cat looking at a mouse. "What do you say, Mr. Swift?"

For a moment Tom did not answer. Then getting up and opening the library door, to indicate that the interview was at an end, the young inventor smiled, and said:

"Tell Mr. Peters that I thank him, but that I have nothing for him to exploit, or with which to form a company to market."

"Wha—what!" faltered the visitor. "Do you mean to say you will not take advantage of his remarkable offer?"

"That's just what I mean to say," replied Tom, with a smile.

"You won't do business with Mr. Peters? You won't let him do you good?"

"No," said Tom, quietly.

"Why—why, that's the strangest—the most preposterous thing I ever heard of!" protested Mr. Boylan. "What—what shall I say to Mr. Peters?"

"Tell him," said Tom, "tell him, from me, and excuse the slang, if you like, but tell him there is—nothing doing!"

CHAPTER VIII

TOM IS BAFFLED

Amazement held Mr. Boylan silent for a moment, and then, staring at Tom, as though he could not believe what he had heard the young inventor say, the representative of Mr. Peters exclaimed:

"Nothing doing?"

"That's what I said," repeated Tom, calmly.

"But—but you don't understand, I'm afraid."

"Oh, but indeed I do."

"Then you refuse to let my friend, Mr. Peters, exploit some of your inventions?"

"I refuse absolutely."

"Oh, come now. Take an invention that hasn't been very successful."

"Well, I don't like to boast," said Tom with a smile, "but all of my inventions have been successful. They don't need any aid from Mr. Peters, thank you."

"But this one!" went on the visitor eagerly, "this one about some new kind of telephone," and he motioned to the drawings on the table. "Has that been a success? Excuse me for having looked at the plans, but I did not think you would mind. Has that telephone been a success? If it has not perhaps Mr. Peters could form a company to—"

"How did you know those drawings referred to a telephone?" asked Tom, suspiciously, for the papers did not make it clear just what the invention was.

"Why, I understood—I heard, in fact, that you were working on a new photo telephone, and—"

"Who told you?" asked Tom quickly.

"Oh, no one in particular. The colored man who sent me here mentioned—"

"Eradicate!" thought Tom. "He must have been talking. That isn't like him. I must look into this."

Then to his caller he said:

"Really, you must excuse me, Mr. Boylan, but I don't care to do any business with Mr. Peters. Tell him, with my thanks, that there is really nothing doing in his line. I prefer to exploit my own inventions."

"That is your last word?"

"Yes," returned Tom, as he gathered up the drawings.

"Well," said Mr. Boylan, and Tom could not help thinking there was a veiled threat in his tones, "you will regret this. You will be sorry for not having accepted this offer."

"I think not," replied Tom, confidently. "Good-day."

The young inventor sat for some time thinking deeply, when his visitor had gone. He called Eradicate to him, and gently questioned the old colored man, for Eradicate was ageing fast of late, and Tom did not want him to feel badly.

It developed that the servant had been closely cross-questioned by Mr. Boylan, while he was waiting for Tom, and it was small wonder that the old colored man had let slip a reference to the photo telephone. But he really knew nothing of the details of the invention, so he could have given out no secrets.

"But at the same time," mused Tom, "I must be on guard against these fellows. That Boylan seems a pretty slick sort of a chap. As for Peters, he's a big 'bluff,' to be perfectly frank. I'm glad I had Mr. Damon's warning in mind, or I might have been tempted to do business with him."

"Now to get busy at this photo telephone again. I'm going to try a totally different system of transmission. I'll use an alternating current on the third wire, and see if that makes it any better. And I'll put in the most sensitive selenium plate I can make. I'm going to have this thing a success."

Tom carefully examined the drawings of his invention, at which papers Mr. Boylan had confessed to looking. As far as the young inventor could tell none was missing, and as they were not completed it would be hard work for anyone not familiar with them to have gotten any of Tom's ideas.

"But at the same time I'm going to be on my guard," mused Tom. "And now for another trial."

Tom Swift worked hard during the following week, and so closely did he stick to his home and workshop that he did not even pay a visit to Mr. Damon, so he did not learn in what condition that gentleman's affairs were. Tom even denied himself to his chum Ned, so taken up was the young inventor with working out the telephone problem, until Ned fairly forced himself into the shop one day, and insisted on Tom coming out.

"You need some fresh air!" exclaimed Ned. "Come on out in the motor boat again. She's all fixed now; isn't she?"

"Yes," answered Tom, "but—"

"Oh, 'but me no buts,' as Mr. Shakespeare would say. Come on, Tom. It will do you good. I want a spin myself."

"All right, I will go for a little while," agreed Tom. "I am feeling a bit rusty, and my head seems filled with cobwebs."

"Can't get the old thing to come out properly; eh?"

"No. I guess dad was more than half right when he said it couldn't be done. But I haven't given up. Maybe I'll think of some new plan if I take a little run. Come along."

They went down to the boat house, and soon were out on the lake in the *Kilo*.

"She runs better since you had her fixed," remarked Ned.

"Yes, they did a good job."

"Did you sue Peters?"

"Didn't have to. He sent the money," and Tom told of his interview with Mr. Boylan. This was news to Ned, as was also the financial trouble of Mr. Damon.

"Well," said the young banker, "that bears out what I had heard of Peters—that he was a get-rich-quick chap, and a good one to steer clear of."

"Speaking of steering clear," laughed Tom, "there he is now, in his big boat," and he pointed to a red blur coming up the lake. "I'll give him a wide enough berth this time."

But though Mr. Peters, in his powerful motor boat, passed close to Tom's more modest craft, the big man did not glance toward our hero and his chum. Nor did Mr. Boylan, who was with his friend, look over.

"I guess they've had enough of you," chuckled Ned.

"Probably he wishes he hadn't paid me that money," said Tom. "Very likely he thought, after he handed it over, that I'd be only too willing to let him manage one of my inventions. But he has another guess coming."

Tom and Ned rode on for some distance, thoroughly enjoying the spin on the lake that fine Summer day. They stopped for lunch at a picnic resort, and coming back in the cool of the evening they found themselves in the midst of a little flotilla of pleasure craft, all decorated with Japanese lanterns.

"Better slow down a bit," Ned advised Tom, for many of the pleasure craft were canoes and light row boats. "Our wash may upset some of them."

"Guess you're right, old man," agreed Tom, as he closed the gasolene throttle, to reduce speed. Hardly had he done so than there broke in upon the merry shouts and singing of the pleasureseekers the staccato exhaust of a powerful motor boat, coming directly behind Tom's craft.

Then came the shrill warning of an electrical siren horn.

"Somebody's in a hurry," observed Tom.

"Yes," answered Ned. "It sound's like Peters's boat, too."

"It is!" exclaimed Tom. "Here he comes. He ought to know better than to cut through this raft of boats at that speed."

"Is he headed toward us?"

"No, I guess he's had enough of that. But look at him!"

With undiminished speed the burly promoter was driving his boat on. The big vibrating horn kept up its clamor, and a powerful searchlight in front dazzled the eyes.

"Look out! Look out!" cried several.

Many of the rowers and paddlers made haste to clear a lane for the big, speedy motor craft, and Peters and his friends (for there were several men in his boat now) seemed to accept this as a matter of course, and their right.

"Somebody'll be swamped!" exclaimed Ned.

Hardly had he spoken than, as the big red boat dashed past in a smother of foam, there came a startled cry in girls' voices.

"Look!" cried Tom. "That canoe's upset! Speed her up, Ned! We've got to get 'em!"

CHAPTER IX

A GLEAM OF HOPE

"Where are they?"

"Who are they?"

"Over this way! There's their canoe!"

"Look out for that motor boat!"

"Who was it ran them down? They ought to be arrested!"

These were only a few of the cries that followed the upsetting of the frail canoe by the wash from the powerful red boat. On Tom's *Kilo* there was a small, electrical searchlight which he had not yet switched on. But, with his call to Ned Newton to speed up the motor, that had been slowed down, Tom, with one turn of his fingers, set the lamp aglow, while, with the other hand, he whirled the wheel over to head his craft for the spot where he saw two figures struggling in the water.

Fortunately the lanterns on the various canoes and row-boats, as well as the light on the bow of Tom's *Kilo*, made an illumination that gave the rescuers a good chance to work. Many other boats besides Tom's had headed for the scene, but his was the more practical, since the others—all quite small ones—were pretty well filled.

"There they are, Ned!" Tom suddenly cried. "Throw out the clutch! I'll get 'em!"

"Want any help?"

"No, you stay at the engine, and mind what I say. Reverse now! We're going to pass them!"

Ned threw in the backing gear, and the screw churned the water to foam under the stern of the *Kilo*.

Tom leaned over the bow, and made a grab for the gasping, struggling figure of a girl in the water. At the same time he had tossed overboard a cork life ring, attached to a rope which, in turn, was made fast to the forward deck-cleat. "Grab that!" cried Tom. "Hold on, and I'll have you out in a second! That's enough, Ned! Shut her off!"

The *Kilo* came to a standstill, and, a second later, Tom had pulled into his boat one of the girls. She would have collapsed, and fallen in a heap on the bottom boards, had not Ned, who had come forward from the engine, caught her.

Then Tom, again leaning over the side, pulled in the other girl, who was clinging to the life ring.

"You're all right," Tom assured her, as she came up, gasping, choking and crying hysterically. "You're all right!"

"Is—is Minnie saved?" she sobbed.

"Yes, Grace! I'm here," answered the one Ned was supporting.

"Oh, wasn't it terrible!" cried the second girl Tom had saved.

"I thought we would be drowned, even though we can swim."

"Yes, it—it was so—so sudden!" gasped her companion. "What happened?"

"The wash from that big boat upset you," explained Tom. "That fellow ought to be ashamed of himself, rushing along the way he did. Now, can I take you girls anywhere? Your canoe seems to have drifted off."

"I have it!" someone called. "It's turned over, but I can tow it to shore."

"And I'll take the girls home," offered a gentleman in a large row-boat. "My wife will look after them. They live near us," and he mentioned his own name and the names of the two girls Tom had saved. The young inventor did not know them, but he introduced himself and Ned.

"This is the annual moonlight outing of our little boat club," explained the man who had offered to look after the girls, "and it is the first time we ever had an accident. This was not our fault, though."

"Indeed it was not," agreed Tom, after he had helped the two dripping young ladies into the rowboat. "It was due to Mr. Peters's speed mania."

"I shall make a complaint against him to the navigation authorities," said Mr. Ralston, who was looking after the girls. "He must think he, alone, has any rights on this lake."

With renewed thanks to Tom and Ned, the rescued girls were rowed off to their homes, while the interrupted water carnival was continued.

"Some little excitement; eh, Tom?" remarked Ned, when they were once more under way.

"Yes. We seem to run into that fellow Peters, or some of his doings, quite often lately."

"And it isn't a good sign, either," murmured Ned.

For some minutes after that Tom did not speak. In fact he was so silent that Ned at last inquired:

"What's the matter, Tom—in love?"

"Far from it. But, Ned, I've got an idea."

"And I've got a wet suit of clothes where that nice young lady fainted in my arms. I'm soaked."

"That's what gave me the idea—the water, I mean. I noticed how everything was reflected in it, and, do you know, Ned, I believe I have been working on the wrong principle for my photo telephone."

"Wrong, Tom, how is that?"

"Why, I've been using a dry plate, and I think I should have used a wet one. You know how even in a little puddle of water on the sidewalk you can see yourself reflected?"

"Yes, I've often seen that."

"Well then, 'bless my watch chain!' as Mr. Damon would say, I think I've got just what I want. I'm going to try a wet plate now, and I think it will work. Come on now. Speed up! I'm in a great big hurry to get home and try it!"

"Well, Tom, I sure will be glad if you've got the right idea," laughed Ned. "It will be worth getting wet through for, if you strike something. Good luck!"

Tom could hardly wait to fasten up his boat for the night, so eager was he to get to his shop laboratory and try the new idea. A gleam of hope had come to him.

It was still early evening, and Tom, when enticed out by Ned, had left his photo telephone apparatus in readiness to go on with his trials as soon as he should have come back.

"Now for it, Ned!" exclaimed the young inventor, as he took off his coat. "First I'll sensitize a selenium plate, and then I'll wet it. Water is always a good conductor of electricity, and it's a wonder that I forgot that when I was planning this photo telephone. But seeing the sparkle of lights, and the reflection of ourselves in the lake tonight, brought it back to me. Now then, you haven't anything special to do; have you?"

"Not a thing, Tom."

"That's good. Then you get in this other telephone closet—the one in the casting shop. I'll put a prepared plate in there, and one in the booth where I'm to sit. Then I'll switch on the current, and we'll see if I can make you out, and you notice whether my image appears on your plate."

It took some little time to make ready for this new test. Tom was filled with enthusiasm, and he was sure it was going to be successful this time. Ned watched him prepare the selenium plates—plates that were so sensitive to illumination that, in the dark, the metal would hardly transmit a current of electricity, but in the light would do so readily, its conductivity depending on the amount of light it received.

"There, I guess we're all ready, Ned," announced Tom, at last. "Now you go to your little coop, and I'll shut myself up in mine. We can talk over the telephone."

Seated in the little booth in one of the smaller of Tom's shops, Ned proceeded with his part in the new experiment. A small shelf had been fitted up in the booth, or closet, and on this was the apparatus, consisting of a portable telephone set, and a small box, in which was set a selenium plate. This plate had been wet by a spray of water in order to test Tom's new theory.

In a similar booth, several hundred feet away, and in another building, Tom took his place. The two booths were connected by wires, and in each one was an electric light.

"All ready, Ned?" asked Tom, through the telephone.

"All ready," came the answer.

"Now then, turn on your switch—the one I showed you—and look right at the sensitized plate. Then turn out your light, and slowly turn it on. It's a new kind, and the light comes up gradually, like gas or an oil lamp. Turn it on easily."

"I get you, Tom."

Ned did as requested. Slowly the illumination in the booth increased.

"Do you get anything, Tom?" asked Ned, over the wire.

"Not yet," was the somewhat discouraged answer. "Go ahead, turn on more light, and keep your face close to the plate."

Ned did so.

"How about it now?" he asked, a moment later.

"Nothing—yet," was the answer. And then suddenly Tom's voice rose to a scream over the wire.

"Ned—Ned! Quick!" he called. "Come here—I—I—"

The voice died off into a meaningless gurgle.

CHAPTER X

MIDNIGHT VISITORS

Ned Newton never knew exactly how he got out of the telephone booth. He seemed to give but one jump, tearing the clamped receiver from his ear, and almost upsetting the photo apparatus in his mad rush to help Tom. Certain it is, however, that he did get out, and a few seconds later he was speeding toward the shop where Tom had taken his position in a booth.

Ned burst in, crying out:

"Tom! What is it? What happened? What's the matter?"

There was no answer. Fearing the worst, Ned hurried to the small booth, in one corner of the big, dimly lighted shop. He could see Tom's lamp burning in the telephone compartment.

"Tom! Tom!" called the young banker.

Still there was no answer, and Ned, springing forward, threw open the double, sound-proof door of the booth. Then he saw Tom lying unconscious, with his head and arms on the table in front of him, while the low buzzing of the electrical apparatus in the transmitting box told that the current had not been shut off.

"Tom! Tom!" cried Ned in his chum's ear. He shook him by the shoulder.

"Are you hurt? What is the matter?"

The young inventor seemed unconscious, and for a moment Ned had a wild idea that Tom had been shocked to death, possibly by some crossed live wire coming in contact with the telephone circuit.

"But that couldn't have happened, or I'd have been shocked myself," mused Ned.

Then he became aware of a curious, sweet, sickish odor in the booth. It was overpowering. Ned felt himself growing dizzy.

"I have it—chloroform!" he gasped. "In some way Tom has been overcome by chloroform. I've got to get him to the fresh air."

Once he had solved the puzzle of Tom's unconsciousness, Ned was quick to act. He caught Tom under the arms, and dragged him out of the booth, and to the outer door of the shop. Almost before Ned had reached there with his limp burden, Tom began to revive, and soon the fresh, cool night air completed the work.

"I—I," began the young inventor. "Ned, I—I—"

"Now take it easy, Tom," advised his chum. "You'll be all right in a few minutes. What happened? Shall I call your father, or Koku?"

"No—don't. It would only—only alarm dad," faltered Tom. "I'm getting all right now. But he—he nearly had me, Ned!"

"He had you? What do you mean, Tom? Who had you?"

"I don't know who it was, but when I was talking to you over the wire, all of a sudden I felt a hand behind me. It slipped over my mouth and nose, and I smelled chloroform. I knew right away something was wrong, and I called to you. That's all I remember. I guess I must have gone off."

"You did," spoke Ned. "You were unconscious when I got to you. I couldn't imagine what had happened. First I thought it was an electrical shock. Then I smelled that chloroform. But who could it have been, Tom?"

"Give it up, Ned! I haven't the slightest idea."

"Could they have been going to rob you?"

"I haven't a thing but a nickel watch on me," went on Tom. "I left all my cash in the house. If it was robbery, it wasn't me, personally, they were after."

"What then? Some of your inventions?"

"That's my idea now, Ned. You remember some years ago Jake Burke and his gang held me up and took one of dad's patents away from me?"

"Yes, I've heard you mention that. It was when you first got your motor cycle; wasn't it?"

"That's right. Well, what I was going to say was that they used chloroform on me then, and—"

"You think this is the same crowd? Why, I thought they were captured."

"No, they got away, but I haven't heard anything of them in years. Now it may be they have come back for revenge, for you know we got back the stolen property."

"That's right. Say, Tom, it might be so. What are you going to do about it?"

"I hardly know. If it was Jake Burke, alias Happy Harry, and his crowd, including Appleson, Morse and Featherton, they're a bad lot. I wouldn't want father to know they were around, for he'd be sure to worry himself sick. He never really got over the time they attacked me, and got the patent away. Dad sure thought he was ruined then."

"Now if I tell him I was chloroformed again tonight, and that I think it was Burke and his crowd, he'd be sure to get ill over it. So I'm just going to keep mum."

"Well, perhaps it's the best plan. But you ought to do something."

"Oh, I will, Ned, don't worry about that. I feel much better now."

"How did it happen?" asked Ned, his curiosity not yet satisfied.

"I don't know, exactly. I was in the booth, talking to you, and not paying much attention to anything else. I was adjusting and readjusting the current, trying to get that image to appear on the plate. All at once, I felt someone back of me, and, before I could turn, that hand, with the chloroform sponge, was over my mouth and nose. I struggled, and called out, but it wasn't much use."

"But they didn't do anything else—they didn't take anything; did they, Tom?"

"I don't know, Ned. We'll have to look around. They must have sneaked into the shop. I left the door open, you see. It would have been easy enough."

"How many were there?"

"I couldn't tell. I only felt one fellow at me; but he may have had others with him."

"What particular invention were they after, Tom?"

"I'm sure I don't know. There are several models in here that would be valuable. I know one thing, though, they couldn't have been after my photo telephone," and Tom laughed grimly.

"Why not?" Ned wanted to know.

"Because it's a failure—that's what! It's a dead, sure failure, Ned, and I'm going to give it up!" and Tom spoke bitterly.

"Oh, don't say that!" urged his chum. "You may be right on the verge of perfecting it, Tom. Didn't you see any image at all on the plate?"

"Not a shadow. I must be on the wrong track. Well, never mind about that now. I'm going to look around, and see if those fellows took any-thing."

Tom was feeling more like himself again, the effects of the chloro-form having passed away. He had breathed the fumes of it for only a little while, so no harm had been done. He and Ned made an examination of the shop, but found nothing missing.

There were no traces of the intruders, however, though the two chums looked carefully about outside the building.

"You were too quick for them, Ned," said Tom. "You came as soon as I called. They heard me speaking, and must have known that I had given the alarm."

"Yes, I didn't lose any time," admitted Ned, "but I didn't see a sign of anyone as I ran up."

"They must have been pretty quick at getting away. Well, now to decide what's best to do tonight."

After some consultation and consideration it was decided to set the burglar alarms in every building of the Swift plant. Some time previous, when he had been working on a number of valuable inventions, unscrupulous men had tried to steal his ideas and models. To prevent this Tom had arranged a system of burglar alarms, and had also fitted up a wizard camera that would take moving pictures of anyone coming within its focus. The camera could be set to work at night, in connection with the burglar alarms.

The apparatus was effective, and thus an end was put to the efforts of the criminals. But now it seemed Tom would have to take new precautionary measures. His camera, however, was not available, as he had loaned it to a scientific society for exhibition.

"But we'll attach the burglar wires," decided Tom, "and see what happens."

"It might be a good plan to have Koku on guard," said Tom's chum. "That giant could handle four or five of the chaps as easily as you and I could tackle one."

"That's right," agreed Tom. "I'll put him on guard. Whew! That chloroform is giving me a headache. Guess I'll go to bed. I wish you'd stay over tonight, Ned, if you haven't anything else to do. I may need you."

"Then of course I'll stay, Tom. I'll telephone home that I won't be in."

A little later Tom had put away his new photo telephone apparatus, and had prepared for the warm reception of any unbidden callers.

"I wish I hadn't started on this new invention," said Tom, half bitterly, as he locked up the main parts of his machine, "I know it will never work."

"Oh, yes it will," spoke Ned, cheerfully. "You never failed yet, Tom Swift, in anything you undertook, and you're not going to now."

"Well, that's good of you to say, Ned, but I think you're wrong this time. But I'm not going to think any more about it tonight, anyhow. Now to find Koku and put him on watch."

The giant listened carefully to Tom's simple instructions.

"If any bad men come in the night, Koku," said the young inventor, "you catch them!"

"Yes, master, me catch!" said Koku, grimly. "Me catch!" and he stretched out his powerful arms, and clenched his big hands in a way that boded no good to evildoers.

Nothing was said to Mr. Swift, to Mrs. Baggert, or to Eradicate about what had happened, for Tom did not want to worry them. The burglar alarms were set, Koku took his place where he could watch the signals, and at the same time be ready to rush out, for, somehow, Tom had an idea that the men who had attacked him would come back.

Tom and Ned occupied adjoining rooms, and soon were ready for bed. But, somehow, Tom could not sleep. He lay awake, tossing from side to side, and, in spite of his resolution not to think about his photo telephone invention, his mind ran on nothing but that.

"I can't see what next to do to make it work," he told himself, over and over again. "Something is wrong—but what?"

At length he fell into a fitful doze, and he had a wild dream that he was sliding down hill on a big mirror in which all sorts of reflections were seen—reflections that he could not get to show in the selenium plates.

Then Tom felt the mirror bobbing up and down like a motor boat in a storm. He felt the vibration, and he heard a voice calling in his ear:

"Get up, Tom! Get up!"

"Yes! What is it?" he sleepily exclaimed,

"Hush!" was the caution he heard, and then he realized that his dream had been caused by Ned shaking him.

"Well?" whispered Tom, in tense tones.

"Midnight visitors!" answered his chum "The burglar alarm has just gone off! The airship hangar drop fell. Koku has gone out. Come on!"

CHAPTER XI

THE AIRSHIP IS TAKEN

Tom leaped silently out of bed, and stood for a moment half dazed, so soundly had he been sleeping.

"Come on!" urged Ned softly, realizing that his chum had not fully comprehended. "Koku will hold them until we get there. I haven't roused anyone else."

"That's right," whispered Tom, as he began putting on his clothes. "I don't want father to know. When did it happen?"

"Just a little while ago. I couldn't sleep very well, but I fell into a doze, and then I heard the buzzer of the alarm go off. I saw that the drop, showing that the hangar had been entered, had fallen. I got to the window in time to see Koku going toward the shed from his little coop. Then I came to you."

"Glad you did," answered Tom. "I didn't think I was sleeping so soundly."

Together the two chums made their way from their rooms down the dimly-lighted hall to a side door, whence they could reach the airship hangar, or shed.

"Won't we need something—a gun or—" began Ned.

"Clubs are better—especially at night when you can't see to aim very well," whispered back Tom. "I've got a couple of good ones downstairs. I could use my electric rifle, and set it merely to disable temporarily whoever the charge hit, but it's a little too risky. Koku has a habit of getting in the way at the most unexpected times. He's so big, you know. I think clubs will be best."

"All right, Tom, just as you say," agreed Ned. "But who do you think it can be?"

"I haven't the least idea. Probably the same fellows who were after me before, though. This time I'll find out what their game is, and what they're after."

The chums reached the lower hall, and there Tom picked out two African war clubs which he had brought back with him from one of his many trips into wild lands.

"These are just the thing!" exclaimed Ned, swinging his about.

"Careful," cautioned Tom, "If you hit something you'll rouse the house, and I don't want my father and Mrs. Baggert, to say nothing of Eradicate, awakened."

"Excuse me," murmured Ned. "But we'd better be getting a move on."

"That's right," agreed Tom. He dropped into a side pocket a small but powerful electric flash lamp, and then he and Ned let themselves out.

There had been a bright moon, but it was now overcast by clouds. However, there was sufficient light to enable the two lads to see objects quite clearly. All about them were the various buildings that made up the manufacturing and experimental plant of Tom Swift and his father. Farthest away from the house was the big shed where once Tom had kept a balloon, but which was now given over to his several airships. In front of it was a big, level grassy space, needed to enable the aircraft to get a "running start" before they could mount into the clouds.

"See anything of Koku?" whispered Ned.

"No," answered Tom, in the same cautious voice. "I guess he must be hiding—"

"There he goes now!" hissed Ned, pointing to a big figure that was approaching the hangar. It was undoubtedly that of the giant, and he could be seen, in the dim light, stalking cautiously along.

"I wonder where the uninvited guests are?" asked Tom.

"Probably in the airship shed," answered Ned. "Koku was after them as soon as the alarm went off, and they couldn't have gotten away. They must be inside there yet. But what can their game be?"

"It's hard to say," admitted Tom. "They may be trying to get something belonging to me, or they may imagine they can pick up some valuable secrets. Or they may—" He stopped suddenly, and then exclaimed:

"Come on, Ned! They're after one of the airships! That's it! My big biplane is all ready to start, and they can get it in motion inside of a few seconds. Oh, why didn't I hurry?" he added, bitterly.

But the hangar was still some distance away, and it would take two or three minutes of running to reach it.

Meanwhile, and at the instant Tom had his thought of the possible theft of his biggest aircraft, something happened.

The doors of the shed were suddenly thrown open, and the two boys could see the large airship being wheeled out. The hazy light of the moon behind the clouds shone on the expanse of white planes, and on the fishtail rudder, one of Tom's latest ideas.

"Hey, there!" cried Tom, warningly.

"Leave that alone!" yelled Ned.

"Koku! Koku!" shouted Tom, shrilly. "Get after those fellows!"

"Me get!" boomed out the giant, in his deep voice.

He had been standing near the entrance to the hangar, probably waiting for developments, and watching for the arrival of Tom and Ned. The big form was seen to leap forward, and then several dark shadows swarmed from around the airship, and were seen to fling themselves upon the giant.

"That's a fight!" cried Ned. "They're attacking him!"

"Koku can take care of himself!" murmured Tom. "But come on. I don't see what their game is."

He understood a moment later, however, for while several of the midnight visitors were engaged in a hand-to-hand tussle with the giant there came a sharp, throbbing roar of the airship motor in motion. The propellers were being whirled rapidly about.

"Koku! Koku!" cried Tom, for he was still some distance off. "Never mind them! Don't let the airship be taken!"

But Koku could only grunt. Big and strong as he was, half a dozen men attacking him at once hampered him. He threw them from him, one after another, and was gradually making his way toward the now slowly-moving airship. But would he be in time?

Tom and Ned could not hope to reach the machine before Koku, though they were running at top speed.

"Koku! Koku!" yelled Tom. "Don't let them get away!"

But Koku could only grunt—harder this time—for he fell heavily, being tripped by a stick thrust between his legs. He lay for a moment stunned.

"They're going to get away!" panted Tom, making an effort to increase his speed.

"That's what!" agreed Ned.

Even as they spoke the roar of the airship motor increased. Several of the dark forms which had been engaged in the struggle with Koku were seen to pick themselves up, and run toward the airship, that was now in motion, moving on the bicycle wheels over the grass plot, preparatory to mounting upward in the sky.

"Stop! Stop!" commanded Tom. But it was all in vain.

The men leaped aboard the airship, which could carry six persons, and a moment later, with a deafening roar, as the engine opened up full, the big craft shot upward, taking away all but two of the midnight visitors. These, who had seemingly been stunned by Koku, now arose from the ground, and staggered off in the darkness.

"Get them!" cried Tom.

"We must see to Koku!" added Ned, "Look, there goes your airship, Tom!"

"Yes, I know. But we can't stop that now. Let's see if we can get a clue in these fellows!"

He pointed toward the two who had run off in the dark underbrush surrounding the hangar plaza, and he and Ned trailed them as well as they could. But from the first they knew it would be useless, for there were many hiding places, and, a little way beyond, was a clump of trees.

After a short search, Tom gave up reluctantly and came back to where Koku was now sitting on the ground.

"Are you hurt?" he asked of the giant.

"My mind hurt—that all," said the big man.

"I guess he means his feelings are hurt," Tom explained. "Do you know who they were, Koku?"

"No, master."

"But we must do something!" cried Ned. "They've got your airship, Tom."

"I know it," said the young inventor calmly. "But we can't do anything now. You can hardly hear her, let alone see her. She's moving fast!"

He pointed upward to the darkness. Like some black bird of prey, the airship was already lost to sight, though it would have seemed as if her white planes might render her visible. But she had moved so swiftly that, during the short search, she had already disappeared.

"Aren't you going to do anything?" asked Ned.

"Certainly," spoke Tom. "I'm going to telephone an alarm to all the nearby towns. This is certainly a queer game, Ned."

CHAPTER XII

A STRANGE DISAPPEARANCE

Disappointed and puzzled, Tom and Ned went to where Koku was standing in rather a dazed attitude. The giant, like all large bodies, moved slowly, not only bodily but mentally. He could understand exactly what had happened, except that he had not prevailed over the "pygmies" who had attacked him. They had been too many for him.

"Let's take a look inside," suggested Tom, when, by another glance upward, he had made sure that all trace of his big airship was gone. "Maybe we can get a clue. Then, Koku, you tell us what happened."

"It all happened to me," said the giant, simply. "Me no make anything happen to them."

"That's about right," laughed Tom, ruefully. "It all happened to us."

The lights in the hangar were switched on, but a careful search revealed little. The men, half a dozen or more, had come evidently well prepared for the taking away of Tom Swift's airship, and they had done so.

Entrance had been effected by forcing a small side door. True, the burglar alarm had given notice of the presence of the men, but Tom and Ned had not acted quite quickly enough. Koku had been at the hangar almost as soon as the men themselves, but he had watched and waited for orders, instead of going in at once, and this had given the intruders time to wheel out the craft and start the motor.

"Why didn't you jump right in on them when you saw what they were up to, Koku?" asked Tom.

"Me wait for master. Me think master want to see who men were. Me go in—they run."

"Well, of course that's so, in a way," admitted Tom. "They probably would have run, but they'd have run *without* my airship instead of *with* it, if they hadn't had time to get it outside the hangar. However, there's no use in crying over lost biplanes. The next thing is how to get her back. Did you know any of the men, Koku?"

"No, master."

"Then we haven't any clue that way. They laid their plans well. They just let you tangle yourself up with them, Koku, while the head ones got the motor going; an easy matter, since it was all ready to start. Then they tripped you, Koku, and as many of them as could, made a jump for the machine. Then they were off."

"Well, what's the next thing to do?" asked Ned, when another look about the shed had shown that not the slightest clue was available.

"I'm going to do some telephoning," Tom stated. "A big airship like mine can't go scooting around the country without being noticed. And those fellows can't go on forever. They've got to have gasolene and oil, and to get them they'll have to come down. I'll get it back, sooner or later; but the question is: Why did they take her?"

"To sell," suggested Ned.

"I think not," Tom said. "A big airship like mine isn't easy to sell. People who would buy it would ask questions that might not easily be answered. I'm inclined to think that some other reason made them take her, and it's up to us to find out what it was. Let's go into the house."

"Hark!" suddenly exclaimed Ned, holding up his hand for silence. They all heard footsteps outside the hangar.

Tom sprang to the door, flashing his electric light, and a voice exclaimed:

"Golly! Chicken thieves!"

"Oh, is it you, Eradicate?" asked the young inventor, with a laugh. "No, it isn't chicken thieves—they were after bigger game this time."

"Suffin happen?" asked the colored man. "Massa Swift he heah a noise, an' see a light, an' he sent me out yeah t' see what all am gwine on."

"Yes, something happened," admitted Tom. "They got the *Eagle*, Rad."

"What! Yo' big airship?"

"Yes."

"Huh! Dat's too bad, Massa Tom. I suah am sorry t' heah dat. Who done it?"

"We don't know, Rad."

"Maybe it was dat low-down cousin ob mine what tried t' git mah chickens, onct!"

"No, Rad, it wasn't your cousin. But I'll telephone the alarm to the police. They may be able to help me get the *Eagle* back."

Within the next hour several messages were sent to the authorities of nearby towns, asking them to be on the watch for the stolen airship. This was about all that could be done, and after Mr. Swift had been told the story of the night's happenings, everyone went back to bed again.

Further search the next morning brought forth no clues, though Tom, Ned and the others beat about in the bushes where the men had disappeared.

One or two reports were heard from surrounding towns, to the effect that several persons had heard a strange throbbing sound in the night, that, possibly, was caused by the passage of the airship overhead. One such report came from Waterford, the home town of Mr. Damon.

"Let's go over there," suggested Ned, to his chum. "I'd like to see our friend, and maybe we can get some other clues by circulating around there."

"Oh, I don't know," spoke Tom, rather listlessly.

"Why not?" Ned wanted to know.

"Well, I ought to be working on my photo telephone," was the answer. "I've got a new idea now. I'm going to try a different kind of current, and use a more sensitive plate. And I'll use a tungsten filament lamp in the sending booth."

"Oh, let your experiments go for a little while, Tom," suggested Ned. "Come on over to Mr. Damon's. The trouble with you is that you keep too long at a thing, once you start."

"That's the only way to succeed," remarked Tom. "Really, Ned, while I feel sorry about the airship, of course, I ought to be working on my telephone. I'll get the *Eagle* back sooner or later."

"That's not the way to talk, Tom. Let's follow up this clue."

"Well, if you insist on it I suppose I may as well go. We'll take the little monoplane. I've fixed her up to carry double. I guess—"

Tom Swift broke off suddenly, as the telephone at his elbow rang.

"Hello," he said, taking off the receiver. "Yes, this is Tom Swift. Oh, good morning, Mrs. Damon! Eh! What's that? Mr. Damon has disappeared? You don't tell me! Disappeared! Yes, yes, I can come right over. Be there in a few minutes. Eh? You don't know what to make of it? Oh, well, maybe it can easily be explained. Yes, Ned Newton and I will be right over. Don't worry."

Tom hung up the receiver and turned to his chum.

"What do you think of that?" he asked.

"What is it?"

"Why, Mr. Damon mysteriously vanished last night, and this morning word came from his bankers that every cent of his fortune had disappeared! He's lost everything!"

"Maybe—maybe—" hesitated Ned.

"No, Mr. Damon isn't that kind of a man," said Tom, stoutly. "He hasn't made away with himself."

"But something is wrong!"

"Evidently, and it's up to us to find out what it is. I shouldn't be surprised but that he knew of this coming trouble and started out to prevent it if he could."

"But he wouldn't disappear and make his wife worry."

"No, that's so. Well, we'll have to go over there and find out all about it."

"Say, Tom!" exclaimed Ned, as they were getting the small, but swift monoplane ready for the flight, "could there be any connection with the disappearance of Mr. Damon and the taking of the *Eagle*?"

Tom started in surprise.

"How could there be?" he asked.

"Oh, I don't know," answered Ned. "It was only an idea."

"Well, we'll see what Mrs. Damon has to say," spoke the young inventor, as he took his seat beside Ned, and motioned to Koku to twirl the propeller.

CHAPTER XIII

THE TELEPHONE PICTURE

"Oh, Tom Swift! I'm so glad to see you!"

Mrs. Damon clasped her arms, in motherly fashion, about the young inventor. He held her close, and his own eyes were not free from tears as he witnessed the grief of his best friend's wife.

"Now, don't worry, Mrs. Damon," said Tom, sympathetically. "Everything will be all right," and he led her to a chair.

"All right, Tom! How can it be?" and the lady raised a tear-stained face. "My husband has disappeared, without a word! It's just as if the earth had opened and swallowed him up! I can't find a trace of him! How can it be all right?"

"Well, we'll find him, Mrs. Damon. Don't worry. Ned and I will get right to work, and I'll have all the police and detectives within fifty miles on the search—if we have to go that far."

"Oh, it's awfully good of you, Tom. I—I didn't know who else to turn to in my trouble but you."

"And why shouldn't you come to me? I'd do anything for you and Mr. Damon. Now tell me all about it."

Tom and Ned had just arrived at the Damon home in the airship, to find the wife of the eccentric man almost distracted over her husband's strange disappearance.

"It happened last night," Mrs. Damon said, when she was somewhat composed. "Last night about twelve o'clock."

"Twelve o'clock!" cried Tom, in surprise "Why that's about the time—"

He stopped suddenly.

"What were you going to say?" asked Mrs. Damon.

"Oh—nothing," answered Tom. "I—I'll tell you later. Go on, please."

"It is all so confusing," proceeded Mrs. Damon. "You know my husband has been in trouble of late—financial trouble?"

"Yes," responded Tom, "he mentioned it to me."

"I don't know any of the details," sighed Mrs. Damon, "but I know he was mixed up with a man named Peters."

"I know him, too," spoke Tom, grimly.

"My husband has been very gloomy of late," went on Mrs. Damon. "He foolishly entrusted almost his entire fortune to that man, and last night he told me it was probably all gone. He said he saw only the barest chance to save it, but that he was going to take that chance."

"Did he go into details?" asked Tom.

"No, that was all he said. That was about ten o'clock. He didn't want to go to bed. He just sat about, and he kept saying over and over again: 'Bless my tombstone!' 'Bless the cemetery!' and all such stuff as that. You know how he was," and she smiled through her tears.

"Yes," said Tom. "I know. Only it wasn't like him to bless such grewsome things. He was more jolly."

"He hasn't been, of late," sighed his wife. "Well, he sat about all the evening, and he kept figuring away, trying, I suppose, to find some way out of his trouble."

"Why didn't he come to my father?" cried Tom. "I told him he could have all the money he needed to tide him over."

"Well, Mr. Damon was queer that way," said his wife. "He wanted to be independent. I urged him to call you up, but he said he'd fight it out alone."

"As I said, we sat there, and he kept feeling more and more blue, and blessing his funeral, and the hearse and all such things as that. He kept looking at the clock, too, and I wondered at that."

"'Are you expecting someone?' I asked him. He said he wasn't, exactly, but I made sure he was, and finally, about half-past eleven, he put on his hat and went out."

"'Where are you going?' I asked him."

"'Oh, just to get a breath of air. I can't sleep,' he said. I didn't think much of that, as he often used to go out and walk about a bit before going to bed. So he went out, and I began to see about locking up, for I never trust the servants."

"It must have been about an hour later when I heard voices out in front. I looked, and I saw Mr. Damon talking to a man."

"Who was he?" asked Tom, eagerly, on the alert for the slightest clue.

"I thought at the time," said Mrs. Damon, "that it was one of the neighbors. I have learned since, however, that it was not. Anyhow, this man and Mr. Damon stood talking for a little while, and then they went off together. I didn't think it strange at the time, supposing he was merely strolling up and down in front with Mr. Blackson, who lives next door, He often had done that before."

"Well, I saw that the house was locked up, and then I sat down in a chair to wait for Mr. Damon to come back. I was getting sleepy, for we don't usually stay up so late. I suppose I must have dozed off, but I was suddenly awakened by hearing a peculiar noise. I sat up in alarm, and then I realized that Mr. Damon had not come in."

"I was frightened then, and I called my maid. It was nearly one o'clock, and my husband never stays out as late as that. We went next door, and found that Mr. Blackson had not been out of his house that evening. So it could not have been he to whom Mr. Damon was speaking."

"We roused up other neighbors, and they searched all about the grounds, thinking he might have been overcome by a sudden faint. But we could not find him. My husband had disappeared—mysteriously disappeared!" and the lady broke into sobs.

"Now don't worry," said Tom, soothingly, as he put his arms about her as he would have done to his own mother, had she been alive, "We'll get him back!"

"But how can you? No one knows where he is."

"Oh, yes!" said Tom, confidently, "Mr. Damon himself knows where he is, and unless he has gone away voluntarily, I think you will soon hear from him."

"What do you mean by—voluntarily?" asked the wife.

"First let me ask you a question," came from Tom. "You said you were awakened by a peculiar noise. What sort of a sound was it?"

"Why, a whirring, throbbing noise, like—like—"

She paused for a comparison.

"Like an airship?" asked Tom, with a good deal of eagerness.

"That was it!" cried Mrs. Damon. "I was trying to think where I had heard the sound before. It was just like the noise your airship makes, Tom!"

"That settles it!" exclaimed the young inventor.

"Settles what?" asked Ned.

"The manner of Mr. Damon's disappearance. He was taken away—or went away—in my airship—the airship that was stolen from my shed last night!"

Mrs. Damon stared at Tom in amazement.

"Why—why—how could that be?" she asked.

Quickly Tom told of what had happened at his place.

"I begin to see through it," he said. "There is some plot here, and we've got to get to the bottom of it. Mr. Damon either went with these men in the airship willingly, or he was taken away by force. I'm inclined to think he went of his own accord, or you would have heard some out-cry, Mrs. Damon."

"Well, perhaps so," she admitted. "But would he go away in that manner without telling me?"

"He might," said Tom, willing to test his theory on all sides. "He might not have wanted you to worry, for you know you dislike him to go up an airships."

"Yes, I do. Oh, if I only thought he did go away of his own accord, I could understand it. He went, if he did, to try and save his fortune."

"It does look as though he had an appointment with someone, Tom," suggested Ned. "His looking at the clock, and then going out, and all that."

"Yes," admitted the young inventor, "and now I'm inclined to change my theory a bit. It may have been some other airship than mine that was used."

"How so?" asked Ned.

"Because the men who took mine were unprincipled fellows. Mr. Damon would not have gone away with men who would steal an airship."

"Not if he knew it," admitted Ned. "Well, then, let's consider two airships—yours and the other that came to keep the appointment with Mr. Damon. If the last is true, why should he want to go away in an airship at midnight? Why couldn't he take a train, or an auto?"

"Well, we don't know all the ins and outs," admitted Tom. "Taking a midnight airship ride is rather strange, but that may have been the only course open. We'll have to let the explanation go until later. At any rate, Mrs. Damon, I feel sure that your husband did go off through the air—either in my *Eagle* or in some other craft."

"Well, I'm glad to hear you say so, Tom Swift, though it sounds a dreadful thing to say. But if he did go off of his own accord, I know he did it for the best. And he may not have told me, for fear I would worry. I can understand that. But why isn't he back now?"

Tom had been rather dreading that question. It was one he had asked himself, and he had found no good answer for it. If there had been such need of haste, that an airship had to be used, why had not Mr. Damon come back ere this? Unless, as Tom feared to admit, even to himself, there had been some accident.

Half a dozen theories flashed through his mind, but he could not select a good, working one,—particularly as there were no clues. Disappearing in an airship was the one best means of not leaving a trace behind. An auto, a motor boat, a train, a horse and carriage—all these could be more or less easily traced. But an airship—

If Mr. Damon wanted to cover up his tracks, or if he had been taken away, and his captors wanted to baffle pursuit, the best means had been adopted.

"Now don't you worry," advised Tom to Mrs. Damon. "I know it looks funny, but I think it will come out all right. Ned and I will do all we can. Mr. Damon must have known what he was about. But, to be on the safe side, we'll send out a general alarm through the police."

"Oh, I don't know what I'd done if you hadn't come to help me!" exclaimed Mrs. Damon.

"Just you leave it to me!" said the young inventor, cheerfully. "I'll find Mr. Damon!"

But, though he spoke thus confidently, Tom Swift had not the slightest notion, just then, of how to set about his difficult task. He had had hard problems to solve before, so he was not going to give up this one. First he wanted to think matters out, and arrange a plan of action.

He and Ned made a careful examination of the grounds of the Damon homestead. There was little they could learn, though they did find where an airship had landed in a meadow, not far away, and where it had made a flying start off again.

Carefully Tom looked at the marks made by the wheels of the airship.

"They're the same distance apart as those on the *Eagle*," he said to his chum, "and the tires are the same. But that isn't saying anything, as lots of airships have the same equipment. So we won't jump to any conclusions that way."

Tom and Ned interviewed several of the neighbors, but beyond learning that some of them had heard the throbbing of the midnight airship, that was as far as they got on that line.

There was nothing more they could do in Waterford, and, leaving Mrs. Damon, who had summoned a relative to stay with her, the two chums made a quick trip back through the air to Shopton. As Eradicate came out to help put away the monoplane Tom noticed that the colored man was holding one hand as though it hurt him.

"What's the matter, Rad?" asked the young investor.

"Oh, nuffin—jest natcherly nuffin, Massa Tom."

But Eradicate spoke evasively and in a manner that roused Tom's suspicions.

"Boomerang, your mule, didn't kick you; did he?"

"No, sah, Massa Tom, no sah. 'Twern't nuffin laik dat."

"But what was it? Your hand is hurt!"

"Well, Massa Tom, I s'pose I done bettah tell yo' all. I'se had a shock!"

"A shock?"

"Yas, sah. A shock. A lickrish shock."

"Oh, you mean an electrical shock. That's too bad. I suppose you must have touched a live wire."

"No, sah. 'Twern't dat way."

"How was it, then?"

"Well, yo' see, Massa Tom, I were playin' a joke on Koku."

"Oh, you were; eh? Then I suppose Koku shocked you," laughed Tom.

"No, sah. I—I'll tell you. Dat giant man he were in de telefoam boof in de pattern shop—you know—de one where yo' all been tryin' to make pishures."

"Yes, I know. Go on!" exclaimed Tom, impatiently.

"Well, he were in dere, Massa Tom, an' I slipped into de boof in de next shop—de odder place where yo' all been 'speermentin'. I called out on de telefoam, loud laik de Angel Gabriel gwine t' holler at de last trump: 'Look out, yo' ole sinnah!' I yell it jest t' scare Koku."

"I see," said Tom, a bit severely, for he did not like Eradicate interfering with the instruments. "And did you scare Koku?"

"Oh, yas, sah, Massa Tom. I skeered him all right; but suffin else done happen. When I put down de telefoam I got a terrible shock. It hurts yit!"

"Well," remarked Tom, "I suppose I ought to feel sorry for you, but I can't. You should let things alone. Now I've got to see if you did any damage. Come along, Ned."

Tom was the first to enter the telephone booth where Eradicate had played the part of the Angel Gabriel. He looked at the wires and apparatus, but could see nothing wrong.

Then he glanced at the selenium plate, on which he hoped, some day, to imprint an image from over the wire. And, as he saw the smooth surface he started, and cried.

"Ned! Ned, come here quick!"

"What is it?" asked his chum, Crowding into the booth.

"Look at that plate! Tell me what you see!"

Ned looked.

"Why—why it's Koku's picture!" he gasped.

"Exactly!" cried Tom. "In some way my experiment has succeeded when I was away. Eradicate must have made some new connection by his monkeying. Ned, it's a success! I've got my first photo telephone picture! Hurray!"

CHAPTER XIV

MAKING IMPROVEMENTS

Tom Swift was so overjoyed and excited that for a few moments he capered about, inside the booth, and outside, knocking against his chum Ned, clapping him on the back, and doing all manner of boyish "stunts."

"It's a success, Ned! I've struck it!" cried Tom, in delight.

"Ouch! You struck *me*, you mean!" replied Ned, rubbing his shoulder, where the young inventor had imparted a resounding blow of joy.

"What of it?" exclaimed Tom. "My apparatus works! I can send a picture by telephone! It's great, Ned!"

"But I don't exactly understand how it happened," said Ned, in some bewilderment, as he gazed at the selenium plate.

"Neither do I," admitted Tom, when he had somewhat calmed down. "That is, I don't exactly understand what made the thing succeed now, when it wouldn't work for me a little while ago. But I've got to go into that. I'll have to interview that rascal Eradicate, and learn what he did when he played that trick on Koku. Yes, and I'll have to see Koku, too. We've got to get at the bottom of this, Ned."

"I suppose so. You've got your hands full, Tom, with your photo telephone, and the disappearance of Mr. Damon."

"Yes, and my own airship, too. I must get after that. Whew! A lot of things to do! But I like work, Ned. The more the better."

"Yes, that's like you, Tom. But what are you going to get at first?"

"Let me see; the telephone, I think. I'll have Rad and Koku in here and talk to them. I say, you Eradicate!" he called out of the door of the shop, as he saw the colored man going past, holding his shocked arm tenderly.

"Yas, sah, Massa Tom, I'se comin'! What is it yo' all wants, Massa Tom?"

"I want you to show me exactly what you did to the wires, and other things in here, when you played that Angel Gabriel trick on your partner Koku."

"Partner! He ain't mah partner!" exclaimed Eradicate with a scowl, for there was not the best of feeling between the two. Eradicate had served in the Swift family many years, and he rather resented the coming of the giant, who performed many services formerly the province of the colored man.

"Well, never mind what he is, Rad," laughed Tom. "You just show me what you did. Come now, something happened in here, and I want to find out what it was."

"Oh, suffin done happened all right, Massa Tom. Yas, sah! Suffin done happened!" cried Eradicate, with such odd emphasis that Tom and Ned both laughed.

"An' suffin happened to me," went on the colored man, rubbing his shocked arm.

"Well, tell us about it," suggested Tom.

"It was dish yeah way," proceeded Eradicate. And he told more in detail how, seeing Koku cleaning and sweeping out the other telephone booth, he had thought of the trick to play on him. Both telephones had what are called "amplifiers" attached, that could be switched on when needed. These amplifiers were somewhat like the horn of a phonograph—they increased, or magnified the sound, so that one could hear a voice from any part of the shop, and need not necessarily have the telephone receiver at his ear.

Seeing Koku near the instrument, Eradicate had switched on the amplifier, and had called into his instrument, trying to scare the giant.

And he did startle Koku, for the loud voice, coming so suddenly, sent the giant out of the booth on the run.

"But you must have done something else," insisted Tom. "Look here, Rad," and the young inventor pointed to the picture on the plate.

"Mah gracious sakes!" gasped the colored man. "Why dat's Koku hisse'f!" and he looked in awe at the likeness.

"That's what you did, Rad!"

"Me? I done dat? No, sah, Massa Tom. I neber did! No, sah!" Eradicate spoke emphatically.

"Yes you did, Rad. You took that picture of Koku over my photo telephone, and I want you to show me exactly what you did—what wires and switches you touched and changed, and all that."

"Yo—yo' done say I tuck dat pishure, Massa Tom?"

"You sure did, Rad."

"Well—well, good land o' massy! An' I done dat!"

Eradicate stared in wonder at the image of the giant on the plate, and shook his head doubtingly.

"I—I didn't know I could do it. I never knowed I had it in me!" he murmured.

Tom and Ned laughed long and loud, and then the young inventor said:

"Now look here, Rad. You've done me a mighty big service, though you didn't know it, and I want to thank you. I'm sorry about your arm, and I'll have the doctor look at it. But now I want you to show me all the things you touched when you played that joke on Koku. In some way you did what I haven't been able to do, You took the picture. There's probably just one little thing I've overlooked, and you stumbled on it by accident. Now go ahead and show me."

Eradicate thought for a moment, and then said:

"Well, I done turned on de current, laik I seen you done, Massa Tom."

"Yes, go on. You connected the telephone."

"Yas, sah. Den I switched on that flyer thing yo' all has rigged up."

"You switched on the amplifier, yes. Go on."

"An'—an' den I plugged in dish year wire," and the colored man pointed to one near the top of the booth.

"You switched on that wire, Rad! Why, great Scott, man! That's connected to the arc light circuit—it carries over a thousand volts. And you switched that into the telephone circuit?"

"Dat's what I done did, Massa Tom; yas, Bah!"

"What for?"

"Why, I done want t' make mah voice good an' loud t' skeer dat rascal Koku!"

Tom stared at the colored man in amazement.

"No wonder you got a shock!" exclaimed the young inventor. "You didn't get all the thousand volts, for part of it was shunted off; but you got a good charge, all right. So that's what did the business; eh? It was the combination of the two electrical circuits that sent the photograph over the wire."

"I understand it now, Rad; but you did more than I've been able to do. I never, in a hundred years, would have thought of switching on that current. It never occurred to me. But you, doing it by accident, brought out the truth. It's often that way in discoveries. And Koku was standing in the other telephone booth, near the plate there, when you switched in this current, Rad?"

"Yas, sah, Massa Tom. He were. An' yo' ought t' see him hop when he heard mah voice yellin' at him. Ha! ha! ha!"

Eradicate chuckled at the thought. Then a pain in his shocked arm made him wince. A wry look passed over his face.

"Yas, sah, Koku done jump about ten feet," he said. "An'—an' den I jump too. Ain't no use in denyin' dat fact. I done jump when I got dat shock!"

"All right, Rad. You may go now. I think I'm on the right track!" exclaimed Tom. "Come on, Ned, we'll try some experiments, and we'll see what we can do."

"No shocks though—cut out the shocks, Tom," stipulated his chum.

"Oh, sure! No shocks! Now let's bet busy and improve on Eradicate's Angel Gabriel system."

Tom made a quick examination of the apparatus.

"I understand it, I think," he said. "Koku was near the plate in the other booth when Rad put on the double current. There was a light there, and in an instant his likeness was sent over the wire, and imprinted on this plate. Now let's see what we can do. You go to that other booth, Ned. I'll see if I can get your picture, and send you mine. Here, take some extra selenium plates along. You know how to connect them."

"I think so," answered Ned.

"This image is really too faint to be of much use," went on Tom, as he looked at the one of Koku. "I think I can improve on it. But we're on the right track."

A little later Ned stood in the other booth, while Tom arranged the wires, and made the connections in the way accidently discovered by Eradicate. The young inventor had put in a new plate, carefully putting away the one with the picture of the giant, This plate could be used again, when the film, into which the image was imprinted, had been washed off.

"All ready, Ned," called Tom, over the wire, when he was about to turn the switch. "Stand still, and I'll get you."

The connection was made, and Tom uttered a cry of joy. For there, staring at him from the plate in front of him was the face of Ned.

It was somewhat reduced in size, of course, and was not extra clear, but anyone who knew Ned could have told he was at the other end of the wire.

"Do you get me, Tom?" called Ned, over the telephone.

"I sure do! Now see if you can get me."

Tom made other connections, and then looked at the sending plate of his instrument, there being both a sending and receiving plate in each booth, just as there was a receiver and a transmitter to the telephone.

"Hurray! I see you, Tom!" cried Ned, over the wire. "Say, this is great!"

"It isn't as good as I want it," went on Tom. "But it proves that I'm right. The photo telephone is a fact, and now persons using the wire can be sure of the other person they are conversing with. I must tell dad. He wouldn't believe I could do it!"

And indeed Mr. Swift was surprised when Tom proved, by actual demonstration, that a picture could be sent over the wire.

"Tom, I congratulate you!" declared the aged inventor. "It is good news!"

"Yes, but we have bad news of Mr. Damon," said Tom, and he told his father of the disappearance of the eccentric man. Mr. Swift at once telephoned his sympathy to Mrs. Damon, and offered to do anything he could for her.

"But Tom can help you more than I can," he said. "You can depend on Tom."

"I know that," replied Mrs. Damon, over the wire.

And certainly Tom Swift had many things to do now. He hardly knew at what to begin first, but now, since he was on the right road in regard to his photo telephone, he would work at improving it.

And to this end he devoted himself, after he had sent out a general alarm to the police of nearby towns, in regard to the disappearance of Mr. Damon. The airship clue, he believed, as did the police, would be a good one to work on.

For several days after this nothing of moment occurred. Mr. Damon could not be located, and Tom's airship might still be sailing above the clouds as far as getting any trace of it was concerned.

Meanwhile the young inventor, with the help of Ned, who was given a leave of absence from the bank, worked hard to improve the photo telephone.

CHAPTER XV

THE AIRSHIP CLEW

"Now Ned, we'll try again. I'm going to use a still stronger current, and this is the most sensitive selenium plate I've turned out yet. We'll see if we can't get a better likeness of you—one that will be plainer."

It was Tom Swift who was speaking, and he and his chum had just completed some hard work on the new photo telephone. Though the apparatus did what Tom had claimed for it, still he was far from satisfied. He could transmit over the wire the picture of a person talking at the telephone, but the likeness was too faint to make the apparatus commercially profitable.

"It's like the first moving pictures," said Tom. "They moved, but that was about all they did."

"I say," remarked Ned, as he was about to take his place in the booth where the telephone and apparatus were located, "this double-strength electrical current you're speaking of won't shock me; will it? I don't want what happened to Eradicate to happen to me, Tom."

"Don't worry. Nothing will happen. The trouble with Rad was that he didn't have the wires insulated when he turned that arc current switch by mistake—or, rather, to play his joke. But he's all right now."

"Yes, but I'm not going to take any chances," insisted Ned. "I want to be insulated myself."

"I'll see to that," promised Tom. "Now get to your booth."

For the purpose of experiments Tom had strung a new line between two of his shops, They were both within sight, and the line was not very long; but, as I have said, Tom knew that if his apparatus would work over a short distance, it would also be successful over a long one, provided he could maintain the proper force of current, which he was sure could be accomplished.

"And if they can send pictures from Monte Carlo to Paris I can do the same," declared Tom, though his system of photo telephony was different from sending by a telegraph system—a reproduction of a picture on a copper plate. Tom's apparatus transmitted the likeness of the living person.

It took some little time for the young inventor, and Ned working with him, to fix up the new wires and switch on the current. But at last it was complete, and Ned took his place at one telephone, with the two sensitive plates before him. Tom did the same, and they proceeded to talk over the wire, first making sure that the vocal connection was perfect.

"All ready now, Ned! We'll try it," called Tom to his chum, over the wire. "Look straight at the plate. I want to get your image first, and then I'll send mine, if it's a success."

Ned did as requested, and in a few minutes he could hear Tom exclaim, joyfully:

"It's better, Ned! It's coming out real clear. I can see you almost as plainly as if you were right in the booth with me. But turn on your light a little stronger."

Tom could hear, through the telephone, his chum moving about, and then he caught a startled exclamation.

"What's the matter?" asked Tom anxiously.

"I got a shock!" cried Ned. "I thought you said you had this thing fixed. Great Scott, Tom! It nearly yanked the arm off me! Is this a joke?"

"No, old man. No, of course not! Something must be wrong. I didn't mean that. Wait, I'll take a look. Say, it does seem as if everything was going wrong with this invention. But I'm on the right track, and soon I'll have it all right. Wait a second. I'll be right over."

Tom found that it was only a simple displacement of a wire that had given Ned a shock, and he soon had this remedied.

"Now we'll try again," he said. This time nothing wrong occurred, and soon Tom saw the clearest image he had yet observed on his telephone photo plate.

"Switch me on now, Ned," he called to his chum, and Ned reported that he could see Tom very plainly.

"So far—so good," observed Tom, as he came from the booth. "But there are several things I want yet to do."

"Such as what?" questioned Ned.

"Well, I want to arrange to have two kinds of pictures come over the wire. I want it so that a person can go into a booth, call up a friend, and then switch on the picture plate, so he can see his friend as well as talk to him. I want this plate to be like a mirror, so that any number of images can be made to appear on it. In that way it can be used over and over again. In fact it will be exactly like a mirror, or a telescope. No matter how far two persons may be apart they can both see and talk to one another."

"That's a big contract, Tom."

"Yes, but you've seen that it can be done. Then another thing I want to do is to have it arranged so that I can make a photograph of a person over a wire."

"Meaning what?"

"Meaning that if a certain person talks to me over the wire, I can turn my switch, and get a picture of him here at my apparatus connected with my telephone. To do that I'll merely need a sending apparatus at the other end of the telephone line—not a receiving machine."

"Could you arrange it so that the person who was talking to you would have his picture taken whether he wanted it or not?" asked Ned.

"Yes, it might be done," spoke Tom, thoughtfully. "I could conceal the sending plate somewhere in the telephone booth, and arrange the proper light, I suppose."

"That might be a good way in which to catch a criminal," went on Ned. "Often crooks call up on the telephone, but they know they are safe. The authorities can't see them—they can only hear them. Now if you could get a photograph of them while they were telephoning—"

"I see!" cried Tom, excitedly. "That's a great idea! I'll work on that, Ned."

And, all enthusiasm, Tom began to plan new schemes with his photo telephone.

The young inventor did not forget his promise to help Mrs. Damon. But he could get absolutely no clue to her husband's whereabouts. Mr. Damon had completely and mysteriously disappeared. His fortune, too, seemed to have been swallowed up by the sharpers, though lawyers engaged by Tom could fasten no criminal acts on Mr. Peters, who indignantly denied that he had done anything unlawful.

If he had, he had done it in such a way that he could not be brought to justice. The promoter was still about Shopton, as well groomed as ever, with his rose in his buttonhole, and wearing his silk hat. He still speeded up and down Lake Carlopa in his powerful motor boat. But he gave Tom Swift a wide berth.

Late one night, when Tom and Ned had been working at the new photo telephone, after all the rest of the household had retired, Tom suddenly looked up from his drawings and exclaimed:

"What's that?"

"What's what?" inquired Ned.

"That sound? Don't you hear it? Listen!"

"It's an airship—maybe yours coming back!" cried the young banker.

As he spoke Ned did hear, seemingly in the air above the house, a curious, throbbing, pulsating sound.

"That's so! It is an airship motor!" exclaimed Tom. "Come on out!"

Together they rushed from the house, but, ere they reached the yard, the sound had ceased. They looked up into the sky, but could see nothing, though the night was light from a full moon.

"I certainly heard it," said Tom.

"So did I," asserted Ned. "But where is it now?"

They advanced toward the group of work-buildings. Something showing white in the moonlight, before the hangar, caught Ned's eyes.

"Look!" he exclaimed. "There's an airship, Tom!"

The two rushed over to the level landing place before the big shed. And there, as if she had just been run out for a flight, was the *Eagle*. She had come back in the night, as mysteriously as she had been taken away.

CHAPTER XVI

SUCCESS

"Well, this gets me!" exclaimed Tom.

"It sure is strange," agreed Ned. "How did she come here?"

"She didn't come alone—that's sure," went on Tom. "Someone brought her here, made a landing, and got away before we could get out."

The two chums were standing near the *Eagle*, which had come back so mysteriously.

"Just a couple of seconds sooner and we'd have seen who brought her here," went on Tom. "But they must have shut off the motor some distance up, and then they volplaned down. That's why we didn't hear them."

Ned went over and put his hand on the motor.

"Ouch!" he cried, jumping back. "It's hot!"

"Showing that she's been running up to within a few minutes ago," said Tom. "Well, as I said before, this sure does get me. First these mysterious men take my airship, and then they bring her back again, without so much as thanking me for the use of her."

"Who in the world can they be?" asked Ned.

"I haven't the least idea. But I'm going to find out, if it's at all possible. We'll look the machine over in the morning, and see if we can get any clues. No use in doing that now. Come on, we'll put her back in the hangar."

"Say!" exclaimed Ned, as a sudden idea came to him. "It couldn't be Mr. Damon who had your airship; could it, Tom?"

"I don't know. Why do you ask that?"

"Well, he might have wanted to get away from his enemies for a while, and he might have taken your *Eagle*, and—"

"Mr. Damon wouldn't trail along with a crowd like the one that took away my airship," said Tom, decidedly. "You've got another guess coming, Ned. Mr. Damon had nothing to do with this."

"And yet the night he disappeared an airship was heard near his house."

"That's so. Well, I give up. This is sure a mystery. We'll have a look at it in the morning. One thing I'll do, though, I'll telephone over to Mr. Damon's house and see if his wife has heard any news. I've been doing that quite often of late, so she won't think anything of it. In that way we can find out if he had anything to do with my airship. But let's run her into the shed first."

This was done, and Koku, the giant, was sent to sleep in the hangar to guard against another theft. But it was not likely that the mysterious men, once having brought the airship back, would come for it again.

Tom called up Mrs. Damon on the telephone, but there was no news of the missing man. He expressed his sympathy, and said he would come and see her soon. He told Mrs. Damon not to get discouraged, adding that he, and others, were doing all that was possible. But, in spite of this, Mrs. Damon, naturally, did worry.

The next morning the two chums inspected the airship, so mysteriously returned to them. Part after part they went over, and found nothing wrong. The motor ran perfectly, and there was not so much as a bent spoke in the landing wheels. For all that could be told by an inspection of the craft she might never have been out of the hangar.

"Hello, here's something!" cried Tom, as he got up from the operator's seat, where he had taken his place to test the various controls.

"What is it?" asked Ned.

"A button. A queer sort of a button. I never had any like that on my clothes, and I'm sure you didn't. Look!" and Tom held out a large, metal button of curious design.

"It must have come off the coat of one of the men who had your airship, Tom," said his chum. "Save it. You may find that it's a clue."

"I will. No telling what it may lead to. Well, I guess that's all we can find."

And it was. But Tom little realized what a clue the button was going to be. Nothing more could be learned by staring at the returned airship, so he and Ned went back to the house.

Tom Swift had many things to do, but his chief concern was for the photo telephone. Now that he was near the goal of success he worked harder than ever. The idea Ned had given him of being able to take the picture of a person at the instrument—without the knowledge of that person—appealed strongly to Tom.

"That's going to be a valuable invention!" he declared, but little he knew how valuable it would prove to him and to others.

It was about a week later when Tom was ready to try the new apparatus. Meanwhile he had prepared different plates, and had changed his wiring system. In the days that had passed nothing new had been learned concerning the whereabouts of Mr. Damon, nor of the men who had so mysteriously taken away Tom's airship.

All was in readiness for the trial. Tom sent Ned to the booth that he had constructed in the airship hangar, some distance away from the house. The other booth Tom had placed in his library, an entirely new system of wires being used.

"Now Ned," explained Tom, "the idea is this! You go into that booth, just as if it were a public one, and ring me up in the regular way. Of course we haven't a central here, but that doesn't matter. Now while I'm talking to you I want to see you. You don't know that, of course."

"The point is to see if I can get your picture while you're talking to me, and not let you know a thing about it."

"Think you can do it, Tom?"

"I'm going to try. We'll soon know. Go ahead."

A little later Ned was calling up his chum, as casually as he could, under the circumstances.

"All right!" called Tom to his chum. "Start in and talk. Say anything you like—it doesn't matter. I want to see if I can get your picture. Is the light burning in your booth?"

"Yes, Tom."

"All right then. Go ahead."

Ned talked of the weather—of anything. Meanwhile Tom was busy. Concealed in the booth occupied by Ned was a sending plate. It could not be seen unless one knew just where to look for it. In Tom's booth was a receiving plate.

The experiment did not take long. Presently Tom called to Ned that he need stay there no longer.

"Come on to the house," invited the young inventor, "and we'll develope this plate." For in this system it was necessary to develope the receiving plate, as is done with an ordinary photographic one. Tom wanted a permanent record.

Eagerly the chums in the dark room looked down into the tray containing the plate and the developing solution.

"Something's coming out!" cried Ned, eagerly.

"Yes! And it's you!" exclaimed Tom. "See, Ned, I got your picture over the telephone. Success! I've struck it! This is the best yet!"

At that moment, as the picture came out more and more plainly, someone knocked on the door of the dark room.

"Who is it?" asked Tom.

"Gen'man t' see you," said Eradicate. "He say he come from Mistah Peters!"

"Mr. Peters—that rascally promoter!" whispered Tom to his chum. "What does this mean?"

CHAPTER XVII

THE MYSTERIOUS MESSAGE

Tom Swift and his chum looked at one another strangely for a moment in the dim, red light of the dark room. Then the young inventor spoke:

"I'm not going to see him. Tell him so, Rad!"

"Hold on a second," suggested Ned. "Maybe you had better see him, Tom. It may have something to with Mr. Damon's lost fortune."

"That's so! I didn't think of that. And I may get a clue to his disappearance, though I don't imagine Peters had anything to do with that. Wait, Rad. Tell the gentleman I'll see him. Did he give any name, Rad?"

"Yas, sah. Him done say him Mistah Boylan."

"The same man who called to see me once before, trying to get me to do some business with Peters," murmured Tom. "Very well, I'll see him as soon as this picture is fixed. Tell him to wait, Rad."

A little later Tom went to where his caller awaited in the library. This time there were no plans to be looked at, the young inventor having made a practice of keeping all his valuable papers locked in a safe.

"You go into the next room, Ned," Tom had said to his chum. "Leave the door open, so you can hear what is said."

"Why, do you think there'll be trouble? Maybe we'd better have Koku on hand to—"

"Oh, no, nothing like that," laughed Tom. "I just want you to listen to what's said so, if need be, you can be a witness later. I don't know what their game is, but I don't trust Peters and his crowd. They may want to get control of some of my patents, and they may try some underhanded work. If they do I want to be in a position to stop them."

"All right," agreed Ned, and he took his place.

But Mr. Boylan's errand was not at all sensational, it would seem. He bowed to Tom, perhaps a little distantly, for they had not parted the best of friends on a former occasion.

"I suppose you are surprised to see me," began Mr. Boylan.

"Well, I am, to tell the truth," Tom said, calmly.

"I am here at the request of my employer, Mr. Peters," went on the caller. "He says he is forming a new and very powerful company to exploit airships, and he wants to know whether you would not reconsider your determination not to let him do some business for you."

"No, I'm afraid I don't care to go into anything like that," said Tom.

"It would be a good thing for you," proceeded Mr. Boylan, eagerly. "Mr. Peters is able to command large capital, and if you would permit the use of your airships—or one of them—as a model, and would supervise the construction of others, we could confidently expect large sales. Thus you would profit, and I am frank to admit that the company, and Mr. Peters, also, would make money. Mr. Peters is perfectly free to confess that he is in business to make money, but he is also willing to let others share with him. Come now, what do you say?"

"I am sorry, but I shall have to say the same thing I said before," replied Tom. "Nothing doing!"

Mr. Boylan glanced rather angrily at the young inventor, and then, with a shrug of his shoulders, remarked:

"Well, you have the say, of course. But I would like to remind you that this is going to be a very large airship company, and if your inventions are not exploited some others will be. And Mr. Peters also desired me to say that this is the last offer he would make you."

"Tell him," said Tom, "that I am much obliged, but that I have no business that I can entrust to him. If he wishes to make some other type of airship, that is his affair. Good-day."

As Mr. Boylan was going out Tom noticed a button dangling from the back of his caller's coat. It hung by a thread, being one of the pair usually sewed on the back of a cutaway garment.

"I think you had better take off that button before it falls," suggested Tom. "You may lose it, and perhaps it would be hard to match."

"That's so. Thank you!" said Mr. Boylan. He tried to reach around and get it, but he was too stout to turn easily, especially as the coat was tight-fitting.

"I'll get it for you," offered Tom, as he pulled it off. "There is one missing, though," he said, as he handed the button to the man. And then Tom started as he saw the pattern of the one in his hand.

"One gone? That's too bad," murmured Mr. Boylan. "Those buttons were imported, and I doubt if I can replace them. They are rather odd."

"Yes," agreed Tom, gazing as if fascinated at the one he still held. "They are rather odd."

And then, as he passed it over, like a flash it came to him where he had seen a button like that before. He had found it in his airship, which had been so mysteriously taken away and returned.

Tom could hardly restrain his impatience until Mr. Boylan had gone. The young inventor had half a notion to produce the other button, matching the one he had just pulled off his visitor's coat, and tell where he had found it. But he held himself back. He wanted to talk first to Ned.

And, when his chum came in, Tom cried:

"Ned, what do you think? I know who had my airship!"

"How?" asked Ned, in wonder.

"By that button clue! Yes, it's the same kind—they're as alike as twins!" and Tom brought out the button which he had put away in his desk. "See, Boylan had one just like this on the back of his coat. The other was missing. Here it is—it was in the seat of my airship, where it was probably pulled off as he moved about. Ned, I think I've got the right clue at last."

Ned said nothing for several seconds. Then he remarked slowly:

"Well, Tom, it proves one thing; but not the other."

"What do you mean?"

"I mean that it may be perfectly true that the button came off Mr. Boylan's coat, but that doesn't prove that he wore it. You can be reasonably sure that the coat was having a ride in your *Eagle*, but was Boylan in the coat? That's the question."

"In the coat? Of course he was in it!" cried Tom.

"You can't be sure. Someone may have borrowed his coat to take a midnight ride in the airship."

"Mr. Boylan doesn't look to be the kind of a man who would lend his clothes," remarked Tom.

"You never can tell. Someone may have borrowed it without his knowledge. You'd better go a bit slow, Tom."

"Well, maybe I had. But it's a clue, anyhow."

Ned agreed to this.

"And all I've got to do is to find out who was in the coat when it was riding about in my airship," went on Tom.

"Yes," said Ned, "and then maybe you'll have some clue to the disappearance of Mr. Damon."

"Right you are! Come on, let's get busy!"

"As if we hadn't been busy all the while!" laughed Ned. "I'll lose my place at the bank if I don't get back soon."

"Oh, stay a little longer—a few days," urged Tom. "I'm sure that something is going to happen soon. Anyhow my photo telephone is about perfected. But I've just thought of another improvement."

"What is it?"

"I'm going to arrange a sort of dictaphone, or phonograph, so I can get a permanent record of what a person says over the wire, as well as get a picture of him saying it. Then everything will be complete. This last won't be hard to do, as there are several machines on the market now, for preserving a record of telephone conversations. I'll make mine a bit different, though."

"Tom, is there any limit to what you're going to do?" asked Ned, admiringly.

"Oh, yes, I'm going to stop soon, and retire," laughed the young inventor.

After talking the matter over, Tom and his chum decided to wait a day or so before taking any action in regard to the button clue to the takers of the airship. After all, no great harm had been done, and Tom was more anxious to locate Mr. Damon, and try to get back his fortune, as well as to perfect his photo telephone, than he was to discover those who had helped themselves to the *Eagle*.

Tom and Ned put in some busy days, arranging the phonograph attachment. It was easy, compared to the hard work of sending a picture over the wire. They paid several visits to Mrs. Damon, but she had no news of her missing husband, and, as the days went by, she suffered more and more under the strain.

Finally Tom's new invention was fully completed. It was a great success, and he not only secured pictures of Ned and others over the wire, as he talked to them, but he imprinted on wax cylinders, to be reproduced later, the very things they said.

It was a day or so after he had demonstrated his new attachment for the first time, that Tom received a most urgent message from Mrs. Damon.

"Tom," she said, over the telephone, "I wish you would call. Something very mysterious has happened."

"Mr. Damon hasn't come back; has he?" asked Tom eagerly.

"No—but I wish I could say he had. This concerns him, however. Can you come?"

"I'll be there right away."

In his speedy monoplane Tom soon reached Waterford. Ned did not accompany him this time.

"Now what is it, Mrs. Damon?" asked the young inventor.

"About half an hour before I called you," she said, "I received a mysterious message."

"Who brought it?" asked Tom quickly.

"No one. It came over the telephone. Someone, whose voice I did not know, said to me: 'Sign the land papers, and send them to us, and your husband will be released.' "

"That message came over the wire?" cried Tom, excitedly.

"Yes," answered Mrs. Damon. "Oh, I am so frightened! I don't know what to do!" and the lady burst into tears.

CHAPTER XVIII

ANOTHER CALL

Tom Swift, for the moment, did not know what to do. It was a strange situation, and one he had never thought of. What did the mysterious message mean? He must think it all out, and plan some line of action. Clearly Mrs. Damon was not able to do so.

"Now let's get at this in some kind of order," suggested the youth, when Mrs. Damon had calmed herself. It was his habit to have a method about doing things. "And don't worry," he advised. "I am certain some good will come of this. It proves one thing, that's sure."

"What is it, Tom?"

"That Mr. Damon is alive and well. Otherwise the message would not have said he would be 'released.' It wasn't from anyone you know; was it?"

"No, I'm sure I never heard the voice before."

Tom paused a moment to think how useful his photo telephone and phonograph arrangement might have been in this case.

"How did the telephone call come in?" inquired the young inventor.

"In the usual way," answered Mrs. Damon. "The bell rang, and, as I happened to be near the instrument, I answered it, as I often do, when the maid is busy. A voice asked if I was Mrs. Damon, and of course I said I was. Then I heard this: 'Sign the land papers, and send them to us, and your husband will be released.' "

"Was that all?" Tom asked.

"I think so—I made a note of it at the time." Mrs. Damon looked into a small red book. "No, that wasn't all," she said, quickly. "I was so astonished, at hearing those strange words about my husband, that I didn't know what to say. Before I could ask any questions the voice went on to say, rather abruptly: 'We will call you again.'"

"That's good!" cried Tom. "I only hope they do it while I am here. Perhaps I can get some clue as to who it was called you. But was this all you heard?"

"Yes, I'm sure that was all. I had forgotten about the last words, but I see I have them written down in my note book."

"Did you ask any questions?" inquired Tom.

"Oh, indeed I did! As soon as I got over being stunned by what I heard, I asked all sorts of questions. I demanded to know who was speaking, what they meant, where they were, and all that. I begged them to tell me something of my husband."

"And what did they say?"

"Not a thing. There wasn't a sound in the telephone. The receiver was hung up, breaking the connection after that message to me—that mysterious message."

"Yes, it was mysterious," agreed Tom, thoughtfully. "I can't understand it. But didn't you try to learn from the central operator where the call had come from?"

"Oh, yes, indeed, Tom! As soon as I found out the person speaking to me had rung off, I got the girl in the exchange."

"And what did she say?"

"That the call came from an automatic pay station in a drug store in town. I have the address. It was one of those telephones where you put your money for the call in a slot."

"I see. Well, the first thing to do is for me to go to that drug store and find out, if I can, who used the telephone about that time. It's a slim chance, but we'll have to take it. Was it a man's voice, or a woman's?"

"Oh, a man's, I'm sure. It was very deep and heavy. No woman could speak like that."

"So much is settled, anyhow. Now about the land papers—what was meant?"

"I'll tell you," said Mrs. Damon. "You know part of our property—considerable land and some buildings—is in my name. Mr. Damon had it fixed so a number of years ago, in order to protect me. No one could get this property, and land, unless I signed the deeds, or agreed to sign them. Now all of Mr. Damon's fortune is tied up in some of Mr. Peters's companies. That is why my husband has disappeared."

"He didn't disappear—he was taken away against his will; I'm positive of that!" exclaimed Tom.

"Perhaps so," agreed Mrs. Damon, sadly. "But those are the papers referred to, I'm sure."

"Probably," assented Tom. "The rascals want to get control of everything—even your possessions. Not satisfied with ruining Mr. Damon, they want to make you a beggar, too. So they are playing on your fears. They promise to release your husband if you will give them the land."

"Yes, that must be it, Tom. What would you advise me to do? I am so frightened over this!"

"Do? Don't you do anything!" cried Tom. "We'll fool these rascals yet. If they got those papers they might release Mr. Damon, or they might not—fearing he would cause their arrest later. But we'll have him released anyhow, and we'll save what is left of your fortune. Put those land papers in a safe-deposit box, and let me do the rest. I'm going to catch those fellows!"

"But how, Tom? You don't know who they are. And a mere message over a telephone won't give you a clue to where they are."

"Perhaps not an ordinary message," agreed Tom. "But I'm going to try some of my new inventions. You said they told you they were going to call again?"

"That's what they said, Tom."

"Well, when they do, I want to be here. I want to listen to that message. If you will allow me, I'll take up my residence here for a while, Mrs. Damon."

"Allow you? I'll be only too glad if you will, Tom. But I thought you were going to try to get some clue from the drug store where the mysterious message came from."

"I'll let Ned Newton do that. I want to stay here."

Tom telephoned to Ned to meet him at Mrs. Damon's house, and also to bring with him certain things from the laboratory. And when Ned arrived in an auto, with various bits of apparatus, Tom put in some busy hours.

Meanwhile Ned was sent to the drug store, to see if any clues could be obtained there as to who had sent the message. As Tom had feared, nothing could be learned. There were several automatic 'phones in the place, and they were used very often during the day by the public. The drug clerks took little or no notice of the persons entering or leaving the booths, since the dropping of a coin in the slot was all that was necessary to be connected with central.

"Well, we've got to wait for the second call here," said Tom, who had been busy during Ned's absence. He had fitted to Mrs. Damon's telephone a recording wax phonograph cylinder, to get a record of the speaker's voice. And he had also put in an extension telephone, so that he could listen while Mrs. Damon talked to the unknown.

"There, I guess we're ready for them," said Tom, late that afternoon. But no queer call came in that day. It was the next morning, about ten o'clock, after Mrs. Damon had passed a restless night, that the telephone bell rang. Tom, who was on the alert, was at his auxiliary instrument in a flash. He motioned to Mrs. Damon to answer on the main wire.

"Hello," she spoke into the transmitter. "Who is this?"

"Are you Mrs. Damon?" Tom heard come over the wire in a deep voice, and by the manner in which Mrs. Damon signalled the young inventor knew that, at the other end of the line, was the mysterious man who had spoken before.

CHAPTER XIX

THE BUZZING SOUND

"Are you Mrs. Damon?" came the question again—rather more impatiently this time, Tom thought.

"Yes," answered the lady, glancing over at Tom. The extension telephone was in the same room. Softly Tom switched on the phonograph attachment. The little wax cylinder began to revolve noiselessly, ready to record the faintest word that came over the wire.

"You got a message from me yesterday," went on the hoarse voice. In vain Tom tried to recall whether or not he had heard it before. He could not place it.

"Who are you?" asked Mrs. Damon. She and Tom had previously agreed on a line of talk. "Tell me your name, please."

"There's no need for any names to be used," went on the unknown at the other end of the wire. "You heard what I said yesterday. Are you willing to send me those land title papers, if we release your husband?"

"But where shall I send them?" asked Mrs. Damon, to gain time.

"You'll be told where. And listen—no tricks! You needn't try to find out who I am, nor where I am. Just send those papers if you want to see your husband again."

"Oh, how is he? Tell me about him! You are cruel to keep him a prisoner like this! I demand that you release him!"

Tom had not told Mrs. Damon to say this. It came out of her own heart—she could not prevent the agonized outburst.

"Never mind about that, now," came the gruff voice over the wire. "Are you willing to send the papers?"

Mrs. Damon looked over to Tom for silent instructions. He nodded his head in assent.

"Yes, I—I will send them if you tell me where to get them to you—if you will release Mr. Damon," said the anxious wife. "But tell me who you are—and where you are!" she begged.

"None of that! I'm not looking to be arrested. You get the papers ready, and I'll let you know tomorrow, about this time, where to send them."

"Wait a minute!" called Mrs. Damon, to gain more time. "I must know just what papers you want."

"All right, I'll tell you," and he began to describe the different ones.

It took a little time for the unknown to give this information to Mrs. Damon. The man was very particular about the papers. There were trust deeds, among other things, and he probably thought that once he had possession of them, with Mrs. Damon's signature, even though it had been obtained under a threat, he could claim the property. Later it was learned that such was not the case, for Mrs. Damon, with Tom's aid, could have proved the fraud, had the scoundrels tried to get the remainder of the Damon fortune.

But at the time it seemed to the helpless woman that everything she owned would be taken from her. Though she said she did not care, as long as Mr. Damon was restored to her.

As I have said, the telephoning of the instructions about the papers took some time. Tom had counted on this, and had made his plans accordingly.

As soon as the telephone call had come in, Tom had communicated with a private detective who was in waiting, and this man had gone to the drug store whence the first call had come. He was going to try to make the arrest of the man telephoning.

But for fear the scoundrel would go to a different instrument, Tom took another precaution. This was to have one of the operators in the central exchange on the watch. As soon as Mrs. Damon's house was in connection with another telephone, the location of the latter would be noted, and another private detective would be sent there. Thus Tom hoped to catch the man at the 'phone.

Meanwhile Tom listened to the hoarse voice at the other end of the wire, giving the directions to Mrs. Damon. Tom hoped that soon there would be an arrest made.

Meanwhile the talk was being faithfully recorded on the phonograph cylinder. And, as the man talked on, Tom became aware of a curious undercurrent of sound. It was a buzzing noise, that Tom knew did not come from the instrument itself. It was not the peculiar tapping, singing noise heard in a telephone receiver, caused by induced electrical currents, or by wire trouble.

"This is certainly different," mused Tom. He was trying to recall where he had heard the noise before. Sometimes it was faint, and then it would gradually increase, droning off into faintness once more. Occasionally it was so loud that Mrs. Damon could not hear the talk about the papers, and the man would have to repeat.

But finally he came to an end.

"This is all now," he said, sharply. Tom heard the words above the queer, buzzing, humming sound. "You are keeping me too long. I think you are up to some game, but it won't do you any good, Mrs. Damon. I'll 'phone you tomorrow where to send the papers. And if you don't send them—if you try any tricks—it will be the worse for you and Mr. Damon!"

There was a click, that told of a receiver being placed back on the hook, and the voice ceased. So, also, did the queer, buzzing sound over which Tom puzzled.

"What can it have been?" he asked. "Did you hear it, Mrs. Damon?"

"What, Tom?"

"That buzzing sound."

"Yes, I heard, but I didn't know what it was. Oh, Tom, what shall I do?"

"Don't worry. We'll see if anything happened. They may have caught that fellow. If not I'll plan another scheme."

Tom's first act was to call up the telephone exchange to learn where the second call had come from. He got the information at once. The address was in the suburbs. The man had not gone to the drug store this time.

"Did the detective get out to that address?" asked Tom eagerly of the manager.

"Yes. As soon as we were certain that he was the party you wanted, your man got right after him, Mr. Swift."

"That's good, I hope he catches him!" cried the young inventor. "We'll have to wait and find out."

"He said he'd call up and let you know as soon as he reached the place," the telephone manager informed Tom.

There was nothing to do but wait, and meanwhile Tom did what he could to comfort Mrs. Damon. She was quite nervous and inclined to be hysterical, and the youth thought it wise to have a cousin, who had come to stay with her, summon the doctor.

"But, Tom, what shall I do about those papers?" Mrs. Damon asked him. "Shall I send them?"

"Indeed not!"

"But I want Mr. Damon restored to me," she pleaded. "I don't care about the money. He can make more."

"Well, we'll not give those scoundrels the satisfaction of getting any money out of you. Just wait now, I'll work this thing out, and find a way to catch that fellow. If I could only think what that buzzing sound was—"

Then, in a flash, it came to Tom.

"A sawmill! A planing mill!" he cried. "That's what it was! That fellow was telephoning from some place near a sawmill!"

The telephone rang in the midst of Tom's excited comments.

"Yes—yes!" he called eagerly. "Who is it—what is it?"

"This is Larsen—the private detective you sent."

"Oh, yes, you were at the drug store."

"Yes, Mr. Swift. Well, that party didn't call up from here."

"I know, Larsen. It was from another station. We're after him. Much obliged to you. Come on back."

Tom was sure his theory was right. The man had called up the Damon house from some telephone near a sawmill. And a little later Tom's theory was proved to be true. He got a report from the second detective. Unfortunately the man had not been able to reach the telephone station before the unknown speaker had departed.

"Was the place near a sawmill?" asked Tom, eagerly.

"It was," answered the detective over the wire. "The telephone is right next door to one. It's an automatic pay station and no one seems to have noticed who the man was who telephoned. I couldn't get a single clue. I'm sorry."

"Never mind," said Tom, as cheerfully as he could. "I think I'm on the right track now. I'm going to lay a trap for this fellow."

CHAPTER XX

SETTING THE TRAP

Troublesome problems seemed to be multiplying for Tom Swift. He admitted as much himself after the failure to capture the man who had telephoned to Mrs. Damon. He had hoped that his plan of sending detectives to the location of the telephones would succeed. Since it had not the youth must try other means.

"Now, Ned," he said to his chum, when they were on their way from Mrs. Damon's, it being impossible to do anything further there. "Now, Ned, we've got to think this thing out together."

"I'm willing, Tom. I'll do what I can."

"I know you will. Now the thing to do is to go at this thing systematically. Otherwise we'll be working around in a circle, and won't get anywhere. In the first place, let's set down what we do know. Then we'll put down what we don't know, and go after that."

"Put down what you don't know?" exclaimed Ned. "How are you going to put down a thing when you don't know it?"

"I mean we can put a question mark after it, so to speak. For instance we don't know where Mr. Damon is, but we want to find out."

"Oh, I see. Well, let's start off with the things we do know."

The two friends were at Tom's house by now, having come from Waterford in Tom's airship. After thinking over all the exciting happenings of the past few days, Tom remarked: "Now, Ned, for the things we do know. In the first place Mr. Damon is missing, and his fortune is about gone. There is considerable left to Mrs. Damon, however, but those scoundrels may get that away from her, if we don't watch out. Secondly, my airship was taken and brought back, with a button more than it had when it went away. Said button exactly matched one off Mr. Boylan's coat."

"Thirdly, Mr. Damon was either taken away or went away, in an airship—either in mine or someone else's. Fourthly, Mrs. Damon has received telephonic communications from the man, or men, who have her husband. Fifthly, Mr. Peters, either legally or illegally, is responsible for the loss of Mr. Damon's fortune. Now: there you are—for the things we do know."

"Now for the things we don't know. We don't know who has taken Mr. Damon away, nor where he is, to begin with the most important."

"Hold on, Tom, I think you're wrong," broke in Ned.

"In what way?"

"About not knowing who is responsible for the taking away of Mr. Damon. I think it's as plain as the nose on your face that Peters is responsible."

"I can't see it that way," said Tom, quickly. "I will admit that it looks as though Boylan had been in my airship, but as for Peters taking Mr. Damon away—why, Peters is around town all the while, and if he had a hand in the disappearance of Mr. Damon, do you think he'd stay here, when he knows we are working on the case? And would he send Boylan to see me if Boylan had been one of those who had a hand in it? They wouldn't dare, especially as they know I'm working on the case."

"Peters is a bad lot. I'll grant you, though, he was fair enough to pay for my motor boat. I don't believe he had anything to do with taking Mr. Damon away."

"Do you think he was the person who was talking to Mrs. Damon about the papers?"

"No, Ned. I don't. I listened to that fellow's voice carefully. It wasn't like Peters's. I'm going to put it in the phonograph, too, and let you listen to it. Then see what you say."

Tom did this, a little later. The record of the voice, as it came over the wire, was listened to from the wax cylinder, and Ned had to admit that it was not much like that of the promoter.

"Well, what's next to be done?" asked the young banker.

"I'm going to set a trap," replied Tom, with a grin.

"Set a trap?"

"Yes, a sort of mouse-trap. I'm glad my photo telephone is now perfected, Ned."

"What has that got to do with it?"

"That's going to be my trap, Ned. Here is my game. You know this fellow—this strange unknown—is going to call up Mrs. Damon tomorrow. Well, I'll be ready for him. I'm going to put in the booth where he will telephone from, one of my photo telephones—that is, the sending apparatus. In Mrs. Damon's house, attached to her telephone, will be the receiving plate, as well as the phonograph cylinder."

"When this fellow starts to talk he'll be sending us his picture, though he won't know it, and we'll be getting a record of his voice. Then we'll have him just where we want him."

"Good!" cried Ned. "But, Tom, there's a weak spot in your mouse-trap."

"What is it?"

"How are you going to know which telephone the unknown will call up from? He may go to any of a hundred, more or less."

"He might—yes. But that's a chance we've got to take. It isn't so much of a chance, though when you stop to think that he will probably go to some public telephone in an isolated spot, and, unless I'm much mistaken he will go to a telephone near where he was today. He knows that was safe, since we didn't capture him, and he's very likely to come back."

"But to make the thing as sure as possible, I'm going to attach my apparatus to a number of public telephones in the vicinity of the one near the sawmill. So if the fellow doesn't get caught in one, he will in another. I admit it's taking a chance; but what else can we do?"

"I suppose you're right, Tom. It's like setting a number of traps."

"Exactly. A trapper can't be sure where he is going to get his catch, so he picks out the place, or run-way, where the game has been in the habit of coming. He hides his traps about that place, and trusts to luck that the animal will blunder into one of them."

"Criminals, to my way of thinking, are a good bit like animals. They seem to come back to their old haunts. Nearly any police story proves this. And it's that on which I am counting to capture this criminal. So I'm going to fit up as many telephones with my photo and phonograph outfit, as I can in the time we have. You'll have to help me. Luckily I've got plenty of selenium plates for the sending end. I'll only need one at the receiving end. Now we'll have to go and have a talk with the telephone manager, after which we'll get busy."

"You've overlooked one thing, Tom."

"What's that, Ned?"

"Why, if you know about which telephone this fellow is going to use, why can't you have police stationed near it to capture him as soon as he begins to talk?"

"Well, I did think of that, Ned; but it won't work."

"Why not?"

"Because, in the first place this man, or some of his friends, will be on the watch. When he goes into the place to telephone there'll be a look-out, I'm sure, and he'd either put off talking to Mrs. Damon, or he'd escape before we had any evidence against him."

"You see I've got to get evidence that will stand in the courts to convict this fellow, and if he's scared off before we get that, the game will be up."

"That's what my photo telephone will do—it will get the evidence, just as a dictaphone does. In fact, I'm thinking of working it out on those lines, after I clear up this business."

"Just suppose we had detectives stationed at all the telephones near the sawmill, where this fellow would be likely to go. In the first place no one has seen him, as far as we know, so there's no telling what sort of a chap he is. And you can't go up to a perfect stranger and arrest him because you think he is the man who has spirited away Mr. Damon."

"Another thing. Until this fellow has talked, and made his offer to Mrs. Damon, to restore her husband, in exchange for certain papers, we have no hold over him."

"But he has done that, Tom. You heard him, and you have his voice down on the wax cylinder."

"Yes, but I haven't had a glimpse of his face. That's what I want, and what I'm going to get. Suppose he does go into the telephone booth, and tell Mrs. Damon an address where she is to send the papers. Even if a detective was near at hand he might not catch what was said. Or, if he did, on what ground could he arrest a man who, very likely, would be a perfect stranger to him? The detective couldn't say: 'I take you into custody for telephoning an address to Mrs. Damon.' That, in itself, is no crime."

"No, I suppose not," admitted Ned. "You've got this all thought out, Tom."

"I hope I have. You see it takes quite a combination to get evidence against a criminal—evidence that will convict him. That's why I have to be so careful in setting my trap."

"I see, Tom. Well, it's about time for us to get busy; isn't it?"

"It sure is. There's lots to do. First we'll go see the telephone people."

Tom explained to the 'phone manager the necessity for what he was about to do. The manager at once agreed to let the young inventor have a free hand. He was much interested in the photo telephone, and Tom promised to give his company a chance to use it on their lines, later.

The telephone near the sawmill was easily located. It was in a general store, and the instrument was in a booth. To this instrument Tom attached his sending plate, and he also substituted for the ordinary incandescent light, a powerful tungsten one, that would give illumination enough to cause the likeness to be transmitted over the wire.

The same thing was done to a number of the public telephones in that vicinity, each one being fitted up so that the picture of whoever talked would be transmitted over the wire when Tom turned the switch. To help the plan further the telephone manager marked a number of other 'phones, "Out of Order," for the time being.

"Now, I think we're done!" exclaimed the young inventor, with a sigh, late that night. He and Ned and the line manager had worked hard.

"Yes," answered the young banker, "the traps are set. The question is: Will our rat be caught?"

CHAPTER XXI

THE PHOTO TELEPHONE

Tom Swift was taking, as he afterward confessed, "a mighty big chance." But it seemed the only way. He was working against cunning men, and had to be as cunning as they.

True, the man he hoped to capture, through the combination of his photo telephone and the phonograph, might go to some other instrument than one of those Tom had adjusted. But this could not be helped. In all he had put his new attachment on eight 'phones in the vicinity of the sawmill. So he had eight chances in his favor, and as many against him as there were other telephones in use.

"It's a mighty small margin in our favor," sighed Tom.

"It sure is," agreed Ned. They were at Mrs. Damon's house, waiting for the call to come in.

"But we couldn't do anything else," went on Tom.

"No," spoke Ned, "and I have a great deal of hope in the proverbial Swift luck, Tom."

"Well, I only hope it holds good this time!" laughed the young inventor.

"There are a good many things that can go wrong," observed Ned. "The least little slip-up may spoil your traps, Tom."

"I know it, Ned. But I've got to take the chance. We've just got to do something for Mrs. Damon. She's wearing herself out by worrying," he added in a low voice, for indeed the wife of his friend felt the absence of her husband greatly. She had lost flesh, she ate scarcely anything, and her nights were wakeful ones of terror.

"What if this fails?" asked Ned.

"Then I'm going to work that button clue to the limit," replied Tom. "I'll go to Boylan and see what he and Peters have to say."

"If you'd done as I suggested you'd have gone to them first," spoke Ned. "You'll find they're mixed up in this."

"Maybe; but I doubt it. I tell you there isn't a clue leading to Peters—as yet."

"But there will be," insisted Ned. "You'll see that that I'm right this time."

"I can't see it, Ned. As a matter of fact, I would have gone to Boylan about that button I found in my airship only I've been so busy on this photo telephone, and in arranging the trap, that I haven't had time. But if this fails—and I'm hoping it won't—I'll get after him," and there was a grim look on the young inventor's face.

It was wearying and nervous work—this waiting. Tom and Ned felt the strain as they sat there in Mrs. Damon's library, near the telephone. It had been fitted up in readiness. Attached to the receiving wires was a sensitive plate, on which Tom hoped would be imprinted the image of the man at the other end of the wire—the criminal who, in exchange for the valuable land papers, would give Mr. Damon his liberty.

There was also the phonograph cylinder to record the man's voice. Several times, while waiting for the call to come in, Tom got up to test the apparatus. It was in perfect working order.

As before, there was an extension telephone, so that Mrs. Damon could talk to the unknown, while Tom could hear as well. But he planned to take no part in the conversation unless something unforeseen occurred.

Mr. Damon was an enthusiastic photographer, and he had a dark room adjoining his library. It was in this dark room that Tom planned to develop the photo telephone plate.

On this occasion he was not going to use the metal plate in which, ordinarily, the image of the person talking appeared. That record was but a fleeting one, as in a mirror. This time Tom wanted a permanent picture that could, if necessary, be used in a court of justice.

Tom's plan was this: If the person who had demanded the papers came to one of the photo telephones, and spoke to Mrs. Damon, Tom would switch on the receiving apparatus. Thus, while the man was talking, his picture would be taken, though he would not know of the thing being done.

His voice would also be recorded on the wax cylinder, and he would be equally unaware of this.

When Tom had imprinted the fellow's image on the prepared plate, he would go quickly to the dark room and develop it. A wet print could be made, and with this as evidence, and to use in identification, a quick trip could be made to the place whence the man had telephoned. Tom hoped thus to capture him.

To this end he had his airship in waiting, and as soon as he had developed the picture he planned to rush off to the vicinity of the sawmill, and make a prisoner of the man whose features would be revealed to him over the wire.

It was a hazardous plan—a risky one—but it was the best that he could evolve. Tom had instructed Mrs. Damon to keep the man in conversation as long as possible, in order to give the young inventor himself time to rush off in his airship. But of course the man might get suspicious and leave. That was another chance that had to be taken.

"If I had thought of it in time," said Tom, musingly, as he paced up and down in the library waiting for the 'phone to ring, "if I had thought of it in time I would have rigged up two plates—one for a temporary, or looking-glass, picture, and the other for a permanent one. In that way I could rush off as soon as I got a glimpse of the fellow. But it's too late to do that now. I'll have to develop this plate."

Waiting is the most wearisome work there is. Tom and Ned found this to be the case, as they sat there, hoping each moment that the telephone bell would ring, and that the man at the other end of the wire would be the mysterious stranger. Mrs. Damon, too, felt the nervous strain.

"This is about the hour he called up yesterday," said Tom, in a low voice, after coming back from a trip to the window to see that his airship was in readiness. He had brought over to help in starting it, for he was using his most powerful and speedy craft, and the propellers were hard to turn.

"Yes," answered Mrs. Damon. "It was just about this hour, Tom. Oh, I do hope—"

She was interrupted by the jingle of the telephone bell. With a jump Tom was at the auxiliary instrument, while Mrs. Damon lifted off the receiver of her own telephone.

"Yes; what is it?" she asked, in a voice that she tried to make calm.

"Do you know who this is?" Tom heard come over the wire.

"Are you the—er—the person who was to give me an address where I am to send certain papers?"

"Yes. I'm the same one. I'm glad to see that you have acted sensibly. If I get the papers all right, you'll soon have your husband back. Now do as I say. Take down this address."

"Very well," assented Mrs. Damon. She looked over at Tom. He was intently listening, and he, too, would note the address given. The trap was about to be sprung. The game had walked into it. Just which telephone was being used Tom could not as yet tell. It was evidently not the one nearest the planing mill, for Tom could not hear the buzzing sound. It was well he had put his attachment on several instruments.

"One moment, please," said Mrs. Damon, to the unknown at the other end of the wire. This was in accordance with the pre-arranged plan.

"Well, what is it?" asked the man, impatiently. "I have no time to waste."

Tom heard again the same gruff tones, and he tried in vain to recognize them.

"I want you take down a message to Mr. Damon," said his wife. "This is very important. It can do you no harm to give him this message; but I want you to get it exact. If you do not promise to deliver it I shall call all negotiations off."

"Oh, all right I'll take the message; but be quick about it. Then I'll give you the address where you are to send the papers."

"This is the message," went on Mrs. Damon. "Please write it down. It is very important to me. Have you a pencil?"

"Yes, I have one. Wait until I get a bit of paper. It's so dark in this booth—wait until I turn on the light."

Tom could not repress a pleased and joyful exclamation. It was just what he had hoped the man would do—turn on the light in the booth. Indeed, it was necessary for the success of the trap that the light be switched on. Otherwise no picture could be transmitted over the wire. And the plan of having the man write down a message to Mr. Damon was arranged with that end in view. The man would need a light to see to write, and Tom's apparatus must be lighted in order to make it work. The plot was coming along finely.

"There!" exclaimed the man at the other end of the wire. "I have a light now. Go ahead with your message, Mrs. Damon. But make it short. I can't stay here long."

Then Mrs. Damon began dictating the message she and Tom had agreed upon. It was as long as they dared make it, for they wanted to keep the man in the booth to the last second.

"Dear Husband," began Mrs. Damon. What the message was does not matter. It has nothing to do with this story. Sufficient to say that the moment the man began writing it down, as Tom could tell over the sensitive wire, by the scratching of the pencil—at that moment Tom, knowing the light was on in the distant telephone booth, switched on the picture-taking apparatus. His receiving apparatus at once indicated that the image was being made on the sensitive plate.

It took only a few seconds of time, and with the plate in the holder Tom hastened to the dark room to develop it. Ned took his chum's place at the telephone, to see that all worked smoothly. The photo telephone had done it's work. Whose image would be found imprinted on the sensitive plate? Tom's hands trembled so that he could scarcely put it in the developing solution.

CHAPTER XXII

THE ESCAPE

Ned Newton, listening at the auxiliary telephone heard the man, to whom Mrs. Damon was dictating her message to her husband, utter an exclamation of impatience.

"I'm afraid I can't take down any more," he called. "That is enough. Now you listen. I want you to send me those papers."

"And I am willing to," went on Mrs. Damon, while Ned listened to the talk, the phonograph faithfully recording it.

"I wonder whose picture Tom will find," mused Ned.

The unknown, at the other end of the wire, began giving Mrs. Damon a description of just what papers he wanted, and how to mail them to him. He gave an address that Ned recognized as that of a cigar store, where many persons received their mail under assumed names. The postal authorities had, for a long time, tried to get evidence against it.

"That's going to make it hard to get him, when he comes for the papers," thought Ned. "He's a foxy criminal, all right. But I guess Tom will turn the trick."

Mrs. Damon was carefully noting down the address. She really intended to send the papers, if it proved that there was no other way in which she could secure the release of her husband. But she did not count on all of Tom's plans. "Why doesn't he develop that plate?" thought Ned. "He'll be too late, in spite of his airship. That fellow will skip."

It was at that moment that Tom came into the library. He moved cautiously, for he realized that a loud sound in the room would carry to the man at the other end of the wire. Tom motioned for Ned to come to him. He held out a dripping photographic plate.

"It's Peters!" said Tom, in a hoarse whisper.

"Peters?" gasped Ned. "How could it be? His voice—"

"I know. It didn't sound a bit like Peters over the 'phone, but there's his picture, all right!"

Tom held up the plate. There, imprinted on it by the wonderful power of the young inventor's latest appliance, was the image of the rascally promoter. As plainly as in life he was shown, even to his silk hat and the flower in his button-hole. He was in a telephone booth—that much could be told from the photograph that had been transmitted over the wire, but which booth could not be said—they were nearly all alike.

"Peters!" gasped Ned. "I thought he was the fellow, Tom."

"Yes, I know. You were right, and I was wrong. But I did not recognize his voice. It was very hoarse. He must have a bad cold." Later this was learned to have been the case. "There's no time to lose," whispered Tom, while Mrs. Damon was doing her best to prolong the conversation in order to hold the man at the other end of the wire. "Ned, get central on the other telephone, and see where this call came from. Then we'll get there as fast as the airship will take us."

A second and temporary telephone line had been installed in the Damon home, and on this Ned was soon talking, while Tom, putting the photographic plate away for future use, rushed out to get his airship in shape for a quick flight. He had modified his plans. Instead of having a detective take a print of the photo telephone image, and make the arrest, Tom was going to try to capture Peters himself. He believed he could do it. One look at the wet plate was enough. He knew Peters, though it upset some of his theories to learn that it was the promoter who was responsible for Mr. Damon's disappearance.

The man at the other end of the wire was evidently getting impatient. Possibly he suspected some trick. "I've got to go now," he called to Mrs. Damon. "If I don't get those papers in the morning it will be the worse for Mr. Damon."

"Oh, I'll send you the papers," she said.

By this time Ned had gotten into communication with the manager of the central telephone exchange, and had learned the location of the instrument Peters was using. It was about a mile from the one near the sawmill.

"Come on!" called Tom to his chum, as the latter gave him this information. "The Firefly is tuned up for a hundred miles an hour! We'll be there in ten minutes! We must catch him red-handed, if possible!"

"He's gone!" gasped Mrs. Damon as she came to the outer door, and watched Tom and Ned taking their places in the airship, while Koku prepared to twirl the propellers.

"Gone!" echoed Tom, blankly.

"Yes, he hung up the receiver."

"See if you can't get him back," suggested the young inventor. "Ask Central to ring that number again. We'll be there in a jiffy. Maybe he'll come to the telephone again. Or he may even call up his partners and tell them the game is working his way. Try to get him back, Mrs. Damon."

"I will," she said.

And, as she hurried back to the instrument, Tom and Ned shot up toward the blue sky in an endeavor to capture the man at the other telephone.

"And to think it was Peters!" cried Tom into Ned's ear, shouting to be heard above the roar of the motor exhaust.

"I thought he'd turn out to be mixed up in the affair," said Ned.

"Well, you were right. I was off, that time," admitted Tom, as he guided his powerful craft above the trees. "I was willing to admit that he had something to do with Mr. Damon's financial trouble, but as for kidnapping him—well, you never can tell."

They drove on at a breath-catching pace, and it seemed hardly a minute after leaving Mrs. Damon's house before Tom called:

"There's the building where the telephone is located."

"And now for that rascal Peters!" cried Ned.

The airship swooped down, to the great astonishment of some work-men nearby.

Hardly had the wheels ceased revolving on the ground, as Tom made a quick landing, than he was out of his seat, and running toward the telephone. He knew the place at once from having heard Ned's descrip-tion, and besides, this was one of the places where he had installed his apparatus.

Into the store Tom burst, and made a rush for the 'phone booth. He threw open the door. The place was empty!

"The man—the man who was telephoning!" Tom called to the pro-prietor of the place.

"You mean that big man, with the tall hat, who was in there so long?"

"Yes, where is he?"

"Gone. About two minutes ago."

"Which way?"

"Over toward Shopton, and in one of the fastest autos that ever scat-tered dust in this section."

"He's escaped us!" said Tom to Ned. "But we'll get him yet! Come on!"

"I'm with you. Say, do you know what this looks like to me?"

"What?"

"It looks as if Peters was scared and was going to run away to stay!"

CHAPTER XXIII

ON THE TRAIL

Such a crowd had quickly gathered about Tom's airship that it was impossible to start it. Men and boys, and even some girls and women, coming from no one knew where, stood about the machine, making won-dering remarks about it.

"Stand back, if you please!" cried Tom, good-naturedly. "We've got to get after the fellow in the auto."

"You'll have hard work catching him, friend, in that rig," remarked a man. "He was fracturing all the speed laws ever passed. I reckon he was going nigh onto sixty miles an hour."

"We can make a hundred," spoke Ned, quietly.

"A hundred! Get out!" cried the man. "Nothing can go as fast as that!"

"We'll show you, if we once get started," said Tom. "I guess we'll have to get one of these fellows to twirl the propellers for us, Ned," he added. "I didn't think, or I'd have brought the selfstarting machine," for this one of Tom's had to be started by someone turning over the propellers, once or twice, to enable the motor to begin to speed. On some of his aircraft the young inventor had attached a starter, something like the ones on the newest autos.

"What are you going to do?" asked Ned, as Tom looked to the priming of the cylinders.

"I'm going to get on the trail of Peters," he said. "He's at the bottom of the whole business; and it's a surprise to me. I'm going to trail him right down to the ground now, and make him give up Mr. Damon and his fortune."

"But you don't know where he is, Tom."

"I'll find out. He isn't such an easy man to miss—he's too conspicuous. Besides, if he's just left in his auto we may catch him before he gets to Shopton."

"Do you think he's going there?"

"I think so. And I think, Ned, that he's become suspicious and will light out. Something must have happened, while he was telephoning, and he got frightened, as big a bluff as he is. But we'll get him. Come on! Will you turn over the propellers, please? I'll show you how to do it," Tom went on to a big, strong man standing close to the blades.

"Sure I'll do it," was the answer. "I was a helper once at an airship meet, and I know how."

"Get back out of the way in time," the young inventor warned him. "They start very suddenly, sometimes."

"All right, friend, I'll watch out," was the reply, and with Tom and Ned in their seats, the former at the steering wheel, the craft of the air was soon throbbing and trembling under the first turn, for the cylinders were still warm from the run from Mrs. Damon's house.

The telephone was in an outlying section of Waterford—a section devoted in the main to shops and factories, and the homes of those employed in various lines of manufacture. Peters had chosen his place well, for there were many roads leading to and from this section, and he could easily make his escape.

"But we'll get after him," thought Tom, grimly, as he let the airship run down the straight road a short distance on the bicycle wheels, to give it momentum enough so that it would rise.

Then, with the tilting of the elevation rudder, the craft rose gracefully, amid admiring cheers from the crowd. Tom did not go up very far, as he wanted to hover near the ground, to pick out the speeding auto containing Peters.

But this time luck was not with Tom. He and Ned did sight a number of cars speeding along the highway toward Shopton, but when they got near enough to observe the occupants they were disappointed not to behold the man they sought. Tom circled about for some time, but it was of no use, and then he headed his craft back toward Waterford.

"Where are you going?" asked Ned, yelling the words into the ear of his chum.

"Back to Mrs. Damon's," answered Tom, in equally loud tones.

It was impossible to talk above the roaring and throbbing of the motor, so the two lads kept silent until the airship had landed near Mrs. Damon's home.

"I want to see if Mrs. Damon is all right," Tom explained, as he jumped from the still moving machine. "Then we'll go to Shopton, and cause Peters's arrest. I can make a charge against him now, and the evidence of the photo telephone will convict him, I'm sure. And I also want to see if Mrs. Damon has had any other word."

She had not, however, though she was more nervous and worried than ever.

"Oh, Tom, what shall I do?" she exclaimed. "I am so frightened! What do you suppose they will do to Mr. Damon?"

"Nothing at all!" Tom assured her. "He will be all right. I think matters are coming to a crisis now, and very likely he'll be with you inside of twenty-four hours. The game is up, and I guess Peters knows it. I'm going to have him arrested at once."

"Shall I send those land papers, Tom?"

"Indeed you must not! But I'll talk to you about that later. Just put away that phonograph record of Peters's talk. I'll take along the photo telephone negative, and have some prints made—or, I guess, since we're going in the airship, that I'd better leave it here for the present. We'll use it as evidence against Peters. Come on, Ned."

"Where to now?"

"Peters's house. He's probably there, arranging to cover up his tracks when he lights out."

But Shallock Peters did better than merely cover up his tracks. He covered himself up, so to speak. For when Ned and Tom, after a quick flight in the airship, reached his house, the promoter had left, and the servants, who were quite excited, did not know where he had gone.

"He just packed up a few clothes and ran out," said one of the maids. "He didn't say anything about our wages, either, and he owes me over a month."

"Me too," said another.

"Well, if he doesn't pay me some of my back wages soon, I'll sue him!" declared the gardener. "He owes me more than three months, but he kept putting me off."

And, so it seemed, Peters had done with several of his employes. When the promoter came to Shopton he had taken an elaborate house and engaged a staff of servants. Peters was not married, but he gave a number of entertainments to which the wealthy men of Shopton and their wives came. Later it was found that the bills for these had never been paid. In short, Peters was a "bluff" in more ways than one.

Tom told enough of his story to the servants to get them on his side. Indeed, now that their employer had gone, and under such queer circumstances, they had no sympathy for him. They were only concerned about their own money, and Tom was given admittance to the house.

Tom made a casual search, hoping to find some clue to the whereabouts of Mr. Damon, or to get some papers that would save his fortune. But the search was unsuccessful.

There was a safe in the room Peters used for an office, but when Tom got there the strong box was open, and only some worthless documents remained.

"He smelled a rat, all right," said Tom, grimly. "After he telephoned to Mrs. Damon something happened that gave him an intimation that someone was after him. So he got away as soon as he could."

"But what are you going to do about it, Tom?"

"Get right after him. He can't have gotten very far. I want him and I want Boylan. We're getting close to the end of the trail, Ned."

"Yes, but we haven't found Mr. Damon yet, and his fortune seems to have vanished."

"Well, we'll do the best we can," said Tom, grimly. "Now I'm going to get a warrant for the arrest of Peters, and one for Boylan, and I'm going to get myself appointed a special officer with power to serve them. We've got our work cut out for us, Ned."

"Well, I'm with you to the end."

"I know you are!" cried Tom.

CHAPTER XXIV

THE LONELY HOUSE

The young inventor had little difficulty in getting the warrants he sought. In the case of Boylan, who seemed to be Peters's righthand man, when it came to criminal work, Tom made a charge of unlawfully taking the airship. This would be enough to hold the man on until other evidence could be obtained against him.

As for Peters, he was accused of taking certain valuable bonds and stocks belonging to Mr. Damon. Mrs. Damon gave the necessary evidence in this case, and the authorities were told that later, when Peters should have been arrested, other evidence so skillfully gotten by Tom's photo telephone, would be brought before the court.

"It's a new way of convicting a man—by a photo telephone—but I guess it's a good one," said the judge who signed the warrants.

"Well, now that we've got what we want, the next thing to do is to get the men—Peters, and the others," said Tom, as he and Ned sat in Tom's library after several hours of strenuous work.

"How are you going to start?" the young banker wanted to know. "It seems a strange thing that a man like Mr. Damon could be made away with, and kept in hiding so long without something being heard of him. I'm afraid, Tom, that something must have happened to him."

"I think so too, Ned. Nothing serious, though," Tom added, quickly, as he saw the look of alarm on his chum's face. "I think Mr. Damon at first went away of his own accord."

"Of his own accord?"

"Yes. I think Peters induced him to go with him, on the pretense that he could recover his fortune. After getting Mr. Damon in their power they kept him, probably to get the rest of his fortune away from him."

"But you stopped that, Tom," said Ned, proud of his chum's abilities.

"Well, I hope so," admitted the young inventor. "But I've still got plenty to do."

"Have you a starting point?"

"For one thing," Tom answered, "I'm going to have Mrs. Damon mail a fake package to the address Peters gave. If he, or any of his men, call for it, we'll have a detective on the watch, and arrest them."

"Good!"

"Of course it may not work," spoke Tom; "but it's something to try, and we can't miss any chances."

Accordingly, the next day, a package containing only blank paper, made up to represent the documents demanded by Peters as the price of releasing Mr. Damon, was mailed to the address Mrs. Damon had received over the wire from the rascally promoter. Then a private detective was engaged to be on the watch, to take into custody whoever called for the bundle. Tom, though, had not much hope of anything coming of this, as it was evident that Peters had taken the alarm, and left.

"And now," said Tom, when he had safely put away the wax record, containing the incriminating talk of Peters, and had printed several photographs, so wonderfully taken over the wire, "now to get on the trail again."

It was not an easy one to follow. Tom began at the deserted home of the alleged financier. The establishment was broken up, for many tradesmen came with bills that had not been paid, and some of them levied on what little personal property there was to satisfy their claims. The servants left, sorrowful enough over their missing wages. The place was closed up under the sheriff's orders.

But of Peters and his men not a trace could be found. Tom and Ned traveled all over the surrounding country, looking for clues, but in vain. They made several trips in the airship, but finally decided that an automobile was more practical for their work, and kept to that.

They did find some traces of Peters. As Tom had said, the man was too prominent not to be noticed. He might have disguised himself, though it seemed that the promoter was a proud man, and liked to be seen in flashy clothes, a silk hat, and with a buttonhole bouquet.

This made it easy to get the first trace of him. He had been seen to take a train at the Shopton station, though he had not bought a ticket. The promoter had paid his fare to Branchford, a junction point, but there all trace of him was lost. It was not even certain that he went there.

"He may have done that to throw us off," said Tom. "Just because he paid his way to Branchford, doesn't say he went there. He may have gotten off at the next station beyond Shopton."

"Do you think he's still lingering around here?" asked Ned.

"I shouldn't be surprised," was Tom's answer. "He knows that there is still some of the Damon property left, and he is probably hungry for that. We'll get him yet, Ned."

But at the end of several days Tom's hopes did not seem in a fair way to be realized. He and Ned followed one useless clue after another. All the trails seemed blind ones. But Tom never gave up.

He was devoting all his time now to the finding of his friend Mr. Damon, and to the recovery of his fortune. In fact the latter was not so important to Tom as was the former. For Mrs. Damon was on the verge of a nervous collapse on account of the absence of her husband.

"If I could only have some word from him, Tom!" she cried, helplessly.

To Tom the matter was very puzzling. It seemed utterly impossible that Mr. Damon could be kept so close a prisoner that he could not manage to get some word to his friends. It was not as if he was a child. He was a man of more than ordinary abilities. Surely he might find a way to outwit his enemies.

But the days passed, and no word came. A number of detectives had been employed, but they were no more successful than Tom. The latter had given up his inventive work, for the time being, to devote all his time to the solution of the mystery.

Tom and Ned had been away from Shopton for three days, following the most promising clue they had yet received. But it had failed at the end, and one afternoon they found themselves in a small town, about a hundred miles from Shopton. They had been motoring.

"I think I'll call up the house," said Tom. "Dad may have received some news, or Mrs. Damon may have sent him some word. I'll get my father on the wire."

Connection to Tom's house was soon made, and Ned, who was listening to his chum's remarks, was startled to hear him cry out:

"What's that you say? My airship taken again? When did it happen? Yes, I'm listening. Go on, Father!"

Then followed a silence while Tom listened, breaking in now and then with an excited remark, Suddenly he called:

"Good-by, Dad! I'm coming right home!"

Tom hung up the receiver with a bang, and turned to his chum.

"What do you think!" he cried. "The *Eagle* was taken again last night! The same way as before. Nobody got a glimpse of the thieves, though. Dad has been trying to get in communication with me ever since. I'm glad I called up. Now we'll get right back to Shopton, and see what we can do. This is the limit! Peters and his crowd will be kidnapping us, next."

"That's right," agreed Ned.

He and Tom were soon off again, speeding in the auto toward Shopton. But the roads were bad, after a heavy rain, and they did not make fast time.

The coming of dusk found them with more than thirty miles to go. They were in an almost deserted section of the country when suddenly, as they were running slowly up a hill, there was a sudden crack, the auto gave a lurch to one side of the roadway and then settled heavily. Tom clapped on both brakes quickly, and gave a cry of dismay.

"Broken front axle!" he said. "We're dished, Ned!"

They got out, being no more harmed than by the jolting. The car was out of commission. The two chums looked around Except for a lonely house, that bore every mark of being deserted, not a dwelling was in sight where they might ask for aid or shelter.

And, as they looked, from that lonely house came a strange cry—a cry as though for help!

CHAPTER XXV

THE AIRSHIP CAPTURE

"Did you hear that?" cried Ned.

"I certainly did," answered Tom. "What was it?"

"Sounded to me like a cry of some sort."

"It was. An animal, I'd say."

The two chums moved away from the broken auto, and looked at each other. Then, by a common impulse, they started toward the lonely house, which was set back some distance from the road.

"Let's see who it was," suggested Tom, "After all, though it looks deserted, there may be someone in the house, and we've got to have some kind of help. I don't want to leave my car on the road all night, though it will have to be repaired before I can use it again."

"It sure is a bad break," agreed Ned.

As they walked toward the deserted house they heard the strange cry again. It was louder this time, and following it the boys heard a sound as if a blow had been struck.

"Someone is being attacked!" cried Tom. "Maybe some poor tramp has taken shelter in there and a dog is after them. Come on, Ned, we've got to help!"

They started on a run for the lonely house, but while still some distance away a curious thing happened.

There was a sudden cry—an appeal for help it seemed—but this time in the open. And, as Tom and Ned looked, they saw several men running from the rear of the old house. Between them they carried an inert form.

"Something's wrong!" exclaimed Tom, "There's crooked work going on here, Ned."

"You're right! It's up to us to stop it! Come on!"

But before the boys had taken half a dozen more steps they heard that which caused them great surprise. For from a shed behind the house came the unmistakable throb and roar of a motor.

"They're going off in an auto!" cried Ned.

"And they're carrying someone with them!" exclaimed Tom.

By this time they had gotten to a point where they could see the shed, and what was their astonishment to see being rolled from it a big biplane. At the sight of it Tom cried:

"It's the *Eagle*! That's my airship, Ned!"

"You're right! How did it get here?"

"That's for us to find out. I shouldn't wonder, Ned, but what we're at last on the trail of Peters and his crowd!"

The men—there were four or five of them, Ned guessed—now broke into a run, still carrying among them the inert form of another. The cries for help had ceased, and it seemed as if the unfortunate one was unconscious.

A moment later, and before the boys could do anything, had they the power, the men fairly jumped aboard Tom Swift's biggest airship. The unconscious one was carried with them.

Then the motor was speeded up. The roar and throbbing were almost deafening.

"Stop that! Hold on! That's my machine!" yelled Tom.

He might as well have spoken to the wind. With a rush and a roar the big *Eagle* shot away and upward, carrying the men and their mysterious, unconscious companion. It was getting too dark for Tom and Ned to make out the forms or features of the strangers.

"We're too late!" said Ned, hopelessly.

"Yes, they got away," agreed Tom. "Oh, if only I had my speedy little monoplane!"

"But who can they be? How did your airship get here? And who is that man they carried out of the house?" cried Ned.

"I don't know the last—maybe one of their crowd who was injured in a fight."

"What crowd?"

"The Peters gang, of course. Can't you see it, Ned?"

Unable to do anything, the two youths watched the flight of the *Eagle*. She did not move at her usual speed, for she was carrying too heavy a load.

Presently from the air overhead, and slightly behind them, the boys heard the sound of another motor. They turned quickly.

"Look!" cried Ned. "Another airship, by all that's wonderful!"

"If we could only stop them!" exclaimed Tom. "That's a big machine, and they could take us aboard. Then we could chase the *Eagle*. We could catch her, too, for she's overloaded!"

Frantically he and Tom waved their caps at the man who was now almost overhead in his airship. The boys did not call. They well knew, with the noise of the motor, the occupant of the airship could not hear them. But they waved and pointed to the slowly-moving *Eagle*.

To their surprise and delight the man above them shut off his engine, and seemed about to come down. Then Tom cried, knowing he could be heard:

"Help us capture that airship? It's mine and they've stolen it!"

"All right! Be with you in a minute!" came back the answer from above.

The second biplane came down to earth, ands as it ceased running along on its bicycle wheels, the occupant jumped out.

"Hello, Tom Swift!" he called, as he took off his goggles.

"Why—why it's Mr. Halling!" cried the young inventor, in delight, recognizing the birdman who had brought him the first news of Mr. Damon's trouble, the day the airship became entangled in the aerials of the wireless on Tom's house.

"What are you doing here, Tom?" asked Mr. Hailing. "What has happened?"

"We're looking for Mr. Damon. That's a bad crowd there," and he pointed toward the other aircraft. "They have my *Eagle*. Can you help me catch them?"

"I certainly can—and will! Get aboard! I can carry four."

"Then you have a new machine?"

"Yes, and a dandy! All the latest improvements—self-starter and all! I'm glad of a chance to show it to you."

"And I'm glad, too!" cried Tom. "It was providential that you happened along. What were you doing here?"

"Just out on a trial spin. But come on, if we're going to catch those fellows!"

Quickly Tom, Ned, and Mr. Halling climbed into the seats of the new airship. It was started from a switch, and in a few seconds it was on the wing, chasing after the *Eagle*.

Then began a strange race, a race in the air after the unknown strangers who had Tom's machine. Had the *Eagle* not been so heavily laden it might have escaped, for Tom's craft was a speedy one. But this time it had to give the palm to Mr. Grant Halling's. Faster and faster in pursuit flew the *Star*, as the new craft was called. Faster and faster, until at last, coming directly over the *Eagle*, Mr. Halling sent his craft down in such a manner as to "blanket" the other. In an instant she began to sink, and with cries of alarm the men shut off the motor and started to volplane to the earth.

But they made an unskillful landing. The *Eagle* tilted to one side, and came down with a crash. There were cries of pain, then silence, and a few seconds later two men ran away from the disabled airship. But there were three senseless forms on the ground beside the craft when Tom, Ned and Mr. Halling ran up. In the fading light Tom saw a face he knew—three faces in fact.

"Mr. Damon!" he cried. "We've found him, Ned!"

"But—too late—maybe!" answered Ned, in a low voice, as he, too, recognized the man who had been missing so long.

Mr. Halling was bending over the unconscious form of his friend.

"He's alive!" he cried, joyfully. "And not much hurt, either. But he has been ill, and looks half starved. Who are these men?"

Tom gave a hasty look.

"Shallock Peters and Harrison Boylan!" he cried. "Ned, at last we've caught the scoundrels!"

It was true. Chance had played into the hands of Tom Swift. While Mr. Halling was looking after Mr. Damon, reviving him, the young inventor and Ned quickly bound the hands and feet of the two plotters with pieces of wire from the broken airship.

Presently Mr. Damon opened his eyes.

"Where am I? What happened? Oh, bless my watch chain—it's Tom Swift! Bless my cigar case, I—"

"He's all right!" cried Tom, joyfully. "When Mr. Damon blesses something beside his tombstone he's all right."

Peters and Boylan soon revived, both being merely stunned, as was Mr. Damon. They looked about in wonder, and then, feeling that they were prisoners, resigned themselves to their fate. Both men were shabbily dressed, and Tom would hardly have known the once spick and span Mr. Peters. He had no rose in his buttonhole now.

"Well, you have me, I see," he said, coolly. "I was afraid we were playing for too high a stake."

"Yes, we've got you," replied Tom,

"But you can't prove much against me," went on Peters. "I'll deny everything."

"We'll see about that," added the young inventor, grimly, and thought of the picture in the plate and the record on the wax cylinder.

"We've got to get Mr. Damon to some place where he can be looked after," broke in Mr. Halling. "Then we'll hear the story."

A passing farmer was prevailed on to take the party in his big wagon to the nearest town, Mr. Hailing going on ahead in his airship. Tom's craft could not be moved, being badly damaged.

Once in town Peters and Boylan were put in jail, on the charges for which Tom carried warrants. Mr. Damon was taken to a hotel and a doctor summoned. It was as Mr. Halling had guessed. His friend had been ill, and so weak that he could not get out of bed. It was this that enabled the plotters to so easily keep him a prisoner.

By degrees Mr. Damon told his story. He had rashly allowed Peters to get control of most of his fortune, and, in a vain hope of getting back some of his losses, had, one night—the night he disappeared, in fact—agreed to meet Peters and some of his men to talk matters over. Of this Mr. Damon said nothing to his wife.

He went out that night to meet Peters in the garden, but the plotters had changed their plans. They boldly kidnapped their victim, chloroformed him and took him away in Tom's airship, which Boylan and some of his tools daringly stole a short time previously. Later they returned it, as they had no use for it at the lonely house.

Mr. Damon was taken to the house, and there kept a prisoner. The men hoped to prevail on the fears of his wife to make her give up the valuable property. But we have seen how Tom foiled Peters.

The experience of Mr. Damon, coupled with rough treatment he received, and lack of good food, soon made him ill. He was so weak that he could not help himself, and with that he was kept under guard. So he had no chance to escape or send his wife or friends any word.

"But I'm all right now, Tom, thanks to you!" said he. "Bless my pocketbook, I don't care if my fortune is lost, as long as I'm alive and can get back to my wife."

"But I don't believe your fortune will be lost," said Tom. "I think I have the picture and other evidence that will save it," and he told of his photo telephone, and of what it had accomplished.

"Bless my eyelashes!" cried Mr. Damon. "What a young man you are, Tom Swift!"

Tom smiled gladly. He knew now that his old friend was himself once more.

There is little left to tell. Chance had aided Tom in a most wonderful way—chance and the presence of Mr. Halling with his airship at just the right moment.

Tom made a diligent effort to find out who it was that had chloroformed him in the telephone booth that time, but learned nothing definite. Peters and Boylan were both examined as to this on their trials, but denied it, and the young inventor was forced to conclude that it must have been some of the unscrupulous men who had taken his father's patent some time before.

"They may have heard of your prosperity, and thought it a good chance to rob you," suggested Ned.

"Maybe," agreed Tom. "Well, we'll let it go at that. Only I hope they don't come again."

Mr. Damon was soon home with his wife again, and Peters and Boylan were held in heavy bail. They had secreted most of Mr. Damon's wealth, falsely telling him it was lost, and they were forced to give back his fortune. The evidence against them was clear and conclusive. When Tom went into court with his phonograph record of the talk of Peters, even though the man's voice was hoarse from a cold when he talked, and when his picture was shown, in the telephone booth, the jury at once convicted him.

Boylan, when he learned of the missing button in Tom's possession, confessed that he and some of his men who were birdmen had taken Tom's airship. They wanted a means of getting Mr. Damon to the lonely house without being traced, and they accomplished it.

As Tom had surmised, Peters had become suspicious after his last talk with Mrs. Damon, and had fled. He disguised himself and went into hiding with the others at the lonely house. Then he learned that the authorities of another city, where he had swindled many, were on his trail, and he decided to decamp with his gang, taking Mr. Damon with them. For this purpose Tom's airship was taken the second time, and a wholesale escape, with Mr. Damon a prisoner, was planned.

But fate was against the plotters. Two of them did manage to get away, but they were not really wanted. The big fish were Peters and Boylan, and they were securely caught in the net of the law. Peters was greatly surprised when he learned of Tom's trap, and of the photo telephone. He had no idea he had been incriminating himself when he talked over the wire.

"Well, it's all over," remarked Ned to Tom, one day, when the disabled auto and the airship had been brought home and repaired. "The plotters are in prison for long terms, and Mr. Damon is found, together with his fortune. The photo telephone did it, Tom."

"Not all of it—but a good bit," admitted the young inventor, with a smile.

"What are you going to do next, Tom?"

"I hardly know. I think—"

Before Tom could finish, a voice was heard in the hall outside the library.

"Bless my overshoes! Where's Tom? I want to thank him again for what he did for me," and Mr. Damon, now fully recovered, came in. "Bless my suspender button, but it's good to be alive, Tom!" he cried.

"It certainly is," agreed Tom. "And the next time you go for a conference with such men as Peters, look out for airships."

"I will, Tom, I will!" exclaimed Mr. Damon. "Bless my watch chain, I will!"

And now, for a time, we will say good-bye to Tom Swift, leaving him to perfect his other inventions.

TOM SWIFT AND HIS AERIAL WARSHIP

Or, THE NAVAL TERROR OF THE SEAS

CHAPTER I

TOM IS PUZZLED

"What's the matter, Tom? You look rather blue!"

"Blue! Say, Ned, I'd turn red, green, yellow, or any other color of the rainbow, if I thought it would help matters any."

"Whew!"

Ned Newton, the chum and companion of Tom Swift, gave vent to a whistle of surprise, as he gazed at the young fellow sitting opposite him, near a bench covered with strange-looking tools and machinery, while blueprints and drawings were scattered about.

Ranged on the sides of the room were models of many queer craft, most of them flying machines of one sort or another, while through the open door that led into a large shed could be seen the outlines of a speedy monoplane.

"As bad as that, eh, Tom?" went on Ned. "I thought something was up when I first came in, but, if you'll excuse a second mention of the color scheme, I should say it was blue—decidedly blue. You look as though you had lost your last friend, and I want to assure you that if you do feel that way, it's dead wrong. There's myself, for one, and I'm sure Mr. Damon—"

"Bless my gasoline tank!" exclaimed Tom, with a laugh, in imitation of the gentleman Ned Newton had mentioned, "I know that! I'm not worrying over the loss of any friends."

"And there are Eradicate, and Koku, the giant, just to mention a couple of others," went on Ned, with a smile.

"That's enough!" exclaimed Tom. "It isn't that, I tell you."

"Well, what is it then? Here I go and get a half-holiday off from the bank, and just at the busiest time, too, to come and see you, and I find you in a brown study, looking as blue as indigo, and maybe you're all yellow inside from a bilious attack, for all I know."

"Quite a combination of colors," admitted Tom. "But it isn't what you think. It's just that I'm puzzled, Ned."

"Puzzled?" and Ned raised his eyebrows to indicate how surprised he was that anything should puzzle his friend.

"Yes, genuinely puzzled."

"Has anything gone wrong?" Ned asked. "No one is trying to take any of your pet inventions away from you, is there?"

"No, not exactly that, though it is about one of my inventions I am puzzled. I guess I haven't shown you my very latest; have I, Ned?"

"Well, I don't know, Tom. Time was when I could keep track of you and your inventions, but that was in your early days, when you started with a motorcycle and were glad enough to have a motorboat. But, since you've taken to aerial navigation and submarine work, not to mention one or two other lines of activity, I give up. I don't know where to look next, Tom, for something new."

"Well, this isn't so very new," went on the young inventor, for Tom Swift had designed and patented many new machines of the air, earth and water. "I'm just trying to work out some new problems in aerial navigation, Ned," he went on.

"I thought there weren't any more," spoke Ned, soberly enough.

"Come, now, none of that!" exclaimed Tom, with a laugh. "Why, the surface of aerial navigation has only been scratched. The science is far from being understood, or even made safe, not to say perfected, as water and land travel have been. There's lots of chance yet."

"And you're working on something new?" asked Ned, as he looked around the shop where he and Tom were sitting. As the young bank employee had said, he had come away from the institution that afternoon to have a little holiday with his chum, but Tom, seated in the midst of his inventions, seemed little inclined to jollity.

Through the open windows came the hum of distant machinery, for Tom Swift and his father were the heads of a company founded to manufacture and market their many inventions, and about their home were grouped several buildings. From a small plant the business had grown to be a great tree, under the direction of Tom and his father.

"Yes, I'm working on something new," admitted Tom, after a moment of silence.

"And, Ned," he went on, "there's no reason why you shouldn't see it. I've been keeping it a bit secret, until I had it a little further advanced, but I've got to a point now where I'm stuck, and perhaps it will do me good to talk to someone about it."

"Not to talk to me, though, I'm afraid. What I don't know about machinery, Tom, would fill a great many books. I don't see how I can help you," and Ned laughed.

"Well, perhaps you can, just the same, though you may not know a lot of technical things about machines. It sometimes helps me just to tell my troubles to a disinterested person, and hear him ask questions. I've got dad half distracted trying to solve the problem, so I've had to let up on him for a while. Come on out and see what you make of it."

"Sure, Tom, anything to oblige. If you want me to sit in front of your photo-telephone, and have my picture taken, I'm agreeable, even if you shoot off a flashlight at my ear. Or, if you want me to see how long I can stay under water without breathing I'll try that, too, provided you don't leave me under too long, lead the way—I'm agreeable as far as I'm able, old man."

"Oh, it isn't anything like that," Tom answered with a laugh. "I might as well give you a few hints, so you'll know what I'm driving at. Then I'll take you out and show it to you."

"What is it—air, earth or water?" asked Ned Newton, for he knew his chum's activities led along all three lines.

"This happens to be air."

"A new balloon?"

"Something like that. I call it my aerial warship, though."

"Aerial warship, Tom! That sounds rather dangerous!"

"It will be dangerous, too, if I can get it to work. That's what it's intended for."

"But a warship of the air!" cried Ned. "You can't mean it. A warship carries guns, mortars, bombs, and—"

"Yes, I know," interrupted Tom, "and I appreciate all that when I called my newest craft an aerial warship."

"But," objected Ned, "an aircraft that will carry big guns will be so large that—"

"Oh, mine is large enough," Tom broke in.

"Then it's finished!" cried Ned eagerly, for he was much interested in his chum's inventions.

"Well, not exactly," Tom said. "But what I was going to tell you was that all guns are not necessarily large. You can get big results with small guns and projectiles now, for high-powered explosives come in small packages. So it isn't altogether a question of carrying a certain amount of weight. Of course, an aerial warship will have to be big, for it will have to carry extra machinery to give it extra speed, and it will have to carry a certain armament, and a large crew will be needed. So, as I said, it will need to be large. But that problem isn't worrying me."

"Well, what is it, then?" asked Ned.

"It's the recoil," said Tom, with a gesture of despair.

"The recoil?" questioned Ned, wonderingly.

"Yes, from the guns, you know. I haven't been able to overcome that, and, until I do, I'm afraid my latest invention will be a failure."

Ned shook his head.

"I'm afraid I can't help you any," he said. "The only thing I know about recoils is connected with an old shotgun my father used to own.

"I took that once, when he didn't know it," Ned proceeded. "It was pretty heavily loaded, for the crows had been having fun in our cornfield, and dad had been shooting at them. This time I thought I'd take a chance.

"Well, I fired the gun. But it must have had a double charge in it and been rusted at that. All I know is that after I pulled the trigger I thought the end of the world had come. I heard a clap of thunder, and then I went flying over backward into a blackberry patch."

"That was the recoil," said Tom.

"The what?" asked Ned.

"The recoil. The recoil of the gun knocked you over."

"Oh, yes," observed Ned, rubbing his shoulder in a reflective sort of way. "I always thought it was something like that. But, at the time I put it down to an explosion, and let it go at that."

"No, it wasn't an explosion, properly speaking," said Tom. "You see, when powder explodes, in a gun, or otherwise, its force is exerted in all directions, up, down and every way."

"This went mostly backward—in my direction," said Ned ruefully.

"You only thought so," returned Tom. "Most of the power went out in front, to force out the shot. Part of it, of course, was exerted on the barrel of the gun—that was sideways—but the strength of the steel held it in. And part of the force went backward against your shoulder. That part was the recoil, and it is the recoil of the guns I figure on putting aboard my aerial warship that is giving me such trouble."

"Is that what makes you look so blue?" asked Ned.

"That's it. I can't seem to find a way by which to take up the recoil, and the force of it, from all the guns I want to carry, will just about tear my ship to pieces, I figure."

"Then you haven't actually tried it out yet?" asked Ned.

"Not the guns, no. I have the warship of the air nearly done, but I've worked out on paper the problem of the guns far enough so that I know I'm up against it. It can't be done, and an aerial warship without guns wouldn't be worth much, I'm afraid."

"I suppose not," agreed Ned. "And is it only the recoil that is bothering you?"

"Mostly. But come, take a look at my latest pet," and Tom arose to lead the way to another shed, a large one in the distance, toward which he waved his hand to indicate to his chum that there was housed the wonderful invention.

The two chums crossed the yard, threading their way through the various buildings, until they stood in front of the structure to which Tom had called attention.

"It's in here," he said. "I don't mind admitting that I'm quite proud of it, Ned; that is, proud as far as I've gone. But the gun business sure has me worried. I'm going to talk it off on you. Hello!" cried Tom suddenly, as he put a key in the complicated lock on the door, "someone has been in here. I wonder who it is?"

Ned was a little startled at the look on Tom's face and the sound of alarm in his chum's voice.

CHAPTER II

A FIRE ALARM

Tom Swift quickly opened the door of the big shed. It was built to house a dirigible balloon, or airship of some sort. Ned could easily tell that from his knowledge of Tom's previous inventions.

"Something wrong?" asked the young bank clerk.

"I don't know," returned Tom, and then as he looked inside the place, he breathed a sigh of relief.

"Oh, it's you, is it, Koku?" he asked, as a veritable giant of a man came forward.

"Yes, master, it is only Koku and your father," spoke the big chap, with rather a strange accent.

"Oh, is my father here?" asked Tom. "I was wondering who had opened the door of this shed."

"Yes, Tom," responded the elder Swift, coming up to them, "I had a new idea in regard to some of those side guy wires, and I wanted to try it out. I brought Koku with me to use his strength on some of them."

"That's all right, Dad. Ned and I came out to wrestle with that recoil problem again. I want to try some guns on the craft soon, but—"

"You'd better not, Tom," warned his father. "It will never work, I tell you. You can't expect to take up quick-firing guns and bombs in an airship, and have them work properly. Better give it up."

"I never will. I'll make it work, Dad!"

"I don't believe you will, Tom. This time you have bitten off more than you can chew, to use a homely but expressive statement."

"Well, Dad, we'll see," began Tom easily. "There she is, Ned," he went on. "Now, if you'll come around here..."

But Tom never finished that sentence, for at that moment there came running into the airship shed an elderly, short, stout, fussy gentleman, followed by an aged colored man. Both of them seemed very much excited.

"Bless my socks, Tom!" cried the short, stout man. "There sure is trouble!"

"I should say So, Massa Tom!" added the colored man. "I done did prognosticate dat some day de combustible material of which dat shed am composed would conflaggrate—"

"What's the matter?" interrupted Tom, jumping forward. "Speak out! Eradicate! Mr. Damon, what is it?"

"The red shed!" cried the short little man. "The red shed, Tom!"

"It's on fire!" yelled the colored man.

"Great thunderclaps!" cried Tom. "Come on—everybody on the job!" he yelled. "Koku, pull the alarm! If that red shed goes—"

Instantly the place was in confusion. Tom and Ned, looking from a window of the hangar, saw a billow of black smoke roll across the yard. But already the private fire bell was clanging out its warning. And, while the work of fighting the flames is under way, I will halt the progress of this story long enough to give my new readers a little idea of who Tom Swift is, so they may read this book more intelligently. Those of you who have perused the previous volumes may skip this part.

Tom Swift, though rather young in years, was an inventor of note. His tastes and talents were developed along the line of machinery and locomotion. Motorcycles, automobiles, motorboats, submarine craft, and, latest of all, craft of the air, had occupied the attention of Tom Swift and his father for some years.

Mr. Swift was a widower, and lived with Tom, his only son, in the village of Shopton, New York State. Mrs. Baggert kept house for them, and an aged colored man, Eradicate Sampson, with his mule, Boomerang, did "odd jobs" about the Shopton home and factories.

Among Tom's friends was a Mr. Wakefield Damon, from a nearby village. Mr. Damon was always blessing something, from his hat to his shoes, a harmless sort of habit that seemed to afford him much comfort. Then there was Ned Newton, a boyhood chum of Tom's, who worked in the Shopton bank. I will just mention Mary Nestor, a young lady of Shopton, in whom Tom was more than ordinarily interested. I have spoken of Koku, the giant. He really was a giant of a man, of enormous strength, and was one of two whom Tom had brought with him from a strange land where Tom was held captive for a time. You may read about it in a book devoted to those adventures.

Tom took Koku into his service, somewhat to the dismay of Eradicate, who was desperately jealous. But poor Eradicate was getting old, and could not do as much as he thought he could. So, in a great measure, Koku replaced him, and Tom found much use for the giant's strength.

Tom had begun his inventive work when, some years before this story opens, he had bargained for Mr. Damon's motorcycle, after that machine had shot its owner into a tree. Mr. Damon was, naturally, perhaps, much disgusted, and sold the affair cheap. Tom repaired it, made some improvements, and, in the first volume of this series, entitled "Tom Swift and His Motor-cycle," you may read of his rather thrilling adventures on his speedy road-steed.

From then on Tom had passed a busy life, making many machines and having some thrilling times with them. Just previous to the opening of this story Tom had made a peculiar instrument, described in the volume entitled "Tom Swift and His Photo-Telephone." With that a person talking could not only see the features of the person with whom he was conversing, but, by means of a selenium plate and a sort of camera, a permanent picture could be taken of the person at either end of the wire.

By means of this invention Tom had been able to make a picture that had saved a fortune. But Tom did not stop there. With him to invent was as natural and necessary as breathing. He simply could not stop it. And so we find him now about to show to his chum, Ned Newton, his latest patent, an aerial warship, which, however, was not the success Tom had hoped for.

But just at present other matters than the warship were in Tom's mind. The red shed was on fire.

That mere statement might not mean anything special to the ordinary person, but to Tom, his father, and those who knew about his shops, it meant much.

"The red shed!" Tom cried. "We mustn't let that get the best of us! Everybody at work! Father, not you, though. You mustn't excite yourself!"

Even in the midst of the alarm Tom thought of his father, for the aged man had a weak heart, and had on one occasion nearly expired, being saved just in time by the arrival of a doctor, whom Tom brought to the scene after a wonderful race through the air.

"But, Tom, I can help," objected the aged inventor.

"Now, you just take care of yourself, Father!" Tom cried. "There are enough of us to look after this fire, I think."

"But, Tom, it—it's the red shed!" gasped Mr. Swift.

"I realize that, Dad. But it can't have much of a start yet. Is the alarm ringing, Koku?"

"Yes, Master," replied the giant, in correct but stilted English. "I have set the indicator to signal the alarm in every shop on the premises."

"That's right." Tom sprang toward the door. "Eradicate!" he called.

"Yais, sah! Heah I is!" answered the colored man. "I'll go git mah mule, Boomerang, right away, an' he—"

"Don't you bring Boomerang on the scene!" Tom yelled. "When I want that shed kicked apart I can do it better than by using a mule's heels. And you know you can't do a thing with Boomerang when he sees fire."

"Now dat's so, Massa Tom. But I could put blinkers on him, an'—"

"No, you let Boomerang stay where he is. Come on, Ned. We'll see what we can do. Mr. Damon—"

"Yes, Tom, I'm right here," answered the peculiar man, for he had come over from his home in Waterford to pay a visit to his friends, Tom and Mr. Swift. "I'll do anything I can to help you, Tom, bless my necktie!" he went on. "Only say the word!"

"We've got to get some of the stuff out of the place!" Tom cried. "We may be able to save it, but I can't take a chance on putting out the fire and letting some of the things in there go up in smoke. Come on!"

Those in the shed where was housed what Tom hoped would prove to be a successful aerial warship rushed to the open. From the other shops and buildings nearby were pouring men and boys, for the Swift plant employed a number of hands now.

Above the shouts and yells, above the crackle of flames, could be heard the clanging of the alarm bell, set ringing by Koku, who had pulled the signal in the airship shed. From there it had gone to every building in the plant, being relayed by the telephone operator, whose duty it was to look after that.

"My, you've got a big enough fire-fighting force, Tom!" cried Ned in his chum's ear.

"Yes, I guess we can master it, if it hasn't gotten the best of us. Say, it's going some, though!"

Tom pointed to where a shed, painted red—a sign of danger—could be seen partly enveloped in smoke, amid the black clouds of which shot out red tongues of flame.

"What have you got it painted red for?" Ned asked pantingly, as they ran on.

"Because—" Tom began, but the rest of the sentence was lost in a yell.

Tom had caught sight of Eradicate and the giant, Koku, unreeling from a central standpipe a long line of hose.

"Don't take that!" Tom cried. "Don't use that hose! Drop it!"

"What's the matter? Is it rotten?" Ned wanted to know.

"No, but if they pull it out the water will be turned on automatically."

"Well, isn't that what you want at a fire—water?" Ned demanded.

"Not at this fire," was Tom's answer. "There's a lot of calcium carbide in that red shed—that's why it's red—to warn the men of danger. You know what happens when water gets on carbide—there's an explosion, and there's enough carbide in that shed to send the whole works sky high.

"Drop that hose!" yelled Tom in louder tones. "Drop it, Rad—Koku! Do you want to kill us all!"

CHAPTER III

A DESPERATE BATTLE

Tom's tones and voice were so insistent that the giant and the colored man had no choice but to obey. They dropped the hose which, half unreeled, lay like some twisted snake in the grass. Had it been pulled out all the way the water would have spurted from the nozzle, for it was of the automatic variety, with which Tom had equipped all his plant.

"But what are you going to do, Tom, if you don't use water?" asked Ned, wonderingly.

"I don't know—yet, but I know water is the worst thing you can put on carbide," returned Tom. For all he spoke Slowly his brain was working fast. Already, even now, he was planning how best to give battle to the flames.

It needed but an instant's thought on the part of Ned to make him understand that Tom was right. It would be well-nigh fatal to use water on carbide. Those of you who have bicycle lanterns, in which that not very pleasant-smelling chemical is used, know that if a few drops of water are allowed to drip slowly on the gray crystals acetylene gas is generated, which makes a brilliant light. But, if the water drips too fast, the gas is generated too quickly, and an explosion results. In lamps, of course, and in lighting plants where carbide is used, there are automatic arrangements to prevent the water flowing too freely to the chemical. But Tom knew if the hose were turned on the fire in the red shed a great explosion would result, for some of the tins of carbide would be melted by the heat.

Yet the fire needed to be coped with. Already the flames were coming through the roof, and the windows and door were spouting red fire and volumes of smoke.

Several other employees of Tom's plant had made ready to unreel more hose, but the warning of the young inventor, shouted to Eradicate and Koku, had had its effect. Every man dropped the line he had begun to unreel.

"Ha! Massa Tom say drop de hose, but how yo' gwine t' squirt watah on a fire wifout a hose; answer me dat?" and Eradicate looked at Koku.

"Me no know," was the slow answer. "I guess Koku go pull shed down and stamp out fire."

"Huh! Maybe yo' could do dat in cannibal land, where yo' all come from," spoke Eradicate, "but yo' can't do dat heah! 'Sides, de red shed will blow up soon. Dere's suffin' else in dere except carbide, an' dat's gwine t' go up soon, dat's suah!"

"Maybe you get your strong man-mule, Boomerang," suggested Koku. "Nothing ever hurt him—explosion or nothing. He can kick shed all to pieces, and put out fire."

"Dat's what I wanted t' do, but Massa Tom say I cain't," explained the colored man. "Golly! Look at dat fire!"

Indeed the blaze was now assuming alarming proportions. The red shed, which was not a small structure, was blazing on all sides. About it stood the men from the various shops.

"Tom, you must do something," said Mr. Swift. "If the flames once reach that helmanite—"

"I know, Father. But that explosive is in double vacuum containers, and it will be safe for some time yet. Besides, it's in the cellar. It's the carbide I'm most worried about. We daren't use water."

"But something will have to be done!" exclaimed Mr. Damon. "Bless my red necktie, if we don't—"

"Better get back a way," suggested Tom. "Something may go off!"

His words of warning had their effect, and the whole circle moved back several paces.

"Is there anything of value in the shed?" asked Ned.

"I should say there was!" Tom answered. "I hoped we could get some of them out, but we can't now—until the fire dies down a bit, at any rate."

"Look, Tom! The pattern shop roof is catching!" shouted Mr. Swift, pointing to where a little spurt of flame showed on the roof of a distant building.

"It's from sparks!" Tom said.

"Any danger of using water there?" Ned wanted to know.

"No, use all you like! That's the only thing to do. Come on, you with the hose!" Tom yelled. "Save the other buildings!"

"But are you going to let the red shed burn?" asked Mr. Swift. "You know what it means, Tom."

"Yes, Father, I know. And I'm going to fight that fire in a new way. But we must save the other buildings, too. Play water on all the other sheds and structures!" ordered the young inventor. "I'll tackle this one myself. Oh, Ned!" he called.

"Yes," answered his chum. "What is it?"

"You take charge of protecting the place where the new aerial warship is stored. Will you? I can't afford to lose that."

"I'll look after it, Tom. No harm in using water there, though; is there?"

"Not if you don't use too much. Some of the woodwork isn't varnished yet, and I wouldn't want it to be wet. But do the best you can. Take Koku and Eradicate with you. They can't do any good here."

"Do you mean to say you're going to give up and let this burn?"

"Not a bit of it, Ned. But I have another plan I want to try. Lively now! The wind's changing, and it's blowing over toward my aerial warship shed. If that catches—"

Tom shook his head protestingly, and Ned set off on the run, calling to the colored man and the giant to get out another line of hose.

"I wonder what Tom is going to do?" mused Ned, as he neared the big shed he and the others had left on the alarm of fire.

Tom, himself, seemed in no doubt as to his procedure With one look at the blazing red shed, as if to form an opinion as to how much longer it could burn without getting entirely beyond control, Tom set off on a run toward another large structure. Ned, glancing toward his chum, observed:

"The dirigible shed! I wonder what his game is? Surely that can't be in danger—it's too far off!"

Ned was right as to the last statement. The shed, where was housed a great dirigible balloon Tom had made, but which he seldom used of late, was sufficiently removed from the zone of fire to be out of danger.

Meanwhile several members of the fire-fighting force that had been summoned from the various shops by the alarm, had made an effort to save from the red shed some of the more valuable of the contents. There were some machines in there, as well as explosives and chemicals, in addition to the store of carbide.

But the fire was now too hot to enable much to be done in the way of salvage. One or two small things were carried out from a little addition to the main structure, and then the rescuers were driven back by the heat of the flames, as well as by the rolling clouds of black smoke.

"Keep away!" warned Mr. Swift. "It will explode soon. Keep back!"

"That's right!" added Mr. Damon. "Bless my powder-horn! We may all be going sky-high soon, and without aid from any of Tom Swift's aeroplanes, either."

Warned by the aged inventor, the throng of men began slowly moving away from the immediate neighborhood of the blazing shed. Though it may seem to the reader that some time has elapsed since the first sounding of the alarm, all that I have set down took place in a very short period—hardly three minutes elapsing since Tom and the others came rushing out of the aerial warship building.

Suddenly a cry arose from the crowd of men near the red shed. Ned, who stood ready with several lines of hose, in charge of Koku, Eradicate and others, to turn them on the airship shed, in case of need, looked in the direction of the excited throng.

The young bank clerk saw a strange sight. From the top of the dirigible balloon shed a long, black, cigar-shaped body arose, floating gradually upward. The very roof of the shed slid back out of the way, as Tom pressed the operating lever, and the dirigible was free to rise—as free as though it had been in an open field.

"He's going up!" cried Ned in surprise. "Making an ascent at a time like this, when he ought to stay here to fight the fire! What's gotten into Tom, I'd like to know? I wonder if he can be—"

Ned did not finish his half-formed sentence. A dreadful thought came into his mind. What if the sudden fire, and the threatened danger, as well as the prospective loss that confronted Tom, had affected his mind?

"It certainly looks so," mused Ned, as he saw the big balloon float free from the shed. There was no doubt but that Tom was in it. He could be seen standing within the pilot-house, operating the various wheels and levers that controlled the ship of the air.

"What can he be up to?" marveled Ned. "Is he going to run away from the fire?"

Koku, Eradicate and several others were attracted by the sight of the great dirigible, now a considerable distance up in the air. Certainly it looked as though Tom Swift were running away. Yet Ned knew his chum better than that.

Then, as they watched, Ned and the others saw the direction of the balloon change. She turned around in response to the influence of the rudders and propellers, and was headed straight for the blazing shed, but some distance above it.

"What can he be planning?" wondered Ned.

He did not have long to wait to find out.

An instant later Tom's plan was made clear to his chum. He saw Tom circling over the burning red shed, and then the bank clerk saw what looked like fine rain dropping from the lower part of the balloon straight into the flames.

"He can't be dousing water on from up above there," reasoned Ned. "Pouring water on carbide from a height is just as bad as spurting it on from a hose, though perhaps not so dangerous to the persons doing it. But it can't be—"

"By Jove!" suddenly exclaimed Ned, as he had a better view of what was going on. "It's sand, that's what it is! Tom is giving battle to the flames with sand from the ballast bags of the dirigible! Hurray? That's the ticket! Sand! The only thing safe to use in case of an explosive chemical fire.

"Fine for you. Tom Swift! Fine!"

CHAPTER IV

SUSPICIONS

High up aloft, over the blazing red shed, with its dangerous contents that any moment might explode, Tom Swift continued to hold his big dirigible balloon as near the flames as possible. And as he stood outside on the small deck in front of the pilot-house, where were located the various controls, the young inventor pulled the levers that emptied bag after bag of fine sand on the spouting flames that, already, were beginning to die down as a result of this effectual quenching.

"Tom's done the trick!" yelled Ned, paying little attention now to the big airship shed, since he saw that the danger was about over.

"Dhat's what he suah hab done!" agreed Eradicate. "Mah ole mule Boomerang couldn't 'a' done any better."

"Huh! Your mule afraid of fire," remarked Koku.

"What's dat? Mah mule afraid ob fire?" cried the colored man. "Look heah, yo' great, big, overgrowed specimen ob an equilateral quadruped,

I'll hab yo' all understand dat when yo' all speaks dat way about a friend ob mine dat yo'—"

"That'll do, Rad!" broke in Ned, with a laugh. He knew that when Tom's helper grew excited on the subject of his mule there was no Stopping him, and Boomerang was a point on which Eradicate and Koku were always arguing. "The fire is under control now."

"Yes, it seems to have gone visiting," observed Koku.

"Visiting?" queried Ned, in some surprise.

"Yes, that is, it is going out," went on Koku.

"Oh, I understand!" laughed Ned. "Yes, and I hope it doesn't pay us another visit soon. Oh, look at Tom, would you!" he cried, for the young aviator had swung his ship about over the flames, to bring another row of sand bags directly above a place where the fire was hottest.

Down showered more sand from the bags which Tom opened. No fire could long continue to blaze under that treatment. The supply of air was cut off, and without that no fire can exist. Water would have been worse than useless, because of the carbide, but the sand covered it up so that it was made perfectly harmless.

Moving slowly, the airship hovered over every part of the now slowly expiring flames, the burned opening in the roof of the shed making it possible for the sand to reach the spots where it was most needed. The flames died out in section after section, until no more could be seen— only clouds of black smoke.

"How is it now?" came Tom's voice, as he spoke from the deck of the balloon through a megaphone.

"Almost out," answered Mr. Damon. "A little more sand, Tom."

The eccentric man had caught up a piece of paper and, rolling it into a cone, made an improvised megaphone of that.

"Haven't much more sand left," was Tom's comment, as he sent down a last shower. "That will have to do. Hustle that carbide and other explosive stuff out of there now, while you have a chance."

"That's it!" cried Ned, who caught his chums meaning. "Come on, Koku. There's work for you."

"Me like work," answered the giant, stretching out his great arms.

The last of the sand had completely smothered the fire, and Tom, observing from aloft that his work was well done, moved away in the dirigible, sending it to a landing space some little distance away from the shed whence it had arisen. It was impossible to drop it back again through the roof of the hangar, as the balloon was of such bulk that even a little breeze would deflect it so that it could not be accurately anchored. But Tom had it under very good control, and soon it was being held down on the ground by some of his helpers.

As all the sand ballast had been allowed to run out Tom was obliged to open the gas-valves and let some of the lifting vapor escape, or he could not have descended.

"Come on, now!" cried the inventor, as he leaped from the deck of his sky craft. "Let's clean out the red shed. That fire is only smothered, and there may be sparks smoldering under that sand, which will burst into flame, if we're not careful. Let's get the explosives out of the way."

"Bless my insurance policy, yes," exclaimed Mr. Damon. "That was a fine move of yours."

"It was the only way I could think of to put out the fire," Tom replied. "I knew water was out of the question, and sand was the next thing."

"But I didn't know where to get any until I happened to think of the ballast bags of my dirigible. Then I knew, if I could get above the fire, I could do the trick. I had to fly pretty high, though, as the fire was hot, and I was afraid it might explode the gas bag and wreck me."

"You were taking a chance," remarked Ned.

"Oh, well, you have to take chances in this business," observed Tom, with a smile. "Now, then, let's finish this work."

The sand, falling from the ballast bags of the dirigible, had so effectually quenched the fire that it was soon cool enough to permit close approach. Koku, Tom and some of the men who best knew how to handle the explosives, were soon engaged in the work of salvage.

"I wish I could help you, Tom," said his aged father. "I don't seem able to do anything but stand here and look on," and he gazed about him rather sadly.

"Never you mind, Dad!" Tom exclaimed. "We'll get along all right now. You'd better go up to the house. Mr. Damon will go with you."

"Yes, of course!" exclaimed the odd man, catching a wink from Tom, who wanted his father not to get too excited on account of his weak heart. "Come along, Professor Swift. The danger is all over."

"All right," assented the aged inventor, with a look at the still smoking shed.

"And, Dad, when you haven't anything else to do," went on Tom, rather whimsically, "you might be thinking up some plan to take up the recoil of those guns on my aerial warship. I confess I'm clean stumped on that point."

"Your aerial warship will never be a success," declared Mr. Swift. "You might as well give that up, Tom."

"Don't you believe it, Dad!" cried Tom, with more of a jolly air of one chum toward another than as though the talk was between father and son. "You solve the recoil problem for me, and I'll take care of the rest, and make the air warship sail. But we've got something else to do just now. Lively, boys."

While Mr. Swift, taking Mr. Damon's arm, walked toward the house, Tom, Ned, Koku, and some of the workmen began carrying out the explosives which had so narrowly escaped the fire. With long hooks the men pulled the shed apart, where the side walls had partly been burned through. Tom maintained an efficient firefighting force at his works, and the men had the proper tools with which to work.

Soon large openings were made on three sides of the red shed, or rather, what was left of it, and through these the dangerous chemicals and carbide, in sheet-iron cans, were carried out to a place of safety. In a little while nothing remained but a heap of hot sand, some charred embers and certain material that had been burned.

"Much loss, Tom?" asked Ned, as they surveyed the ruins. They were both black and grimy, tired and dirty, but there was a great sense of satisfaction.

"Well, yes, there's more lost than I like to think of," answered Tom slowly, "but it would have been a heap sight worse if the stuff had gone up. Still, I can replace what I've lost, except a few models I kept in this place. I really oughtn't to have stored them here, but since I've been working on my new aerial warship I have sort of let other matters slide. I intended to make the red shed nothing but a storehouse for explosive chemicals, but I still had some of my plans and models in it when it caught."

"Only for the sand the whole place might have gone," said Ned in a low voice.

"Yes. It's lucky I had plenty of ballast aboard the dirigible. You see, I've been running it alone lately, and I had to take on plenty of sand to make up for the weight of the several passengers I usually carry. So I had plenty of stuff to shower down on the fire. I wonder how it started, anyhow? I must investigate this."

"Mr. Damon and Eradicate seem to have seen it first," remarked Ned.

"Yes. At least they gave the alarm. Guess I'll ask Eradicate how he happened to notice. Oh, I say, Rad!" Tom called to the colored man.

"Yais, sah, Massa Tom! I'se comin'!" the darky cried, as he finished piling up, at a safe distance from the fire, a number of cans of carbide.

"How'd you happen to see the red shed ablaze?" Tom asked.

"Why, it was jest dish yeah way, Massa Tom," began the colored man. "I had jest been feedin' mah mule, Boomerang. He were pow'ful hungry, Boomerang were, an', when I give him some oats, wif a carrot sliced up in 'em—no, hole on—did I gib him a carrot t'day, or was it yist'day?—I done fo'got. No, it were yist'day I done gib him de carrot, I 'member now, 'case—"

"Oh, never mind the carrot, or Boomerang, either, Rad!" broke in Tom, "I'm asking you about the fire."

"An' I'se tellin' yo', Massa Tom," declared Eradicate, with a rather reproachful look at his master. "But I wanted t' do it right an' proper. I were comin' from Boomerang's stable, an' I see suffin' red spoutin' up at one corner ob de red shed. I knowed it were fire right away, an' I yelled."

"Yes, I heard you yell," Tom said. "But what I wanted to know is, did you see anyone near the red shed at the time?"

"No, Massa Tom, I done didn't."

"I wonder if Mr. Damon did? I must ask him," went on the young inventor. "Come, on, Ned, we'll go up to the house. Everything is all right here, I think. Whew! But that was some excitement. And I didn't show you my aerial warship after all! Nor have you settled that recoil problem for me."

"Time enough, I guess," responded Ned. "You sure did have a lucky escape, Tom."

"That's right. Well, Koku, what is it?" for the giant had approached, holding out something in his hand.

"Koku found this in red shed," went on the giant, holding out a round, blackened object. "Maybe him powder; go bang-bang!"

"Oh, you think it's something explosive, eh?" asked Tom, as he took the object from the giant.

"Koku no think much," was the answer. "Him look funny."

Tom did not speak for a moment. Then he cried:

"Look funny! I should say it did! See here, Ned, if this isn't suspicious I'll eat my hat!" and Tom beckoned excitedly to his chum, who had walked on a little in advance.

CHAPTER V

A QUEER STRANGER

What Tom Swift held in his hand looked like a small cannon ball, but it could not have been solid or the young aviator would not so easily have held it out at arm's length for his friend Ned Newton to look at.

"This puts a different face on it, Ned," Tom went on, as he turned the object over.

"Is that likely to go off?" the bank clerk asked, as he came to a halt a little distance from his friend.

"Go off? No, it's done all the damage it could, I guess."

"Damage? It looks to me as though it had suffered the most damage itself. What is it, one of your models? Looks like a bomb to me."

"And that's what it is, Ned."

"Not one of those you're going to use on your aerial warship, is it, Tom?"

"Not exactly. I never saw this before, but it's what started the fire in the red shed all right; I'm sure of that."

"Do you really mean it?" cried Ned.

"I sure do."

"Well, if that's the case, I wouldn't leave such dangerous things around where there are explosives, Tom."

"I didn't, Ned. I wouldn't have had this within a hundred miles of my shed, if I could have had my way. It's a fire bomb, and it was set to go off at a certain time. Only I think something went wrong, and the bomb started a fire ahead of time.

"If it had worked at night, when we were all asleep, we might not have put the fire out so easily. This sure is suspicious! I'm glad you found this, Koku."

Tom was carefully examining the bomb, as Ned had correctly named it. The bank clerk, now that he was assured by his chum that the object had done all the harm it could, approached closer.

What he saw was merely a hollow shell of iron, with a small opening in it, as though intended for a place through which to put a charge of explosives and a fuse.

"But there was no explosion, Tom," explained Ned.

"I know it," said Tom quietly. "It wasn't an explosive bomb. Smell that!"

He held the object under Ned's nose so suddenly that the young bank clerk jumped back.

"Oh, don't get nervous," laughed Tom. "It can't hurt you now. But what does that smell like?"

Ned sniffed, sniffed again, thought for a moment, and then sniffed a third time.

"Why," he said slowly, "I don't just know the name of it, but it's that funny stuff you mix up sometimes to put in the oxygen tanks when we go up in the rarefied atmosphere in the balloon or airship."

"Manganese and potash," spoke Tom. "That and two or three other things that form a chemical combination which goes off by itself of spontaneous combustion after a certain time. Only the person who put this bomb together didn't get the chemical mixture just right, and it went off ahead of time; for which we have to be duly thankful."

"Do you really think that, Tom?" cried Ned.

"I'm positive of it," was the quiet answer.

"Why—why—that would mean some one tried to set fire to the red shed, Tom!"

"They not only tried it, but did it," responded Tom, more coolly than seemed natural under the circumstances. "Only for the fact that the mixture went off before it was intended to, and found us all alert and ready—well, I don't like to think what might have happened," and Tom cast a look about at his group of buildings with their valuable contents.

"You mean some one purposely put that bomb in the red shed, Tom?"

"That's exactly what I mean. Some enemy, who wanted to do me an injury, planned this thing deliberately. He filled this steel shell with chemicals which, of themselves, after a certain time, would send out a hot tongue of flame through this hole," and Tom pointed to the opening in the round steel shell.

"He knew the fire would be practically unquenchable by ordinary means, and he counted on its soon eating its way into the carbide and other explosives. Only it didn't."

"Why, Tom!" cried Ned. "It was just like one of those alarm-clock dynamite bombs—set to go off at a certain time."

"Exactly," Tom said, "only this was more delicate, and, if it had worked properly, there wouldn't have been a vestige left to give us a clue. But the fire, thanks to the ballast sand in the dirigible, was put out in time. The fuse burned itself out, but I can tell by the smell that chemicals were in it. That's all, Koku," he went on to the giant who had stood waiting, not understanding all the talk between Tom and Ned. "I'll take care of this now."

"Bad man put it there?" asked the giant, who at least comprehended that something was wrong.

"Well, yes, I guess you could say it was a bad man," replied Tom.

"Ha! If Koku find bad man—bad for that man!" muttered the giant, as he clasped his two enormous hands together, as though they were already on the fellow who had tried to do Tom Swift such an injury.

"I wouldn't like to be that man, if Koku catches him," observed Ned. "Have you any idea who it could be, Tom?"

"Not the least. Of course I know I have enemies, Ned. Every successful inventor has persons who imagine he has stolen their ideas, whether he has ever seen them or not. It may have been one of those persons, or some half-mad crank, who was jealous. It would be impossible to say, Ned."

"It wouldn't be Andy Foger, would it?"

"No; I don't believe Andy has been in this neighborhood for some time. The last lesson we gave him sickened him, I guess."

"How about those diamond-makers, whose secret you discovered? They wouldn't be trying to get back at you, would they?"

"Well, it's possible, Ned. But I don't imagine so. They seem to have been pretty well broken up. No, I don't believe it was the diamond-makers who put this fire bomb in the red shed. Their line of activities didn't include this branch. It takes a chemist to know just how to blend the things contained in the bomb, and even a good chemist is likely to fail—as this one did, as far as time went."

"What are you going to do about it?" Ned asked.

"I don't know," and Tom spoke slowly, "I hoped I was done with all that sort of thing," he went on; "fighting enemies whom I have never knowingly injured. But it seems they are still after me. Well, Ned, this gives us something to do, at all events."

"You mean trying to find out who these fellows are?"

"Yes; that is, if you are willing to help."

"Well, I guess I am!" cried the bank clerk with sparkling eyes. "I wouldn't ask anything better. We've been in things like this before, Tom, and we'll go in again—and win! I'll help you all I can. Now, let's see if we can pick up any other clues. This is like old times!" and Ned laughed, for he, like Tom, enjoyed a good "fight," and one in which the odds were against them.

"We sure will have our hands full," declared the young inventor. "Trying to solve the problem of carrying guns on an aerial warship, and finding out who set this fire."

"Then you're not going to give up your aerial warship idea?"

"No, indeed!" Tom cried. "What made you think that?"

"Well, the way your father spoke—"

"Oh, dear old dad!" exclaimed Tom affectionately. "I don't want to argue with him, but he's dead wrong!"

"Then you are going to make a go of it?"

"I sure am, Ned! All I have to solve is the recoil proposition, and, as soon as we get straightened out from this fire, we'll tackle that problem again—you and I. But I sure would like to know who put this in my red shed," and Tom looked in a puzzled manner at the empty fire bomb he still held.

Tom paused, on his way to the house, to put the bomb in one of his offices.

"No use letting dad know about this," he went on. "It would only be something else for him to worry about."

"That's right," agreed Ned.

By this time nearly all evidences of the fire, except for the blackened ruins of the shed, had been cleared away. High in the air hung a cloud of black smoke, caused by some chemicals that had burned harmlessly save for that pall. Tom Swift had indeed had a lucky escape.

The young inventor, finding his father quieted down and conversing easily with Mr. Damon, who was blessing everything he could think of, motioned to Ned to follow him out of the house again.

"We'll leave dad here," said Tom, "and do a little investigating on our own account. We'll look for clues while they're fresh."

But, it must be confessed, after Tom and Ned had spent the rest of that day in and about the burned shed, they were little wiser than when they started. They found the place where the fire bomb had evidently been placed, right inside the main entrance to the shed. Tom knew it had been there because there were peculiar marks on the charred wood, and a certain queer smell of chemicals that confirmed his belief.

"They put the bomb there to prevent anyone going in at the first alarm and saving anything," Tom said. "They didn't count on the roof burning through first, giving me a chance to use the sand. I made the roof of the red shed flimsy just on that account, so the force of the explosion if one ever came, would be mostly upward. You know the expanding gases, caused by an explosion or by rapid combustion, always do just as electricity does, seek the shortest and easiest route. In this case I made the roof the easiest route."

"A lucky provision," observed Ned.

That night Tom had to confess himself beaten, as far as finding clues was concerned. The empty fire bomb was the only one, and that seemed valueless.

Close questioning of the workmen failed to disclose anything. Tom was particularly anxious to discover if any mysterious strangers had been seen about the works. There was a strict rule about admitting them to the plant, however, and it could not be learned that this had been violated.

"Well, we'll just have to lay that aside for a while," Tom said the next day, when Ned again came to pay a visit. "Now, what do you say to tackling, with me, that recoil problem on the aerial warship?"

"I'm ready, if you are," Ned agreed, "though I know about as much of those things as a snake does about dancing. But I'm game."

The two friends walked out toward the shed where Tom's new craft was housed. As yet Ned had not seen it. On the way they saw Eradicate walking along, talking to himself, as he often did.

"I wonder what he has on his mind," remarked Ned musingly.

"Something does seem to be worrying him," agreed Tom.

As they neared the colored man, they could hear him saying:

"He suah did hab nerve, dat's what he did! De idea ob askin' me all dem questions, an' den wantin' t' know if I'd sell him!"

"What's that, Eradicate?" asked Tom.

"Oh, it's a man I met when I were comin' back from de ash dump," Eradicate explained. One of the colored man's duties was to cart ashes away from Tom's various shops, and dump them in a certain swampy lot. With an old ramshackle cart, and his mule, Boomerang, Eradicate did this task to perfection.

"A man—what sort of a man?" asked Tom, always ready to be suspicious of anything unusual.

"He were a queer man," went on the aged colored helper. "First he stopped me an' asted me fo' a ride. He was a dressed-up gen'man, too, an' I were suah s'prised at him wantin' t' set in mah ole ash cart," said Eradicate. "But I done was polite t' him, an' fixed a blanket so's he wouldn't git too dirty. Den he asted me ef I didn't wuk fo' yo', Massa Tom, an' of course I says as how I did. Den he asted me about de fire, an' how much damage it done, an' how we put it out. An' he end up by sayin' he'd laik t' buy mah mule, Boomerang, an' he wants t' come heah dis arternoon an' talk t' me about it."

"He does, eh?" cried Tom. "What sort of a man was he, Rad?"

"Well, a gen'man sort ob man, Massa Tom. Stranger t' me. I nebber seed him afo'. He suah was monstrous polite t' ole black Eradicate, an' he gib me a half-dollar, too, jest fo' a little ride. But I aint' gwine t' sell Boomerang, no indeedy, I ain't!" and Eradicate shook his gray, kinky head decidedly.

"Ned, there may be something in this!" said Tom, in an excited whisper to his chum. "I don't like the idea of a mysterious stranger questioning Eradicate!"

CHAPTER VI

THE AERIAL WARSHIP

Ned Newton looked at Tom questioningly. Then he glanced at the unsuspicious colored man, who was industriously polishing the half-dollar the mysterious stranger had given him.

"Rad, just exactly what sort of a man was this one you speak of?" asked Tom.

"Why, he were a gen'man—"

"Yes, I know that much. You've said it before. But was he an English-man, an American—or—"

Tom paused and waited for an answer.

"I think he were a Frenchman," spoke Eradicate. "I done didn't see him eat no frogs' laigs, but he smoked a cigarette dat had a funny smell, and he suah was monstrous polite. He suah was a Frenchman. I think."

Tom and Ned laughed at Eradicate's description of the man, but Tom's face was soon grave again.

"Tell us more about him, Rad," he suggested. "Did he seem especially interested in the fire?"

"No, sah, Massa Tom, he seemed laik he was more special interested in mah mule, Boomerang. He done asted how long I had him, an' how much I wanted fo' him, an' how old he was."

"But every once in a while he put in some question about the fire, or about our shops, didn't he, Rad?" Tom wanted to know.

The colored man scratched his kinky head, and glanced with a queer look at Tom.

"How yo' all done guess dat?" he asked.

"Answer my question," insisted Tom.

"Yes, sah, he done did ask about yo', and de wuks, ebery now and den," Rad confessed. "But how yo' all knowed dat, Massa Tom, when I were a-tellin' yo' all about him astin' fo' mah mule, done gets me—dat's what it suah does."

"Never mind, Rad. He asked questions about the plant, that's all I want to know. But you didn't tell him much, did you?"

Eradicate looked reproachfully at his master.

"Yo' all done knows me bettah dan dat, Massa Tom," the old colored man said. "Yo' all know yo' done gib orders fo' nobody t' talk about yo' projections."

"Yes, I know I gave those orders," Tom said, with a smile, "but I want to make sure that they have been followed."

"Well, I done follered 'em, Massa Tom."

"Then you didn't tell this queer stranger, Frenchman, or whatever he is, much about my place?"

"I didn't tell him nuffin', sah. I done frowed dust in his eyes."

Ned uttered an exclamation of surprise.

"Eradicate is speaking figuratively," Tom said, with a laugh.

"Dat's what I means," the colored man went on. "I done fooled him. When he asted me about de fire I said it didn't do no damage at all—in fack dat we'd rather hab de fire dan not hab it, 'case it done gib us a chance t' practice our hose drill."

"That's good," laughed Tom. "What else?"

"Well, he done sort ob hinted t' me ef we all knowed how de fire done start. I says as how we did, dat we done start it ourse'ves fo' practice, an dat we done expected it all along, an' were ready fo' it. Course I knows dat were a sort of fairy story, Massa Tom, but den dat cigarette-smokin' Frenchman didn't hab no right t' asted me so many questions, did he?"

"No, indeed, Rad. And I'm glad you didn't give him straight answers. So he's coming here later on, is he?"

"T' see ef I wants t' sell mah mule, Boomerang, yais, sah. I sort ob thought maybe you'd want t' hab a look at dat man, so I tole him t' come on. Course I doan't want t' sell Boomerang, but ef he was t' offer me a big lot ob money fo' him I'd take it."

"Of course," Tom answered. "Very well, Rad. You may go on now, and don't say anything to anyone about what you have told me."

"I won't, Massa Tom," promised the colored man, as he went off muttering to himself.

"Well, what do you make of it, Tom?" asked Ned of his chum, as they walked on toward the shed of the new, big aerial warship.

"I don't know just what to think, Ned. Of course things like this have happened before—persons trying to worm secrets out of Eradicate, or some of the other men."

"They never succeeded in getting much, I'm glad to say, but it always keeps me worried for fear something will happen," Tom concluded.

"But about this Frenchman?"

"Well, he must be a new one. And, now I come to think of it, I did hear some of the men speaking about a foreigner—a stranger—being around town last week. It was just a casual reference, and I paid little attention to it. Now it looks as though there might be something in it."

"Do you think he'll come to bargain with Eradicate about the mule?" Ned asked.

"Hardly. That was only talk to make Eradicate unsuspicious. The stranger, whoever he was, sized Rad up partly right. I surmised, when Rad said he asked a lot of questions about the mule, that was only to divert suspicion, and that he'd come back to the subject of the fire every chance he got."

"And you were right."

"Yes, so it seems. But I don't believe the fellow will come around here. It would be too risky. All the same, we'll be prepared for him. I'll just rig up one of my photo-telephone machines, so that, if he does come to have a talk with Rad, we can both see and hear him."

"That's great, Tom! But do you think this fellow had anything to do with the fire?"

"I don't know. He knew about it, of course. This isn't the first fire we've had in the works, and, though we always fight them ourselves, still news of it will leak out to the town. So he could easily have known about it. And he might be in with those who set it, for I firmly believe the fire was set by someone who has an object in injuring me."

"It's too bad!" declared Ned. "Seems as though they might let you alone, if they haven't gumption enough to invent things for themselves."

"Well, don't worry. Maybe it will come out all right," returned Tom. "Now, let's go and have a look at my aerial warship. I haven't shown it to you yet. Then we'll get ready for that mysterious Frenchman, if he comes—but I don't believe he will."

The young inventor unlocked the door of the shed where he kept his latest "pet," and at the sight which met his eyes Ned Newton uttered an exclamation of surprise.

"Tom, what is it?" he cried in an awed voice.

"My aerial warship!" was the quiet answer.

Ned Newton gave vent to a long whistle, and then began a detailed examination of the wonderful craft he saw before him. That is, he made as detailed an examination as was possible under the circumstances, for it was a long time before the young bank clerk fully appreciated all Tom Swift had accomplished in building the Mars, which was the war-like name painted in red letters on the big gas container that tugged and swayed overhead.

"Tom, however did you do it?" gasped Ned at length.

"By hard work," was the modest reply. "I've been at this for a longer time than you'd suppose, working on it at odd moments. I had a lot of help, too, or I never could have done it. And now it is nearly all finished, as far as the ship itself is concerned. The only thing that bothers me is to provide for the recoil of the guns I want to carry. Maybe you can help me with that. Come on, now, I'll explain how the affair works, and what I hope to accomplish with it."

In brief Tom's aerial warship was a sort of German Zeppelin type of dirigible balloon, rising in the air by means of a gas container, or, rather, several of them, for the section for holding the lifting gas element was divided by bulkheads.

The chief difference between dirigible balloons and ordinary aeroplanes, as you all know, is that the former are lifted from the earth by a gas, such as hydrogen, which is lighter than air, while the aeroplane lifts itself by getting into motion, when broad, flat planes, or surfaces, hold it up, just as a flat stone is held up when you sail it through the air. The moment the stone, or aeroplane, loses its forward motion, it begins to fall.

This is not so with a dirigible balloon. It is held in the air by means of the lifting gas, and once so in the air can be sent in any direction by means of propellers and rudders.

Tom's aerial warship contained many new features. While it was as large as some of the war-type Zeppelins, it differed from them materially. But the details would be of more interest to a scientific builder of such things than to the ordinary reader, so I will not weary you with them.

Sufficient to say that Tom's craft consisted first of a great semi-rigid bag, or envelope, made of specially prepared oiled silk and aluminum, to hold the gas, which was manufactured on board. There were a number of gas-tight compartments, so that if one, or even if a number of them burst, or were shot by an enemy, the craft would still remain afloat.

Below the big gas bag was the ship proper, a light but strong and rigid framework about which were built enclosed cabins. These cabins, or compartments, housed the driving machinery, the gas-generating plant, living, sleeping and dining quarters, and a pilot-house, whence the ship could be controlled.

But this was not all.

Ned, making a tour of the Mars, as she swayed gently in the big shed, saw where several aluminum pedestals were mounted, fore and aft and on either beam of the ship.

"They look just like places where you intend to mount guns," said Ned to Tom.

"And that's exactly what they are," the young inventor replied. "I have the guns nearly ready for mounting, but I can't seem to think of a way of providing for the recoil. And if I don't take care of that, I'm likely to find my ship coming apart under me, after we bombard the enemy with a broadside or two."

"Then you intend to fight with this ship?" asked Ned.

"Well, no; not exactly personally. I was thinking of offering it to the United States Government. Foreign nations are getting ready large fleets of aerial warships, so why shouldn't we? Matters in Europe are mighty uncertain. There may be a great war there in which aerial craft will play a big part. I am conceited enough to think I can build one that will measure up to the foreign ones, and I'll soon be in a position to know."

"What do you mean?"

"I mean I have already communicated with our government experts, and they are soon to come and inspect this craft. I have sent them word that it is about finished. There is only the matter of the guns, and some of the ordnance officers may be able to help me out with a suggestion, for I admit I am stuck!" exclaimed Tom.

"Then you're going to do the same with this aerial warship as you did with your big lantern and that immense gun you perfected?" asked Ned.

"That's right," confirmed Tom. My former readers will know to what Ned Newton referred, and those of you who do not may learn the details of how Tom helped Uncle Sam, by reading the previous volumes, "Tom Swift and His Great Searchlight," and "Tom Swift and His Giant Cannon."

"When do you expect the government experts?" Ned asked.

"Within a few days, now. But I'll have to hustle to get ready for them, as this fire has put me back. There are quite a number of details I need to change. Well, now, let me explain about that gun recoil business. Maybe you can help me."

"Fire away," laughed Ned. "I'll do the best I can."

Tom led the way from the main shed, where the aerial warship was housed, to a small private office. As Ned entered, the door, pulled by a strong spring, swung after him. He held back his hand to prevent it from slamming, but there was no need, for a patent arrangement took up all the force, and the door closed gently. Ned looked around, not much surprised, for the same sort of door-check was in use at his bank. But a sudden idea came to him.

"There you are, Tom!" he cried. "Why not take up the recoil of the guns on your aerial warship by some such device as that?" and Ned pointed to the door-check.

CHAPTER VII

WARNINGS

For a moment or two Tom Swift did not seem to comprehend what Ned had said. He remained staring, first at his chum, who stood pointing, and from him Tom's gaze wandered to the top of the door. It may have been, and probably was, that Tom was thinking of other matters at that instant. But Ned said again:

"Wouldn't that do, Tom? Check the recoil of the gun with whatever stuff is in that arrangement!"

A sudden change came over Tom's face. It was lighted up with a gleam of understanding.

"By Jove, Ned, old man!" he cried. "I believe you've struck it! And to think that has been under my nose, or, rather, over my head, all this while, and I never thought of it. Hurray! That will solve the problem!"

"Do you think it will?" asked Ned, glad that he had contributed something, if only an idea, to Tom's aerial warship.

"I'm almost sure it will. I'll give it a trial right away."

"What's in that door-check?" Ned asked. "I never stopped before to think what useful things they are, though at the bank, with the big, heavy doors, they are mighty useful."

"They are a combination of springs and hydrostatic valves," began Tom.

"Good-night!" laughed Ned. "Excuse the slang, Tom, but what in the world is a hydrostatic valve?"

"A valve through which liquids pass. In this door-check there may be a mixture of water, alcohol and glycerine, the alcohol to prevent freezing in cold weather, and the glycerine to give body to the mixture so it will not flow through the valves too freely."

"And do you think you can put something like that on your guns, so the recoil will be taken up?" Ned wanted to know.

"I think so," spoke Tom. "I'm going to work on it right away, and we'll soon see how it will turn out. It's mighty lucky you thought of that, for I sure was up against it, as the boys say."

"It just seemed to come to me," spoke Ned, "seeing how easily the door closed."

"If the thing works I'll give you due credit for it," promised Tom. "Now, I've got to figure out how much force a modified hydrostatic valve check like that will take up, and how much recoil my biggest gun will have."

"Then you're going to put several guns on the Mars?" asked Ned.

"Yes, four quick-firers, at least, two on each side, and heavier guns at the bow and stern, to throw explosive shells in a horizontal or upward direction. For a downward direction we won't need any guns, we can simply drop the bombs, or shells, from a release clutch."

"Drop them on other air craft?" Ned wanted to know.

"Well, if it's necessary, yes. Though I guess there won't be much chance of doing that to a rival aeroplane or dirigible. But in flying over cities or forts, explosive bombs can be dropped very nicely. For use in attacking other air craft I am going to depend on my lateral fire, from the guns mounted on either beam, and in the bow and stern."

"You speak as though you, yourself, were going into a battle of the air," said Ned.

"No, I don't believe I'll go that far," Tom replied. "Though, if the government wants my craft, I may have to go aloft and fire shots at targets for them to show them how things work.

"Please don't think that I am in favor of war, Ned," went on Tom earnestly. "I hate it, and I wish the time would come when all nations would disarm. But if the other countries are laying themselves out to have aerial battleships, it is time the United States did also. We must not be left behind, especially in view of what is taking place in Europe."

"I suppose that's right," agreed Ned. "Have you any of your guns ready?"

"Yes, all but the mounting of them on the supports aboard the Mars. I haven't dared do that yet, and fire them, until I provided some means of taking up the recoil. Now I'm going to get right to work on that problem."

There was considerable detailed figuring and computation work ahead of Tom Swift, and I will not weary you by going into the details of higher mathematics. Even Ned lost interest after the start of the problem, though he was interested when Tom took down the door-check and began measuring the amount of force it would take up, computing it on scales and spring balances.

Once this had been done, and Tom had figured just how much force could be expected to be taken up by a larger check, with stronger hydrostatic valves, the young inventor explained:

"And now to see how much recoil force my guns develop!"

"Are you really going to fire the guns?" asked Ned.

"Surely," answered Tom. "That's the only way to get at real results. I'll have the guns taken out and mounted in a big field. Then we'll fire them, and measure the recoil."

"Well, that may be some fun," spoke Ned, with a grin. "More fun than all these figures," and he looked at the mass of details on Tom's desk.

This was the second or third day after the fire in the red shed, and in the interim Tom had been busy making computations. These were about finished. Meanwhile further investigation bad been made of clues leading to the origin of the blaze in the shed, but nothing had been learned.

A photo-telephone had been installed near Eradicate's quarters, in the hope that the mysterious stranger might keep his promise, and come to see about the mule. In that case something would have been learned about him. But, as Tom feared, the man did not appear.

Ned was much interested in the guns, and, a little later, he helped Tom and Koku mount them in a vacant lot. The giant's strength came in handy in handling the big parts.

Mr. Swift strolled past, as the guns were being mounted for the preliminary test, and inquired what his son was doing.

"It will never work, Tom, never!" declared the aged inventor, when informed. "You can't take up those guns in your air craft, and fire them with any degree of safety."

"You wait, Dad," laughed Tom. "You haven't yet seen how the Newton hydrostatic recoil operates."

Ned smiled with pleasure at this.

It took nearly a week to get all the guns mounted, for some of them required considerable work, and it was also necessary to attach gauges to them to register the recoil and pressure. In the meanwhile Tom had been in further communication with government experts who were soon to call on him to inspect the aerial warship, with a view to purchase.

"When are they coming?" asked Ned, as he and Tom went out one morning to make the first test of the guns.

"They will be here any day, now. They didn't set any definite date. I suppose they want to take us unawares, to see that I don't 'frame-up' any game on them. Well, I'll be ready any time they come. Now, Koku, bring along those shells, and don't drop any of them, for that new powder is freakish stuff."

"Me no drop any, Master," spoke the giant, as he lifted the boxes of explosives in his strong arms.

The largest gun was loaded and aimed at a distant hill, for Tom knew that if the recoil apparatus would take care of the excess force of his largest gun, the problem of the smaller ones would be easy to solve.

"Here, Rad, where are you going?" Tom asked, as he noticed the colored man walking away, after having completed a task assigned to him.

"Where's I gwine, Massa Tom?"

"Yes, Rad, that's what I asked you."

"I—I'se gwine t' feed mah mule, Boomerang," said the colored man slowly. "It's his eatin' time, jest now, Massa Tom."

"Nonsense! It isn't anywhere near noon yet."

"Yais, sab, Massa Tom, I knows dat," said Eradicate, as he carefully edged away from the big gun, "but I'se done changed de eatin' hours ob dat mule. He had a little touch ob indigestion de udder day, an' I'se feedin' him diff'rent now. So I guess as how yo'll hab t' 'scuse me now, Massa Tom."

"Oh, well, trot along," laughed the young inventor. "I guess we won't need you. Is everything all right there, Koku?"

"All right, Master."

"Now, Ned, if you'll stand here," went on Tom, "and note the extreme point to which the hand on the pressure gauge goes, I'll be obliged to you. Just jot it down on this pad."

"Here comes someone," remarked the bank clerk, as he saw that his pencil was sharpened. He pointed to the field back of them.

"It's Mr. Damon," observed Tom. "We'll wait until he arrives. He'll be interested in this."

"Bless my collar button, Tom! What's going on?" asked the eccentric man, as he came up. "Has war been declared?"

"Just practicing," replied the young inventor. "Getting ready to put the armament on my aerial warship."

"Well, as long as I'm behind the guns I'm all right, I suppose?"

"Perfectly," Tom replied. "Now then, Ned, I think we'll fire."

There was a moment of inspection, to see that nothing had been forgotten, and then the big gun was discharged. There was a loud report, not as heavy, though, as Ned had expected, but there was no puff of smoke, for Tom was using smokeless powder. Only a little flash of flame was observed.

"Catch the figure, Ned!" Tom cried.

"I have it!" was the answer. "Eighty thousand!"

"Good! And I can build a recoil check that will take up to one hundred and twenty thousand pounds pressure. That ought to be margin of safety enough. Now we'll try another shot."

The echoes of the first had hardly died away before the second gun was ready for the test. That, too, was satisfactory, and then the smaller ones were operated. These were not quite so satisfactory, as the recoil developed was larger, in proportion to their size, than Tom had figured.

"But I can easily put a larger hydrostatic check on them," he said. "Now, we'll fire by batteries, and see what the total is."

Then began a perfect bombardment of the distant hillside, service charges being used, and explosive shells sent out so that dirt, stones and gravel flew in all directions. Danger signs and flags had been posted, and a cordon of Tom's men kept spectators away from the hill, so no one would be in the danger zone.

The young inventor was busy making some calculations after the last of the firing had been completed. Koku was packing up the unfired shells, and Mr. Damon was blessing his ear-drums, and the pieces of cotton he had stuffed in to protect them, when a tall, erect man was observed strolling over the fields in the direction of the guns.

"Somebody's coming, Tom," warned Ned.

"Yes, and a stranger, too," observed Tom. "I wonder if that can be Eradicate's Frenchman?"

But a look at the stranger's face disproved that surmise. He had a frank and pleasant countenance, obviously American.

"I beg your pardon," he began, addressing everyone in general, "but I am looking for Tom Swift. I was told he was here."

"I am Tom Swift," replied our hero.

"Ah! Well, I am Lieutenant Marbury, with whom you had some correspondence recently about—"

"Oh, yes, Lieutenant Marbury, of the United States Navy," interrupted Tom. "I'm glad to see you," he went on, holding out his hand. "We are just completing some tests with the guns. You called, I presume, in reference to my aerial warship?"

"That is it—yes. Have you it ready for a trial flight?"

"Well, almost. It can be made ready in a few hours. You see, I have been delayed. There was a fire in the plant."

"A fire!" exclaimed the officer in surprise. "How was that? We heard nothing of it in Washington."

"No, I kept it rather quiet," Tom explained. "We had reason to suspect that it was a fire purposely set, in a shed where I kept a quantity of explosives."

"Ha!" exclaimed Lieutenant Marbury. "This fits in with what I have heard. And did you not receive warning?" he asked Tom.

"Warning? No. Of what?"

"Of foreign spies!" was the unexpected answer. "I am sorry. Some of our Secret Service men unearthed something of a plot against you, and I presumed you had been told to watch out. If you had, the fire might not have occurred. There must have been some error in Washington. But let me tell you now, Tom Swift—be on your guard!"

CHAPTER VIII

A SUSPECTED PLOT

The officer's words were so filled with meaning that Tom started. Ned Newton, too, showed the effect he felt.

"Do you really mean that?" asked the young inventor, looking around to make sure his father was not present. On account of Professor Swift's weak heart, Tom wished to spare him all possible worry.

"I certainly do mean it," insisted Lieutenant Marbury. "And, while I am rather amazed at the news of the fire, for I did not think the plotters would be so bold as that, it is in line with what I expected, and what we suspected in Washington."

"And that was—what?" asked Tom.

"The existence of a well-laid plot, not only against our government, but against you!"

"And why have they singled me out?" Tom demanded.

"I might as well tell it from the beginning," the officer went on. "As long as you have not received any official warning from Washington you had better hear the whole story. But are you sure you had no word?"

"Well, now, I won't be so sure," Tom confessed. "I have been working very hard, the last two days, making some intricate calculations. I have rather neglected my mail, to tell you the truth.

"And, come to think of it, there were several letters received with the Washington postmark. But, I supposed they had to do with some of my patents, and I only casually glanced over them. There was one letter, though, that I couldn't make head or tail of."

"Ha! That was it!" cried the lieutenant. "It was the warning in cipher or code. I didn't think they would neglect to send it to you."

"But what good would it do me if I couldn't read it?" asked Tom.

"You must also have received a method of deciphering the message," the officer said. "Probably you overlooked that. The Secret Service men sent you the warning in code, so it would not be found out by the plotters, and, to make sure you could understand it, a method of translating the cipher was sent in a separate envelope. It is too bad you missed it."

"Yes, for I might have been on my guard," agreed Tom. "The red shed might not have burned, but, as it was, only slight damage was done."

"Owing to the fact that Tom put the fire out with sand ballast from his dirigible!" cried Ned. "You should have seen it!"

"I should have liked to be here," the lieutenant spoke. "But, if I were you, Tom Swift, I would take means to prevent a repetition of such things."

"I shall," Tom decided. "But, if we want to talk, we had better go to my office, where we can be more private. I don't want the workmen to hear too much."

Now that the firing was over, a number of Tom's men from the shops had assembled around the cannon. Most of them, the young inventor felt, could be trusted, but in so large a gathering one could never be sure.

"Did you come on from Washington yesterday?" asked Tom, as he, Ned and the officer strolled toward the shed where was housed the aerial warship.

"Yes, and I spent the night in New York. I arrived in town a short time ago, and came right on out here. At your house I was told you were over in the fields conducting experiments, so I came on here."

"Glad you did," Tom said. "I'll soon have something to show you, I hope. But I am interested in hearing the details of this suspected plot. Are you sure one exists?"

"Perfectly sure," was the answer. "We don't know all the details yet, nor who are concerned in it, but we are working on the case. The Secret Service has several agents in the field.

"We are convinced in Washington," went on Lieutenant Marbury, when he, Tom and Ned were seated in the private office, "that foreign spies are at work against you and against our government."

"Why against me?" asked Tom, in wonder.

"Because of the inventions you have perfected and turned over to Uncle Sam—notably the giant cannon, which rivals anything foreign European powers have, and the great searchlight, which proved so effective against the border smugglers. The success of those two alone, to say nothing of your submarine, has not only made foreign nations jealous, but they fear you—and us," the officer went on.

"Well, if they only take it out in fear—"

"But they won't!" interrupted the officer—"They are seeking to destroy those inventions. More than once, of late, we have nipped a plot just in time."

"Have they really tried to damage the big gun?" asked Tom, referring to one he had built and set up at Panama.

"They have. And now this fire proves that they are taking other measures—they are working directly against you."

"Why, I wonder?"

"Either to prevent you from making further inventions, or to stop you from completing your latest—the aerial warship."

"But I didn't know the foreign governments knew about that," Tom exclaimed. "It was a secret."

"Few secrets are safe from foreign Spies," declared Lieutenant Marbury. "They have a great ferreting-out system on the other side. We are just beginning to appreciate it. But our own men have not been idle."

"Have they really learned anything?" Tom asked. "Nothing definite enough to warrant us in acting," was the answer of the government man. "But we know enough to let us see that the plot is far-reaching."

"Are the French in it?" asked Ned impulsively.

"The French! Why do you ask that?"

"Tell him about Eradicate, and the man who wanted to buy the mule, Tom," suggested Ned.

Thereupon the young inventor mentioned the story told by Eradicate. He also brought out the fire-bomb, and explained his theory as to how it had operated to set the red shed ablaze.

"I think you are right," said Lieutenant Marbury. "And, as regards the French, I might say they are not the only nation banded to obtain our secrets—yours and the government's!"

"But I thought the French and the English were friendly toward us!" Ned exclaimed.

"So they are, in a certain measure," the officer went on. "And Russia is, too. But, in all foreign countries there are two parties, the war party, as it might be called, and the peace element.

"But I might add that it is neither France, England, nor Russia that we must fear. It is a certain other great nation, which at present I will not name."

"And you think spies set this fire?"

"I certainly do."

"But what measures shall I adopt against this plot?" Tom asked.

"We will talk that over," said Lieutenant Marbury. "But, before I go into details, I want to give you another warning. You must be very careful about—"

A sudden knock on the door interrupted the speaker.

CHAPTER IX

THE RECOIL CHECK

"Who is that?" asked Ned Newton, with a quick glance at his chum.

"I don't know," Tom answered. "I left orders we weren't to be disturbed unless it was something important."

"May be something has happened," suggested the navy officer, "another fire, perhaps, or a—"

"It isn't a fire," Tom answered. "The automatic alarm would be ringing before this in that case."

The knock was repeated. Tom went softly to the door and opened it quickly, to disclose, standing in the corridor, one of the messengers employed about the shops.

"Well, what is it?" asked Tom a bit sharply.

"Oh, if you please, Mr. Swift," said the boy, "a man has applied for work at the main office, and you know you left orders there that if any machinists came along, we were to—"

"Oh, so I did," Tom exclaimed. "I had forgotten about that," he went on to Lieutenant Marbury and Ned. "I am in need of helpers to rush through the finishing touches on my aerial warship, and I left word, if any applied, as they often do, coming here from other cities, that I wanted to see them. How many are there?" Tom asked of the messenger.

"Two, this time. They both say they're good mechanics."

"That's what they all say," interposed Tom, with a smile. "But, though they may be good mechanics in their own line, they need to have special qualifications to work on airships. Tell them to wait, Rodney," Tom went on to the lad, "and I'll see them presently."

As the boy went away, and Tom closed the door, he turned to Lieutenant Marbury.

"You were about to give me another warning when that interruption came. You might complete it now."

"Yes, it was another warning," spoke the officer, "and one I hope you will heed. It concerns yourself, personally."

"Do you mean he is in danger?" asked Ned quickly.

"That's exactly what I do mean," was the prompt reply. "In danger of personal injury, if not something worse."

Tom did not seem as alarmed as he might reasonably have been under the circumstances.

"Danger, eh?" he repeated coolly. "On the part of whom?"

"That's just where I can't warn you," the officer replied. "I can only give you that hint, and beg of you to be careful."

"Do you mean you are not allowed to tell?" asked Ned

"No, indeed; it isn't that!" the lieutenant hastened to assure the young man. "I would gladly tell, if I knew. But this plot, like the other one, directed against the inventions themselves, is so shrouded in mystery that I cannot get to the bottom of it.

"Our Secret Service men have been working on it for some time, not only in order to protect you, because of what you have done for the government, but because Uncle Sam wishes to protect his own property, especially the searchlight and the big cannon. But, though our agents have worked hard, they have not been able to get any clues that would put them on the right trail.

"So we can only warn you to be careful, and this I do in all earnestness. That was part of my errand in coming here, though, of course, I am anxious to inspect the new aerial warship you have constructed.

So watch out for two things—your inventions, and, more than all, your life!"

"Do you really think they would do me bodily harm?" Tom asked, a trifle skeptical.

"I certainly do. These foreign spies are desperate. If they cannot secure the use of these inventions to their own country, they are determined not to let this country have the benefit of them."

"Well, I'll be careful," Tom promised. "I'm no more anxious than anyone else to run my head into danger, and I certainly don't want any of my shops or inventions destroyed. The fire in the red shed was as close as I want anything to come."

"That's right!" agreed Ned. "And, if there's anything I can do, Tom, don't hesitate to call on me."

"All right, old man. I won't forget. And now, perhaps, you would like to see the Mars," he said to the lieutenant.

"I certainly would," was the ready answer. "But hadn't you better see those men who are waiting to find out about positions here?"

"There's no hurry about them," Tom said. "We have applicants every day, and it's earlier than the hour when I usually see them. They can wait. Now I want your opinion on my new craft. But, you must remember that it is not yet completed, and only recently did I begin to solve the problem of mounting the guns. So be a little easy with your criticisms."

Followed by Ned and Lieutenant Marbury, Tom led the way into the big airship shed. There, Swaying about at its moorings, was the immense aerial warship. To Ned's eyes it looked complete enough, but, when Tom pointed out the various parts, and explained to the government officer how it was going to work, Ned understood that considerable yet remained to be done on it.

Tom showed his official guest how a new system of elevation and depressing rudders had been adopted, how a new type of propeller was to be used and indicated several other improvements. The lower, or cabin, part of the aircraft could be entered by mounting a short ladder from the ground, and Tom took Ned and Lieutenant Marbury through the engine-room and other compartments of the Mars.

"It certainly is most complete," the officer observed. "And when you get the guns mounted I shall be glad to make an official test. You understand," he went on, to Tom, "that we are vitally interested in the guns, since we now have many aircraft that can be used purely for scouting purposes. What we want is something for offense, a veritable naval terror of the seas."

"I understand," Tom answered. "And I am going to begin work on mounting the guns at once. I am going to use the Newton recoil check," he added. "Ned, here, is responsible for that."

"Is that so?" asked the lieutenant, as Tom clapped his chum on the back.

"Yes, that's his invention."

"Oh, it isn't anything of the sort," Ned objected. "I just—"

"Yes, he just happened to solve the problem for me!" interrupted Tom, as he told the story of the door-spring.

"A good idea!" commented Lieutenant Marbury.

Tom then briefly described the principle on which his aerial warship would work, explaining how the lifting gas would raise it, with its load of crew, guns and explosives, high into the air; how it could then be sent ahead, backward, to either side, or around in a circle, by means of the propellers and the rudders, and how it could be raised or lowered, either by rudders or by forcing more gas into the lifting bags, or by letting some of the vapor out.

And, while this was being done by the pilot or captain in charge, the crew could be manning the guns with which hostile airships would be attacked, and bombs dropped on the forts or battleships of the enemy.

"It seems very complete," observed the lieutenant. "I shall be glad when I can give it an official test."

"Which ought to be in about a week," Tom said. "Meanwhile I shall be glad if you will be my guest here."

And so that was arranged.

Leaving Ned and the lieutenant to entertain each other, Tom went to see the mechanics who had applied for places. He found them satisfactory and engaged them. One of them had worked for him before. The other was a stranger, but he had been employed in a large aeroplane factory, and brought good recommendations.

There followed busy days at the Swift plant, and work was pushed on the aerial warship. The hardest task was the mounting of the guns, and equipping them with the recoil check, without which it would be impossible to fire them with the craft sailing through the air.

But finally one of the big guns, and two of the smaller ones were in place, with the apparatus designed to reduce the recoil shock, and then Tom decided to have a test of the Mars.

"Up in the air, do you mean?" asked Ned, who was spending all his spare time with his chum.

"Well, a little way up in the air, at least," Tom answered. "I'll make a sort of captive balloon of my craft, and see how she behaves. I don't want to take too many chances with that new recoil check, though it seems to work perfectly in theory."

The day came when, for the first time, the Mars was to come out of the big shed where she had been constructed. The craft was not completed for a flight as yet, but could be made so in a few days, with rush work. The roof of the great shed slid back, and the big envelope containing the buoyant gas rose slowly upward. There was a cry of surprise from the many workmen in the yard, as they saw, most of them for the first time, the wonderful new craft. It did not go up very high, being held in place with anchor ropes.

The sun glistened on the bright brass and nickel parts, and glinted from the gleaming barrels of the quick-firing guns.

"That's enough!" Tom called to the men below, who were paying out the ropes from the windlasses. "Hold her there."

Tom, Ned, Lieutenant Marbury and Mr. Damon were aboard the captive Mars.

Looking about, to see that all was in readiness, Tom gave orders to load the guns, blank charges being used, of course.

The recoil apparatus was in place, and it now remained to see if it would do the work for which it was designed.

"All ready?" asked the young inventor.

"Bless my accident insurance policy!" exclaimed Mr. Damon. "I'm as ready as ever I shall be, Tom. Let 'em go!"

"Hold fast!" cried Tom, as he prepared to press the electrical switch which would set off the guns. Ned and Lieutenant Marbury stood near the indicators to notice how much of the recoil would be neutralized by the check apparatus.

"Here we go!" cried the young inventor, and, at the same moment, from down below on the ground, came a warning cry:

"Don't shoot, Massa Tom. Don't shoot! Mah mule, Boomerang—"

But Eradicate had spoken too late. Tom pressed the switch; there was a deafening crash, a spurt of flame, and then followed wild cries and confused shouts, while the echoes of the reports rolled about the hills surrounding Shopton.

CHAPTER X

THE NEW MEN

"What was the matter down there?"

"Was anyone hurt?"

"Don't forget to look at those pressure gauges!"

"Bless my ham sandwich!"

Thus came the cries from those aboard the captive Mars. Ned, Lieutenant Marbury and Tom had called out in the order named. And, of course, I do not need to tell you what remark Mr. Damon made. Tom glanced toward where Ned and the government man stood, and saw that they had made notes of the pressure recorded on the recoil checks directly after the guns were fired. Mr. Damon, blessing innumerable objects under his breath, was looking over the side of the rail to discover the cause of the commotion and cries of warning from below.

"I don't believe it was anything serious, Tom," said the odd man. "No one seems to be hurt." "Look at Eradicate!" suddenly exclaimed Ned.

"And his mule! I guess that's what the trouble was, Tom!"

They looked to where the young bank employee pointed, and saw the old colored man, seated on the seat of his ramshackle wagon, doing his best to pull down to a walk the big galloping mule, which was dragging the vehicle around in a circle.

"Whoa, dere!" Eradicate was shouting, as he pulled on the lines. "Whoa, dere! Dat's jest laik yo', Boomerang, t' run when dere ain't no call fo' it, nohow! Ef I done wanted yo' t' git a move on, yo'd lay down 'side de road an' go to sleep. Whoa, now!"

But the noise of the shots had evidently frightened the long-eared animal, and he was in no mood for stopping, now that he had once started. It was not until some of the workmen ran out from the group where they had gathered to watch Tom's test, and got in front of Boomerang, that they succeeded in bringing him to a halt.

Eradicate climbed slowly down from the seat, and limped around until he stood in front of his pet.

"Yo'—yo're a nice one, ain't yo'?" he demanded in sarcastic tones. "Yo' done enough runnin' in a few minutes fo' a week ob Sundays, an' now I won't be able t' git a move out ob ye! I'se ashamed ob yo', dat's what I is! Puffickly ashamed ob yo'. Go 'long, now, an' yo' won't git no oats dish yeah day! No sah!" and, highly indignant, Eradicate led the now slowly-ambling mule off to the stable.

"I won't shoot again until you have him shut up, Rad!" laughed Tom. "I didn't know you were so close when I set off those guns."

"Dat's all right, Mass a Tom," was the reply. "I done called t' you t' wait, but yo' didn't heah me, I 'spects. But it doan' mattah, now. Shoot all yo' laik, Boomerang won't run any mo' dis week. He done runned his laigs off now. Shoot away!"

But Tom was not quite ready to do this. He wanted to see what effect the first shots had had on his aerial warship, and to learn whether or not the newly devised recoil check had done what was expected of it.

"No more shooting right away," called the young inventor. "I want to see how we made out with the first round. How did she check up, Ned?"

"Fine, as far as I can tell."

"Yes, indeed," added Lieutenant Marbury. "The recoil was hardly noticeable, though, of course, with the full battery of guns in use, it might be more so."

"I hope not," answered Tom. "I haven't used the full strength of the recoil check yet. I can tune it up more, and when I do, and when I have it attached to all the guns, big and little, I think we'll do the trick. But now for a harder test."

The rest of that day was spent in trying out the guns, firing them with practice and service charges, though none of the shells used contained projectiles. It would not have been possible to shoot these, with the Mars held in place in the midst of Tom's factory buildings.

"Well, is she a success, Tom?" asked Ned, when the experimenting was over for the time being.

"I think I can say so—yes," was the answer, with a questioning look at the officer.

"Indeed it is—a great success! We must give the Newton shock absorber due credit."

Ned blushed with pleasure.

"It was only my suggestion," he said. "Tom worked it all out."

"But I needed the Suggestion to start with," the young inventor replied.

"Of course something may develop when you take your craft high in the air, and discharge the guns there," said the lieutenant. "In a rarefied atmosphere the recoil check may not be as effective as at the earth's surface. But, in such case doubtless, you can increase the strength of the springs and the hydrostatic valves."

"Yes, I counted on that," Tom explained. "I shall have to work out that formula, though, and be ready for it. But, on the whole, I am pretty well satisfied."

"And indeed you may well feel that way," commented the government official.

The Mars was hauled back into the shed, and the roof slid shut over the craft. Much yet remained to do on it, but now that Tom was sure the important item of armament was taken care of, he could devote his entire time to the finishing touches.

As his plant was working on several other pieces of machinery, some of it for the United States Government, and some designed for his own use, Tom found himself obliged to hire several new hands. An advertisement in a New York newspaper brought a large number of replies, and for a day or two Tom was kept busy sifting out the least desirable, and arranging to see those whose answers showed they knew something of the business requirements.

Meanwhile Lieutenant Marbury remained as Tom's guest, and was helpful in making suggestions that would enable the young inventor to meet the government's requirements.

"I'd like, also, to get on the track of those spies who, I am sure, wish to do you harm," said the lieutenant, "but clues seem to be scarce around here."

"They are, indeed," agreed Tom. "I guess the way in which we handled that fire in the red shed sort of discouraged them."

Lieutenant Marbury shook his head.

"They're not so easily discouraged as that," he remarked. "And, with the situation in Europe growing more acute every day, I am afraid some of those foreigners will take desperate measures to gain their ends."

"What particular ends do you mean?"

"Well, I think they will either try to so injure you that you will not be able to finish this aerial warship, or they will damage the craft itself, steal your plans, or damage some of your other inventions."

"But what object would they have in doing such a thing?" Tom wanted to know. "How would that help France, Germany or Russia, to do me an injury?"

"They are seeking to strike at the United States through you," was the answer. "They don't want Uncle Sam to have such formidable weapons as your great searchlight, the giant cannon, or this new warship of the clouds."

"But why not, as long as the United States does not intend to go to war with any of the foreign nations?" Tom inquired.

"No, it is true we do not intend to go to war with any of the conflicting European nations," admitted Lieutenant Marbury, "but you have no idea how jealous each of those foreign nations is of all the others. Each one fears that the United States will cease to be neutral, and will aid one or the other."

"Oh, so that's' it?" exclaimed Tom.

"Yes, each nation, which may, at a moments notice, be drawn into a war with one or more rival nations, fears that we may throw in our lot with its enemies."

"And, to prevent that, they want to destroy some of my inventions?" asked Tom.

"That's the way I believe it will work out. So you must be careful, especially since you have taken on so many new men."

"That's so," agreed the young inventor. "I have had to engage more strangers than ever before, for I am anxious to get the Mars finished and give it a good test. And, now that you have mentioned it, there are some of those men of whom I am a bit suspicious."

"Have they done anything to make you feel that way?" asked the lieutenant.

"Well, not exactly; it is more their bearing, and the manner in which they go about the works. I must keep my eye on them, for it takes only a few discontented men to spoil a whole shop full. I will be on my guard."

"And not only about your new airship and other inventions," said the officer, "but about yourself, personally. Will you do that?"

"Yes, though I don't imagine anything like that will happen."

"Well, be on your guard, at all events," warned Lieutenant Marbury.

As Tom had said, he had been obliged to hire a number of new men. Some of these were machinists who had worked for him, or his father, on previous occasions, and, when tasks were few, had been dismissed, to go to other shops. These men, Tom felt sure, could be relied upon.

But there were a number of others, from New York, and other large cities, of whom Tom was not so sure.

"You have more foreigners than I ever knew you to hire before, Tom," his father said to him one day, coming back from a tour of the shops.

"Yes, I have quite a number," Tom admitted. "But they are all good workmen. They stood the test."

"Yes, some of them are too good," observed the older inventor. "I saw one of them making up a small motor the other day, and he was winding the armature a new way. I spoke to him about it, and he tried to prove that his way was an improvement on yours. Why, he'd have had it short-circuited in no time if I hadn't stopped him."

"Is that so?" asked Tom. "That is news to me. I must look into this."

"Are any of the new men employed on the Mars?" Mr. Swift asked.

"No, not yet, but I shall have to shift some there from other work I think, in order to get finished on time."

"Well, they will bear watching I think," his father said.

"Why, have you seen anything—do you—" began the young man, for Mr. Swift had not been told of the suspicions of the lieutenant.

"Oh, it isn't anything special," the older inventor went on. "Only I wouldn't let a man I didn't know much about get too much knowledge of my latest invention."

"I won't, Dad. Thanks for telling me. This latest craft is sure going to be a beauty."

"Then you think it will work, Tom?"

"I'm sure of it, Dad!"

Mr. Swift shook his head in doubt.

CHAPTER XI

A DAY OFF

Tom Swift pondered long and intently over what his father had said to him. He sat for several minutes in his private office, after the aged inventor had passed out, reviewing in his mind the talk just finished.

"I wonder," said Tom slowly, "if any of the new men could have obtained work here for the purpose of furthering that plot the lieutenant suspects? I wonder if that could be true?"

And the more Tom thought of it, the more he was convinced that such a thing was at least possible.

"I must make a close inspection, and weed out any suspicious characters," he decided, "though I need every man I have working now, to get the Mars finished in time. Yes, I must look into this."

Tom had reached a point in his work where he could leave much to his helpers. He had several good foremen, and, with his father to take general supervision over more important details, the young inventor had more time to himself. Of course he did not lay too many burdens on his father's shoulders since Mr. Swift's health was not of the best.

But Tom's latest idea, the aerial warship, was so well on toward completion that his presence was not needed in that shop more than two or three times a day.

"When I'm not there I'll go about in the other shops, and sort of size up the situation," he decided. "I may be able to get a line on some of those plotters, if there are any here."

Lieutenant Marbury had departed for a time, to look after some personal matters, but he was to return inside of a week, when it was hoped to give the aerial warship its first real test in flight, and under some of the conditions that it would meet with in actual warfare.

As Tom was about to leave his office, to put into effect his new resolution to make a casual inspection of the other shops, he met Koku, the giant, coming in. Koku's hands and face were black with oil and machine filings.

"Well, what have you been doing?" Tom wanted to know. "Did you have an accident?" For Koku had no knowledge of machinery, and could not even be trusted to tighten up a simple nut by himself. But if some one stood near him, and directed him how to apply his enormous strength, Koku could do more than several machines.

"No accident, Master," he replied. "I help man lift that hammer-hammer thing that pounds so. It get stuck!"

"What, the hammer of the drop forger?" cried Tom. "Was that out of order again?"

"Him stuck," explained Koku simply.

There was an automatic trip-hammer in one of the shops, used for pounding out drop forgings, and this hammer seemed to take especial delight in getting out of order. Very often it jammed, or "stuck," as Koku described it, and if the hammer could not be forced back on the channel or upright guide-plates, it meant that it must be taken apart, and valuable time lost. Once Koku had been near when the hammer got out of order, and while the workmen were preparing to dismantle it, the giant seized the big block of steel, and with a heave of his mighty shoulders forced it back on the guides.

"And is that what you did this time?" asked Tom.

"Yes, Master. Me fix hammer," Koku answered. "I get dirty, I no care. Man say I no can fix. I show him I can!"

"What man said that?"

"Man who run hammer. Ha! I lift him by one finger! He say he no like to work on hammer. He want to work on airship. I tell him I tell you, maybe you give him job—he baby! Koku can work hammer. Me fix it when it get stuck."

"Well, maybe you know what you're talking about, but I don't," said Tom, with a pleasant smile at his big helper. "Come on, Koku, we'll go see what it all means."

"Koku work hammer, maybe?" asked the giant hope fully.

"Well, I'll see," half promised Tom. "If it's going to get out of gear all the while it might pay me to keep you at it so you could get it back in place whenever it kicked up a fuss, and so save time. I'll see about it."

Koku led the way to the shop where the triphammer was installed. It was working perfectly now, as Tom could tell by the thundering blows it struck. The man operating it looked up as Tom approached, and, at a gesture from the young inventor, shut off the power.

"Been having trouble here?" asked Tom, noting that the workman was one of the new hands he had hired.

"Yes, sir, a little," was the respectful answer. "This hammer goes on a strike every now and then, and gets jammed. Your giant there forced it back into place, which is more than I could do with a big bar for a lever. He sure has some muscle."

"Yes," agreed Tom, "he's pretty strong. But what's this you said about wanting to give up this job, and go on the airship construction."

The man turned red under his coat of grime.

"I didn't intend him to repeat that to you, Mr. Swift," he said. "I was a little put out at the way this hammer worked. I lose so much time at it that I said I'd like to be transferred to the airship department. I've worked in one before But I'm not making a kick," he added quickly. "Work is too scarce for that."

"I understand," said Tom. "I have been thinking of making a change. Koku seems to like this hammer, and knows how to get it in order once it gets off the guides. You say you have had experience in airship construction?"

"Yes, sir. I've worked on the engines, and on the planes."

"Know anything about dirigible balloons?"

"Yes, I've worked on them, too, but the engineering part is my specialty. I'm a little out of my element on a trip-hammer."

"I see. Well, perhaps I'll give you a trial. Meanwhile you might break Koku in on operating this machine. If I transfer you I'll put him on this hammer."

"Thank you, Mr. Swift! I'll show him all I know about it. Oh, there goes the hammer again!" he exclaimed, for, as he started it up, as Tom turned away, the big piece of steel once more jammed on the channel-plates.

"Me fix!" exclaimed the giant eagerly, anxious for a chance to exhibit his great strength.

"Wait a minute!" exclaimed Tom. "I want to get a look at that machine."

He inspected it carefully before he signaled for Koku to force the hammer back into place. But, if Tom saw anything suspicious, he said nothing. There was, however, a queer look on his face as he turned aside, and he murmured to himself, as he walked away:

"So you want to be transferred to the airship department, do you? Well, we'll see about that We'll see."

Tom had more problems to solve than those of making an aerial warship that would be acceptable to the United States Government.

Ned Newton called on his chum that evening. The two talked of many things, gradually veering around to the subject uppermost in Tom's mind—his new aircraft.

"You're thinking too much of that." Ned warned him. "You're as bad as the time you went for your first flight."

"I suppose I am," admitted Tom. "But the success of the Mars means a whole lot to me. And that's something I nearly forgot. I've got to go out to the shop now. Want to come along, Ned?"

"Sure, though I tell you that you're working too hard—burning the electric light at both ends."

"This is just something simple," Tom said. "It won't take long."

He went out, followed by his chum.

"But this isn't the way to the airship shed," objected the young bank clerk, as he noted in which direction Tom was leading him.

"I know it isn't," Tom replied. "But I want to look at one of the trip-hammers in the forge shop when none of the men is around. I've been having a little trouble there."

"Trouble!" exclaimed his chum. "Has that plot Lieutenant Marbury spoke of developed?"

"Not exactly. This is something else," and Tom told of the trouble with the big hammer.

"I had an idea," the young inventor said, "that the man at the machine let it get out of order purposely, so I'd change him. I want to see if my suspicions are correct."

Tom carefully inspected the hammer by the light of a powerful portable electric lamp Ned held.

"Ha! There it is!" Tom suddenly exclaimed.

"Something wrong?" Ned inquired.

"Yes. This is what's been throwing the hammer off the guides all the while," and Tom pulled out a small steel bolt that had been slipped into an oil hole. A certain amount of vibration, he explained to Ned, would rattle the bolt out so that it would force the hammer to one side, throwing it off the channel-plates, and rendering it useless for the time being.

"A foxy trick," commented Tom. "No wonder the machine got out of kilter so easily."

"Do you think it was done purposely?"

"Well, I'm not going to say. But I'm going to watch that man. He wants to be transferred to the airship department. He put this in the hammer, perhaps, to have an excuse for a change. Well, I'll give it to him."

"You don't mean that you'd take a fellow like that and put him to work on your new aerial warship, do you, Tom?"

"Yes, I think I will, Ned. You see, I look at it this way: I haven't any real proof against him now. He could only laugh at me if I accused him. But you've heard the proverb about giving a calf rope enough and he'll hang himself, haven't you?"

"I think I have."

"Well, I'm going to give this fellow a little rope. I'll transfer him, as he asks, and I'll keep a close watch on him."

"But won't it be risky?"

"Perhaps, but no more so than leaving him in here to work mischief. If he is hatching a plot, the sooner it's over with the better I shall like it. I don't like a shot to hang fire. I'm warned now, and I'll be ready for him. I have a line on whom to suspect. This is the first clue," and Tom held up the incriminating bolt.

"I think you're taking too big a risk, Tom," his chum said. "Why not discharge the man?"

"Because that might only smooth things over for a time. If this plot is being laid the sooner it comes to a head, and breaks, the better. Have it done, short, sharp and quick, is my motto. Yes, I'll shift him in the morning. Oh, but I wish it was all over, and the Mars was accepted by Uncle Sam!" and Tom put his hand to his head with a tired gesture.

"Say, old man!" exclaimed Ned, "what you want is a day off, and I'm going to see that you get it. You need a little vacation."

"Perhaps I do," assented Tom wearily.

"Then you'll have it!" cried Ned. "There's going to be a little picnic tomorrow. Why can't you go with Mary Nestor? She'd like you to take her, I'm sure. Her cousin, Helen Randall, is on from New York, and she wants to go, also."

"How do you know?" asked Tom quickly.

"Because she said so," laughed Ned. "I was over to the house to call. I have met Helen before, and I suggested that you and I would take the two girls, and have a day off. You'll come, won't you?"

"Well, I don't know," spoke Tom slowly. "I ought to—"

"Nonsense! Give up work for one day!" urged Ned. "Come along. It'll do you good—get the cobwebs out of your head."

"All right, I'll go," assented Tom, after a moment's thought.

The next day, having instructed his father and the foremen to look well to the various shops, and having seen that the work on the new aerial warship was progressing favorably, Tom left for a day's outing with his chum and the two girls.

The picnic was held in a grove that surrounded a small lake, and after luncheon the four friends went for a ride in a launch Tom hired. They went to the upper end of the lake, in rather a pretty but lonesome locality.

"Tom, you look tired," said Mary. "I'm sure you've been working too hard!"

"Why, I'm not working any harder than usual," Tom insisted.

"Yes, he is, too!" declared Ned, "and he's running more chances, too."

"Chances?" repeated Mary.

"Oh, that's all bosh!" laughed Tom. "Come on, let's go ashore and walk."

"That suits me," spoke Ned. Helen and Mary assented, and soon the four young persons were strolling through the shady wood.

After a bit the couples became separated, and Tom found himself walking beside Mary in a woodland path. The girl glanced at her companion's face, and ventured:

"A penny for your thoughts, Tom."

"They're worth more than that," he replied gallantly. "I was thinking of—you."

"Oh, how nicely you say it!" she laughed. "But I know better! You're puzzling over some problem. Tell me, what did Ned mean when he hinted at danger? Is there any, Tom?"

"None at all," he assured her. "It's just a soft of notion—"

Mary made a sudden gesture of silence.

"Hark!" she whispered to Tom, "I heard someone mention your name then. Listen!"

CHAPTER XII

A NIGHT ALARM

Mary Nestor spoke with such earnestness, and her action in catching hold of Tom's arm to enjoin silence was so pronounced that, though he had at first regarded the matter in the light of a joke, he soon thought otherwise. He glanced from the girl's face to the dense underbrush on either side of the woodland path.

"What is it, Mary?" he asked in a whisper.

"I don't just know. I heard whispering, and thought it was the rustling of the leaves of the trees. Then someone spoke your name quite loudly. Didn't you hear it?"

Tom shook his head in negation.

"It may be Ned and his friend," he whispered, his lips close to Mary's ear.

"I think not," was her answer. "Listen; there it is again."

Distinctly then, Tom heard, from some opening in the screen of bushes, his own name spoken. "Did you hear it?" asked Mary, barely forming the words with her lips. But Tom could read their motion.

"Yes," he nodded. Then, motioning to Mary to remain where she was, he stepped forward, taking care to tread only on grassy places where there were no little twigs or branches to break and betray his presence. He was working his way toward the sound of the unseen voice.

There was a sudden movement in the bushes, just beyond the spot Tom was making for. He halted quickly and peered ahead. Mary, too, was looking on anxiously.

Tom saw the forms of two men, partially concealed by bushes, walking away from him. The men took no pains to conceal their movements, so Tom was emboldened to advance with less caution. He hurried to where he could get a good view, and, at the sight of one of the men, he uttered an exclamation.

"What is it?" asked Mary, who was now at his side. She had seen that Tom had thrown aside caution, and she had come up to join him.

"That man—I know him!" the young inventor exclaimed. "It is Feldman—the one who wanted to be changed from the trip-hammer to the airship department. But who is that with him?"

As Tom spoke the other turned, and at the sight of his face Mary Nestor said:

"He looks like a Frenchman, with that little mustache and imperial."

"So he is!" exclaimed Tom, in a hoarse whisper. "He must be the Frenchman that Eradicate spoke about. I wonder what this can mean? I didn't know Feldman had left the shop."

"You may know what you're talking about, but I don't, Tom," said Mary, with a smile at her companion. "Are they friends of yours?"

"Hardly," spoke the young inventor dryly. "That one, Feldman, is one of my workmen. He had charge of a drop-forge press and trip-hammer that—"

"Spare me the details, Tom!" interrupted Mary. "You know I don't understand a thing about machinery. The wireless you erected on Earthquake Island was as much as I could comprehend."

"Well, a trip-hammer isn't as complicated as that," spoke Tom, with a laugh, as he noticed that the two men were far enough away so they could not hear him. "What I was going to say was, that one of those men works in our shops. The other I don't know, but I agree with you that he does look like a Frenchman, and old Eradicate had a meeting with a man whom he described as being of that nationality."

"And you say they are not friends of yours?"

"I have no reason to believe they are."

"Then they must be enemies!" exclaimed Mary with quick intuition. "Oh, Tom, you will be careful, won't you?"

"Of course I will, little girl," he said, a note of fondness creeping into his voice, as he covered the small hand with his own large one. "But there is no danger."

"Then why were these men discussing you?"

"I don't know that they were, Mary."

"They mentioned your name."

"Well, that may be. Probably one of them, Feldman, who works for me, was speaking to his companion about the chance for a position. My father and I employ a number of men, you know."

"Well, I suppose it is all right, Tom, and I surely hope it is. But you will be careful, won't you? And you look more worried than you used to. Has anything gone wrong?"

"Not a thing, little girl. Everything is going fine. My new aerial warship will soon make a trial flight, and I'd be pleased to have you as a passenger."

"Would you really, Tom?"

"Of course. Consider that you have the first invitation."

"That's awfully nice of you. But you do look worried, Tom. Has anything troubled you?"

"No, not much. Everything is going all right now. We did have a little trouble at a fire in one of my buildings—"

"A fire! Oh, Tom! You never told me!"

"Well, it didn't amount to much—the only suspicious fact about it was that it seemed to have been of incendiary origin."

Mary seemed much alarmed, and again begged Tom to be on his guard, which he promised to do. Had Mary known the warnings uttered by Lieutenant Marbury she might have had more occasion for worry.

"Do you suppose that hammer man of yours came to these woods to meet that Frenchman and talk about you, Tom?" asked his companion, when the two men had strolled out of sight, and the young people were on their way back to the launch.

"Well, it's possible. I have been warned that foreign spies are trying to get hold of some of my patents, and also to hamper the government in the use of some others I have sold. But they'll have their own troubles to get away with anything. The works are pretty well guarded, and you forget I have the giant, Koku, who is almost a personal bodyguard."

"Yes, but he can't be everywhere at once. Oh, you will be careful, won't you, Tom?"

"Yes, Mary, I will," promised the young inventor. "But don't say anything to Ned about what we just saw and heard."

"Why not?"

"Because he's been at me to hire a couple of detectives to watch over me, and this would give him another excuse. Just don't say anything, and I'll adopt all the precautions I think are needful."

"I will on condition that you do that."

"And I promise I will."

With that Mary had to be content. A little later they joined Ned and his friend, and soon they were moving swiftly down the lake in the launch.

"Well, hasn't it done you good to take a day off?" Ned demanded of his chum, when they were on their homeward way.

"Yes, I think it has," agreed Tom.

"You swung your thoughts into a new channel, didn't you?"

"Oh, yes, I found something new to think about," admitted the young inventor, with a quick look at Mary.

But, though Tom thus passed off lightly the little incident of the day, he gave it serious thought when he was alone.

"Those fellows were certainly talking about me," he reasoned. "I wonder what for? And Feldman left the shop without my knowledge. I'll have to look into that. I wonder if that Frenchy looking chap I saw was the one who tried to pump Eradicate? Another point to settle."

The last was easily disposed of, for, on reaching his shops that afternoon, Tom cross-questioned the colored man, and obtained a most accurate description of the odd foreigner. It tallied in every detail with the man Tom had seen in the woods.

"And now about Feldman," mused Tom, as he went to the foreman of the shop where the suspected man had been employed.

"Yes, Feldman asked for a day off," the foreman said in response to Tom's question. "He claimed his mother was sick, and he wanted to go to see her. I knew you wouldn't object, as we were not rushed in his department."

"Oh, that's all right," said Tom quickly. "Did he say where his mother lived?"

"Over Lafayette way."

"Humph!" murmured Tom. To himself he added: "Queer that he should be near Lake Loraine, in an opposite direction from Lafayette. This will bear an investigation."

The next day Tom made it his business to pass near the hammer that was so frequently out of order. He found Feldman busy instructing Koku in its operation. Tom resolved on a little strategy.

"How is it working, Feldman?" he asked.

"Very well, Mr. Swift. There doesn't seem to be any trouble at all, but it may happen any minute. Koku seems to take to it like a duck to water."

"Well, when he is ready to assume charge let me know."

"And then am I to go into the aeroplane shop?"

"I'll see. By the way, how is your mother?" he asked quickly, looking Feldman full in the face.

"She is much better. I took a day off yesterday to go to see her," the man replied quietly enough, and without sign of embarrassment.

"That's good. Let me see, she lives over near Lake Loraine, doesn't she?"

This time Feldman could not repress a start. But he covered it admirably by stooping over to pick up a tool that fell to the floor.

"No, my mother is in Lafayette," he said. "I don't know where Lake Loraine is."

"Oh," said Tom, as he turned aside to hide a smile. He was sure now he knew at least one of the plotters.

But Tom was not yet ready to show his hand. He wanted better evidence than any he yet possessed. It would take a little more time.

Work on the aerial warship was rushed, and it seemed likely that a trial flight could be made before the date set. Lieutenant Marbury sent word that he would be on hand when needed, and in some of the shops, where fittings for the Mars were being made, night and day shifts were working.

"Well, if everything goes well, we'll take her for a trial flight tomorrow," said Tom, coming in from the shops one evening.

"Guns and all?" asked Ned, who had come over to pay his chum a visit. Mr. Damon was also on hand, invoking occasional blessings.

"Guns and all," replied Tom.

Ned had a little vacation from the bank, and was to stay all night, as was Mr. Damon.

What time it was, save that it must be near midnight, Tom could not tell, but he was suddenly awakened by hearing yells from Eradicate:

"Massa Tom! Massa Tom!" yelled the excited colored man. "Git up! Git up! Suffin' turrible am happenin' in de balloon shop. Hurry! An' yo' stan' still, Boomerang, or I'll twist yo' tail, dat's what I will! Hurry, Massa Tom!"

Tom leaped out of bed.

CHAPTER XIII

THE CAPTURE

Tom Swift was something like a fireman. He had lived so long in an atmosphere of constant alarms and danger, that he was always ready for almost any emergency. His room was equipped with the end in view that he could act promptly and effectively.

So, when he heard Eradicate's alarm, though he wondered what the old colored man was doing out of bed at that hour, Tom did not stop to reason out that puzzle. He acted quickly.

His first care was to throw on the main switch, connected with a big storage battery, and to which were attached the wires of the lighting system. This at once illuminated every shop in the plant, and also the grounds themselves. Tom wanted to see what was going on. The use of a storage battery eliminated the running of the dynamo all night.

And once he had done this, Tom began pulling on some clothes and a pair of shoes. At the same time he reached out with one hand and pressed a button that sounded an alarm in the sleeping quarters of Koku, the giant, and in the rooms of some of the older and most trusted men.

All this while Eradicate was shouting away, down in the yard.

"Massa Tom! Massa Tom!" he called. "Hurry! Hurry! Dey is killin' Koku!"

"Killing Koku!" exclaimed Tom, as he finished his hasty dressing. "Then my giant must already be in the fracas. I wonder what it's all about, anyhow."

"What's up, Tom?" came Ned's voice from the adjoining room. "I thought I heard a noise."

"Your thoughts do you credit, Ned!" Tom answered. "If you listen right close, you'll hear several noises."

"By Jove! You're right, old man!"

Tom could hear his chum bound out of bed to the floor, and, at the same time, from the big shed where Tom was building his aerial warship came a series of yells and shouts.

"That's Koku's voice!" Tom exclaimed, as he recognized the tones of the giant.

"I'm coming, Tom!" Ned informed his chum. "Wait a minute."

"No time to wait," Tom replied, buttoning his coat as he sped down the hall.

"Oh, Tom, what is it?" asked Mrs. Baggert, the housekeeper, looking from her room.

"I don't know. But don't let dad get excited, no matter what happens. Just put him off until I come back. I think it isn't anything serious."

Mr. Damon, who roomed next to Ned, came out of his own apartment partially dressed.

"Bless my suspenders!" he cried to Tom, those articles just then dangling over his hips. "What is it? What has happened? Bless my steam gauge, don't tell me it's a fire!"

"I think it isn't that," Tom answered. "No alarm has rung. Koku seems to be in trouble."

"Well, he's big enough to look after himself, that's one consolation," chuckled Mr. Damon. "I'll be right with you."

By this time Ned had run out into the hall, and, together, he and Tom sped down the corridor. They could not hear the shouts of Eradicate so plainly now, as he was on the other side of the house.

But when the two young men reached the front porch, they could hear the yells given with redoubled vigor. And, in the glare of the electric lights, Tom saw Eradicate leading along Boomerang, the old mule.

"What is it, Rad? What is it?" demanded the young inventor breathlessly.

"Trouble, Massa Tom! Dat's what it am! Trouble!"

"I know that—but what kind?"

"De worstest kind, I 'spects, Massa Tom. Listen to it!"

From the interior of the big shed, not far from the house, Tom and Ned heard a confused jumble of shouts, cries and pleadings, mingled with the rattle of pieces of metal, and the banging of bits of wood. And, above all that, like the bellowing of a bull, was noted the rumbling voice of Koku, the giant.

"Come on, Ned!" Tom cried.

"It's suah trouble, all right," went on Eradicate. "Mah mule, Boomerang, had a touch ob de colic, an' I got up t' gib him some hot drops an' walk him around, when I heard de mostest terrific racket-sound, and den I 'spected trouble was comm."

"It isn't coming—it's here!" called Tom, as he sped toward the big shop. Ned was but a step behind him. The big workshop where the aerial warship was being built was, like the other buildings, brilliantly illuminated by the lights Tom had switched on. The young inventor also saw several of his employees speeding toward the same point.

Tom was the first to reach the small door of the shed. This was built in one of the two large main doors, which could be swung open when it was desired to slide the Mars in from the ground, and not admit it through the roof.

"Look!" cried Tom, pointing.

Ned looked over his chum's shoulder and saw the giant, Koku, struggling with four men—powerful men they were, too, and they seemed bent on mischief.

For they came at Koku from four sides, seeking to hold his hands and feet so that he could not fight them back. On the floor near where the struggle was taking place was a coil of rope, and it was evident that it had been the intention of the men to overcome Koku and truss him up, so that he would not interfere with what they intended to do. But Koku was a match for even the four men, powerful as they were.

"We're here, Koku!" cried Tom. "Watch for an opening, Ned!" he called to his chum.

The sound of Tom's voice disconcerted at least two of the attackers, for they looked around quickly, and this was fatal to their chances.

Though such a big man, Koku was exceptionally quick, and no sooner did he see his advantage, as two of the men turned their gaze away from him, than he seized it.

Suddenly tearing loose his hands from the grip of the two men who had looked around, Koku shot out his right and left fists, and secured good hold on the necks of two of his enemies. The other two, at his back, were endeavoring to pull him over, but the giant's sturdy legs still held.

So big was Koku's hands that they almost encircled the necks of his antagonists. Then happened a curious thing.

With a shout that might have done credit to some ancient cave-dweller of the stone age, Koku spread out his mighty arms, and held apart the two men he had grasped. In vain they struggled to free themselves from that terrible grip. Their faces turned purple, and their eyes bulged out.

"He's choking them to death!" shouted Ned.

But Koku was not needlessly cruel.

A moment later, with a quick and sudden motion he bent his arms, bringing toward each other the two men he held as captives. Their heads came together with a dull thud, and a second later Koku allowed two limp bodies to slip from his grip to the floor.

"He's done for them!" Tom cried. "Knocked them unconscious. Good for you, Koku!"

The giant grunted, and then, with a quick motion, slung himself around, hoping to bring the enemies at his back within reach of his powerful arms. But there was no need of this.

As soon as the other two ruffians had seen their companions fall to the floor of the shop they turned and fled, leaping from an open window.

"There they go!" cried Ned.

"Some of the other men can chase them," said the young inventor. "We'll tie up the two Koku has captured."

As he approached nearer to the unconscious captives Tom uttered a cry of surprise, for he recognized them as two of the new men he had employed.

"What can this mean?" he asked wonderingly.

He glanced toward the window through which the two men had jumped to escape, and he was just in time to see one of them run past the open door. The face of this one was under a powerful electric light, and Tom at once recognized the man as Feldman, the worker who had had so much trouble with the trip-hammer.

"This sure is a puzzle," marveled Tom. "My own men in the plot! But why did they attack Koku?"

The giant, bending over the men he had knocked unconscious by beating their heads together, seemed little worse for the attack.

"We tie 'em up," he said grimly, as he brought over the rope that had been intended for himself.

CHAPTER XIV

THE FIRST FLIGHT

Little time was lost in securing the two men who bad been so effectively rendered helpless by Koku's ready, if rough, measures. One of them was showing signs of returning consciousness now, and Tom, not willing to inflict needless pain, even on an enemy, told one of his men, summoned by the alarm, to bring water. Soon the two men opened their eyes, and looked about them in dazed fashion.

"Did—did anything hit me?" asked one meekly.

"It must have been a thunderbolt," spoke the other dreamily. "But it didn't look like a storm."

"Oh, dere was a storm, all right," chuckled Eradicate, who, having left his mule, Boomerang outside, came into the shed. "It was a giant storm all right."

The men put their hands to their heads, and seemed to comprehend. They looked at the rope that bound their feet. Their forearms had been loosened to allow them to take a drink of water.

"What does this mean—Ransom—Kurdy?" asked Tom sternly, when the men seemed able to talk. "Did you attack Koku?"

"It looks as though he had the best of us, whether we did or not," said the man Tom knew as Kurdy. "Whew, how my head aches!"

"Me sorry," said Koku simply.

"Not half as sorry as we are," returned Ransom ruefully.

"What does it mean?" asked Tom sternly. "There were four of you. Feldman and one other got away."

"Oh, trust Feldman for getting away," sneered Kurdy. "He always leaves his friends in the lurch."

"Was this a conspiracy?" demanded Tom.

The two captives looked at one another, sitting bound on the floor of the shop, their backs against some boxes.

"I guess it's all up, and we might as well make a clean breast of it," admitted Kurdy.

"Perhaps it would be better," said Tom quietly. "Eradicate," he went on, to the colored man, "go to the house and tell Mrs. Baggert that every-thing is all right and no one hurt."

"No one hurt, Massa Tom? What about dem dere fellers?" and the colored man pointed to the captives.

"Well, they're not hurt much," and Tom permitted himself a little smile. "I don't want my father to worry. Tell him everything is all right."

"All right, Massa Tom. I'se gwine right off. I'se got t' look after mah mule, Boomerang, too. I'se gwine," and he shuffled away.

"Who else besides Feldman got away?" asked Tom, looking alter-nately at the prisoners.

They hesitated a moment about answering.

"We might as well give up, I tell you," spoke Kurdy to Ransom.

"All right, go ahead, we'll have to take our medicine. I might have known it would turn out this way—going in for this sort of thing. It's the first bit of crooked business I ever tried," the man said earnestly, "and it will be the last—believe me!"

"Who was the fourth man?" Tom repeated.

"Harrison," answered Kurdy, naming one of the most efficient of the new machinists Tom had hired during the rush.

"Harrison, who has been working on the motor?" cried the young inventor.

"Yes," said Ransom.

"I'm sorry to learn that," Tom went on in a low voice. "He was an expert in his line. But what was your object, anyhow, in attacking Koku?"

"We didn't intend to attack him," explained Ransom, "but he came in when we were at work, and as he went for us we tried to stand him off. Then your colored man heard the racket, and—well, I guess you know the rest."

"But I don't understand why you came into this shed at night," went on Tom. "No one is allowed in here. You had no right, and Koku knew that. What did you want?"

"Look here!" exclaimed Kurdy, "I said we'd make a clean breast of it, and we will. We're only a couple of tools, and we were foolish ever to go in with those fellows; or rather, in with that Frenchman, who promised us big money if we succeeded."

"Succeeded in what?" demanded the young inventor.

"In damaging your new aerial warship, or in getting certain parts of it so he could take them away with him."

Tom gave a surprised whistle.

"A frenchman!" he exclaimed. "Is he one of the—?"

"Yes, he's one of the foreign spies," interrupted Ransom. "You'd find it out, anyhow, if we didn't tell you. They are after you, Tom Swift, and after your machines. They had vowed to get them by fair means or foul, for some of the European governments are desperate."

"But we were only tools in their hands. So were Feldman and Harrison, but they knew more about the details. We were only helping them."

"Then we must try to capture them," decided Tom. "Ned, see if the chase had any results. I'll look after these chaps—Koku and I."

"Oh, we give in," admitted Kurdy. "We know when we've had enough," and he rubbed his head gently where the giant had banged it against that of his fellow-conspirator.

"Do you mean that you four came into this shop, at midnight, to damage the Mars?" asked Tom.

"That's about it, Mr. Swift," replied Kurdy rather shamefacedly. "We were to damage it beyond repair, set fire to the whole place, if need be, and, at the same time, take away certain vital parts.

"Harrison, Feldman, Ransom and I came in, thinking the coast was clear. But Koku must have seen us enter, or he suspected we were here, for he came in after us, and the fight began. We couldn't stop him, and he did for us. I'm rather glad of it, too, for I never liked the work. It was only that they tempted me with a promise of big money."

"Who tempted you?" demanded Tom.

"That Frenchman—La Foy, he calls himself, and some other foreigners in your shops."

"Are there foreigners here?" cried Tom.

"Bless my chest protector!" cried Mr. Damon, who had come in and had been a silent listener to this. "Can it be possible?"

"That's the case," went on Kurdy. "A lot of the new men you took on are foreign spies from different European nations. They are trying to learn all they can about your plans, Mr. Swift!"

"Are they friendly among themselves?" asked Tom.

"No; each one is trying to get ahead of the other. So far the Frenchman seems to have had the best of it. But tonight his plan failed."

"Tell me more about it," urged Tom.

"That's about all we know," spoke Ransom. "We were only hired to do the rough work. Those higher up didn't appear. Feldman was only a step above us."

"Then my suspicions of him were justified," thought Tom. "He evidently met La Foy in the woods to make plans. But Koku and Eradicate spoiled them."

The two captives seemed willing enough to make a confession, but they did not know much. As they said, they were merely tools, acting for others. And events had happened just as they had said.

The four conspirators had managed, by means of a false key, and by disconnecting the burglar alarm, to enter the airship shed. They were about to proceed with their work of destruction when Koku came on the scene.

The giant's appearance was due to accident. He acted as a sort of night watchman, making a tour of the buildings, but he entered the shed where the Mars was because, that day, he had left his knife in there, and wanted to get it. Only for that he would not have gone in. When he entered he surprised the four men.

Of course he attacked them at once, and they sprang at him. Then ensued a terrific fight. Eradicate, arising to doctor his mule, as he had said, heard the noise, and saw what was going on. He gave the alarm.

"Well, Ned, any luck?" asked Tom, as his chum came in.

"No, they got away, Tom. I had a lot of your men out helping me search the grounds, but it wasn't of much use."

"Particularly if you depended on some of my men," said Tom bitterly.

"What do you mean?"

"I mean that the place is filled with spies, Ned! But we will sift them out in the morning. This has been a lucky night for me. It was touch and go. Now, then, Koku, take these fellows and lock them up somewhere until morning. Ned, you and I will remain on guard here the rest of the night."

"I'm with you, Tom."

"Will you be a bit easy on us, considering what we told you?" asked Kurdy.

"I'll do the best I can," said Tom, gently, making no promises.

The two captives were put in secure quarters, and the rest of the night passed quietly. During the fight in the airship shed some machinery and tools had been broken, but no great amount of damage was done. Tom and Ned passed the remaining hours of darkness there.

A further search was made in the morning for the two conspirators who had escaped, but no trace of them was found. Tom then realized why Feldman was so anxious to be placed in the aeroplane department—it was in order that he might have easier access to the Mars.

A technical charge was made against the two prisoners, sufficient to hold them for some time. Then Tom devoted a day to weeding out the suspected foreigners in his place. All the new men were discharged, though some protested against this action.

"Probably I am hitting some of the innocent in punishing those who, if they had the chance, would become guilty," Tom said to his chum, "but it cannot be helped—I can't afford to take any chances."

The Mars was being put in shape for her first flight. The guns, fitted with the recoil shock absorbers, were mounted, and Lieutenant Marbury had returned to go aloft in the big aerial warship. He congratulated Tom on discovering at least one plot in time.

"But there may be more," he warned the young inventor. "You are not done with them yet."

The Mars was floated out of her hangar, and made ready for an ascent. Tom, Ned, Lieutenant Marbury, Mr. Damon, and several workmen were to be the first passengers. Tom was busy going over the various parts to see that nothing had been forgotten.

"Well, I guess we re ready," he finally announced. "All aboard!"

"Bless my insurance policy!" exclaimed Mr. Damon. "Now that the time comes I almost wish I wasn't going."

"Nonsense!" exclaimed Tom. "You're not going to back out at the last minute. All aboard! Cast off the ropes!" he cried to the assistants.

A moment later the Mars, the biggest airship Tom Swift had ever constructed, arose from the earth like some great bird, and soared aloft.

CHAPTER XV

IN DANGER

"Well, Tom, we're moving!" cried Ned Newton, clapping his chum on the back, as he stood near him in the pilot-house. "We're going up, old sport!"

"Of course we are," replied Tom. "You didn't think it wouldn't go up, did you?"

"Well, I wasn't quite sure," Ned confessed. "You know you were so worried about—"

"Not about the ship sailing," interrupted Tom. "It was only the effect the firing of the guns might have. But I think we have that taken care of."

"Bless my pin cushion!" cried Mr. Damon, as he looked over the rail at the earth below. "We're moving fast, Tom."

"Yes, we can make a quicker ascent in this than in most aeroplanes," Tom said, "for they have to go up in a slanting direction. But we can't quite equal their lateral speed."

"Just how fast do you think you can travel when you are in first-class shape?" asked Lieutenant Marbury, as he noted how the Mars was behaving on this, the first trip.

"Well, I set a limit of seventy-five miles an hour," the young inventor replied, as he shifted various levers and handles, to change the speed of the mechanism. "But I'm afraid we won't quite equal that with all our guns on board. But I'm safe in saying sixty, I think."

"That will more than satisfy the government requirements," the officer said. "But, of course, your craft will have to come up to expectations and requirements in the matter of armament."

"I'll give you every test you want," declared Tom, with a smile. "And now we'll see what the Mars can do when put to it."

Up and up went the big dirigible aerial warship. Had you been fortunate enough to have seen her you would have observed a craft not unlike, in shape, the German Zeppelins. But it differed from those war balloons in several important particulars.

Tom's craft was about six hundred feet long, and the diameter of the gas bag, amidships, was sixty feet, slightly larger than the largest

Zeppelin. Below the bag, which, as I have explained, was made up of a number of gas-tight compartments, hung from wire cables three cabins. The forward one was a sort of pilot-house, containing various instruments for navigating the ship of the air, observation rooms, gauges for calculating firing ranges, and the steering apparatus.

Amidships, suspended below the great bag, were the living and sleeping quarters, where food was cooked and served and where those who operated the craft could spend their leisure time. Extra supplies were also stored there.

At the stern of the big bag was the motor-room, where gas was generated to fill the balloon compartments when necessary, where the gasoline and electrical apparatus were installed, and where the real motive power of the craft was located. Here, also, was carried the large quantity of gasoline and oil needed for a long voyage. The Mars could carry sufficient fuel to last for over a week, provided no accidents occurred.

There was also an arrangement in the motor compartment, so that the ship could be steered and operated from there. This was in case the forward pilot-house should be shot away by an enemy. And, also, in the motor compartment were the sleeping quarters for the crew.

All three suspended cabins were connected by a long covered runway, so that one could pass from the pilot-house to the motor-room and back again through the amidship cabin.

At the extreme end of the big bag were the various rudders and planes, designed to keep the craft on a level keel, automatically, and to enable it to make headway against a strong wind. The motive power consisted of three double-bladed wooden propellers, which could be operated together or independently. A powerful gasoline engine was the chief motive power, though there was an auxiliary storage battery, which would operate an electrical motor and send the ship along for more than twenty-four hours in case of accident to the gasoline engine.

There were many other pieces of apparatus aboard, some not completely installed, the uses of which I shall mention from time to time, as the story progresses. The gas-generating machine was of importance, for there would be a leakage and shrinking of the vapor from the big bag, and some means must be provided for replenishing it.

"You don't seem to have forgotten anything, Tom," said Ned admiringly, as they soared upward.

"We can tell better after we've flown about a bit," observed the young inventor, with a smile. "I expect we shall have to make quite a number of changes."

"Are you going far?" asked Mr. Damon.

"Why, you're not frightened, are you?" inquired Tom. "You have been up in airships with me before."

"Oh, no, I'm not frightened!" exclaimed the odd man. "Bless my suspenders, no! But I promised my wife I'd be back this evening, and..."

"We'll sail over toward Waterford," broke in Tom, "and I'll drop you down in your front yard."

"No, don't do that! Don't! I beg of you!" cried Mr. Damon. "You see—er—Tom, my wife doesn't like me to make these trips. Of course, I understand there is no danger, and I like them. But it's just as well not to make her worry-you understand!"

"Oh, all right," replied Tom, with a laugh. "Well, we're not going far on this trip. What I want to do, most of all, is to test the guns, and see if the recoil check will work as well when we are aloft as it did down on the ground. You know a balloon isn't a very stable base for a gun, even one of light caliber."

"No, it certainly is not," agreed Lieutenant Marbury, "and I am interested in seeing how you will overcome the recoil."

"We'll have a test soon," announced Tom.

Meanwhile the Mars, having reached a considerable height, being up so far, in fact, that the village of Shopton could scarcely be distinguished, Tom set the signal that told the engine-room force to start the propellers. This would send them ahead.

Some of Tom's most trusted workmen formed the operating crew, the young inventor taking charge of the pilot-house himself.

"Well she seems to run all right," observed Lieutenant Marbury, as the big craft surged ahead just below a stratum of white, fleecy clouds.

"Yes, but not as fast as I'd like to see her go," Tom replied. "Of course the machinery is new, and it will take some little time for it to wear down smooth. I'll speed her up a little now."

They had been running for perhaps ten minutes when Tom shoved over the hand of an indicator that communicated with the engine-room from the pilot-house. At once the Mars increased her speed.

"She can do it!" cried Ned.

"Bless my-hat! I should say so!" cried Mr. Damon, for he was standing outside the pilot-house just then, on the "bridge," and the sudden increase of speed lifted his hat from his head.

"There you are—caught on the fly!" cried Ned, as he put up his hand just in time to catch the article in question.

"Thanks! Guess I'd better tie it fast," remarked the odd man, putting his hat on tightly.

The aerial warship was put through several evolutions to test her stability, and to each one she responded well, earning the praise of the government officer. Up and down, to one side and the other, around in big circles, and even reversing, Tom sent his craft with a true hand and eye. In a speed test fifty-five miles was registered against a slight wind, and the young inventor said he knew he could do better than that as soon as some of the machinery was running more smoothly.

"And now suppose we get ready for the gun tests," suggested Tom, when they had been running for about an hour.

"That's what I'm mostly interested in," said Lieutenant Marbury. "It's easy enough to get several good types of dirigible balloons, but few of them will stand having a gun fired from them, to say nothing of several guns."

"Well, I'm not making any rash promises," Tom went on, "but I think we can turn the trick."

The armament of the Mars was located around the center cabin. There were two large guns, fore and aft, throwing a four-inch projectile, and two smaller calibered quick-firers on either beam. The guns were mounted on pedestals that enabled the weapons to fire in almost any direction, save straight up, and of course the balloon bag being above them prevented this. However, there was an arrangement whereby a small automatic quick-firer could be sent up to a platform built on top of the gas envelope itself, and a man stationed there could shoot at a rival airship directly overhead.

But the main deck guns could be elevated to an angle of nearly forty-five degrees, so they could take care of nearly any hostile aircraft that approached.

"But where are the bombs I heard you speaking of?" asked Ned, as they finished looking at the guns.

"Here they are," spoke Tom, as he pointed to a space in the middle of the main cabin floor. He lifted a brass plate, and disclosed three holes, covered with a strong wire netting that could be removed. "The bombs will be dropped through those holes," explained the young inventor, "being released by a magnetic control when the operator thinks he has reached a spot over the enemy's city or fortification where the most damage will be done. I'll show you how they work a little later. Now we'll have a test of some of the guns."

Tom called for some of his men to take charge of the steering and running of the Mars while he and Lieutenant Marbury prepared to fire the two larger weapons. This was to be one of the most important tests.

Service charges had been put in, though, of course, no projectiles would be used, since they were then flying over a large city not far from Shopton.

"We'll have to wait until we get out over the ocean to give a complete test, with a bursting shell," Tom said.

He and Lieutenant Marbury were beside a gun, and were about to fire it, when suddenly, from the stern of the ship, came a ripping, tearing sound, and, at the same time, confused shouts came from the crew's quarters.

"What is it?" cried Tom.

"One of the propellers!" was the answer. "It's split, and has torn a big hole in the gas bag!"

"Bless my overshoes!" cried Mr. Damon. "We're going down!"

All on board the Mars became aware of a sudden sinking sensation.

CHAPTER XVI

TOM IS WORRIED

"Steady, all!" came in even tones from Tom Swift. Not for an instant had he lost his composure. For it was an accident, that much was certain, and one that might endanger the lives of all on board.

Above the noise of the machinery in the motor room could be heard the thrashing and banging of the broken or loose propeller-blade. Just what its condition was, could not be told, as a bulge of the gas bag hid it from the view of those gathered about the gun, which was about to be fired when the alarm was given.

"We're sinking!" cried Mr. Damon. "We're going down, Tom!"

"That's nothing," was the cool answer. "It is only for a moment. Only a few of the gas compartments can be torn. There will soon enough additional gas in the others to lift us again."

And so it proved. The moment the pressure of the lifting gas in the big oiled silk and aluminum container was lowered, it started the generating machine, and enough extra gas was pumped into the uninjured compartments to compensate for the loss.

"We're not falling so fast now," observed Ned.

"No, and we'll soon stop falling altogether," calmly declared Tom. "Too bad this accident had to happen, though."

"It might have been much worse, my boy!" exclaimed the lieutenant. "That's a great arrangement of yours—the automatic gas machine."

"It's on the same principle as the air brakes of a trolley car," explained Tom, when a look at the indicators showed that the Mars had ceased falling and remained stationary in the air. Tom had also sent a signal to the engine-room to shut off the power, so that the two undamaged propellers, as well as the broken one, ceased revolving.

"In a trolley car, you see," Tom went on, when the excitement had calmed down, "as soon as the air pressure in the tanks gets below a certain point, caused by using the air for a number of applications of the brakes, it lets a magnetized bar fall, and this establishes an electrical connection, starting the air pump. The pump forces more air into the tanks until the pressure is enough to throw the pump switch out of connection, when the pump stops. I use the same thing here."

"And very clever it is," said Mr. Damon. "Do you suppose the danger is all over, Tom?"

"For the time being, yes. But we must unship that damaged propeller, and go on with the two."

The necessary orders were given, and several men from the engine-room at once began the removal of the damaged blades.

As several spare ones were carried aboard one could be put on in place of the broken one, had this been desired. But Tom thought the accident a good chance to see how his craft would act with only two-thirds of her motive force available, so he did not order the damaged propeller replaced. When it was lowered to the deck it was carefully examined.

"What made it break?" Ned wanted to know.

"That's a question I can't answer," Tom replied. "There may have been a defect in the wood, but I had it all carefully examined before I used it."

The propeller was one of the "built-up" type, with alternate layers of ash and mahogany, but some powerful force had torn and twisted the blades. The wood was splintered and split, and some jagged pieces, flying off at a tangent, so great was the centrifugal force, had torn holes in the strong gas bag.

"Did something hit it; or did it hit something?" asked Ned as he saw Tom carefully examining the broken blades.

"Hard to say. I'll have a good look at this when we get back. Just now I want to finish that gun test we didn't get a chance to start."

"You don't mean to say you're going to keep on, and with the balloon damaged; are you?" cried Mr. Damon, in surprise.

"Certainly—why not?" Tom replied. "In warfare accidents may happen, and if the Mars can't go on, after a little damage like this, what is going to happen when she's fired on by a hostile ship? Of course I'm going on!"

"Bless my necktie!" ejaculated the odd man.

"That's the way to talk!" exclaimed Lieutenant Marbury. "I'm with you."

There really was very little danger in proceeding. The Mars was just as buoyant as before, for more gas had been automatically made, and forced into the uninjured compartments of the bag. At the same time enough sand ballast had been allowed to run out to make the weight to be lifted less in proportion to the power remaining.

True, the speed would be less, with two propellers instead of three, and the craft would not steer as well, with the torn ends of the gas bag floating out behind. But this made a nearer approach to war conditions, and Tom was always glad to give his inventions the most severe tests possible.

So, after a little while, during which it was seen that the Mars was proceeding almost normally, the matter of discharging the guns was taken up again.

The weapons were all ready to fire, and when Tom had attached the pressure gauges to note how much energy was expended in the recoil, he gave the word to fire.

The two big weapons were discharged together, and for a moment after the report echoed out among the cloud masses every soul on the ship feared another accident had happened.

For the big craft rolled and twisted, and seemed about to turn turtle. Her forward progress was halted, momentarily, and a cry of fear came from several of the members of the crew, who had had only a little experience in aircraft.

"What's the matter?" cried Ned. "Something go wrong?"

"A little," admitted Tom, with a rueful look on his face. "Those recoil checks didn't work as well in practice as they did in theory."

"Are you sure they are strong enough?" asked Lieutenant Marbury.

"I thought so," spoke Tom. "I'll put more tension on the spring next time."

"Bless my watch chain!" cried Mr. Damon. "You aren't going to fire those guns again; are you, Tom?"

"Why not? We can't tell what's the matter, nor get things right without experimenting. There's no danger."

"No danger! Don't you call nearly upsetting the ship danger?"

"Oh, well, if she turns over she'll right herself again," Tom said. "The center of gravity is low, you see. She can't float in any position but right side up, though she may turn over once or twice."

"Excuse me!" said Mr. Damon firmly. "I'd rather go down, if it's all the same to you. If my wife ever knew I was here I'd never hear the last of it!"

"We'll go down soon," Tom promised. "But I must fire a couple of shots more. You wouldn't call the recoil checks a success, would you?" and the young inventor appealed to the government inspector.

"No, I certainly would not," was the prompt answer. "I am sorry, too, for they seemed to be just what was needed. Of course I understand this is not an official test, and I am not obliged to make a report of this trial. But had it been, I should have had to score against you."

"I realize that, and I'm not asking any favors, but I'll try it again with the recoil checks tightened up. I think the hydrostatic valves were open too much, also."

Preparations were now made for firing the four-inch guns once more. All this while the Mars had been speeding around in space, being about two miles up in the air. Tom's craft was not designed to reach as great an elevation as would be possible in an aeroplane, since to work havoc to an enemy's fortifications by means of aerial bombs they do not need to be dropped from a great height.

In fact, experiments in Germany have shown that bombs falling from a great height are less effective than those falling from an airship nearer the earth. For a bomb, falling from a height of two miles, acquires enough momentum to penetrate far into the earth, so that much of the resultant explosive force is expended in a downward direction, and little damage is done to the fortifications. A bomb dropped from a lower altitude, expending its force on all sides, does much more damage.

On the other hand, in destroying buildings, it has been found desirable to drop a bomb from a good height so that it may penetrate even a protected roof, and explode inside.

Once more Tom made ready to fire, this time having given the recoil checks greater resistance. But though there was less motion imparted to the airship when the guns were discharged, there was still too much for comfort, or even safety.

"Well, something's wrong, that's sure," remarked Tom, in rather disappointed tones as he noted the effect of the second shots. "If we get as much recoil from the two guns, what would happen if we fired them all at once?"

"Don't do it! Don't do it, I beg of you!" entreated Mr. Damon. "Bless my toothbrush—don't do it!"

"I won't—just at present," Tom said, ruefully. "I'm afraid I'll have to begin all over again, and proceed along new lines."

"Well, perhaps you will," said the lieutenant. "But you may invent something much better than anything you have now. There is no great rush. Take your time, and do something good."

"Oh, I'll get busy on it right away," Tom declared. "We'll go down now, and start right to work. I'm afraid, Ned, that our idea of a door-spring check isn't going to work."

"I might have known my idea wouldn't amount to anything," said the young bank clerk.

"Oh, the idea is all right," declared Tom, "but it wants modifying. There is more power to those recoils than I figured, though our first experiments seemed to warrant us in believing that we had solved the problem."

"Are you going to try the bomb-dropping device?" asked the lieutenant.

"Yes, there can't be any recoil from that," Tom said. "I'll drop a few blank ones, and see how accurate the range finders are."

While his men were getting ready for this test Tom bent over the broken propeller, looking from that to the recoil checks, which had not come up to expectations. Then he shook his head in a worried and puzzled manner.

CHAPTER XVII

AN OCEAN FLIGHT

Dropping bombs from an aeroplane, or a dirigible balloon, is a comparatively simple matter. Of course there are complications that may ensue, from the danger of carrying high explosives in the limited quarters of an airship, with its inflammable gasoline fuel, and ever-present electric spark, to the possible premature explosion of the bomb itself. But they seem to be considered minor details now.

On the other hand, while it is comparatively easy to drop a bomb from a moving aeroplane, or dirigible balloon, it is another matter to make the bomb fall just where it will do the most damage to the enemy. It is not easy to gauge distances, high up in the air, and then, too, allowance must be made for the speed of the aircraft, the ever-increasing velocity of a falling body, and the deflection caused by air currents.

The law of velocity governing falling bodies is well known. It varies, of course, according to the height, but in general a body falling freely toward the earth, as all high-school boys know, is accelerated at the rate of thirty-two feet per second. This law has been taken advantage of by the French in the present European war. The French drop from balloons, or aeroplanes, a steel dart about the size of a lead pencil, and sharpened in about the same manner. Dropping from a height of a mile or so, that dart will acquire enough velocity to penetrate a man from his head all the way through his body to his feet.

But in dropping bombs from an airship the damage intended does not so much depend on velocity. It is necessary to know how fast the bomb falls in order to know when to set the time fuse that will explode it; though some bombs will explode on concussion.

At aeroplane meets there are often bomb-dropping contests, and balls filled with a white powder (that will make a dust-cloud on falling, and so show where they strike) are used to demonstrate the birdman's accuracy.

"We'll see how our bomb-release works," Tom went on. "But we'll have to descend a bit in order to watch the effect."

"You're not going to use real bombs, are you, Tom?" asked Ned.

"Indeed not. Just chalk-dust ones for practice. Now here is where the bombs will be placed," and he pointed to the three openings in the floor of the amidship cabin. The wire nettings were taken out and one could look down through the holes to the earth below, the ground being nearer now, as Tom had let out some of the lifting gas.

"Here is the range-finder and the speed calculator," the young inventor went on as he indicated the various instruments. "The operator sits here, where he can tell when is the most favorable moment for releasing the bomb."

Tom took his place before a complicated set of instruments, and began manipulating them. One of his assistants, under the direction of Lieutenant Marbury, placed in the three openings bombs, made of light cardboard, just the size of a regular bomb, but filled with a white powder that would, on breaking, make a dust-cloud which could be observed from the airship.

"I have first to determine where I want to drop the bomb," Tom explained, "and then I have to get my distance from it on the range-finder. Next I have to know how fast I am traveling, and how far up in the air I am, to tell what the velocity of the falling bomb will attain at a certain time. This I can do by means of these instruments, some of which I have adapted from those used by the government," he said, with a nod to the officer.

"That's right—take all the information you can get," was the smiling response.

"We will now assume that the bombs are in place in the holes in the floor of the cabin," Tom went on. "As I sit here I have before me three buttons. They control the magnets that hold the bombs in place. If I press one of the buttons it breaks the electrical current, the magnet no longer has any attraction, and it releases the explosive. Now look down. I am going to try and drop a chalk bomb near that stone fence."

The Mars was then flying over a large field and a stone fence was in plain view.

"Here she goes!" cried Tom, as he made some rapid calculations from his gauge instruments. There was a little click and the chalk bomb dropped. There was a plate glass floor in part of the cabin, and through this the progress of the pasteboard bomb could be observed.

"She'll never go anywhere near the fence!" declared Ned. "You let it drop too soon, Tom!"

"Did I? You just watch. I had to allow for the momentum that would be given the bomb by the forward motion of the balloon."

Hardly had Tom spoken than a puff of white was seen on the very top of the fence.

"There it goes?" cried the lieutenant. "You did the trick, Swift!"

"Yes, I thought I would. Well, that shows my gauges are correct, anyhow. Now we'll try the other two bombs."

In succession they were released from the bottom of the cabin, at other designated objects. The second one was near a tree. It struck within five feet, which was considered good.

"And I'll let the last one down near that scarecrow in the field," said Tom, pointing to a ragged figure in the middle of a patch of corn.

Down went the cardboard bomb, and so good was the aim of the young inventor that the white dust arose in a cloud directly back of the scarecrow.

And then a queer thing happened. For the figure seemed to come to life, and Ned, who was watching through a telescope, saw a very much excited farmer looking up with an expression of the greatest wonder on his face. He saw the balloon over his head, and shook his fist at it, evidently thinking he had had a narrow escape. But the pasteboard bomb was so light that, had it hit him, he would not have been injured, though he might have been well dusted.

"Why, that was a man! Bless my pocketbook!" cried Mr. Damon.

"I guess it was," agreed Tom. "I took it for a scarecrow."

"Well, it proved the accuracy of your aim, at any rate," observed Lieutenant Marbury. "The bomb dropping device of your aerial warship is perfect—I can testify to that."

"And I'll have the guns fixed soon, so there will be no danger of a recoil, too," added Tom Swift, with a determined look on his face.

"What's next?" asked Mr. Damon, looking at his watch. "I really ought to be home, Tom."

"We're going back now, and down. Are you sure you don't want me to drop you in your own front yard, or even on your roof? I think I could manage that."

"Bless my stovepipe, no, Tom! My wife would have hysterics. Just land me at Shopton and I'll take a car home."

The damaged airship seemed little the worse for the test to which she had been subjected, and made her way at good speed in the direction of Tom's home. Several little experiments were tried on the way back. They all worked well, and the only two problems Tom had to solve were the taking care of the recoil from the guns and finding out why the propeller had broken.

A safe landing was made, and the Mars once more put away in her hangar. Mr. Damon departed for his home, and Lieutenant Marbury again took up his residence in the Swift household.

"Well, Tom, how did it go?" asked his father.

"Not so very well. Too much recoil from the guns."

"I was afraid so. You had better drop this line of work, and go at something else."

"No, Dad!" Tom cried. "I'm going to make this work. I never had anything stump me yet, and I'm not going to begin now!"

"Well, that's a good spirit to show," said the aged inventor, with a shake of his head, "but I don't believe you'll succeed, Tom."

"Yes I will, Dad! You just wait."

Tom decided to begin on the problem of the propeller first, as that seemed more simple. He knew that the gun question would take longer.

"Just what are you trying to find out, Tom?" asked Ned, a few nights later, when he found his chum looking at the broken parts of the propeller.

"Trying to discover what made this blade break up and splinter that way. It couldn't have been centrifugal force, for it wasn't strong enough."

Tom was "poking" away amid splinters, and bits of broken wood, when he suddenly uttered an exclamation, and held up something. "Look!" he cried. "I believe I've found it."

"What?" asked Ned.

"The thing that weakened the propeller. Look at this, and smell!" He held out a piece of wood toward Ned. The bank employee saw where a half-round hole had been bored in what remained of the blade, and from that hole came a peculiar odor.

"It's some kind of acid," ventured Ned.

"That's it!" cried Tom. "Someone bored a hole in the propeller, and put in some sort of receptacle, or capsule, containing a corrosive acid. In due time, which happened to be when we took our first flight, the acid ate through whatever it was contained in, and then attacked the wood of the propeller blade. It weakened the wood so that the force used in whirling it around broke it."

"Are you sure of that?" asked Ned.

"As sure as I am that I'm here! Now I know what caused the accident!"

"But who would play such a trick?" asked Ned. "We might all have been killed."

"Yes, I know we might," said Tom. "It must be the work of some of those foreign spies whose first plot we nipped in the bud. I must tell Marbury of this, but don't mention it to dad."

"I won't," promised Ned.

Lieutenant Marbury agreed with Tom that someone had surreptitiously bored a small hole in the propeller blade, and had inserted a corrosive acid that would take many hours to operate. The hole had been varnished over, probably, so it would not show.

"And that means I've got to examine the other two blades," Tom said. "They may be doctored too."

But they did not prove to be. A careful examination showed nothing wrong. An effort was made to find out who had tried to destroy the Mars in midair, but it came to nothing. The two men in custody declared they knew nothing of it, and there was no way of proving that they did.

Meanwhile, the torn gas bag was repaired, and Tom began working on the problem of doing away with the gun recoil. He tried several schemes, and almost was on the point of giving up when suddenly he received a hint by reading an account of how the recoil was taken care of on some of the German Zeppelins.

The guns there were made double, with the extra barrel filled with water or sand, that could be shot out as was the regular charge. As both barrels were fired at the same time, and in opposite directions, with the same amount of powder, one neutralized the other, and the recoil was canceled, the ship remaining steady after fire.

"By Jove! I believe that will do the trick!" cried Tom. "I'm going to try it."

"Good luck to you!" cried Ned.

It was no easy matter to change all the guns of the Mars, and fit them with double barrels. But by working day and night shifts Tom managed it. Meanwhile, a careful watch was kept over the shops. Several new men applied for work, and some of them were suspicious enough in looks, but Tom took on no new hands.

Finally the new guns were made, and tried with the Mars held on the ground. They behaved perfectly, the shooting of sand or water from the dummy barrel neutralizing the shot from the service barrel.

"And now to see how it works in practice!" cried Tom one day. "Are you with me for a long flight, Ned?"

"I sure am!"

The next evening the Mars, with a larger crew than before, and with Tom, Ned, Mr. Damon and Lieutenant Marbury aboard, set sail.

"But why start at night?" asked Ned.

"You'll see in the morning," Tom answered.

The Mars flew slowly all night, life aboard her, at about the level of the clouds, going on almost as naturally as though the occupants of the cabins were on the earth. Excellent meals were served.

"But when are you going to try the guns?" asked Ned, as he got ready to turn in.

"Tell you in the morning," replied Tom, with a smile.

And, in the morning, when Ned looked down through the plate glass in the cabin floor, he uttered a cry.

"Why, Tom! We're over the ocean!" he cried.

"I rather thought we'd be," was the calm reply. "I told George to head straight for the Atlantic. Now we'll have a test with service charges and projectiles!"

CHAPTER XVIII

IN A STORM

Surprise, for the moment, held Mr. Damon, Ned and Lieutenant Marbury speechless. They looked from the heaving waters of the ocean below them to the young pilot of the Mars. He smiled at their astonishment.

"What—what does it mean, Tom?" asked Ned. "You never said you were going to take a trip as far as this."

"That's right," chimed in Mr. Damon. "Bless my nightcap! If I had known I was going to be brought so far away from home I'd never have come."

"You're not so very far from Waterford," put in Tom. "We didn't make any kind of speed coming from Shopton, and we could be back again inside of four hours if we had to."

"Then you didn't travel fast during the night?" asked the government man.

"No, we just drifted along," Tom answered. "I gave orders to run the machinery slowly, as I wanted to get it in good shape for the other tests that will come soon. But I told George, whom I left in charge when I turned in, to head for New York. I wanted to get out over the ocean to try the guns with the new recoil arrangement."

"Well, we're over the ocean all right," spoke Ned, as he looked down at the heaving waters.

"It isn't the first time," replied Tom cheerfully. "Koku, you may serve breakfast now," for the giant had been taken along as a sort of cook and waiter. Koku manifested no surprise or alarm when he found the airship floating over the sea. Whatever Tom did was right to him. He had great confidence in his master.

"No, it isn't the first time we've taken a water flight," spoke Ned. "I was only surprised at the suddenness of it, that's all."

"It's my first experience so far out above the water," observed Lieutenant Marbury, "though of course I've sailed on many seas. Why, we're out of sight of land."

"About ten miles out, yes," admitted Tom. "Far enough to make it safe to test the guns with real projectiles. That is what I want to do."

"And we've been running all night?" asked Mr. Damon.

"Yes, but at slow speed. The engines are in better shape now than ever before," Tom said. "Well, if you're ready we'll have breakfast."

The meal was served by Koku with as much unconcern as though they were in the Swift homestead back in Shopton, instead of floating near the clouds. And while it was being eaten in the main cabin, and while the crew was having breakfast in their quarters, the aerial warship was moving along over the ocean in charge of George Watson, one of Tom's engineers, who was stationed in the forward pilot-house.

"So you're going to give the guns a real test this time, is that it, Tom?" asked Ned, as he pushed back his plate, a signal that he had eaten enough.

"That's about it."

"But don't you think it's a bit risky out over the water this way. Supposing something should—should happen?" Ned hesitated.

"You mean we might fall?" asked Tom, with a smile.

"Yes; or turn upside down."

"Nothing like that could happen. I'm so sure that I have solved the problem of the recoil of the guns that I'm willing to take chances. But if any of you want to get off the Mars while the test is being made, I have a small boat I can lower, and let you row about in that until—"

"No, thank you!" interrupted Mr. Damon, as he looked below. There was quite a heavy swell on, and the ocean did not appear very attractive. They would be much more comfortable in the big Mars.

"I think you won't have any trouble," asserted Lieutenant Marbury. "I believe Tom Swift has the right idea about the guns, and there will be so small a shock from the recoil that it will not be noticeable."

"We'll soon know," spoke Tom. "I'm going to get ready for the test now."

They were now well out from shore, over the Atlantic, but to make certain no ships would be endangered by the projectiles, Tom and the others searched the waters to the horizon with powerful glasses. Nothing was seen and the work of loading the guns was begun. The bomb tubes, in the main cabin, were also to be given a test.

As service charges were to be used, and as the projectiles were filled with explosives, great care was needed in handling them.

"We'll try dropping bombs first," Tom suggested. "We know they will work, and that will be so much out of the way."

To make the test a severe one, small floating targets were first dropped overboard from the Mars. Then the aerial warship, circling about, came on toward them. Tom, seated at the range-finders, pressed the button that released the shells containing the explosives. One after another they dropped into the sea, exploding as they fell, and sending up a great column of salt water.

"Every one a hit!" reported Lieutenant Marbury, who was keeping "score."

"That's good," responded Tom. "But the others won't be so easy. We have nothing to shoot at."

They had to fire the other guns without targets at which to aim. But, after all, it was the absence of recoil they wanted to establish, and this could be done without shooting at any particular object.

One after another the guns were loaded. As has been explained, they were now made double, one barrel carrying the projectile, and the other a charge of water.

"Are you ready?" asked Tom, when it was time to fire. Lieutenant Marbury, Ned and Mr. Damon were helping, by being stationed at the pressure gauges to note the results.

"All ready," answered Ned.

"Do you think we'd better put on life preservers, Tom?" asked Mr. Damon.

"Nonsense! What for?"

"In case—in case anything happens."

"Nothing will happen. Look out now, I'm going to fire."

The guns were to be fired simultaneously by means of an electric current, when Tom pressed a button.

"Here they go!" exclaimed the young inventor.

There was a moment of waiting, and then came a thundering roar. The Mars trembled, but she did not shift to either side from an even keel. From one barrel of the guns shot out the explosive projectiles, and from the other spurted a jet of water, sent out by a charge of powder, equal in weight to that which forced out the shot.

As the projectile was fired in one direction, and the water in one directly opposite, the two discharges neutralized one another.

Out flew the pointed steel shells, to fall harmlessly into the sea, where they exploded, sending up columns of water.

"Well!" cried Tom as the echoes died away. "How was it?"

"Couldn't have been better," declared Lieutenant Marbury. "There wasn't the least shock of recoil. Tom Swift, you have solved the problem, I do believe! Your aerial warship is a success!"

"I'm glad to hear you say so. There are one or two little things that need changing, but I really think I have about what the United States Government wants."

"I am, also, of that belief, Tom. If only—" The officer stopped suddenly.

"Well?" asked Tom suggestively.

"I was going to say if only those foreign spies don't make trouble."

"I think we've seen the last of them," Tom declared. "Now we'll go on with the tests."

More guns were fired, singly and in batteries, and in each case the Mars stood the test perfectly. The double barrel had solved the recoil problem.

For some little time longer they remained out over the sea, going through some evolutions to test the rudder control, and then as their present object had been accomplished Tom gave orders to head back to Shopton, which place was reached in due time.

"Well, Tom, how was it?" asked Mr. Swift, for though his son had said nothing to his friends about the prospective test, the aged inventor knew about it.

"Successful, Dad, in every particular."

"That's good. I didn't think you could do it. But you did. I tell you it isn't much that can get the best of a Swift!" exclaimed the aged man proudly. "Oh, by the way, Tom, here's a telegram that came while you were gone," and he handed his son the yellow envelope.

Tom ripped it open with a single gesture, and in a flash his eyes took in the words. He read:

"Look out for spies during trial flights."

The message was signed with a name Tom did not recognize.

"Any bad news?" asked Mr. Swift.

"No—oh, no," replied Tom, as he crumpled up the paper and thrust it into his pocket. "No bad news, Dad."

"Well, I'm glad to hear that," went on Mr. Swift. "I don't like telegrams."

When Tom showed the message to Lieutenant Marbury, that official, after one glance at the signature, said:

"Pierson, eh? Well, when he sends out a warning it generally means something."

"Who's Pierson?" asked Tom.

"Head of the Secret Service department that has charge of this airship matter. There must be something in the wind, Tom."

Extra precautions were taken about the shops. Strangers were not permitted to enter, and all future work on the Mars was kept secret. Nevertheless, Tom was worried. He did not want his work to be spoiled just when it was about to be a success. For that it was a success, Lieutenant Marbury assured him. The government man said he would have no hesitation in recommending the purchase of Tom's aerial warship.

"There's just one other test I want to see made," he said.

"What is that?" Tom inquired.

"In a storm. You know we can't always count on having good weather, and I'd like to see how she behaves in a gale."

"You shall!" declared the young inventor.

For the next week, during which finishing touches were put on the big craft, Tom anxiously waited for signs of a storm. At last they came. Danger signals were put up all along the coast, and warnings were sent out broadcast by the Weather Bureau at Washington.

One dull gray morning Tom roused his friends early and announced that the Mars was going up.

"A big storm is headed this way," Tom said, "and we'll have a chance to see how she behaves in it."

And even as the flight began, the forerunning wind and rain came in a gust of fury. Into the midst of it shot the big aerial warship, with her powerful propellers beating the moisture-laden air.

CHAPTER XIX

QUEER HAPPENINGS

"Say, Tom, are you sure you're all right?"

"Of course I am! What do you mean?"

It was Ned Newton who asked the question, and Tom Swift who answered it. The chums were in the pilot-house of the dipping, swaying Mars, which was nosing her way into the storm, fighting on an upward slant, trying, if possible, to get above the area of atmospheric disturbance.

"Well, I mean are you sure your craft will stand all this straining, pulling and hauling?" went on Ned, as he clung to a brass hand rail, built in the side of the pilot-house wall for the very purpose to which it was now being put.

"If she doesn't stand it she's no good!" cried Tom, as he clung to the steering wheel, which was nearly torn from his hands by the deflections of the rudders.

"Well, it's taking a big chance, it seems to me," went on Ned, as he peered through the rain-spotted bull's-eyes of the pilot-house.

"There's no danger," declared Tom. "I wanted to give the ship the hardest test possible before I formally offered her to the government. If she can't stand a blow like this she isn't what I thought her, and I'll have to build another. But I'm sure she will stand the racket, Ned. She's built strongly, and even if part of the gas bag is carried away, as it was when our propeller shattered, we can still sail. If you think this is anything, wait until we turn about and begin to fight our way against the wind."

"Are you going to do that, Tom?"

"I certainly am. We're going with the gale now, to see what is the highest rate of speed we can attain. Pretty soon I'm going to turn her around, and see if she can make any headway in the other direction. Of course I know she won't make much, if any speed, against the gale; but I must give her that test."

"Well, Tom, you know best, of course," admitted Ned. "But to me it seems like taking a big risk."

And indeed it did seem, not only to Ned, but to some of the experienced men of Tom's crew, that the young inventor was taking more chances than ever before, and Tom, as my old readers well know, had, in his career, taken some big ones.

The storm grew worse as the day progressed, until it was a veritable hurricane of wind and rain. The warnings of the Weather Bureau had not been exaggerated. But through the fierce blow the Mars fought her way. As Tom had said, she was going with the wind. This was comparatively easy. But what would happen when she headed into the storm?

Mr. Damon, in the main cabin, sat and looked at Lieutenant Marbury, the eccentric man now and then blessing something as he happened to think of it.

"Do you—do you think we are in any danger?" he finally asked.

"Not at present," replied the government expert.

"You mean we will be—later?"

"It's hard to say. I guess Tom Swift knows his business, though."

"Bless my accident insurance policy!" murmured Mr. Damon. "I wish I had stayed home. If my wife ever hears of this—" He did not seem able to finish the sentence.

In the engine-room the crew were busy over the various machines. Some of the apparatus was being strained to keep the ship on her course in the powerful wind, and would be under a worse stress when Tom turned his craft about. But, so far, nothing had given way, and everything was working smoothly.

As hour succeeded hour and nothing happened, the timid ones aboard began to take more courage. Tom never for a moment lost heart. He knew what his craft could do, and he had taken her up in a terrific storm with a definite purpose in view. He was the calmest person aboard, with the exception, perhaps, of Koku. The giant did not seem to know what fear was. He depended entirely on Tom, and as long as his young master had charge of matters the giant was content to obey orders.

There was to be no test of the guns this time. They had worked sufficiently well, and, if need be, could have been fired in the gale. But Tom did not want his men to take unnecessary risks, nor was he foolhardy himself.

"We'll have our hands full when we turn around and head into the wind," he said to his chum. "That will be enough."

"Then you're really going to give the Mars that test?"

"I surely am. I don't want any comebacks from Uncle Sam after he accepts my aerial warship. I've guaranteed that she'll stand up and make headway against a gale, and I'm going to prove it."

Lieutenant Marbury was told of the coming trial, and he prepared to take official note of it. While matters were being gotten in readiness Tom turned the wheel over to his assistant pilot and went to the engine-room to see that everything was in good shape to cope with any emergency. The rudders had been carefully examined before the flight was made, to make sure they would not fail, for on them depended the progress of the ship against the powerful wind.

"I rather guess those foreign spies have given up trying to do Tom an injury," remarked Ned to the lieutenant as they sat in the main cabin, listening to the howl of the wind, and the dash of the rain.

"Well, I certainly hope so," was the answer. "But I wouldn't be too sure. The folks in Washington evidently think something is likely to happen, or they wouldn't have sent that warning telegram."

"But we haven't seen anything of the spies," Ned remarked.

"No, but that isn't any sign they are not getting ready to make trouble. This may be the calm before the storm. Tom must still be on the lookout. It isn't as though his inventions alone were in danger, for they would not hesitate to inflict serious personal injury if their plans were thwarted."

"They must be desperate."

"They are. But here comes Tom now. He looks as though something new was about to happen."

"Take care of yourselves now," advised the young aero-inventor, as he entered the cabin, finding it hard work to close the door against the terrific wind pressure.

"Why?" asked Ned.

"Because we are going to turn around and fight our way back against the gale. We may be turned topsy-turvy for a second or two."

"Bless my shoe-horn!" cried Mr. Damon. "Do you mean upside down, Tom?"

"No, not that exactly. But watch out!"

Tom went forward to the pilot-house, followed by Ned and the lieutenant. The latter wanted to take official note of what happened. Tom relieved the man at the wheel, and gradually began to alter the direction of the craft.

At first no change was noticeable. So strong was the force of the wind that it seemed as though the Mars was going in the same direction. But Ned, noticing a direction compass on the wall, saw that the needle was gradually shifting.

"Hold fast!" cried Tom suddenly. Then with a quick shift of the rudder something happened. It seemed as though the Mars was trying to turn over, and slide along on her side, or as if she wanted to turn about and scud before the gale, instead of facing it. But Tom held her to the reverse course.

"Can you get her around?" cried the lieutenant above the roar of the gale.

"I—I'm going to!" muttered Tom through his set teeth.

Inch by inch he fought the big craft through the storm. Inch by inch the indicator showed the turning, until at last the grip of the gale was overcome.

"Now she's headed right into it!" cried Tom in exultation. "She's nosing right into it!"

And the Mars was. There was no doubt of it. She had succeeded, under Tom's direction, in changing squarely about, and was now going against the wind, instead of with it.

"But we can't expect to make much speed," Tom said, as he signaled for more power, for he had lowered it somewhat in making the turn.

But Tom himself scarcely had reckoned on the force of his craft, for as the propellers whirled more rapidly the aerial warship did begin to make headway, and that in the teeth of a terrific wind.

"She's doing it, Tom! She's doing it!" cried Ned exultingly.

"I believe she is," agreed the lieutenant.

"Well, so much the better," Tom said, trying to be calm. "If she can keep this up a little while I'll give her a rest and we'll go up above the storm area, and beat back home."

The Mars, so far, had met every test. Tom had decided on ten minutes more of gale-fighting, when from the tube that communicated with the engine-room came a shrill whistle.

"See what that is, Ned," Tom directed.

"Yes," called Ned into the mouthpiece. "What's the matter?"

"Short circuit in the big motor," was the reply. "We've got to run on storage battery. Send Tom back here! Something queer has happened!"

CHAPTER XX

THE STOWAWAYS

Ned repeated the message breathlessly.

"Short circuit!" gasped Tom. "Run on storage battery! I'll have to see to that. Take the wheel somebody!"

"Wouldn't it be better to turn about, and run before the wind, so as not to put too great a strain on the machinery?" asked Lieutenant Marbury.

"Perhaps," agreed Tom. "Hold her this way, though, until I see what's wrong!"

Ned and the government man took the wheel, while Tom hurried along the runway leading from the pilot-house to the machinery cabin. The gale was still blowing fiercely.

The young inventor cast a hasty look about the interior of the place as he entered. He sniffed the air suspiciously, and was aware of the odor of burning insulation.

"What happened?" he asked, noting that already the principal motive power was coming from the big storage battery. The shift had been made automatically, when the main motor gave out.

"It's hard to say," was the answer of the chief engineer. "We were running along all right, and we got your word to switch on more power, after the turn. We did that all right, and she was running as smooth as a sewing-machine, when, all of a sudden, she short-circuited, and the storage battery cut in automatically."

"Think you put too heavy a load on the motor?" Tom asked.

"Couldn't have been that. The shunt box would have taken that up, and the circuit-breaker would have worked, saving us a burn-out, and that's what happened-a burn-out. The motor will have to be rewound."

"Well, no use trying to fight this gale with the storage battery," Tom said, after a moment's thought. "We'll run before it. That's the easiest way. Then we'll try to rise above the wind."

He sent the necessary message to the pilot-house. A moment later the shift was made, and once more the Mars was scudding before the storm. Then Tom gave his serious attention to what had happened in the engine room.

As he bent over the burned-out motor, looking at the big shiny connections, he saw something that startled him. With a quick motion Tom Swift picked up a bar of copper. It was hot to the touch—so hot that he dropped it with a cry of pain, though he had let go so quickly that the burn was only momentary.

"What's the matter?" asked Jerry Mound, Tom's engineer.

"Matter!" cried Tom. "A whole lot is the matter! That copper bar is what made the short circuit. It's hot yet from the electric current. How did it fall on the motor connections?"

The engine room force gathered about the young inventor. No one could explain how the copper bar came to be where it was. Certainly no one of Tom's employees had put it there, and it could not have fallen by accident, for the motor connections were protected by a mesh of wire, and a hand would have to be thrust under them to put the bar in place. Tom gave a quick look at his men. He knew he could trust them—every one. But this was a queer happening.

For a moment Tom did not know what to think, and then, as the memory of that warning telegram came to him, he had an idea.

"Were any strangers in this cabin before the start was made?" he asked Mr. Mound.

"Not that I know of," was the answer.

"Well, there may be some here now," Tom said grimly. "Look about."

But a careful search revealed no one. Yet the young inventor was sure the bar of copper, which had done the mischief of short-circuiting the motor, had been put in place deliberately.

In reality there was no danger to the craft, since there was power enough in the storage battery to run it for several hours. But the happening showed Tom he had still to reckon with his enemies.

He looked at the height gauge on the wall of the motor-room, and noted that the Mars was going up. In accordance with Tom's instructions they were sending her above the storm area. Once there, with no gale to fight, they could easily beat their way back to a point above Shopton, and make the best descent possible.

And that was done while, under Tom's direction, his men took the damaged motor apart, with a view to repairing it.

"What was it, Tom?" asked Ned, coming back to join his chum, after George Ventor, the assistant pilot, had taken charge of the wheel.

"I don't exactly know, Ned," was the answer. "But I feel certain that some of my enemies came aboard here and worked this mischief."

"Your enemies came aboard?"

"Yes, and they must be here now. The placing of that copper bar proves it."

"Then let's make a search and find them, Tom. It must be some of those foreign spies."

"Just what I think."

But a more careful search of the craft than the one Tom had casually made revealed the presence of no one. All the crew and helpers were accounted for, and, as they had been in Tom's service for some time, they were beyond suspicion. Yet the fact remained that a seemingly human agency had acted to put the main motor out of commission. Tom could not understand it.

"Well, it sure is queer," observed Ned, as the search came to nothing.

"It's worse than queer," declared Tom, "it's alarming! I don't know when I'll be safe if we have ghosts aboard."

"Ghosts?" repeated Ned.

"Well, when we can't find out who put that bar in place I might as well admit it was a ghost," spoke Tom. "Certainly, if it was done by a man, he didn't jump overboard after doing it, and he isn't here now. It sure is queer!"

Ned agreed with the last statement, at any rate.

In due time the Mars, having fought her way above the storm, came over Shopton, and then, the wind having somewhat died out, she fought her way down, and, after no little trouble, was housed in the hangar.

Tom cautioned his friends and workmen to say nothing to his father about the mysterious happening on board.

"I'll just tell him we had a slight accident, and let it go at that," Tom decided. "No use in causing him worry."

"But what are you going to do about it?" asked Ned.

"I'm going to keep careful watch over the aerial warship, at any rate," declared Tom. "If there's a hidden enemy aboard, I'll starve him out."

Accordingly, a guard, under the direction of Koku, was posted about the big shed, but nothing came of it. No stranger was observed to sneak out of the ship, after it had been deserted by the crew. The mystery seemed deeper than ever.

It took nearly a week to repair the big motor, and, during this time, Tom put some improvements on the airship, and added the finishing touches.

He was getting it ready for the final government test, for the authorities in Washington had sent word that they would have Captain Warner, in addition to Lieutenant Marbury, make the final inspection and write a report.

Meanwhile several little things occurred to annoy Tom. He was besieged with applications from new men who wanted to work, and many of these men seemed to be foreigners. Tom was sure they were either spies of some European nations, or the agents of spies, and they got no further than the outer gate.

But some strangers did manage to sneak into the works, though they were quickly detected and sent about their business. Also, once or twice, small fires were discovered in outbuildings, but they were soon extinguished with little damage. Extra vigilance was the watchword.

"And yet, with all my precautions, they may get me, or damage something," declared Tom. "It is very annoying!"

"It is," agreed Ned, "and we must be doubly on the lookout."

So impressed was Ned with the necessity for caution that he arranged to take his vacation at this time, so as to be on hand to help his chum, if necessary.

The Mars was nearing completion. The repaired motor was better than ever, and everything was in shape for the final test. Mr. Damon was persuaded to go along, and Koku was to be taken, as well as the two government officials.

The night before the trip the guards about the airship shed were doubled, and Tom made two visits to the place before midnight. But there was no alarm.

Consequently, when the Mars started off on her final test, it was thought that all danger from the spies was over.

"She certainly is a beauty," said Captain Warner, as the big craft shot upward. "I shall be interested in seeing how she stands gun fire, though."

"Oh, she'll stand it," declared Lieutenant Marbury. The trip was to consume several days of continuous flying, to test the engines. A large supply of food and ammunition was aboard.

It was after supper of the first day out, and our friends were seated in the main cabin laying out a program for the next day, when sudden yells came from a part of the motor cabin devoted to storage. Koku, who had been sent to get out a barrel of oil, was heard to shout.

"What's up?" asked Tom, starting to his feet. He was answered almost at once by more yells.

"Oh, Master! Come quickly!" cried the giant. "There are many men here. There are stowaways aboard!"

CHAPTER XXI

PRISONERS

For a moment, after hearing Koku's reply, neither Tom nor his friends spoke. Then Ned, in a dazed sort of way, repeated:

"Stowaways!"

"Bless my—" began Mr. Damon, but that was as far as he got.

From the engine compartment, back of the amidship cabin, came a sound of cries and heavy blows. The yells of Koku could be heard above those of the others.

Then the door of the cabin where Tom Swift and his friends were was suddenly burst open, and seven or eight men threw themselves within. They were led by a man with a small, dark mustache and a little tuft of whiskers on his chin—an imperial. He looked the typical Frenchman, and his words, snapped out, bore out that belief.

What he said was in French, as Tom understood, though he knew little of that language. Also, what the Frenchman said produced an immediate result, for the men following him sprang at our friends with overwhelming fierceness.

Before Tom, Ned, Captain Warner, Mr. Damon or Lieutenant Marbury could grasp any weapon with which to defend themselves, had their intentions been to do so, they were seized.

Against such odds little could be done, though our friends did not give up without a struggle.

"What does this mean?" angrily demanded Tom Swift. "Who are you? What are you doing aboard my craft? Who are—"

His words were lost in smothered tones, for one of his assailants put a heavy cloth over his mouth, and tied it there, gagging him. Another man, with a quick motion, whipped a rope about Tom's hands and feet, and he was soon securely bound.

In like manner the others were treated, and, despite the struggles of Mr. Damon, the two government men and Ned, they were soon put in a position where they could do nothing—helplessly bound, and laid on a bench in the main cabin, staring blankly up at the ceiling. Each one was gagged so effectively that he could not utter more than a faint moan.

Of the riot of thoughts that ran through the heads of each one, I leave you to imagine.

What did it all mean? Where had the strange men come from? What did they mean by thus assaulting Tom and his companions? And what had happened to the others of the crew—Koku, Jerry Mound, the engineer, and George Ventor, the assistant pilot?

These were only a few of the questions Tom asked himself, as he lay there, bound and helpless. Doubtless Mr. Damon and the others were asking themselves similar questions.

One thing was certain—whatever the stowaways, as Koku had called them, had done, they had not neglected the Mars, for she was running along at about the same speed, though in what direction Tom could not tell. He strained to get a view of the compass on the forward wall of the cabin, but he could not see it.

It had been a rough-and-tumble fight, by which our friends were made prisoners, but no one seemed to have been seriously, or even slightly, hurt. The invaders, under the leadership of the Frenchman, were rather ruffled, but that was all.

Pantingly they stood in line, surveying their captives, while the man with the mustache and imperial smiled in a rather superior fashion at the row of bound ones. He spoke in his own tongue to the men, who, with the exception of one, filed out, going, as Tom and the others could note, to the engine-room in the rear.

"I hope I have not had to hurt any of you," the Frenchman observed, with sarcastic politeness. "I regret the necessity that caused me to do this, but, believe me, it was unavoidable."

He spoke with some accent, and Tom at once decided this was the same man who had once approached Eradicate. He also recognized him as the man he had seen in the woods the day of the outing.

"He's one of the foreign spies," thought Tom "and he's got us and the ship, too. They were too many for us!"

Tom's anxiety to speak, to hold some converse with the captor, was so obvious that the Frenchman said:

"I am going to treat you as well as I can under the circumstances. You and your other friends, who are also made prisoners, will be allowed to be together, and then you can talk to your hearts' content."

The other man, who had remained with the evident ringleader of the stowaways, asked a question, in French, and he used the name La Foy.

"Ah!" thought Tom. "This is the leader of the gang that attacked Koku in the shop that night. They have been waiting their chance, and now they have made good. But where did they come from? Could they have boarded us from some other airship?"

Yet, as Tom asked himself that question, he knew it could hardly have been possible. The men must have been in hiding on his own craft, they must have been, as Koku had cried out—stowaways—and have come out at a preconcerted signal to overpower the aviators.

"If you will but have patience a little longer," went on La Foy, for that was evidently the name of the leader, "you will all be together. We are just considering where best to put you so that you will not suffer too much. It is quite a problem to deal with so many prisoners, but we have no choice."

The two Frenchmen conversed rapidly in their own language for a few minutes, and then there came into the cabin another of the men who had helped overpower Tom and his friends. What he told La Foy seemed to give that individual satisfaction, for he smiled.

"We are going to put you all together in the largest storeroom, which is partly empty," La Foy said. "There you will be given food and drink, and treated as well as possible under the circumstances. You will also be unbound, and may converse among yourselves. I need hardly point out," he went on, "that calling for help will be useless. We are a mile or so in the air, and have no intention of descending," and he smiled mockingly.

"They must know how to navigate my aerial warship," thought Tom. "I wonder what their game is, anyhow?"

Night had fallen, but the cabin was aglow with electric lights. The foreigners in charge of the Mars seemed to know their way about perfectly, and how to manage the big craft. By the vibration Tom could tell that the motor was running evenly and well.

"But what happened to the others—to Mound, Ventor and Koku?" wondered Tom.

A moment later several of the foreigners entered. Some of them did not look at all like Frenchmen, and Tom was sure one was a German and another a Russian.

"This will be your prison—for a while," said La Foy significantly, and Tom wondered how long this would be the case. A sharp thought came to him—how long would they be prisoners? Did not some other, and more terrible, fate await them?

As La Foy spoke, he opened a storeroom door that led off from the main, or amidship, cabin. This room was intended to contain the supplies and stores that would be taken on a long voyage. It was one of two, being the larger, and now contained only a few odds and ends of little importance. It made a strong prison, as Tom well knew, having planned it.

One by one, beginning with Tom, the prisoners were taken up and placed in a recumbent position on the floor of the storeroom. Then were brought in the engineer and assistant pilot, as well as Koku and a machinist whom Tom had brought along to help him. Now the young inventor and all his friends were together. It took four men to carry Koku in, the giant being covered with a network of ropes.

"On second thought," said La Foy, as he saw Koku being placed with his friends, "I think we will keep the big man with us. We had trouble enough to subdue him. Carry him back to the engine-room."

So Koku, trussed up like some roped steer, was taken out again.

"Now then," said La Foy to his prisoners, as he stood in the door of the room, "I will unbind one of you, and he may loose the bonds of the others."

As he spoke, he took the rope from Tom's hands, and then, quickly slipping out, locked and barred the door.

CHAPTER XXII

APPREHENSIONS

For a moment or two, after the ropes binding his hands were loosed, Tom Swift did nothing. He was not only stunned mentally, but the bonds had been pulled so tightly about his wrists that the circulation was impeded, and his cramped muscles required a little time in which to respond.

But presently he felt the tingle of the coursing blood, and he found he could move his arms. He raised them to his head, and then his first care was to remove the pad of cloth that formed a gag over his mouth. Now he could talk.

"I—I'll loosen you all in just a second," he said, as he bent over to pick at the knot of the rope around his legs. His own voice sounded strange to him.

"I don't know what it's all about, any more than you do," he went on, speaking to the others. "It's a fierce game we're up against, and we've got to make the best of it. As soon as we can move, and talk, we'll decide what's best to do. Whoever these fellows are, and I believe they are the foreign spies I've been warned about, they are in complete possession of the airship."

Tom found it no easy matter to loosen the bonds on his feet. The ropes were well tied, and Tom's fingers were stiff from the lack of circulation of blood. But finally he managed to free himself. When he stood up in the dim storeroom, that was now a prison for all save Koku, he found that he could not walk. He almost toppled over, so weak were his legs from the tightness of the ropes. He sat down and worked his muscles until they felt normal again.

A few minutes later, weak and rather tottery, he managed to reach Mr. Damon, whom he first unbound. He realized that Mr. Damon was the oldest of his friends, and, consequently, would suffer most. And it was characteristic of the eccentric gentleman that, as soon as his gag was removed he burst out with:

"Bless my wristlets, Tom! What does it all mean?"

"That's more than I can say, Mr. Damon," replied Tom, with a mournful shake of his head. "I'm very sorry it happened, for it looks as though I hadn't taken proper care. The idea of those men stowing themselves away on board here, and me not knowing it; and then coming out unexpectedly and getting possession of the craft! It doesn't speak very well for my smartness."

"Oh, well, Tom, anyone might have been fooled by those plotting foreigners," said Mr. Damon. "Now, we'll try to turn matters about and get the best of them. Oh, but it feels good to be free once more!"

He stretched his benumbed and stiffened limbs and then helped Tom free the others. They stood up, looking at each other in their dimly lighted prison.

"Well, if this isn't the limit I don't know what is!" cried Ned Newton.

"They got the best of you, Tom," spoke Lieutenant Marbury.

"Are they really foreign spies?" asked Captain Warner.

"Yes," replied his assistant. "They managed to carry out the plot we tried to frustrate. It was a good trick, too, hiding on board, and coming out with a rush."

"Is that what they did?" asked Mr. Damon.

"It looks so," observed Tom. "The attack must have started in the engine-room," he went on, with a look at Mound and Ventor. "What happened there?" he asked.

"Well, that's about the way it was," answered the engineer. "We were working away, making some adjustments, oiling the parts and seeing that everything was running smoothly, when, all at once, I heard Koku yell. He had gone in the oil room. At first I thought something had gone wrong with the ship, but, when I looked at the giant, I saw he was being attacked by four strange men. And, before I, or any of the other men, could do anything, they all swarmed down on us.

"There must have been a dozen of them, and they simply overwhelmed us. One of them hit Koku on the head with an iron bar, and that took all the fight out of the giant, or the story might have been a different one. As it was, we were overpowered, and that's all I know until we were carried in here, and saw you folks all tied up as we were."

"They burst in on us in the same way," Tom explained. "But where did they come from? Where were they hiding?"

"In the oil and gasoline storeroom that opens out of the motor compartment," answered Mound, the engineer. "It isn't half full, you know, and there's room for more than a dozen men in it. They must have gone in some time last night, when the airship was in the hangar, and remained hidden among the boxes and barrels until they got ready to come out and overpower us."

"That's it," decided Tom. "But I don't understand how they got in. The hangar was well guarded all night."

"Some of your men might have been bribed," suggested Ned.

"Yes, that is so," admitted Tom, and, later, he learned that such had been the case. The foreign spies, for such they were, had managed to corrupt one of Tom's trusted employees, who had looked the other way when La Foy and his fellow-conspirators sneaked into the airship shed and secreted themselves.

"Well, discussing how they got on board isn't going to do us any good now," Tom remarked ruefully. "The question is—what are we going to do?"

"Bless my fountain pen!" cried Mr. Damon. "There's only one thing to do!"

"What is that?" asked Ned.

"Why, get out of here, call a policeman, and have these scoundrels arrested. I'll prosecute them! I'll have my lawyer on hand to see that they get the longest terms the statutes call for! Bless my pocketbook, but I will!" and Mr. Damon waxed quite indignant.

"That's easier said than done," observed Torn Swift, quietly. "In the first place, it isn't going to be an easy matter to get out of here."

He looked around the storeroom, which was then their prison. It was illuminated by a single electric light, which showed some boxes and barrels piled in the rear.

"Nothing in them to help us get out," Tom went on, for he knew what the contents were.

"Oh, we'll get out," declared Ned confidently, "but I don't believe we'll find a policeman ready to take our complaint. The upper air isn't very well patrolled as yet."

"That's so," agreed Mr. Damon. "I forgot that we were in an airship. But what is to be done, Tom? We really are captives aboard our own craft."

"Yes, worse luck," returned the young inventor. "I feel foolish when I think how we let them take us prisoners."

"We couldn't help it," Ned commented. "They came on us too suddenly. We didn't have a chance. And they outnumbered us two to one. If they could take care of big Koku, what chance did we have?"

"Very little," said Engineer Mound. "They were desperate fellows. They know something about aircraft, too. For, as soon as Koku, Ventor and I were disposed of, some of them went at the machinery as if they had been used to running it all their lives."

"Oh, the foreigners are experts when it comes to craft of the air," said Captain Warner.

"Well, they seem to be running her, all right," admitted the young inventor, "and at good speed, too. They have increased our running rate, if I am any judge."

"By several miles an hour," confirmed the assistant pilot. "Though in which direction they are heading, and what they are going to do with us is more than I can guess."

"That's so!" agreed Mr. Damon. "What is to become of us? They may heave us overboard into the ocean!"

"Into the ocean!" cried Ned apprehensively. "Are we near the sea?"

"We must be, by this time," spoke Tom. "We were headed in that direction, and we have come almost far enough to put us somewhere over the Atlantic, off the Jersey coast."

A look of apprehension was on the faces of all. But Tom's face did not remain clouded long.

"We won't try to swim until we have to," he said. "Now, let's take an account of stock, and see if we have any means of getting out of this prison."

CHAPTER XXIII

ACROSS THE SEA

With one accord the hands of the captives sought their pockets. Probably the first thought of each one was a knife—a pocket knife. But blank looks succeeded their first hopeful ones, for the hands came out empty.

"Not a thing!" exclaimed Mr. Damon. "Not a blessed thing! They have even taken my keys and—my fountain pen!"

"I guess they searched us all while they were struggling with us, tying us up," suggested Ned. "I had a knife with a big, strong blade, but it's gone."

"So is mine," echoed Tom.

"And I haven't even a screwdriver, or a pocket-wrench," declared the engineer, "though I had both."

"They evidently knew what they were doing," said Lieutenant Marbury. "I don't usually carry a revolver, but of late I have had a small automatic in my pocket. That's gone, too."

"And so are all my things," went on his naval friend. "That Frenchman, La Foy, was taking no chances."

"Well, if we haven't any weapons, or means of getting out of here, we must make them," said Tom, as hopefully as he could under the circumstances. "I don't know all the things that were put in this storeroom, and perhaps there may be something we can use."

"Shall we make the try now?" asked Ned. "I'm getting thirsty, at least. Lucky we had supper before they came out at us."

"Well, there isn't any water in here, or anything to eat, of so much I am sure," went on Tom "So we will have to depend on our captors for that."

"At least we can shout and ask for water," said Lieutenant Marbury. "They have no excuse for being needlessly cruel."

They all agreed that this might not be a bad plan, and were preparing to raise a united shout, when there came a knock on the door of their prison.

"Are you willing to listen to reason?" asked a voice they recognized as that of La Foy.

"What do you mean by reason?" asked Tom bitterly. "You have no right to impose any conditions on us."

"I have the right of might, and I intend exercising it," was the sharp rejoinder. "If you will listen to reason—"

"Which kind—yours or ours?" asked Tom pointedly.

"Mine, in this case," snapped back the Frenchman. "What I was going to say was that I do not intend to starve you, or cause you discomfort by thirst. I am going to open the door and put in food and water. But I warn you that any attempt to escape will be met with severe measures.

"We are in sufficient force to cope with you. I think you have seen that." He spoke calmly and in perfect English, though with a marked accent. "My men are armed, and will stand here ready to meet violence with violence," he went on. "Is that understood?"

For a moment none of the captives replied.

"I think it will be better to give in to him at least for a while," said Captain Warner in a low voice to Tom. "We need water, and will soon need food. We can think and plan better if we are well nourished."

"Then you think I should promise not to raise a row?"

"For the time being—yes."

"Well, I am waiting!" came in sharp tones from the other side of the portal.

"Our answer is—yes," spoke Tom. "We will not try to get out—just yet," he added significantly.

A key was heard grating in the lock, and, a moment later, the door slid back. Through the opening could be seen La Foy and some of his men standing armed. Others had packages of food and jugs of water. A plentiful supply of the latter was carried aboard the Mars.

"Keep back from the door!" was the stern command of La Foy. "The food and drink will be passed in only if you keep away from the entrance. Remember my men are armed!"

The warning was hardly needed, for the weapons could plainly be seen. Tom had half a notion that perhaps a concerted rush would carry the day for him and his friends, but he was forced to abandon that idea.

While the guards looked on, others of the "pirate crew," as Ned dubbed them, passed in food and water. Then the door was locked again.

They all felt better after drinking the water, which was made cool by evaporation, for the airship was quite high above the earth when Tom's enemies captured it, and the young inventor felt sure it had not descended any.

No one felt much like eating, however, so the food was put away for a time. And then, somewhat refreshed, they began looking about for some means of getting out of their prison.

"Of course we might batter down the door, in time, by using some of these boxes as rams," said Tom. "But the trouble is, that would make a noise, and they could stand outside and drive us back with guns and pistols, of which they seem to have plenty."

"Yes, and they could turn some of your own quick-firers on us," added Captain Warner. "No, we must work quietly, I think, and take them unawares, as they took us. That is our only plan."

"We will be better able to see what we have here by daylight," Tom said. "Suppose we wait until morning?"

That plan was deemed best, and preparations made for spending the night in their prison.

It was a most uncomfortable night for all of them. The floor was their only bed, and their only covering some empty bags that had contained supplies. But even under these circumstances they managed to doze off fitfully.

Once they were all awakened by a violent plunging of the airship. The craft seemed to be trying to stand on her head, and then she rocked violently from side to side, nearly turning turtle. "What is it?" gasped Ned, who was lying next to Tom.

"They must be trying some violent stunts," replied the young inventor, "or else we have run into a storm."

"I think the latter is the case," observed Lieutenant Marbury.

And, as the motion of the craft kept up, though less violently, this was accepted as the explanation. Through the night the Mars flew, but whither the captives knew not.

The first gray streaks of dawn finally shone through the only window of their prison. Sore, lame and stiff, wearied in body and disturbed in mind, the captives awoke. Tom's first move was toward the window. It was high up, but, by standing on a box, he could look through it. He uttered an exclamation.

"What is it?" asked Ned, swaying to and fro from the violent motion ef the aerial warship.

"We are away out over the sea," spoke Tom, "and in the midst of a bad storm."

CHAPTER XXIV

THE LIGHTNING BOLT

Tom turned away from the window, to find his companions regarding him anxiously.

"A storm," repeated Ned. "What sort?"

"It might turn into any sort," replied Tom. "All I can see now is a lot of black clouds, and the wind must be blowing pretty hard, for there's quite a sea on."

"Bless my galvanometer!" cried Mr. Damon. "Then we are out over the ocean again, Tom?"

"Yes, there's no doubt of it."

"What part?" asked the assistant pilot.

"That's more than I can tell," Tom answered.

"Suppose I take a look?" suggested Captain Warner. "I've done quite a bit of sailing in my time."

But, when he had taken a look through the window at which Tom had been standing, the naval officer descended, shaking his head.

"There isn't a landmark in sight," he announced. "We might be over the middle of the Atlantic, for all I could tell."

"Hardly as far as that," spoke Tom. "They haven't been pushing the Mars at that speed. But we may be across to the other side before we realize it."

"How's that?" asked Ned.

"Well, the ship is in the possession of these foreign spies," went on Tom. "All their interests are in Europe, though it would be hard to say what nationality is in command here. I think there are even some Englishmen among those who attacked us, as well as French, Germans, Italians and Russians."

"Yes, it seems to be a combination of European nations against us," admitted Captain Warner. "Probably, after they have made good their seizure of Tom's aerial warship, they will portion her out among themselves, or use her as a model from which to make others."

"Do you think that is their object?" asked Mr. Damon.

"Undoubtedly," was the captain's answer. "It has been the object of these foreign spies, all along, not only to prevent the United States from enjoying the benefits of these progressive inventions, but to use them for themselves. They would stop at nothing to gain their ends. It seems we did not sufficiently appreciate their power and daring."

"Well, they've got us, at any rate," observed Tom, "and they may take us and the ship to some far-off foreign country."

"If they don't heave us overboard half-way there," commented Ned, in rather gloomy tones.

"Well, of course, there's that possibility," admitted Tom. "They are desperate characters."

"Well, we must do something," declared Lieutenant Marbury. "Come, it's daylight now, and we can see to work better. Let's see if we can't find a way to get out of this prison. Say, but this sure is a storm!" he cried, as the airship rolled and pitched violently.

"They are handling her well, though," observed Tom, as the craft came quickly to an even keel. "Either they have a number of expert bird-men on board, or they can easily adapt themselves to a new aircraft. She is sailing splendidly."

"Well, let's eat something, and set to work," proposed Ned.

They brought out the food which had been given to them the night before, but before they could eat this, there came a knock on the door, and more food and fresh water was handed in, under the same precautions as before.

Tom and his companions indignantly demanded to be released, but their protests were only laughed at, and while the guards stood with ready weapons the door was again shut and locked.

But the prisoners were not the kind to sit idly down in the face of this. Under Tom's direction they set about looking through their place of captivity for something by which they could release themselves. At first they found nothing, and Ned even suggested trying to cut a way through the wooden walls with a fingernail file, which he found in one of his pockets, when Tom, who had gone to the far end of the storeroom, uttered a cry.

"What is it—a way out?" asked Lieutenant Marbury anxiously.

"No, but means to that end," Tom replied. "Look, a file and a saw, left here by some of my workmen, perhaps," and he brought out the tools. He had found them behind a barrel in the far end of the compartment.

"Hurray!" cried Ned. "That's the ticket! Now we'll soon show these fellows what's what!"

"Go easy!" cautioned Tom. "We must work carefully. It won't do to slam around and try to break down the door with these. I think we had better select a place on the side wall, break through that, and make an opening where we can come out unnoticed. Then, when we are ready, we can take them by surprise. We'll have to do something like that, for they outnumber us, you know."

"That is so," agreed Captain Warner. "We must use strategy."

"Well, where would be a good place to begin to burrow out?" asked Ned.

"Here," said Tom, indicating a place far back in the room. "We can work there in turns, sawing a hole through the wall. It will bring us out in the passage between the aft and amidship cabins, and we can go either way."

"Then let's begin!" cried Ned enthusiastically, and they set to work.

While the aerial warship pitched and tossed in the storm, over some part of the Atlantic, Tom and his friends took turns in working their way to freedom. With the sharp end of the file a small hole was made, the work being done as slowly as a rat gnaws, so as to make no noise that would be heard by their captors. In time the hole was large enough to admit the end of the saw.

But this took many hours, and it was not until the second day of their captivity that they had the hole nearly large enough for the passage of one person at a time. They had not been discovered, they thought.

Meanwhile they had been given food and water at intervals, but to all demands that they be released, or at least told why they were held prisoners, a deaf ear was turned.

They could only guess at the fate of Koku. Probably the giant was kept bound, for once he got the chance to use his enormous strength it might go hard with the foreigners.

The Mars continued to fly through the air. Sometimes, as Tom and his friends could tell by the motion, she was almost stationary in the upper regions, and again she seemed to be flying at top speed. Occasionally there came the sound of firing.

"They're trying my guns," observed Tom grimly.

"Do you suppose they are being attacked?" asked Ned, hopefully.

"Hardly," replied Captain Warner. "The United States possesses no craft able to cope with this one in aerial warfare, and they are hardly engaging in part of the European war yet. I think they are just trying Tom's new guns."

Later our friends learned that such was the case.

The storm had either passed, or the Mars had run out of the path of it, for, after the first few hours of pitching and tossing, the atmosphere seemed reduced to a state of calm.

All the while they were secretly working to gain their freedom so they might attack and overpower their enemies, they took occasional observations from the small window. But they could learn nothing of their whereabouts. They could only view the heaving ocean, far below them, or see a mass of cloud-mist, which hid the earth, if so be that the Mars was sailing over land.

"But how much longer can they keep it up?" asked Ned.

"Well, we have fuel and supplies aboard for nearly two weeks," Tom answered.

"And by the end of that time we may all be dead," spoke the young bank clerk despondently.

"No, we'll be out of here before then!" declared Lieutenant Marbury.

Indeed the hole was now almost large enough to enable them to crawl out one at a time. They could not, of course, see how it looked from the outside, but Tom had selected a place for its cutting so that the sawdust and the mark of the panel that was being removed, would not ordinarily be noticeable.

Their set night as the time for making the attempt—late at night, when it was hoped that most of their captors would be asleep.

Finally the last cut was made, and a piece of wood hung over the opening only by a shred, all ready to knock out.

"We'll do it at midnight," announced Tom.

Anxious, indeed, were those last hours of waiting. The time had almost arrived for the attempt, when Tom, who had been nervously pacing to and fro, remarked:

"We must be running into another storm. Feel how she heaves and rolls!"

Indeed the Mars was most unsteady.

"It sure is a storm!" cried Ned, "and a heavy one, too," for there came a burst of thunder, that seemed like a report of Tom's giant cannon.

In another instant they were in the midst of a violent thunderstorm, the airship pitching and tossing in a manner to almost throw them from their feet.

As Tom reached up to switch on the electric light again, there came a flash of lightning that well nigh blinded them. And so close after it as to seem simultaneous, there came such a crash of thunder as to stun them all. There was a tingling, as of a thousand pins and needles in the body of each of the captives, and a strong smell of sulphur. Then, as the echoes of the clap died away, Tom yelled:

"She's been struck! The airship has been struck!"

CHAPTER XXV

FREEDOM

For a moment there was silence, following Tom's wild cry and the noise of the thunderclap. Then, as other, though less loud reverberations of the storm continued to sound, the captives awoke to a realization of what had happened. They had been partially stunned, and were almost as in a dream.

"Are—are we all right?" stammered Ned.

"Bless my soul! What has happened?" cried Mr. Damon.

"We've been struck by lightning!" Tom repeated. "I don't know whether we're all right or not."

"We seem to be falling!" exclaimed Lieutenant Marbury.

"If the whole gas bag isn't ripped to pieces we're lucky," commented Jerry Mound.

Indeed, it was evident that the Mars was sinking rapidly. To all there came the sensation of riding in an elevator in a skyscraper and being dropped a score of stories.

Then, as they stood there in the darkness, illuminated only by flashes from the lightning outside the window, waiting for an unknown fate, Tom Swift uttered a cry of delight.

"We've stopped falling!" he cried. "The automatic gas machine is pumping. Part of the gas bag was punctured, but the unbroken compartments hold!"

"If part of the gas leaked out I don't see why it wasn't all set on fire and exploded," observed Captain Warner.

"It's a non-burnable gas," Tom quickly explained. "But come on. This may be our very chance. There seems to be something going on that may be in our favor."

Indeed the captives could hear confused cries and the running to and fro of many feet.

He made for the sawed panel, and, in another instant, had burst out and was through it, out into the passageway between the after and amidship cabins. His companions followed him.

They looked into the rear cabin, or motor compartment, and a scene of confusion met their gaze. Two of the foreign men who had seized the ship lay stretched out on the floor near the humming machinery, which had been left to run itself. A look in the other direction, toward the main cabin, showed a group of the foreign spies bending over the inert body of La Foy, the Frenchman, stretched out on a couch.

"What has happened?" cried Ned. "What does it all mean?'

"The lightning!" exclaimed Tom. "The bolt that struck the ship has knocked out some of our enemies! Now is the time to attack them!"

The Mars seemed to have passed completely through a narrow storm belt. She was now in a quiet atmosphere, though behind her could be seen the fitful play of lightning, and there could be heard the distant rumble of thunder.

"Come on!" cried Tom. "We must act quickly, while they are demoralized! Come on!"

His friends needed no further urging. Jerry Mound and the machinist rushed to the engine-room, to look after any of the enemy that might be there, while Tom, Ned and the others ran into the middle cabin.

"Grab 'em! Tie 'em up!" cried Tom, for they had no weapons with which to make an attack.

But none were needed. So stunned were the foreigners by the lightning bolt, which had miraculously passed our friends, and so unnerved by the striking down of La Foy, their leader, that they seemed like men half asleep. Before they could offer any resistance they were bound with the same ropes that had held our friends in bondage. That is, all but the big Frenchman himself. He seemed beyond the need of binding.

Mound, the engineer, and his assistant, came hurrying in from the motor-room, followed by Koku.

"We found him chained up," Jerry explained, as the big giant, freed from his captivity, rubbed his chafed wrists.

"Are there any of the foreigners back there?'

"Only those two knocked out by the lightning," the engineer explained. "We've made them secure. I see you've got things here in shape."

"Yes," replied Tom. "And now to see where we are, and to get back home. Whew! But this has been a time! Koku, what happened to you?"

"They no let anything happen. I be in chains all the while," the giant answered. "Jump on me before I can do anything!"

"Well, you're out, now, and I think we'll have you stand guard over these men. The tables are turned, Koku."

The bound ones were carried to the same prison whence our friends had escaped, but their bonds were not taken off, and Koku was put in the place with them. By this time La Foy and the two other stricken men showed signs of returning life. They had only been stunned.

The young inventor and his friends, once more in possession of their airship, lost little time in planning to return. They found that the spies were all expert aeronauts, and had kept a careful chart of their location. They were then halfway across the Atlantic, and in a short time longer would probably have been in some foreign country. But Tom turned the Mars about.

The craft had only been slightly damaged by the lightning bolt, though three of the gas bag compartments were torn, The others sufficed, however, to make the ship sufficiently buoyant.

When morning came Tom and his friends had matters running almost as smoothly as before their capture.

The prisoners had no chance to escape, and, indeed, they seemed to have been broken in spirit. La Foy was no longer the insolent, mocking Frenchman that he had been, and the two chief foreign engineers seemed to have lost some of their reason when the lightning struck them.

"But it was a mighty lucky and narrow escape for us," said Ned, as he and Tom sat in the pilot-house the second day of the return trip.

"That's right," agreed his chum.

Once again they were above the earth, and, desiring to get rid as soon as possible of the presence of the spies, a landing was made near New York City, and the government authorities communicated with. Captain Warner and Lieutenant Marbury took charge of the prisoners, with some Secret Service men, and the foreigners were soon safely locked up.

"And now what are you going to do, Tom?" asked Ned, when, once more, they had the airship to themselves.

"I'm going back to Shopton, fix up the gas bag, and give her another government trial," was the answer.

And, in due time, this was done. Tom added some improvements to the aircraft, making it better than ever, and when she was given the test required by the government, she was an unqualified success, and the rights to the Mars were purchased for a large sum. In sailing, and in the matter of guns and bombs, Tom's craft answered every test.

"So you see I was right, after all, Dad," the young inventor said, when informed that he had succeeded. "We can shoot off even bigger guns than I thought from the deck of the Mars."

"Yes, Tom," replied the aged inventor, "I admit I was wrong."

Tom's aerial warship was even a bigger success than he had dared to hope. Once the government men fully understood how to run it, in which Tom played a prominent part in giving instructions, they put the Mars to a severe test. She was taken out over the ocean, and her guns trained on an obsolete battleship. Her bombs and projectiles blew the craft to pieces.

"The Mars will be the naval terror of the seas in any future war," predicted Captain Warner.

The Secret Service men succeeded in unearthing all the details of the plot against Tom. His life, at times, had been in danger, but at the last minute the man detailed to harm him lost his nerve.

It was Tom's enemies who had set on fire the red shed, and who later tried to destroy the ship by putting a corrosive acid in one of the propellers. That plot, though, was not wholly successful. Then came the time when one of the spies hid on board, and dropped the copper bar on the motor, short-circuiting it. But for the storage-battery that scheme might have wrought fearful damage. The spy who had stowed himself away on the craft escaped at night by the connivance of one of Tom's corrupt employees.

The foreign spies were tried and found guilty, receiving merited punishment. Of course the governments to which they belonged disclaimed any part in the seizure of Tom's aerial warship.

It came out at the trial that one of Tom's most trusted employees had proved a traitor, and had the night before the test, allowed the foreign spies to secrete themselves on board, to rush out at an opportune time to overpower our hero and his friends. But luck was with Tom at the end.

"Well, what are you going to tackle next, Tom?" asked Ned, one day about a month after these exciting experiences.

"I don't know," was the slow answer. "I think a self-swinging hammock, under an apple tree, with a never-emptying pitcher of ice-cold lemonade would be about the thing."

"Good, Tom! And, if you'll invent that, I'll share it with you."

"Well, come on, let's begin now," laughed Tom. "I need a vacation, anyhow."

But it is very much to be doubted if Tom Swift, even on a vacation, could refrain from trying to invent something, either in the line of airships, water, or land craft. And so, until he again comes to the front with something flew, we will take leave of him.

TOM SWIFT AND HIS BIG TUNNEL

Or, THE HIDDEN CITY OF THE ANDES

CHAPTER I

AN APPEAL FOR AID

Tom Swift, seated in his laboratory engaged in trying to solve a puzzling question that had arisen over one of his inventions, was startled by a loud knock on the door. So emphatic, in fact, was the summons that the door trembled, and Tom started to his feet in some alarm.

"Hello there!" he cried. "Don't break the door, Koku!" and then he laughed. "No one but my giant would knock like that," he said to himself. "He never does seem able to do things gently. But I wonder why he is knocking. I told him to get the engine out of the airship, and Eradicate said he'd be around to answer the telephone and bell. I wonder if anything has happened?"

Tom shoved back his chair, pushed aside the mass of papers over which he had been puzzling, and strode to the door. Flinging it open he confronted a veritable giant of a man, nearly eight feet tall, and big in proportion. The giant, Koku, for that was his name, smiled in a good-natured way, reminding one of an overgrown boy.

"Master hear my knock?" the giant asked cheerfully.

"Hear you, Koku? Say, I couldn't hear anything else!" exclaimed Tom. "Did you think you had to arouse the whole neighborhood just to let me know you were at the door? Jove! I thought you'd have it off the hinges."

"If me break, me fix," said Koku, who, from his appearance and from his imperfect command of English, was evidently a foreigner.

"Yes, I know you can fix lots of things, Koku," Tom went on, kindly enough. "But you musn't forget what enormous strength you have. That's the reason I sent you to take the engine out of the airship. You can lift it without using the chain hoist, and I can't get the chain hoist fast unless I remove all the superstructure. I don't want to do that. Did you get the engine out?"

"Not quite. Almost, Master."

"Then why are you here? Has anything gone wrong?"

"No, everything all right, Master. But man come to machine shop and say he must have talk with you. I no let him come past the gate, but I say I come and call you."

"That's right, Koku. Don't let any strangers past the gate. But why didn't Eradicate come and call me. He isn't doing anything, is he? Unless, indeed, he has gone to feed his mule, Boomerang."

"Eradicate, he come to call you, but that black man no good!" and Koku chuckled so heartily that he shook the floor of the office.

"What's the matter with Eradicate?" asked Tom, somewhat anxiously. "I hope you and he haven't had another row?" Eradicate had served Tom and his father long before Koku, the giant, had been brought back from one of the young inventor's many strange trips, and ever since then there had been a jealous rivalry between the twain as to who should best serve Tom.

"No trouble, Master," said Koku. "Eradicate he start to come and tell you strange man want to have talk, but Eradicate he no come fast enough. So I pick him up, and I set him down by gate to stand on guard, and I come to tell you. Koku come quick!"

"Oh, I knew it must be something like that!" exclaimed Tom in some vexation. "Now I'll have Eradicate complaining to me that you mauled him. Picked him up and set him down again."

"Sure. One hand!" boasted the giant. "Eradicate him not be heavy. More as a sack of flour now."

"No, poor Eradicate is getting pretty old and thin," commented Tom. "He can't move very quickly. But you should have let him come, Koku. It makes him feel badly when he thinks he can't be of service to me any more."

"Man say he in hurry." The giant spoke softly, as though he felt the gentle rebuke Tom administered. "Koku run quick tell you—bang on door."

"Yes, you banged all right, Koku. Well, it can't be helped, I reckon. Where is this strange man? Who is he? Did you ever see him before?"

"Me no can tell, Master. Not sure. But him now be at the outer gate. Eradicate watch."

"All right. I'll go and see who it is. I don't want any strangers poking around here, especially with the plans of my new gyroscope lying in plain view."

Before he left the laboratory Tom swept into a desk drawer the mass of papers and blue prints, and locked the receptacle.

"No use taking any chances," he remarked. "I've had too much trouble with people trying to get inside information about dad's and my patents. Now, Koku, I'll go and see this man."

The buildings composing the plant of Tom Swift and his father at Shopton were enclosed by a high, board fence, and at one of the entrances was a sort of gate-house, where some one was always on guard. Only those who could give a good account of themselves, workmen in the plant, or those known to the sentinel were admitted.

It happened that the colored man, Eradicate, was on guard at the gates this day when the stranger asked to see Tom. Koku, working on the airship engine not far away, saw the stranger. Hearing the man say he was in a hurry and noting the slow progress of the aged Eradicate, who was troubled with rheumatism, the giant took matters into his own hands.

Tom Swift entered the gate-house and saw, seated in a chair, a man who was impatiently tapping the floor with his thick-soled shoe.

"Looks like a detective or a policeman in disguise," thought Tom, for, almost invariably, members of this profession wear very thick-soled shoes. Opposite the stranger sat Eradicate, a much-injured look on his honest, black face.

"Oh, Massa Tom!" exclaimed Eradicate, as soon as the young inventor entered. "Dat Koku he—he—he done gone and cotch me by de collar ob mah coat, an' den he lif' me up, an' he sot me down so hard— so hard—dat he jar loose all mah back teef!" and Eradicate opened his mouth wide to display his gleaming ivories.

"Eradicate, he no can come quick. He walk like so fashion!" and Koku, who had followed the young inventor, imitated the limping gait of the colored man with such a queer effect that Tom could not help laughing, and the stranger smiled.

"Ef I gits holt on yo'—ef I does, yo' great, big, overgrown lummox, Ah'll—Ah'll—" began the colored man, stammeringly.

"There. That will do now!" interrupted Tom. "Don't quarrel in here. Koku, get back to that engine and lift out the motor. Eradicate, didn't father tell you to whitewash the chicken coops today?"

"Dat's what he done, Massa Tom."

"Well, go and see about that. I'll stay here for a while, and when I leave I'll call one of you, or some one else, to be on guard. Skip now!"

Having thus disposed of the warring factions, Tom turned to the stranger and after apologizing for the little interruption, asked:

"You wished to see me?"

"If you're Tom Swift; yes."

"Well, I'm Tom Swift," and the young owner of the name smiled.

"I hope you will pardon a stranger for calling on you," resumed the man, "but I'm in a lot of trouble, and I think you are the only one who can help me out."

"What sort of trouble?" Tom inquired.

"Contracting trouble—tunnel blasting, to be exact. But if you have a few minutes to spare perhaps you will listen to my story. You will then be better able to understand my difficulty."

Tom Swift considered a moment. He was used to having appeals for help made to him, and usually they were of a begging nature. He was often asked for money to help some struggling inventor complete his machine.

In many cases the machines would have been of absolutely no use if perfected. In other cases the inventions were of the utterly hopeless class, incapable of perfection, like some perpetual motion apparatus. In these cases Tom turned a deaf ear, though if the inventor were in want our hero relieved him.

But this case did not seem to be like anything Tom had ever met with before.

"Contracting trouble—blasting," repeated the youth, as he mused over what he had heard.

"That's it," the man went on. "Permit me to introduce myself" and he held out a card, on which was the name

MR. JOB TITUS

Down   in   the   lower   left-hand   corner   was   a   line:

"Titus Brothers, Contractors."

"I am glad to meet you, Mr. Titus," Tom said warmly, offering his hand. "I don't know anything about the contracting business, but if you do blasting I suppose you use explosives, and I know a little about them."

"So I have heard, and that's why I came to you," the contractor went on. "Now if you'll give me a few minutes of your time—"

"You had better come up to the house," interrupted Tom. "We can talk more quietly there."

Calling a young fellow who was at work near by to occupy the gatehouse, Tom led Mr. Titus toward the Swift homestead, and, a little later, ushered him into the library.

"Now I'll listen to you," the youth said, "though I can't promise to aid you."

"I realize that," returned Mr. Titus. "This is a sort of last chance I'm taking. My brother and I have heard a lot about you, and when he wrote to me that he was unable to proceed with his contract of tunneling the Andes Mountains for the Peruvian government, I made up my mind you were the one who could help us if you would."

"Tunneling the Andes Mountains!" exclaimed Tom.

"Yes. The firm represented by my brother and myself have a contract to build a railroad for the Peruvian government. At a point some distance back in the district east of Lima, Peru, we are making a tunnel under the mountain. That is, we have it started, but now we can't advance any further."

"Why not?"

"Because of the peculiar character of the rock, which seems to defy the strongest explosive we can get. Now I understand you used a powder in your giant cannon that—"

Mr. Titus paused in his explanation, for at that moment there arose such a clatter out on the front piazza as effectually to drown conversation. There was a noise of the hoofs of a horse, the fall of a heavy body, a tattoo on the porch floor and then came an excited shout:

"Whoa there! Whoa! Stop! Look out where you're kicking! Bless my saddle blanket! Ouch! There I go!"

CHAPTER II

EXPLANATIONS

"What in the world is that?" cried Mr. Job Titus, in alarm.

Tom Swift did not answer. Instead he jumped up from his chair and ran toward the front door. Mr. Titus followed. They both saw a strange sight.

Standing on the front porch, which he seemed to occupy completely, was a large horse, with a saddle twisted underneath him. The animal was looking about him as calmly as though he always made it a practice to come up on the front piazza when stopping at a house.

Off to one side, with a crushed hat on the back of his head, with a coat split up the back, with a broken riding crop in one hand and a handkerchief in the other, sat a dignified, elderly gentleman.

That is, he would have been dignified had it not been for his position and condition. No gentleman can look dignified with a split coat and a crushed hat on, sitting under the nose of a horse on a front piazza, with his raiment otherwise much disheveled, while he wipes his scratched and bleeding face with a handkerchief.

"Bless my—bless my—" began the elderly gentleman, and he seemed at a loss what particular portion of his anatomy or that of the horse, to bless, or what portion of the universe to appeal to, for he ended up with: "Bless everything, Tom Swift!"

"I heartily agree with you, Mr. Damon!" cried Tom. "But what in the world happened?"

"That!" exclaimed Mr. Damon, pointing with his broken crop at the horse on the piazza. "I was riding him when he ran away—just as my motorcycle tried to climb a tree. No more horses for me! I'll stick to airships," and slamming his riding crop down on the porch floor with such force that the horse started back, Mr. Damon arose, painfully enough if the contortions on his face and his grunts of pain went for anything.

"Let me help you!" begged Tom, striding forward. "Mr. Titus, perhaps you will kindly lead the horse down off the piazza?"

"Certainly!" answered the tunnel contractor. "Whoa now!" he called soothingly, as the steed evinced a disposition to sit down on the side railing. "Steady now!"

The horse finally allowed himself to be led down the broad front steps, sadly marking them, as well as the floor of the piazza, with his sharp shoes.

"*Ouch!* Oh, my back!" exclaimed Mr. Damon, as Tom helped him to stand up.

"Is it hurt?" asked Tom, anxiously.

"No, I've just got what old-fashioned folks call a 'crick' in it," explained the elderly horseman. "But it feels more like a river than a 'crick.' I'll be all right presently."

"How did it happen?" asked Tom, as he led his guest toward the hall. Meanwhile Mr. Titus, wondering what it was all about, had tied the horse to a post out near the street curb, and had re-entered the library.

"I was riding over to see you, Tom, to ask you if you wouldn't go to South America with me," began Mr. Damon, rubbing his leg tenderly.

"South America?" cried Tom, with a sudden look at Mr. Titus.

"Yes, South America. Why, there isn't anything strange in that, is there? You've been to wilder countries, and farther away than that."

"Yes, I know—it's just a coincidence. Go on."

"Let me get where I can sit down," begged Mr. Damon. "I think that crick in my back is running down into my legs, Tom. I feel a bit weak. Let me sit down, and get me a glass of water. I shall be all right presently."

Between them Tom and Mr. Titus assisted the horseman into an easy chair, and there, under the influence of a cup of hot tea, which Mrs. Baggert, the housekeeper, insisted on making for him, he said he felt much better, and would explain the reason for his call which had culminated in such a sensational manner.

And while Mr. Damon is preparing his explanation I will take just a few moments to acquaint my new readers with some facts about Tom Swift, and the previous volumes of this series in which he has played such prominent parts.

Tom Swift was the son of an inventor, and not only inherited his father's talents, but had greatly added to them, so that now Tom had a wonderful reputation.

Mr. Swift was a widower, and he and Tom lived in a big house in Shopton, New York State, with Mrs. Baggert for a housekeeper. About the house, from time to time, shops and laboratories had been erected, until now there was a large and valuable establishment belonging to Tom and his father.

The first volume of this series is entitled, "Tom Swift and His Motor Cycle." It was through a motor cycle that Tom became acquainted with Mr. Wakefield Damon, who lived in a neighboring town. Mr. Damon had bought the motor cycle for himself, but, as he said, one day in riding it the machine tried to climb a tree near the Swift house.

The young inventor (for even then he was working on several patents) ministered to Mr. Damon, who, disgusted with the motor cycle, and wishing to reward Tom, let the young fellow have the machine.

Tom's career began from that hour. For he learned to ride the motor cycle, after making some improvements in it, and from then on the youth had led a busy life. Soon afterward he secured a motor boat and from that it was but a step to an airship.

The medium of the air having been conquered, Tom again turned his attention to the water, or rather, under the water, and he and his father made a submarine. Then he built an electric runabout, the speediest car on the road.

It was when Ton Swift had occasion to send his wireless message from a lonely island where he had been shipwrecked that he was able to do Mr. and Mrs. Nestor a valuable service, and this increased the regard which Miss Mary Nestor felt for the young inventor, a regard that bid fair, some day, to ripen into something stronger.

Tom Swift might have made a fortune when he set out to discover the secret of the diamond makers. But Fate intervened, and soon after that quest he went to the caves of ice, where he and his friends met with disaster. In his sky racer Tom broke all records for speed, and when he went to Africa to rescue a missionary, had it not been for his electric rifle the tide of battle would have gone against him and his party.

Marvelous, indeed, were the adventures underground, which came to Tom when he went to look for the city of gold, but the treasure there was not more valuable than the platinum which Tom sought in dreary Siberia by means of his air glider.

Tom thought his end had come when he fell into captivity among the giants; but even that turned out well, and he brought two of the giants away with him. Koku, one of the two giants, became devotedly attached to the lad, much to the disgust of Eradicate Sampson, the old negro who had worked for the Swifts for a generation, and who, with his mule Boomerang, "eradicated" from the place as much dirt as possible.

With his wizard camera Tom did much to advance the cause of science. His great searchlight was of great help to the United States government in putting a stop to the Canadian smugglers, while his giant cannon was a distinct advance in ordnance, not excepting the great German guns used in the European war.

When Tom perfected his photo telephone the last objection to rendering telephonic conversation admissible evidence in a law court was done away with, for by this invention a person was able to see, as well as to hear, over the telephone wire. One practically stood face to face with the person, miles away, to whom one was talking.

The volume immediately preceding this present one is called: "Tom Swift and His Aerial Warship." The young inventor perfected a marvelous aircraft that was the naval terror of the seas, and many governments, recognizing what an important part aircraft were going to play in all future conflicts, were anxious to secure Tom's machine. But he was true to his own country, though his rivals were nearly successful in their plots against him.

The Mars, which was the name of Tom's latest craft, proved to be a great success, and the United States government purchased it. It was not long after the completion of this transaction that the events narrated in the first chapter of this book took place.

Mr. Damon and Tom had been firm friends ever since the episode of the motor cycle, and the eccentric gentleman (who blessed so many things) often went with Tom on his trips. Besides Mary Nestor, Tom had other friends. The one, after Miss Nestor, for whom he cared most (if we except Mr. Damon) was Ned Newton, who was employed in a Shopton bank. Ned also had often gone with Tom, though lately, having a better position, he had less time to spare.

"Well, do you feel better, Mr. Damon?" asked Tom, after a bit.

"Yes, very much, thank you. Bless my pen wiper! but I thought I was done for when I saw my horse bolt for your front stoop. He rushed up it, fell down, but, fortunately, I managed to get out of his way, though the saddle girth slipped. And all I could think of was that my wife would say: 'I told you so!' for she warned me not to ride this animal.

"But he never ran away with me before, and I was in a hurry to get over to see you, Tom. Now then, let's get down to business. Will you go to South America with me?"

"Whereabout in South America are you going, Mr. Damon, and why?" Tom asked.

"To Peru, Tom."

"What a coincidence!" exclaimed Mr. Titus.

"I beg your pardon?" said Mr. Damon, interrogatively.

"I said what a coincidence. I am going there myself."

"Excuse me," interposed Tom, "I don't believe, in the excitement of the moment, I introduced you gentlemen. Allow me—Mr. Damon—Mr. Titus."

The presentation over, Mr. Damon went on:

"You see, Tom, I have lately invested considerable money in a whole-sale drug concern. We deal largely in Peruvian remedies, principally the bark of the cinchona tree, from which quinine is made. Of late there has been some trouble over our concession from the Peruvian government, and the company has decided to send me down there to investigate.

"Of course, as soon as I made up my mind to go I thought of you. So I came over to see if you would not accompany me. All went well until I reached your front gate. Then my horse became frightened by a yellow toy balloon some boy was blowing up in the street and bolted with me. I suppose if it had been a red or green balloon the effect would have been the same. However, here I am, somewhat the worse for wear. Now Tom, what do you say? Will you go to South America—to Peru—with me, and help look up this Quinine business?"

Once more Mr. Titus and Tom looked at each other.

CHAPTER III

A FACE AT THE WINDOW

"What is the matter?" asked Mr. Damon, catching the glance between Tom and the contractor. "Is there anything wrong with South

America—Peru? I know they have lots of revolutions in those countries, but I don't believe Peru is what they call a 'banana republic'; is it?"

"No," and Mr. Titus shook his head. "It isn't a question of revolutions."

"But it's something!" insisted Mr. Damon. "Bless my ink bottle! but it's something. As soon as I mention Peru, Tom, you and Mr. Titus eye each other as if I'd said something dreadful. Out with it! What is it?"

"It's just—just a coincidence," Tom said. "But go on, Mr. Damon. Finish what you have to say and then we'll explain."

"Well, I guess I've told you all you need to know for the present. I went into this wholesale drug concern, hoping to make some money, but now, on account of the trouble down in Peru, we stand to lose considerable unless I can get back the cinchona concession."

"What does that mean?" Tom asked.

"Well, it means that our concern secured from the Peruvian government the right to take this quinine-producing bark from the trees in a certain tropical section. But there has been a change in the government in the district where our men were working, and now the privilege, or concession, has been withdrawn. I'm going down to see if I can't get it back. And I want you to go with me."

"And I came here for very nearly the same thing," went on Mr. Titus. "That is where the coincidence comes in. It is strange that we should both appeal to Mr. Swift at the same time."

"Well, Tom's a valuable helper!" exclaimed Mr. Damon. "I know him of old, for I've been on many a trip with him."

"This is the first time I have had the pleasure of meeting him," resumed the tunnel contractor, "but I have heard of him. I did not ask him to go to South America for us. I only wanted to get some superior explosive for my brother, who is in charge of driving the railroad tunnel through a spur of the Andes. I look after matters up North here, but I may have to go to Peru myself.

"As I told Mr. Swift, I had read of his invention of the giant cannon and the special powder he used in it to send a projectile such a distance. The cannon is now mounted as one of the pieces of ordnance for the defense of the Panama Canal, is it not?" he asked Tom.

The young inventor nodded in assent.

"Having heard of you, and the wonderful explosive used in your big cannon," the contractor went on, "I wrote to my brother that I would try and get some for him.

"You see," he resumed, "this is the situation. Back in the Andes Mountains, a couple of hundred miles east of Lima, the government is building a short railroad line to connect two others. If this is done it will mean that the products of Peru—quinine bark, coffee, cocoa, sugar, rubber, incense and gold can more easily be transported. But to connect the two railroad lines a big tunnel must be constructed.

"My brother and I make a specialty of such work, and when we saw bids advertised for, our firm put in an estimate. There was some trouble with a rival firm, which also bid, but we secured the contract, and bound ourselves to have the tunnel finished within a certain time, or forfeit a large sum.

"That was over a year ago. Since then our men, aided by the native Indians of Peru, have been tunneling the mountain, until, about a month back, we struck a snag."

"What sort of snag?" Tom asked.

"A snag in the shape of extra hard rock," replied the tunnel contractor. "Briefly, Paleozoic rocks make up the eastern part of the Andean Mountains in Peru, while the western range is formed of Mesozoic beds, volcanic ashes and lava of comparatively recent date. Near the coast the lower hills are composed of crystalline rocks, syenite and granite, with, here and there, a strata of sandstone or limestone. These are, undoubtedly, relics of the lower Cretaceous age, and we, or rather, my brother, states that he has found them covered with marine Tertiary deposits.

"Now this Mesozoic band varies greatly. Porphyritic tuffs and massive limestone compose the western chain of the Andes above Lima, while in the Oroya Valley we find carbonaceous sandstones. Some of the tuffs may be of the Jurassic age, though the Cretaceous period is also largely represented.

"Now while these different masses of rock formation offer hard enough problems to the tunnel digger, still we are more or less prepared to meet them, and we figured on a certain percentage of them. Up to the present time we have met with just about what we expected, but what we did not expect was something we came upon when the tunnel had been driven three miles into the mountain."

"What did you find?" asked Tom, who knew enough about geology to understand the terms used. Mr. Damon did not, however, and when Mr. Titus rolled off some of the technical words, the drug investor softly murmured such expressions as

"Bless my thermometer! Bless my porous plaster!"

"We found," resumed Mr. Titus, "after we had bored for a considerable distance into the mountain, a mass of volcanic rock which is so hard that our best diamond drills are dulled in a short time, and the explosives we use merely shatter the face of the cutting, and give us hardly any progress at all.

"It was after several trials, and when my brother found that he was making scarcely any progress, compared to the energy of his men and the blasting, that he wrote to me, explaining matters. I at once thought of you, Tom Swift, and your powerful explosive, for I had read about it.

"Now then, will you sell us some of your powder—explosive or whatever you call it—Mr. Swift, or tell us where we can get it? We need it soon, for we are losing valuable time."

Mr. Titus paused to draw on a piece of paper a rough map of Peru, and the district where the tunnel was being constructed. He showed where the two railroad lines were, and where the new route would bring them together, the tunnel eliminating a big grade up which it would have been impossible to haul trains of any weight.

"What do you say, Mr. Swift?" the contractor concluded. "Will you let us have some of your powder? Or, better still, will you come to Peru yourself? That would suit us immensely, for you could be right on the ground. And you could carry out your plan of going with your friend here," and Mr. Titus nodded toward Mr. Damon. "That is, if you were thinking of going."

"Well, I was thinking of it," Tom admitted. "Mr. Damon and I have been on so many trips together that it seems sort of natural for us to 'team it.' I have never been to Peru, and I should like to see the country. There is only one matter though, that bothers me."

"What is it?" asked Mr. Titus quickly. "If it is a question of money dismiss it from your mind. The Peruvian government is paying a large sum for this tunnel, and we stand to make considerable, even if we were the lowest bidders. We can afford to pay you well—that is, we shall be able to if we can complete the bore on time. That is what is bothering me now—the unexpected strata of hard rock we have met with, which seems impossible to blast. But I feel sure we can do it with the explosive used in your giant cannon."

"That is just the point!" Tom exclaimed. "I am not so sure my explosive would do."

"Why not?" the tunnel contractor asked. "It's powerful enough; isn't it?"

"Yes, it is powerful enough, but whether it will have the right effect on volcanic rock is hard to say. I should like to see a rock sample."

"I can telegraph to have some sent here to you," said Mr. Titus eagerly. "Meantime, here is a description of it. I can read you that"; and, taking a letter from his pocket, he read to Tom a geological description of the hard rock.

"Hum! Yes," mused Tom, as he listened. "It seems to be of the nature of obsidian."

"Bless my watch chain!" cried Mr. Damon. "What's that?"

"Obsidian is a volcanic rock—a sort of combination of glass and flint for hardness," Tom explained. "It is brittle, black in color, and the natives of the Admiralty Islands use it for tipping their spears with which they slay victims for their cannibalistic feasts."

"Bless my—bless my ear-drums!" gasped Mr. Damon. "Cannibals!"

"Obsidian was also used by the ancient Mexicans to make knives and daggers," Tom went on. "When Cortez conquered Mexico he found the priests cutting the hearts from their living victims with knives made from this volcanic glass-like rock, known as obsidian. It may be that your brother has met with a vein of that in the tunnel," Tom said to the contractor.

"Possibly," admitted Mr. Titus.

"In that case," Tom stated, "I may have to use a new kind of explosive. That used for my giant cannon would merely crumble the hard rock for a short distance."

"Then will you accept the contract, and help us out?" asked Mr. Titus eagerly. "We will pay you well. Will you come to Peru and look over the ground?"

"And kill two birds with one stone, and come with me also?" put in Mr. Damon.

Tom pondered for a moment. He was about to answer when the tunnel contractor, who was looking from the library window, suddenly jumped from his chair crying:

"There he is again! Once more dogging me!"

As he rushed from the room, Tom and Mr. Damon had a glimpse of a face at one of the low library windows—a face that had an evil look. It disappeared as Mr. Titus ran from the room.

CHAPTER IV

TOM'S EXPERIMENTS

"Bless my looking glass, Tom, what does that mean?" exclaimed Mr. Damon. "That face!"

"I don't know," answered the young inventor. "But the sight of some one looking in here seemed to disturb Mr. Titus. We must follow him."

"Perhaps he saw your giant Koku looking in," suggested the odd, little man who blessed everything he could think of. "The sight of his face, to any one not knowing him, Tom, would be enough to cause fright."

"It wasn't Koku who looked in the window," said Tom, decidedly. "It was some stranger. Come on."

The young inventor and Mr. Damon hurried out after the tunnel contractor, who was running down the road that led in front of the Swift homestead.

"He's chasing some one, Tom," called Mr. Damon.

"Yes, I see he is. But who?"

"I can't see any one," reported Mr. Damon, who had run down to the gate, at which his horse was still standing. Mr. Damon had washed the dirt from his hands and face, and was wearing one of Mr. Swift's coats in place of his own split one.

Tom joined the eccentric man and together they looked down the road after the running Mr. Titus. They were in half a mind to join him, when they saw him pull up short, raise his hands as though he had given over the pursuit, and turn back.

"I guess he got away, whoever he was," remarked Tom. "We'll walk down and meet Mr. Titus, and ask him what it all means."

Shortly afterward they came up to the contractor, who was breathing heavily after his run, for he was evidently not used to such exercise.

"I beg your pardon, Tom Swift, for leaving you and Mr. Damon in such a fashion," said Mr. Titus, "but I had to act quickly or lose the chance of catching that rascal. As it was, he got away, but I think I gave him a scare, and he knows that I saw him. It will make him more cautious in the future."

"Who was it?" asked Tom.

"Well, I didn't have as close a look as I could have wished for," the contractor said, as he walked back toward the house with Tom and Mr. Damon, "but I'm pretty sure the face that peered in at us through the library window was that of Isaac Waddington."

"And who is he, if it isn't asking information that ought not be given out?" inquired Mr. Damon.

"Oh, no, certainly. I can tell you," said the contractor. "Only perhaps we had better wait until we get back to the house.

"Since one of their men was seen lurking around here there may be others," went on Mr. Titus, when the three were once more seated in the Swift library. "It is best to be on the safe side. The face I saw, I'm sure, was that of Waddington, who is a tool of Blakeson & Grinder, rival tunnel contractors. They put in a bid on this Andes tunnel, but we were lower in our figures by several thousand dollars, and the contract was awarded to us.

"Blakeson & Grinder tried, by every means in their power, to get the job away from us. They even invoked the aid of some Peruvian revolutionists and politicians, but we held our ground and began the work. Since then they have had spies and emissaries on our trail, trying their best to make us fail in our work, so the Peruvian officials might abrogate the contract and give it to them.

"But, so far, we've managed to come out ahead. This Waddington is a sort of spy, and I've found him dodging me several times of late. I suppose he wants to find out my plans so as to be ready to jump in the breach in case we fail."

"Do you think your rivals had anything to do with the difficulties you are now meeting with in digging the tunnel?" asked Mr. Damon. Mr. Titus shook his head.

"The present difficulties are all of Nature's doing," he said. "It's just the abnormally hard rock that is bothering us. Only for that we'd be all right, though we might have petty difficulties because of the mean acts of Blakeson & Grinder. But I don't fear them."

"How do you think this Waddington, if it was he, knew you were coming here?" asked Tom.

"I can only guess. My brother and I have had some correspondence regarding you, Tom Swift. That is, I announced my intention of coming to see you, and my brother wrote me to use my discretion. I wrote back that I would consult you.

"Our main office is in New York, where we employ a large clerical and expert force. There is nothing to prevent one of our stenographers, for instance, turning traitor and giving copies of the letters of my brother and myself to our rivals.

"Mind you, I don't say this was done, and I don't suspect any of our employees, but it would be an easy matter for any one to know my plans. I never thought of making a secret of them, or of my trip here. In some way Waddington found out about the last, and he must have followed me here. Then he sneaked up under the window, and tried to hear what we said."

"Do you think he did?" asked Tom.

"I wouldn't be surprised. We took no pains to lower our voices. But, after all, he hasn't learned much that he didn't know before, if he knew I was coming here. He didn't learn the secret of the explosive that must be used, and that is the vital thing. For I defy him, or any other contractor, to blast that hard rock with any known explosive. We've tried every kind on the market and we've failed. We'll have to depend on you, Tom Swift, to help us out with some of your giant cannon powder."

"And I'm not sure that will work," said the young inventor. "I think I'll have to experiment and make a new explosive, if I conclude to go to Peru."

"Oh, you'll go all right!" declared Mr. Titus with a smile. "I can see that you are eager for the adventures I am sure you'll find there, and, besides, your friend here, Mr. Damon, needs you."

"That's what I do, Tom!" exclaimed the odd man. "Bless my excursion ticket, but you must come!"

"I'll have to invent the new powder first," Tom said.

"That's what I like to hear!" exclaimed Mr. Titus. "It shows you are thinking of coming with us."

Tom only smiled.

"I am so anxious to get the proper explosive," went on Mr. Titus, "that I would even purchase it from our rivals, Blakeson & Grinder, if I thought they had it. But I'm sure they have not, though they may think they can get it.

"That may be the reason they are following me so closely. They may want to know just when we will fail, and have to give up the contract, and they may think they can step in and finish the work. But I don't believe, without your help, Tom Swift, that they can blast that hard rock, and—"

"Well, I'll say this," interrupted Tom, "first come, first served with me, other things being equal. You have applied to me and, like a lawyer, I won't go over to the other side now. I consider myself retained by your firm, Mr. Titus, to invent some sort of explosive, and if I am successful I shall expect to be paid."

"Oh, of course!" cried the contractor eagerly.

"Very good," Tom went on. "You needn't fear that I'll help the other fellows. Now to get down to business. I must see some samples of this rock in order to know what kind of explosive force is needed to rend it."

"I have some in New York," went on the contractor. "I'll have it sent to you at once. I would have brought it, only it is too heavy to carry easily, and I was not sure I could engage you."

"Did that fellow—Waddington, I believe you called him—get away from you?" asked Mr. Damon.

"Clean away," the contractor answered. "He was a better runner than I."

"It doesn't matter much," Tom said. "He didn't hear anything that would benefit him, and I'll give my men orders to be on the lookout for him. What sort of fellow is he, Mr. Titus?"

The contractor described the eavesdropper, and Mr. Damon exclaimed:

"Bless my turkey wish-bone! I'm sure I passed that chap when I was riding over to see you a while ago, Tom."

"You did?"

"Yes, on the highway. He inquired the way to your place. But there was nothing strange in that, since you employ a number of men, and I thought this one was coming to look for work. I can't say I liked his appearance, though."

"No, he isn't a very prepossessing individual," commented Mr. Titus. "Well, now what's the first thing to be done, Tom Swift?"

"Get me some samples of the rock, so I can begin my experiments."

"I'll do that. And now let us consider about going to Peru. For I'm sure you will be successful in your experiments, and will find for us just the powder or explosive we need."

"We can go together." said Mr. Damon. "I shall certainly feel more at home in that wild country if I know Tom Swift is with me, and I will appreciate the help of you and your friends, Mr. Titus, in straightening out the tangles of our drug business."

"I'll do all I can for you, Mr. Damon."

The three then talked at some length regarding possible plans. Tom sent out word to one of his men to keep a sharp watch around the house and grounds, against the possible return of Waddington, but nothing more was seen of him, at least for the time being.

Mr. Titus drew up a sort of tentative agreement with Tom, binding his firm to pay a large sum in case the young inventor was successful, and then the contractor left, promising to have the rock samples come on later by express.

Mr. Damon, after blessing a few dozen more or less impersonal objects, took his departure, his fractious horse having quieted down in the meanwhile, and Tom was left to himself.

"I wonder what I've let myself in for now," the youth mused, as he went back to his laboratory. "It's a new field for me—tunnel blasting. Well, perhaps something may come of it."

But of the strange adventure that was to follow his agreement to help Mr. Titus, our hero, Tom Swift, had not the least inkling.

Tom went back to his labors over the gyroscope problem, but he could arrive at no satisfactory conclusion, and, tossing aside the papers, covered with intricate figures, he exclaimed:

"Oh, I'm going for a walk! This thing is getting on my nerves."

He strolled through the Shopton streets, and as he reached the outskirts of the town, he saw just ahead of him the figure of a girl. Tom quickened his pace, and presently was beside her.

"Where are you going, Mary?" he asked.

"Oh, Tom! How you startled me!" she exclaimed, turning around. "I was just thinking of you."

"Thanks! Something nice?"

"I shan't tell you!" and she blushed. "But where are you going?"

"Walking with you!"

Tom was nothing if not bold.

"Hadn't you better wait until you're asked?" she retorted, mischievously.

"If I did I might not get an invitation. So I'm going to invite myself, and then I'm going to invite you in here to have an ice cream soda," and he and Miss Nestor were soon seated at a table in a candy shop.

Tom had nearly finished his ice cream when he glanced toward the door, and started at the sight of a man who was entering the place.

"What's the matter?" asked Mary. "Did you drop some ice cream, Tom?"

"No, Mary. But that man—"

Mary turned in time to see an excited man hurry out of the candy shop after a hasty glance at Tom Swift.

"Who was he?" the girl asked.

"I—er—oh, some one I thought I knew, but I guess I don't," said Tom, quickly. "Have some more cream, Mary?"

"No, thank you. Not now."

Tom was glad she did not care for any, as he was anxious to get outside, and have a look at the man, for he thought he had recognized the face as the same that had peered in his window. But when he and Miss Nestor reached the front of the shop the strange man was not in sight.

"I guess he came in to cool off after his run," mused Tom, "but when he saw me he didn't care about it. I wonder if that was Waddington? He's a persistent individual if it was he."

"Are you undertaking any new adventures, Tom?" asked Mary.

"Well, I'm thinking of going to Peru."

"Peru!" she cried. "Oh, what a long way to go! And when you get there will you write to me? I'm collecting stamps, and I haven't any from Peru."

"Is that—er—the only reason you want me to write?" asked Tom.

"No," said Mary softly, as she ran up the walk.

Tom smiled as he turned away.

Three days later he received a box from New York. It contained the samples from the Andes tunnel, and Tom at once began his experiments to discover a suitable explosive for rending the hard stone.

"It is compressed molten lava," said Mr. Swift. "You'll never get an explosive that will successfully blast that, Tom."

"We'll see," declared the young inventor.

CHAPTER V

MARY'S PRESENT

Outside a rudely-constructed shack, in the middle of a large field, about a mile away from the nearest of the buildings owned by Tom Swift and his father, were gathered a group of figures one morning. From the shack, trailing over the ground, were two insulated wires, which led to a pile of rocks and earth some distance off. Out of the temporary building came Koku, the giant, bearing in his arms a big rock, of peculiar formation.

"That's it, Koku!" exclaimed Tom Swift. "Now don't drop it on your toes."

"No, Master, me no drop," the giant said, as he strode off with the heavy load as easily as a boy might carry a stone for his sling-shot.

Koku placed the big rock on top of the pile of dirt and stones and came back to the hut, just as Eradicate, the colored man-of-all-work, emerged. Koku was not looking ahead, and ran into Eradicate with such force that the latter would have fallen had not the giant clasped his big arms about him.

"Heah now! Whut yo' all doin' t' me?" angrily demanded Eradicate. "Yo' done gone an' knocked de breff outen me, dat's whut yo' all done! I'll bash yo' wif a rock, dat's what I'll do!"

Koku, laughing, tried to explain that it was all an accident, but Eradicate would not listen. He looked about for a stone to throw at the giant, though it was doubtful, with his feeble strength, and considering the great frame of the big man, if any damage would have been done. But Eradicate saw no rocks nearer than the pile in which ended the two insulated wires, and, with mutterings, the negro set off in that direction, shuffling along on his rheumatic legs.

From the shack Tom Swift hailed:

"Hi there, Rad! Come back! Where are you going?"

"I'se gwine t' git a rock, Massa Tom, an' bash de haid ob dat big lummox ob a giant! He done knocked de breff outen me, so he did."

"You come back from that stone pile!" Tom ordered. "I'm going to blow it up in a minute, and if you get too near you'll have the breath knocked out of you worse than Koku did it. Come back, I say!"

But Eradicate was obstinate and kept on. Tom, who was adjusting a firing battery in the shack, laughed, and then in exasperation cried:

"Koku, go and get him and bring him back. Carry him if he won't come any other way. I don't want the dear old chump to get the fright of his life, and he sure will if he goes too close. Bring him back!"

"Koku bring, Master," was the giant's answer.

He ran toward Eradicate, who, seeing his tormentor approaching, redoubled his shuffling pace toward the stone pile. But he was no match for the giant, who, ignoring his struggles, picked up Eradicate, and, flinging him over his shoulder like a sack of meal, brought him to the shack.

"There him be, Master!" said the giant.

"So I see," laughed Torn. "Now you stay here, Rad."

"No, sah! No, sah, Massa Tom! I—I'se gwine t' git a rock an'—an' bash his haid—dat's what I'se gwine t' do!" and the colored man tried to struggle to his feet.

"Look out now!" cried Tom, suddenly. "If things go right there won't be a rock left for you to 'bash' anybody's head with, Rad. Look out!"

The three cowered inside the shack, which, though it was rudely made, was built of heavy logs and planks, with a fronting of sod and bags of sand.

Tom turned a switch. There was a loud report, and where the stone pile had been there was a big hole in the ground, while the air was filled with fragments of rock and dirt. These came down in a shower on the roof of the shack, and Eradicate covered his ears with his trembling hands.

"Am—am de world comin' to de end, Massa Tom?" he asked. "Am dat Gabriel's trump I done heah?"

"No, you dear old goose!" laughed the young inventor. "That was just a charge of my new explosive—a small charge, too. But it seems to have done the work."

He ran from the shack to the place where the rock pile had been, and picked up several small fragments.

"Busted all to pieces!" exulted Tom Swift. "Not a piece left as big as a hickory nut. That's going some! I've got the right mixture at last. If an ounce did that, a few hundred pounds ought to knock that Andes tunnel through the mountain in no time. I'll telegraph to Mr. Titus."

Leaving Koku and Rad to collect the wires and firing apparatus, there being no danger now, as no explosive was left in the shack, Tom made his way back to the house. His father met him.

"Well, Tom," he asked, "another failure?"

"No, Dad! Success! This time I turned the trick. I seem to have gotten just the right mixture. Look, these are some of the pieces left from the big rock—one of the samples Mr. Titus sent me. It was all cracked up as small as this," and he held out the fragments he had picked up in the field.

Mr. Swift regarded them for a few moments.

"That's better, Tom," he said. "I didn't think you could get an explosive that would successfully shatter that hard rock, but you seem to have done it. Have you the formula all worked out?"

"All worked out, Dad. I only made a small quantity, but the same proportions will hold good for the larger amounts. I'm going to start in and make it now. And then—Ho! for Peru!"

Tom struck an attitude, such as some old discoverer might have assumed, and then he hurried into the house to telephone a telegram to the Shopton office. The message was to Mr. Titus, and read:

"Explosive success. Start making it at once. Ready for Peru in month's time."

"Thirteen words," repeated Tom, as the operator called them back to him. "I hope that doesn't mean bad luck."

The experiment which Tom Swift had just brought to a successful conclusion was one of many he had conducted, extending over several wearying weeks.

As soon as Tom had received the samples of the rock he had begun to experiment. First he tried some of the explosive that was so successful in the giant cannon. As he had feared, it was not what was needed. It cracked the rock, but did not disintegrate it, and that was what was needed. The hard rock must be broken up into fragments that could be easily handled. Merely to crack it necessitated further explosions, which would only serve to split it more and perhaps wedge it fast in the tunnel.

So Tom tried different mixtures, using various chemicals, but none seemed to be just right. The trials were not without danger, either. Once, in mixing some ingredients, there was an explosion that injured one man, and blew Tom some distance away. Fortunately for him, there was an open window in the direction in which he was propelled, and he went through that, escaping with only some cuts and bruises.

Another time there was a hang-fire, and the explosive burned instead of detonating, so that one of the shops caught, and there was no little work in subduing the flames.

But Tom would not give up, and finally, after many trials, he hit on what he felt to be the right mixture. This he took out to the big lot, and having made a miniature tunnel with some of the sample rock, and having put some of the explosive in a hole bored in the big chunk Koku carried, Tom fired the charge. The result we have seen. It was a success.

A day after receiving Tom's message Mr. Titus came on and a demonstration was given of the powerful explosive.

"Tom, that's great!" cried the tunnel contractor. "Our troubles are at an end now."

But, had he known it, new ones were only just beginning.

Tom at once began preparations for making the explosive on a large scale, as much of it would be needed in the Andes tunnel. Then, having turned the manufacturing end of it over to his men, Tom began his preparations for going to Peru.

Mr. Damon was also getting ready, and it was arranged that he, with Tom and Mr. Titus, should take a vessel from San Francisco, crossing the continent by train. The supply of explosive would follow them by special freight.

"We might have gone by Panama except for the slide in the canal," Tom said. "And I suppose I could take you across the continent in my airship, Mr. Titus, if you object to railroad travel."

"No, thank you, Tom. If it's just the same to you, I'd rather stay on the ground," the contractor said. "I'm more used to it."

A day or so before the start for San Francisco was to be made, Tom, passing a store in Shopton, saw something in the window he thought Mary Nestor would like. It was a mahogany work-box, of unique design, beautifully decorated, and Tom purchased it.

"Shall I have it sent?" asked the clerk.

"No, thank you," Tom answered.

He knew the young lady who had waited on him, and, for reasons of his own, he did not want her to know that Mary was to get the box.

Carrying the present to his laboratory, Tom prepared to wrap it up suitably to send to Mary, with a note. Just, however, as he was looking for a box suitable to contain the gift, he received a summons to the telephone. Mr. Titus, in New York, wanted to speak to him.

"Here, Rad!" Tom called. "Just box this up for me, like a good fellow, and then take it to Miss Nestor at this address; will you?" and Tom handed his man the addressed letter he had written to Mary. "Be careful of it," Tom cautioned.

"Oh, I'll be careful, Massa Tom," was the reply. "I'll shore be careful."

And Eradicate was—all too careful.

CHAPTER VI

MR. NESTOR'S LETTER

"Got t' git a good strong box fo' dish yeah," murmured Eradicate, as he looked at the beautiful mahogany present Tom had turned over to him to take to Mary. "Mah Landy! Dat suttinly am nice; Ah! Um! Jest laik some ob de old mahogany furniture dat was in our fambily down Souf." Eradicate did not mean his family, exactly, but the one in which he had been a slave.

"Yassum, dat shore am nice!" he went on, talking to himself as he admired the present. "I shore got t' put dat in a good box! An' dish year note, too. Let's see what it done say on de outside."

Eradicate held the envelope carefully upside down, and read—or rather pretended to read—the name and address. Eradicate knew well enough where Mary lived, for this was not the first time he had gone there with messages from his young master.

"Massa Tom shore am a fine writer," mused the negro, as he slowly turned the envelope around. "I cain't read nobody's writin' but hisen, nohow."

Had Eradicate been strictly honest with himself, he would have confessed that he could not read any writing, or printing either. His education had been very limited, but one could show him, say, a printed sign and tell him it read "Danger" or "Five miles to Branchville," or anything like that, and the next time he saw it, Eradicate would know what that sign said. He seemed to fix a picture of it in his mind, though the letters and figures by themselves meant nothing to him. So when Tom told him the envelope contained the name and address of Miss Nestor, Eradicate needed nothing more.

He rummaged about in some odds and ends in the corner of the laboratory, and brought out a strong, wooden box, which had a cover that screwed down.

"Dat'll be de ticket!" Eradicate exclaimed. "De mahogany present will jest fit." Eradicate took some excelsior to pad the box, and then, dropping inside it the gift, already wrapped in tissue paper, he proceeded to screw on the cover.

There was something printed in red letters on the outside box, but Eradicate could not read, so it did not trouble him.

"Dat Miss Nestor shore will laik her present," he murmured. "An' I'll be mighty keerful ob it' laik Massa Tom tole me. He wouldn't trust dat big lummox Koku wif anyt'ing laik dis."

Screwing on the cover, and putting a piece of wrapping paper outside the rough, wooden box, with the letter in his hand, Eradicate, full of his own importance, set off for Miss Nestor's house. Tom had not returned from the telephone, over which he was talking to Mr. Titus.

The message was an important one. The contractor said he had received word from his brother in Peru that his presence was urgently needed there.

"Could you arrange to get off sooner than we planned, Tom?" asked Mr. Titus. "I am afraid something has happened down there. Have you sent the first shipment of explosive?"

"Yes, that went three days ago. It ought to arrive at Lima soon after we do. Why yes, I can start tonight if we have to. I'll find out if Mr. Damon can be with us on such short notice."

"I wish you would," came from Mr. Titus. "And say, Tom, do you think you could take that giant Koku with you?"

"Why?"

"Well, I think he'd come in handy. There are some pretty rough characters in those Andes Mountains, and your big friend might be useful."

"All right. I was thinking of it, anyhow. Glad you mentioned it. Now I'll call up Mr. Damon, and I'll let you know, in an hour or so, if he can make it."

"Bless my hair brush, yes, Tom!" exclaimed the eccentric man, when told of the change in plans. "I can leave tonight as well as not."

Word to this effect was sent on to Mr. Titus, and then began some hurrying on the part of Tom Swift. He told Koku to get ready to leave for New York at once, where he and the giant would join Mr. Titus and Mr. Damon, and start across the continent to take for steamer for Lima, Peru.

"Rad, did you send that present to Miss Nestor?" asked Tom, later, as he finished packing his grip.

"Yas, sah. I done did it. Took it mase'f!"

"That's good! I guess I'll have to say good-bye to Mary over the telephone. I won't have time to call. I'm glad I thought of the present."

Tom got the Nestor house on the wire. But Mary was not in.

"There's a package here for her," said the girl's mother. "Did you—?"

"Yes, I sent that," Tom said. "Sorry I won't be able to call and say good-bye, but I'm in a terrible rush. I'll see her as soon as I get back, and I'll write as soon as I arrive."

"Do," urged Mrs. Nestor. "We'll all be glad to hear from you," for Tom and Mary were tentatively engaged to be married.

Tom and Koku went on with their hurried preparations to leave for New York. Eradicate begged to be taken along, but Tom gently told the faithful old servant that it was out of the question.

"Besides, Rad," he said, "it's dangerous in those Andes Mountains. Why, they have birds there, as big as cows, and they can swoop down and carry off a man your size."

"Am dat shorely so, Massa Tom?"

"Of course it is! You get the dictionary and read about the condors of the Andes Mountains."

"Dat's what I'll do, Massa Tom. Birds as big as cows what kin pick up a man in dere beaks, an' carry him off! Oh, my! No, sah, Massa Tom! I don't want t' go. I'll stay right yeah!"

Shortly before Tom and Koku departed for the railroad station, where they were to take a train for New York, Mary Nestor returned home.

"Tom called you on the telephone to say good-bye," her mother informed her, "and said he was sorry he could not see you. But he sent some sort of gift."

"Oh, how sweet of him!" Mary exclaimed. "Where is it?"

"On the dining room table. Eradicate brought it with a note."

Mary read the note first.

In it Tom begged Mary to accept the little token, and to think of him when she used it.

"Oh! I wonder what it can be," she cried in delight.

"Better open it and see," advised Mr. Nestor, who had come in at that moment.

Mary cut the string of the outside paper, and folded back the wrapper. A wooden box was exposed to view, a solid, oblong, wooden box, and on the top, in bold, red letters Mary, her father and her mother read:

DYNAMITE! HANDLE WITH CARE!

"Oh! Oh!" murmured Mrs. Nestor.

"Dynamite! Handle with care!" repeated Mr. Nestor, in a sort of dazed voice. "Quick! Get a pail of water! Dump it in the bathtub! Soak it good, and then telephone for the police. Dynamite! What does this mean?"

He rushed toward the kitchen, evidently with the intention of getting a pail of water, but Mary clasped him by the arm.

"Father!" she exclaimed. "Don't get so excited!"

"Excited!" he cried. "Who's excited? Dynamite! We'll all be blown up! This is some plot! I don't believe Tom sent this at all! Look out! Call the police! Excited! Who's getting excited?"

"You are, Daddy dear!" said Mary calmly. "This is some mistake. Tom did send this—I know his writing. And wasn't it Eradicate who brought this package, Mother?"

"Yes, my dear. But your father is right. Let him put it in water, then it will be safe. Oh, we'll all be blown up. Get the water!"

"No!" cried Mary. "There is some mistake. Tom wouldn't send me dynamite. There must be a present for me in there. Tom must have put it in the wrong box by mistake. I'm going to open it."

Mary's calmness had its effect on her parents. Mr. Nestor cooled down, as did his wife, and a closer examination of the outer box did not seem to show that it was an infernal machine of any kind.

"It's all a mistake, Daddy," Mary said. "I'll show you. Get me a screw driver."

After some delay one was found, and Mr. Nestor himself opened the box. When the tissue paper wrappings of the mahogany gift were revealed he gave a sigh of relief, and when Mary undid the wrappings, and saw what Tom had sent her, she cried:

"Oh, how perfectly dear! Just what I wanted! I wonder how he knew? Oh, I just love it!" and she hugged the beautiful box in her arms.

"Humph!" exclaimed Mr. Nestor, a slowly gathering light of anger showing in his eyes. "It is a nice present, but that is a very poor sort of joke to play, in my estimation."

"Joke! What joke?" asked Mary.

"Putting a present in a box labeled Dynamite, and giving us such a scare," went on her father.

"Oh, Father, I'm sure he didn't mean to do it!" Mary said, earnestly.

"Well, maybe he didn't! He may have thought it a joke, and he may not have! But, at any rate, it was a piece of gross carelessness on his part, and I don't care to consider for a son-in-law a young man as careless as that!"

"Oh, Daddy!" expostulated Mary.

"Now, now! Tut, tut!" exclaimed Mr. Nestor. "It isn't your fault, Mary, but this Tom Swift must be taught a lesson. He was careless, if nothing worse, and, for all he knew, there might have been some stray bits of dynamite in that packing box. It won't do! It won't do! I'll write him a letter, and give him a piece of my mind!"

And in spite of all his wife and his daughter could say, Mr. Nestor did write Tom a scathing letter. He accused him of either perpetrating a joke, or of being careless, or both, and he intimated that the less he saw of Tom at the Nestor home hereafter the better pleased he would be.

"There! I guess that will make him wish he hadn't done it!" exclaimed Mr. Nestor, as he called a messenger and sent the letter to Tom's house.

Mary and her mother did not know the contents of the note, but Mary tried to get Tom on the wire and explain. However, she was unable to reach him, as Tom was on the point of leaving.

The messenger, with Mr. Nestor's letter, arrived just as our hero was receiving the late afternoon mail from the postman, and just as Tom and Koku were getting in an automobile to leave for the depot.

"Good-bye, Dad!" Tom called. "Good-bye, Mrs. Baggert!" He thrust Mr. Nestor's letter, unopened, together with some other mail matter, which he took to be merely circulars, into an inner pocket, and jumped into the car.

Tom and Koku were off on the first stage of their journey.

CHAPTER VII

OFF FOR PERU

"Well, Tom Swift, you're on time I see," was Mr. Job Titus' greeting, when our hero, and Koku, the giant, alighted from a taxicab in New York, in front of the hotel the contractor had appointed as a meeting place.

"Yes, I'm here."

"Did you have a good trip?"

"Oh, all right, yes. Nothing happened to speak of, though we were delayed by a freight wreck. Has Mr. Damon got here yet?"

"Not yet, Tom. But I had a message saying he was on his way. Come on up to the rooms I have engaged. Hello, what's all the crowd here for?" asked the contractor in some surprise, for a throng had gathered at the hotel entrance.

"I expect it's Koku they're staring at," announced Tom, and the giant it was who had attracted the attention. He was carrying his own big valise, and a small steamer trunk belonging to Tom, as easily as though they weighed nothing, the trunk being under one arm.

"I guess they don't see men of his size outside of circuses," commented the contractor. "We can pretty nearly, though not quite match him, down in Peru though, Tom. Some of the Indians are big fellows."

"We'll get up a wrestling match between one of them and Koku," suggested Tom. "Come on!" he called to the giant, who was surrounded by a crowd.

Koku pushed his way through as easily as a bull might make his way through a throng of puppies about his heels, and as Tom, Mr. Titus and the giant were entering the hotel corridor, the chauffeur of the taxicab called out with a laugh:

"I say, boss, don't you think you ought to pay double rates on that chap," and he nodded in the direction of the giant.

"That's right!" added some one in the crowd with a laugh. "He might have broken the springs."

"All right," assented Tom, good-naturedly, tossing the chauffeur a coin. "Here you are, have a cigar on the giant."

There was more laughter, and even Koku grinned, though it is doubtful if he knew what about, for he could not understand much unless Tom spoke to him in a sort of code they had arranged between them.

"Sorry to have hastened your departure," began Mr. Titus when he and Tom sat in the comfortable hotel rooms, while Koku stood at a window, looking out at what to him were the marvelous wonders of the New York streets.

"It didn't make any difference," replied the young inventor. "I was about ready to come anyhow. I just had to hustle a little," and he thought of how he had had to send Mary's present to her instead of taking it himself. As yet he was all unaware of the commotion it had caused.

"Did you get the powder shipment off all right?"

"Yes, and it will be there almost as soon as we. Other shipments will follow as we need them. My father will see to that."

"I'm glad you hit on the right kind of powder," went on the contractor. "I guess I didn't make any mistake in coming to you, Tom."

"Well, I hope not. Of course the explosive worked all right in experimental charges with samples of the tunnel rock. It remains to be seen what it will do under actual conditions, and in big service charges."

"Oh, I've no doubt it will work all right."

"What time do we leave here?" Tom asked.

"At two-thirty this afternoon. We have just time to get a good dinner and have our baggage transferred to the Chicago limited. In less than a week we ought to be in San Francisco and aboard the steamer. I hope Mr. Damon arrives on time."

"Oh, you can generally depend on him," said Tom. "I telephoned him, just before I started from Shopton, and he said—"

"Bless my carpet slippers!" cried a voice outside the hotel apartment. "But I can find my way all right. I know the number of the room. No! you needn't take my bag. I can carry it my self!"

"There he is!" laughed Tom, opening the door to disclose the eccentric gentleman himself, struggling to keep possession of his valise against the importunities of a bellboy.

"Ah, Tom—Mr. Titus! Glad to see you!" exclaimed Mr. Damon. "I—I am a little late, I fear—had an accident—wait until I get my breath," and he sank, panting, into a chair.

"Accident?" cried Tom. "Are you—?"

"Yes—my taxicab ran into another. Nobody hurt though."

"But you're all out of breath," said Mr. Titus. "Did you run?"

"No, but I walked upstairs."

"What! Seven flights?" exclaimed Tom. "Weren't the hotel elevators running?"

"Yes, but I don't like them. I'd rather walk. And I did—carried my valise—bellboy tried to take it away from me every step—here you are, son—it wasn't the tip I was trying to get out of," and he tossed the waiting and grinning lad a quarter.

"There, I'm better now," went on Mr. Damon, when Tom had given him a glass of water. "Bless my paper weight! The drug concern will have to vote me an extra dividend for what I've gone through. Well, I'm here, anyhow. How is everything?"

"Fine!" cried Tom. "We'll soon be off for Peru!"

They talked over plans and made sure nothing had been forgotten. Their railroad tickets had been secured by Mr. Titus so there was nothing more to do save wait for train-time.

"I've never been to Peru," Tom remarked shortly before lunch. "What sort of country is it?"

"Quite a wonderful country," Mr. Titus answered. "I have been very much interested in it since my brother and I accepted this tunnel contract. Peru seems to have taken its name from Peru, a small river on the west coast of Colombia, where Pizarro landed. The country, geographically, may be divided into three sections longitudinally. The coast region is a sandy desert, with here and there rivers flowing through fertile valleys. The sierra region is the Andes division, about two hundred and fifty miles in width."

"Is that where we're going?" asked Tom.

"Yes. And beyond the Andes (which in Peru consist of great chains of mountains, some very high, interspersed with table lands, rich plains and valleys) there is the montana region of tropical forests, running down to the valley of the Amazon.

"That sounds interesting," commented Mr. Damon.

"It is interesting," declared Mr. Titus. "For it is from this tropical region that your quinine comes, Mr. Damon, though you may not have to go there to straighten out your affairs. I think you can do better bargaining with the officials in Lima, or near there."

"Are there any wild animals in Peru?" Tom inquired.

"Well, not many. Of course there are the llamas and alpacas, which are the beasts of burden—almost like little camels you might say, though much more gentle. Then there is the wild vicuna, the fleece of which is made into a sort of wool, after which a certain kind of cloth is named.

"Then there is the taruco, a kind of deer, the viscacha, which is a big rat, the otoc, a sort of wild dog, or fox, and the ucumari, a black bear with a white nose. This bear is often found on lofty mountain tops, but only when driven there in search of food.

"The condors, of course, are big birds of prey in the Andes. You must have read about them; how they seem to lie in the upper regions of the air, motionless, until suddenly they catch sight of some dead animal far down below when they sweep toward it with the swiftness of the wink. There is another bird of the vulture variety, with wings of black and white feathers. The ancient Incas used to decorate their head dresses with these wing feathers."

"Well, I'm glad I'm going to Peru," said Tom. "I never knew it was such an interesting country. But I don't suppose we'll have time to see much of it."

"Oh, I think you will," commented Mr. Titus. "We don't always have to work on the tunnel. There are numerous holidays, or holy-days, which our Indian workers take off, and we can do nothing without them. I'll see that you have a chance to do some exploring if you wish."

"Good!" exclaimed Tom. "I brought my electric rifle with me, and I may get a chance to pop over one of those bears with a white nose. Are they good to eat?"

"The Indians eat them, I believe, when they can get them, but I wouldn't fancy the meat," said the contractor.

Luncheon over, the three travelers departed with their baggage for the Chicago Limited, which left from the Pennsylvania Station at Twenty-third Street. As usual, Koku attracted much attention because of his size.

The trip to San Francisco was without incident worth narrating and in due time our friends reached the Golden Gate where they were to go aboard their steamer. They had to wait a day, during which time Tom and

Mr. Titus made inquiries regarding the first powder shipment. They had had unexpected good luck, for the explosive, having been sent on ahead by fast freight, was awaiting them.

"So we can take it with us on the Bellaconda," said, Tom, naming the vessel on which they were to sail.

The powder was safely stowed away, and our friends having brought their baggage aboard, putting what was wanted on the voyage in their staterooms, went out on deck to watch the lines being cast off.

A bell clanged and an officer cried:

"All ashore that's going ashore!"

There were hasty good-byes, a scramble on the part of those who had come to bid friends farewell, and preparations were made to haul in the gangplank.

Just as the tugs were slowly pushing against the Bellaconda to get her in motion to move her away from the wharf, there was a shout down the pier and a taxicab, driven at reckless speed, dashed up.

"Wait a minute! Hold that gangway. I have a passenger for you!" cried the chauffeur.

He pulled up with a screeching of brakes, and a man with a heavy black beard fairly leaped from the vehicle, running toward the plank which was all but cast off.

"My fare! My fare!" yelled the taxicab driver.

"Take it out of that! Keep the change!" cried the bearded man over his shoulder, tossing a crumpled bill to the chauffeur. And then, clutching his valise in a firm hand, the belated passenger rushed up the gangplank just in time to board the steamer which was moving away from the dock.

"Close shave—that," observed Tom.

"That's right," assented Mr. Titus.

"Well, we're off for Peru!" exclaimed Mr. Damon, as the vessel moved down the bay.

CHAPTER VIII

THE BEARDED MAN

Travel to Tom and Mr. Damon presented no novelties. They had been on too many voyages over the sea, under the sea and even in the air above the sea to find anything unusual in merely taking a trip on a steamer.

Mr. Titus, though he admitted he had never been in a submarine or airship, had done considerable traveling about the world in his time, and had visited many countries, either for business or pleasure, so he was an old hand at it.

But to Koku, who, since he had been brought from the land where Tom Swift had been made captive, had gone about but little, everything was novel, and he did not know at what to look first.

The giant was interested in the ship, in the water, in the passengers, in the crew and in the sights to be seen as they progressed down the harbor.

And the big man himself was a source of wonder to all save his own party. Everywhere he went about the decks, or below, he was followed by a staring but respectful crowd. Koku took it all good-naturedly, however, and even consented to show his great strength by lifting heavy weights. Once when several sailors were shifting one of the smaller anchors (a sufficiently heavy one for all that) Koku pushed them aside with a sweep of his big arm, and, picking up the big "hook," turned to the second mate and asked:

"Where you want him?"

"Good land, man!" cried the astonished officer. "You'll kill yourself!"

But Koku carried the anchor where it ought to go, and from then on he was looked up to with awe and admiration by the sailors.

From San Francisco to Callao, Peru (the latter city being the seaport of Lima, which is situated inland), is approximately nine hundred miles. But as the Bellaconda was a coasting steamer, and would make several stops on her trip, it would be more than a week before our friends would land at Callao, then to proceed to Lima, where they expected to remain a day or so before striking into the interior to where the tunnel was being bored through the mountain.

The first day was spent in getting settled, becoming used to their new surroundings, finding their places and neighbors at table, and in making acquaintances. There were some interesting men and women aboard the Bellaconda, and Tom Swift, Mr. Damon and Mr. Titus soon made friends with them. This usually came about through the medium of Koku, the giant. Persons seeing him would inquire about him, and when they learned he was Tom Swift's helper it was an easy topic with which to open conversation.

Tom told, modestly enough, how he had come to get Koku in his escape from captivity, but Mr. Damon was not so simple in describing Tom's feats, so that before many days had passed our hero found himself regarded as a personage of considerable importance, which was not at all to his liking.

"But bless my fountain pen!" cried Mr. Damon, when Tom objected to so much notoriety. "You did it all; didn't you?"

"Yes, I know. But these people won't believe it."

"Oh, yes they will!" said the odd man. "I'll take good care that they believe it."

"If any one say it not so, you tell me!" broke Koku, shaking his huge fist.

"No, I guess I'd better keep still," said Tom, with a laugh.

The weather was pleasant, if we except a shower or two, and as the vessel proceeded south, tropical clothing became the order of the day, while all who could, spent most of their time on deck under the shade of awnings.

"Did you ever hear anything more of that fellow, Waddington?" asked Tom of Mr. Titus one day.

"Not a thing. He seems to have dropped out of sight."

"And are your rivals, Blakeson & Grinder, making any trouble?"

"Not that I've heard of. Though just what the situation may be down in Peru I don't know. I fancy everything isn't going just right or my brother would not be so anxious for me to come on in such a hurry."

"Do you anticipate any real trouble?"

Mr. Titus paused a moment before answering.

"Well, yes," he said, finally, "I do!"

"What sort?" asked Tom.

"That I can't say. I'll be perfectly frank with you, Tom. You know I told you at the time that we were in for difficulties. I didn't want you to go into this thing blindly."

"Oh, I'm not afraid of trouble," Tom hastened to assure his friend. "I've had more or less of it in my life, and I'm willing to meet it again. Only I like to know what kind it is."

"Well, I can't tell you—exactly," went an the tunnel contractor. "Those rivals of ours, Blakeson & Grinder, are unscrupulous fellows. They feel very bitter about not getting the contract, I hear. And they would be only too glad to have us fail in the work. That would mean that they, as the next lowest bidders, would be given the job. And we would have to make up the difference out of our pockets, as well as lose all the work we have, so far, put on the tunnel."

"And you don't want that to happen!"

"I guess not, my boy! Well, it won't happen if we get there in time with this new explosive of yours. That will do the business I'm sure."

"I hope so," murmured Tom. "Well, we'll soon see. And now I think I'll go and write a few letters. We are going to put in at Panama, and I can mail them there."

Tom started for his stateroom, and rapidly put his hand in the inner pocket of his coat. He drew out a bundle of letters and papers, and, as he looked at them, a cry of astonishment came from his lips.

"What's the matter?" asked Mr. Titus.

"Matter!" cried Tom. "Why here's a letter from Mary—from Mr. Nestor," he went on, as he scanned the familiar handwriting. "I never opened it! Let's see—when did I get that?"

His memory went back to the day of his departure from Shopton when he had sent Mary the gift, and he recalled that the letter had arrived just as he was getting into the automobile.

"I stuck it in my pocket with some other mail," he mused, "and I never thought of it again until just now. But this is the first time I've worn this coat since that day. A letter from Mr. Nestor! Probably Mary wrote, thanking me for the box, and her father addressed the envelope for her. Well, let's see what it says."

Tom retired to the privacy of his stateroom to read the note, but he had not glanced over more than the first half of it before he cried out:

"Dynamite! Great Scott! What does this mean? 'Gross carelessness! Poor idea of a joke! No person with your idea of responsibility will ever be my son-in-law!' Box labeled 'open with care!' Why—why—what does it all mean?"

Tom read the letter over again, and his murmurs of astonishment were so loud that Mr. Damon, in the next room, called out:

"What's the matter, Tom? Get bad news?"

"Bad news? I should say so! Mary—her father—he forbids me to see her again. Says I tried to dynamite them all—or at least scare them into believing I was going to. I can't understand it!"

"Tell me about it, Tom," suggested Mr. Damon, coming into Tom's stateroom. "Bless my gunpowder keg! what does it mean?"

Thereupon Tom told of having purchased the gift for Mary, and of having, at the last minute, told Eradicate to put it in a box and deliver it at the Nestor home.

"Which he evidently did," Tom went on, "but when it got there Mary's present was in a box labeled 'Dynamite. Handle with care.' I never sent that."

Mr. Damon read over Mr. Nestor's letter which had lain so long in Tom's pocket unopened.

"I think I see how it happened," said the old man. "Eradicate can't read; can he, Tom?"

"No, but he pretends he can."

"And did you have any empty boxes marked dynamite in your laboratory?"

"Why yes, I believe I did. I used dynamite as one of the ingredients of my new explosive."

"Well then, it's as clear as daylight. Eradicate, being unable to read, took one of the empty dynamite boxes in which to pack Mary's present. That's how it happened."

Tom thought for a moment. Then he burst into a laugh.

"That's it," he said, a bit ruefully. "That's the explanation. No wonder Mr. Nestor was roiled. He thought I was playing a joke. I'll have to explain. But how?"

"By letter," said Mr. Damon.

"Too slow. I'll send a wireless," decided Tom, and he began the composition of a message that cost him considerable in tolls before he had hit on the explanation that suited him.

"That ought to clear the atmosphere," he said when the wireless had shot his message into the ether. "Whew! And to think, all this while, Mary and her folks have believed that I tried to play a miserable joke on them! My! My! I wonder if they'll ever forgive me. When I get hold of Eradicate—"

"Better teach him to read if he's going to do up love packages," interrupted Mr. Damon, dryly.

"I will," decided the young inventor.

The Bellaconda stopped at Panama and then kept on her way south. Soon after that she ran into a severe tropical storm, and for a time there was some excitement among the passengers. The more timid of them put on life preservers, though the captain and his officers assured them there was no danger.

Tom and Mr. Titus, descending from the deck, whence they had been warned by one of the mates, were on their way to their stateroom, walking with some difficulty owing to the roll of the ship.

As they approached their quarters the door of a stateroom farther up the passage opened, and a head was thrust out.

"Will you send a steward to me?" a man requested. "I am feeling very ill, and need assistance."

"Certainly," Tom answered, and at that moment he heard Mr. Titus utter an exclamation.

"What is it?" asked Tom, for the man who had appealed for help, had withdrawn his head.

"That—that man!" exclaimed the contractor. "That was Waddington, the tool of our rivals."

"Waddington!" repeated Tom, with a look at the now closed door. "Why, the bearded man has that stateroom—the bearded man who so nearly lost the steamer. He isn't Waddington!"

"And I tell you Waddington is in that room!" insisted the contractor. "I only saw the upper part of his face, but I'd know his eyes anywhere. Waddington is spying on us!"

CHAPTER IX

THE BOMB

Tom Swift and Mr. Titus withdrew a little way down the corridor, around a bulkhead and out of sight of any one who might look out from the stateroom whence had come the appeal for help. But, at the same time, they could keep watch over it.

"I tell you Waddington is in there!" insisted Mr. Titus, hoarsely whispering.

"Well, perhaps he may be," admitted Tom. "But several times I have seen the bearded man going in there, and it's only a single stateroom, for it's so marked on the deck plan."

"Waddington might be disguised with a false beard, Tom."

"Yes, he might. But did the man who just now looked out have a beard?"

"I couldn't tell, as I saw only the upper part of his face. But those were Waddington's shifty eyes, I'm positive."

"If Waddington were on board don't you suppose you would have seen him before this?"

"Not positively, no. If he and the bearded man are one and the same that would account for it. But I haven't noticed the bearded man once since he came aboard in such a hurry."

"Nor have I, now that I come to think of it," Tom admitted. "However, there is an easy way to prove who is in there."

"How?"

"We'll knock on the door and go in."

"Perhaps he won't let us."

"He'll think it's the steward he called for. Come, you know Waddington better than I do. You knock and go in."

"I don't know Waddington very well," admitted the contractor. "I have only seen him a few times, but I am sure that was he. But what shall I do when he sees I'm not the steward?"

"Tell him you have sent for one. I'll go with the message, so it will be true enough. Even if you have only a momentary glance at him in close quarters you ought to be able to tell whether or not he has on a false beard, and whether or not it is Waddington."

Mr. Titus considered for a moment, and then he said:

"Yes, I guess that is a good plan. You go for the steward, Tom, and I'll see if I can get in that stateroom. But I'm sure I'm not mistaken. I'll find Waddington in there, perhaps in the person of the bearded man, disguised. Or else they are using a single stateroom as a double one." And while Tom went off down the pitching and rolling corridor to find a steward, Mr. Titus, not without some apprehension, advanced to knock on the door of the suspect.

"If it is Waddington he'll know me at once, of course," thought the contractor, "and there may be a row. Well, I can't help it. The success of my brother and myself depends on finishing that tunnel, and we can't have Waddington, and those whose tool he is, interfering. Here goes!"

He tapped on the door, and a faint voice called:

"Come in!"

The contractor entered, and saw the bearded man lying in his berth.

"Is there anything I can do for you?" asked the contractor, bending close over the man. He wanted to see if the beard were false. Somewhat to his surprise the contractor saw that undoubtedly it was real.

"Steward, will you kindly get me—Oh, you're not the steward!" the bearded man exclaimed.

"No, my friend and I heard you call," replied the contractor. "He has gone for the steward, who will be here soon. Can I do anything for you in the meanwhile?"

"No—not a thing!" was the rather snappish answer, and the man turned his face away. "I beg your pardon," he went on, as if conscious that he had acted rudely, "but I am suffering very much. The steward knows just what I want. I have had these attacks before. I am a poor sailor. If you will send the steward to me I will be obliged to you. He can fix me up."

"Very well," assented Mr. Titus. "But if there is anything I can do—"

At that moment footsteps and voices were heard in the corridor, and as the door of the bearded man's stateroom was opened, Mr. Titus had a glimpse of Tom and one of the stewards.

"Yes, I'll look after him," the steward said "He's been this way before. Thank you, sir, for calling me."

"I guess the steward has been well tipped," thought Tom. As Mr. Titus came out and the door was shut, the young inventor asked in a whisper,

"Well, was it he?"

The contractor shook his head.

"No," he answered. "I never was more surprised in my life. I felt sure it was Waddington in there, but it wasn't. That man's beard is real, and while he has a look like Waddington about the eyes and upper part of his face, the man is a stranger to me. That is I think so, but in spite of all that, I have a queer feeling that I have met him before."

"Where?" Tom inquired.

"That I can't say," and the tunnel contractor shook his head. "Whew! That was a bad one!" he exclaimed, as the steamer pitched and tossed in an alarming manner.

"Yes, the storm seems to be getting worse instead of better," agreed Tom. "I hope none of the cargo shifts and comes banging up against my new explosive. If it does, there'll be no more tunnel digging for any of us."

"Better not mention the fact of the explosives on board," suggested Mr. Titus.

"I won't," promised Tom. "The passengers are frightened enough as it is. But I watched the powder being stored away. I guess it is safe."

The storm raged for two days before it began to die away. Meanwhile, nothing was seen, on deck or in the dining cabins, of the bearded man.

Tom and Mr. Titus made some guarded inquiries of the steward who had attended the sick man, and from him learned that he was down on the passenger list as Senor Pinto, from Rio de Janeiro, Brazil. He was traveling in the interests of a large firm of coffee importers of the United States, and was going to Lima.

"And there's no trace of Waddington?" asked Tom of Mr. Titus, as they were discussing matters in their stateroom one day.

"Not a trace. He seems to have dropped out of sight, and I'm glad of it."

"Perhaps Blakeson & Grinder have given up the fight against you."

"I wish they had, though I don't look for any such good luck. But I'm willing to fight them, now that we have an even chance, thanks to your explosive."

The storm blew itself out. The Bellaconda "crossed the line," and there was the usual horseplay among the sailors when Father Neptune came aboard to hold court. Those who had never before been below the equator were made to undergo more or less of an initiation, being lathered and shaved, and then pushed backward into a canvas tank of water on deck.

While Tom enjoyed the voyage, with the possible exception of the storm, he was anxious, and so was Mr. Titus, for the time to come when they should get to the tunnel and try the effect of the new explosive. Mr. Damon found an elderly gentleman as fond of playing chess as was the eccentric man himself, and his days were fully occupied with castles, pawns, knights, kings, queens and so on. As for Koku he was taken in charge by the sailors and found life forward very agreeable.

Senor Pinto had recovered from his seasickness, the steward told Tom and Mr. Titus, but still he kept to his stateroom.

It was when the Bellaconda was within a day or two of Callao that a wireless message was received for Mr. Titus. It was from his brother. The message read:

"Have information from New York office that rivals are after you. Look out for explosive."

"What does that mean?" asked Tom.

"Well, I presume it means our rival contractors know we have a supply of your new powder on board, and they may try to get it away from us."

"Why?" Tom demanded.

"To prevent our using it to complete the tunnel. In that case they'll get the secret of it to use for themselves, when the contract goes to them by default. Can we do anything to protect the powder, Tom?"

"Well, I don't know that we'll need to while it's stowed away in the cargo. They can't get at it any more than we can, until the ship unloads. I guess it's safe enough. We'll just have to keep our eyes open when it's taken out of the hold, though."

Tom and Mr. Titus, both of whom were fond of fresh air and exercise, had made it a practice to get up an hour before breakfast and take a constitutional about the steamer deck. They did this as usual the morning after the wireless warning was received, and they were standing near the port rail, talking about this, when they heard a thud on the deck behind them. Both turned quickly, and saw a round black object rolling toward them. From the object projected what seemed to be a black cord, and the end of this cord was glowing and smoking.

For a moment neither Tom nor Mr. Titus spoke. Then, as a slow motion of the ship rolled the round black thing toward Tom, he cried:

"It a bomb!"

He darted toward it, but Mr. Titus pulled him back.

"Run!" yelled the contractor.

Before either of them could do anything, a queer figure of an elderly gentleman stepped partly from behind a deck-house, and stooped over the smoking object.

"Look out!" yelled Mr. Titus, crouching low. "That's an explosive bomb! Toss it overboard!"

CHAPTER X

PROFESSOR BUMPER

Fairly fascinated by the spluttering fuse, neither Tom nor Mr. Titus moved for a second, while the deadly fire crept on through the black string-like affair, nearer and nearer to the bomb itself.

Then, just as Tom, holding back his natural fear, was about to thrust the thing overboard with his foot, hardly realizing that it might be even more deadly to the ship in the water than it was on the deck, the foot of the newcomer was suddenly thrust out from behind the deck-house, and the sizzling fuse was trodden upon.

It went out in a puff of smoke, but the owner of the foot was not satisfied with that for a hand reached down, lifted the bomb, the fuse of which still showed a smouldering spark of fire, and calmly pulled out the "tail" of the explosive. It was harmless then, for the fuse, with a trail of smoke following, was tossed into the sea, and the little man came out from behind the deck-house, holding the unexploded bomb.

For a moment neither Tom nor Mr. Titus could speak. They felt an inexpressible sense of relief. Then Tom managed to gasp out:

"You—you saved our lives!"

The little man who had stepped on the fuse, and had then torn it from the bomb, looked at the object in his hand as though it were the most natural thing in the world to pick explosives up off the deck of passenger steamers, as he remarked:

"Well, perhaps I did. Yes, I think it would have gone off in another second or two. Rather curious; isn't it?"

"Curious? Curious!" asked and exclaimed Mr. Titus.

"Why, yes," went on the little man, in the most matter of fact tone. "You see, most explosive bombs are round, made that way so the force will be equal in all directions. But this one, you notice, has a bulge, or protuberance, on one side, so to speak. Very curious!

"It might have been made that way to prevent its rolling overboard, or the bomb's walls might be weaker near that bulge to make sure that the force of the explosion would be in that direction. And the bulge was pointed toward you gentlemen, if you noticed."

"I should say I did!" cried Mr. Titus. "My dear sir, you have put us under a heavy debt to you! You saved our lives! I—I am in no frame of mind to thank you now, but—"

He strode over to the little man, holding out his hand.

"No, no, I'd better keep it," went on the person who had rendered the bomb ineffective. "You might drop it you know. You are nervous—your hand shakes."

"I want to shake hands with you!" exclaimed Mr. Titus—"to thank you!"

"Oh, that's it. I thought you wanted the bomb. Shake hands? Certainly!"

And while this ceremony was being gone through with, Tom had a moment to study the appearance of the man who had saved their lives. He had seen the passenger once or twice before, but had taken no special notice of him. Now he had good reason to observe him.

Tom beheld a little, thin man, little in the sense of being of the "bean pole" construction. His head was as bald as a billiard ball, as the young inventor could notice when the stranger took off his hat to bow formally in response to the greeting of some ladies who passed, while Mr. Titus was shaking hands with him.

The bald head was sunk down between two high shoulders, and when the owner wished to observe anything closely, as he was now observing the bomb, the head was thrust forward somewhat as an eagle might do. And Tom noticed that the eyes of the little man were as bright as those of an eagle. Nothing seemed to escape them.

"I want to add my thanks to those of Mr. Titus for saving our lives," said Tom, as he advanced. "We don't know what to make of it all, but you certainly stopped that bomb from going off."

"Yes, perhaps I did," admitted the little man coolly and calmly, as though preventing bomb explosions was his daily exercise before breakfast.

Tom and Mr. Titus introduced themselves by name.

"I am Professor Swyington Bumper," said the bomb-holder, with a bow, removing his hat, and again disclosing his shiny bald head. "I am very glad to have met you indeed."

"And we are more than glad," said Tom, fervently, as he glanced at the explosive.

"Now that the danger is over," went on Mr. Titus, "suppose we make an investigation, and find out how this bomb came to be here."

"Just what I was about to suggest," remarked Professor Bumper. "Bombs, such as this, do not sprout of themselves on bare decks. And I take it this one is explosive."

"Let me look at it," suggested Tom. "I know something of explosives."

It needed but a casual examination on the part of one who had done considerable experimenting with explosives to disclose the fact that it had every characteristic of a dangerous bomb. Only the pulling out of the fuse had rendered it harmless.

"If it had gone off," said Tom, "we would both have been killed, or, at least, badly injured, Mr. Titus."

"I believe you, Tom. And we owe our lives to Professor Bumper."

"I'm glad I could be of service, gentlemen," the scientist remarked, in an easy tone. "Explosives are out of my line, but I guessed it was rather dangerous to let this go off. Have you any idea how it got here?"

"Not in the least," said Tom. "But some one must have placed it here, or dropped it behind us."

"Would any one have an object in doing such a thing?" the professor asked.

Tom and Mr. Titus looked at one another.

"Waddington!" murmured the contractor. "If he were on board I should say he might have done it to get us out of the way, though I would not go so far as to say he meant to kill us. It may be this bomb has only a light charge in it, and he only meant to cripple us."

"We'll find out about that," said Tom. "I'll open it."

"Better be careful," urged Mr. Titus.

"I will," the young inventor promised. "I beg your pardon," he went on to Professor Bumper. "We have been talking about something of which you know nothing. Briefly, there is a certain man who is trying to interfere in some work in which Mr. Titus and I are interested, and we think, if he were on board, he might have placed this bomb where it would injure us."

"Is he here?" asked the professor.

"No. And that is what makes it all the more strange," said Mr. Titus. "At one time I thought he was here, but I was mistaken."

Tom took the now harmless bomb to his stateroom, and there, after taking the infernal machine apart, he discovered that it was not as dangerous as he had at first believed.

The bomb contained no missiles, and though it held a quantity of explosive, it was of a slow burning kind. Had it gone off it would have sent out a sheet of flame that would have severely burned him and Mr. Titus, but unless complications had set in death would not have resulted.

"They just wanted to disable us," said the contractor. "That was their game. Tom, who did it?"

"I don't know. Did you ever see this Professor Bumper before?"

"I never did."

"And did it strike you as curious that he should happen to be so near at hand when the bomb fell behind us?"

"I hadn't thought of that," admitted the contractor. "Do you mean that he might have dropped it himself?"

"Well, I wouldn't go so far as to say that," replied Tom, slowly. "But I think it would be a good idea to find out all we can of Professor Swyington Bumper."

"I agree with you, Tom. We'll investigate him."

CHAPTER XI

IN THE ANDES

Professor Swyington Bumper seemed to live in a region all by himself. Though he was on board the Bellaconda, he might just as well have been in an airship, or riding along on the back of a donkey, as far as his knowledge, or recognition, of his surroundings went. He seemed to be thinking thoughts far, far away, and he was never without a book—either a bound volume or a note-book. In the former he buried his hawk-like nose, and Tom, looking over his shoulder once, saw that the book was printed in curious characters, which, later, he learned were Sanskrit. If he had a note-book the bald-headed professor was continually jotting down memoranda in it.

"I can hardly think of him as a conspirator against us," said Tom to Mr. Titus.

"After you have been in the contracting business as long as I have you'll distrust every one," was the answer. "Waddington isn't on board, or I'd distrust him. That Spaniard, Senor Pinto, seems to be out of consideration, and there only remains the professor. We must watch him."

But Professor Bumper proved to be above suspicion. Carefully guarded inquiries made of the captain, the purser and other ships' officers, brought out the fact that he was well known to all of them, having traveled on the line before.

"He is making a search for something, but he won't say what it is," the captain said. "At first we thought it was gold or jewels, for he goes away off into the Andes Mountains, where both gold and jewels have been found. He never looks for treasure, though, for though some of his party have made rather rich discoveries, he takes no interest in them."

"What is he after then?" asked Mr. Titus.

"No one knows, and he won't tell. But whatever it is he has never found it yet. Always, when he comes back, unsuccessful, from a trip to the interior and goes back North with us, he will remark that he has not the right directions. That he must seek again.

"Back he comes next season, as full of hope as before, but only to be disappointed. Each time he goes to a new place in the mountains where he digs and delves, so members of the parties he hires tell me, but with no success. He carries with him something in a small iron box, and, whatever this is, he consults it from time to time. It may be directions for finding whatever he is after. But there seems to be something wrong."

"This is quite a mystery," remarked Tom.

"It certainly is. But Professor Bumper is a fine man. I have known him for years."

"This seems to dispose of the theory that he planted the bomb, and that he is one of the plotters in the pay of Blakeson & Grinder," said Mr. Titus, when he and Tom were alone.

"Yes, I guess it does. But who can have done it?"

That was a question neither could answer.

Tom had a theory, which he did not disclose to Mr. Titus, that, after all, the somewhat mysterious Senor Pinto might, in some way, be mixed up in the bomb attempt. But a close questioning of the steward on duty near the foreigner's cabin at the time disclosed the fact that Pinto had been ill in his berth all that day.

"Well, unless the bomb fell from some passing airship, I don't see how it got on deck," said Tom with a shake of his head. "And I'm sure no airship passed over us."

They had kept the matter secret, not telling even Mr. Damon, for they feared the eccentric man would make a fuss and alarm the whole vessel. So Mr. Damon, occasionally blessing his necktie or his shoe laces, played chess with his elderly gentleman friend and was perfectly happy.

That Professor Bumper not only had kept his promise about not mentioning the bomb, but that he had forgotten all about it, was evident a day or two after the happening. Tom and Mr. Titus passed him on deck, and bowed cordially. The professor returned the salutation, but looked at the two in a puzzled sort of fashion.

"I beg your pardon," he remarked, "but your faces are familiar, though I cannot recall your names. Haven't I seen you before?"

"You have," said Tom, with a smile. "You saved our lives from a bomb the other day."

"Oh, yes! So I did! So I did!" exclaimed Professor Bumper. "I felt sure I had seen you before. Are you all right?"

"Yes. There haven't been any more bombs thrown at us," the contractor said. "By the way, Professor Bumper, I understand you are quite a traveler in the Andes, in the vicinity of Lima."

"Yes, I have been there," admitted the bald-headed scientist in guarded tones.

"Well, I am digging a tunnel in that vicinity," went on Mr. Titus, "and if you ever get near Rimac, where the first cutting is made, I wish you would come and see me—Tom too, as he is associated with me."

"Rimac-Rimac," murmured the professor, looking sharply at the contractor. "Digging a tunnel there? Why are you doing that?" and he seemed to resent the idea.

"Why, the Peruvian government engaged me to do it to connect the two railroad lines," was the answer. "Do you know anything about the place?"

"Not so much as I hope to later on," was the unexpected answer. "As it happens I am going to Rimac, and I may visit your tunnel."

"I wish you would," returned Mr. Titus.

Later on, in their stateroom, the contractor remarked to the young inventor:

"Sort of queer; isn't it?"

"What?" asked Tom. "His not remembering us?"

"No, though that was odd. But I suppose he is forgetful, or pretends to be. I mean it's queer he is going to Rimac."

"What do you mean?" asked Tom.

"Well, I don't know exactly what I mean," went on the tunnel contractor, "but our tunnel happens to start at Rimac, which is a small town at the base of the mountains."

"Maybe the professor is a geologist," suggested Tom, "and he may want to get some samples of that hard rock."

"Maybe," admitted Mr. Titus. "But I shall keep my eyes on him all the same. I'm not going to have any strangers, who happen to be around when bombs drop near us, get into my tunnel."

"I think you're wrong to doubt Professor Bumper," Tom said.

A few days after this, when Tom and Mr. Titus were casually discussing the weather on deck and wondering how much longer it would be before they reached Callao, Mr. Damon, who had been playing numberless games of chess, came up for a breath of air.

"Mr. Damon," called Tom, "come over here and meet a friend of ours, Professor Bumper," and he was about to introduce them, for the two, as far as Tom knew, had not yet met. But no sooner had the professor and Mr. Damon caught sight of each other than there was a look of mutual recognition.

"Bless my fountain pen!" cried the eccentric man. "If it isn't my old friend!"

"Mr. Damon!" cried the professor. "I am delighted to see you again. I did not know you were on board!"

"Nor I you. Bless my apple dumpling! Are you still after those Peruvian antiquities?"

"I am, Mr. Damon. But I did not know you were acquainted with Mr. Swift."

"Oh, Tom and I are old friends."

"Professor Bumper saved the lives of Mr. Titus and myself," said Tom, "or at least he saved us from severe injury by a bomb."

"Pray do not mention it, my friends," put in the professor, casually. "It was nothing."

Of course he did not mean it just that way.

Then, naturally, Mr. Damon had to be told all about the bomb for the first time, and his wonder was great. He blessed everything he could think of.

"And to think it should be my old friend, Professor Bumper, who saved you," said the odd man to Tom and Mr. Titus later that day.

"Do you know him well?" asked Mr. Titus.

"Very well indeed. Our drug concern sells him many chemicals for his experiments."

"Well, if you know him I guess he can't be what I thought he was," the contractor went on. "I'm glad to know it. Why is he going to the Andes?"

"Oh, for many years he has been interested in collecting Peruvian antiquities. He has a certain theory in regard to something or other about their ancient civilization, but just what it is I have, at this moment, forgotten. Only I know you can thoroughly trust Professor Bumper, for a finer man never lived, though he is a bit absent-minded at times. But you will like him very much."

Thus the last lingering doubt of Professor Bumper was removed. Mr. Damon told something of how the scientist had been honored by degrees from many colleges and was regarded as an authority on Peruvian matters.

But who had placed the bomb on deck remained a mystery.

In due time Callao, the seaport of Lima, was reached and our friends disembarked. Tom saw to the unloading of the explosive, which was to be sent direct to the tunnel at Rimac. Mr. Titus, Tom and Mr. Damon would remain in Lima a day or so.

Professor Bumper disembarked with our friends, and stopped at the same hotel. Tom kept a lookout for Senor Pinto, but did not see him, and concluded that the Spaniard was ill, and would be carried ashore on a stretcher, perhaps.

Lima, the principal city and capital of Peru, proved an interesting place. It was about eight miles inland and was built on an arid plain about five hundred feet above sea level. Yet, though it was on what might be termed a desert, the place, by means of irrigation, had been made into a beauty spot.

Tom found the older part of the city was laid out with mathematical regularity, each street crossing the other at right angles. But in the new portions there was not this adherence to straightness.

"Bless my transfer! Why, they have electric cars here!" exclaimed Mr. Damon, catching sight of one on the line between Callao and the capital.

"What did you think they'd have?" asked Mr. Titus, "elephants or camels?"

"I—I didn't just know," was the answer.

"Oh, you'll find a deal of civilization here," the contractor said. "Of course much of the population is negro or Indian, but they are often rich and able to buy what they want. There is a population of over 150,000, and there are two steam railroads between Callao and Lima, while there is one running into the interior for 130 miles, crossing the Andes at an elevation of over three miles. It is a branch of that road, together with a branch of the one running to Ancon, that I am to connect with a tunnel."

Tom found some beautiful churches and cathedrals in Lima, and spent some time visiting them. He and Mr. Damon also visited, in the outskirts, the tobacco, cocoa and other factories.

Three days after reaching the capital, Mr. Titus having attended to some necessary business while Mr. Damon set on foot matters connected with his affairs, it was decided to strike inland to Rimac, and to try the effect of Tom Swift's explosive on the tunnel.

The journey was to be made in part by rail, though the last stages of it were over a rough mountain trail, with llamas for beasts of burden, while our friends rode mules.

As Tom, Mr. Damon, Koku, and Mr. Titus were going to the railroad station they saw Professor Bumper also leaving the hotel.

"I believe our roads lie together for a time," said the bald-headed scientist, "and, if you have no objections, I will accompany you."

"Come, and welcome!" exclaimed Mr. Titus, all his suspicions now gone.

"And it may be that you will be able to help me," the scientist went on.

"Help you—how?" asked Tom.

"I will tell you when we reach the Andes," was the mysterious answer.

It was a day later when they left the train at a small station, and struck off into the foothills of the great Andes Mountains, where the tunnel was started, that the professor again mentioned his object.

"Friends," he said, as he gazed up at the towering cliffs and crags, "I am searching for the lost city of Pelone, located somewhere in these mountains. Will you help me to find it?"

CHAPTER XII

THE TUNNEL

Mr. Damon, of the three who heard Professor Bumper make this statement, showed the least sign of astonishment. It would have been more correct to say that he showed none at all. But Tom could not restrain himself.

"The lost city of Pelone!" he exclaimed.

"Is it here—in these mountains?" asked Mr. Titus.

"I have reason to hope that it is," went on the professor. "The golden tablets are very vague, but I have tried many locations, and now I am about to try here. I hope I shall succeed. At any rate, I shall have agreeable company, which has not always been my luck on my previous expeditions seeking to find the lost city."

"Oh, Professor, are you still on that quest?" asked Mr. Damon, in a matter-of-fact tone.

"Yes, Mr. Damon, I am. And now that I look about me, and see the shape of these mountains, I feel that they conform more to the description on the golden plates than any location I have yet tried. Somehow I feel that I shall be successful here."

"Did you know Professor Bumper was searching for a lost city of the Andes?" asked Tom, of his eccentric friend.

"Why yes," answered Mr. Damon. "He has been searching for years to locate it."

"Why didn't you tell us?" inquired Mr. Titus.

"Why, I never thought of it. Bless my memorandum book! it never occurred to me. I did not think you would be interested. Tell them your story, Professor Bumper."

"I will soon. Just now I must see to my equipment. The story will keep."

And though Tom and Mr. Titus were both anxious to hear about the lost city, they, too, had much to do to get ready for the trip into the interior.

The beginning of the tunnel under one of the smaller of the ranges of the Andes lay two days journey from the end of the railroad line. And the trip must be made on mules, with llamas as beasts of burden, transporting the powder and other supplies.

"We'll only need to take enough food with us for the two days," said Mr. Titus. "We have a regular camp at the tunnel mouth, and my brother has supplies of grub and other things constantly coming in. We also have shacks to live in; but on this trip we will use tents, as the weather at this season is fine."

It was quite a little expedition that set off up the mountain trail that afternoon, for they had arrived at the end of the railroad line shortly before dinner, and had eaten at a rather poor restaurant.

Professor Bumper had made up his own exploring party, consisting of himself and three native Indian diggers with their picks and shovels. They were to do whatever excavating he decided was necessary to locate the hidden city.

Several mules and llamas, laden with the new explosive, and burdened with camp equipment and food, and a few Indian servants made up the cavalcade of Tom, the contractor, Mr. Damon and Koku. The giant was almost as much a source of wonder to the Peruvians as he had been on board the ship. And he was a great help, too. For some of the Indians were under-sized, and could not lift the heavy boxes and packages to the backs of the beasts of burden.

But Koku, thrusting the little men aside, grasped with one hand what two of them had tried in vain to lift, and set it on the back of mule or llama.

The way was rough but they took their time to it, for the trail was an ascending one. Above and beyond them towered the great Andes, and Tom, gazing up into the sky, which in places seemed almost pierced by the snow-covered peaks, saw some small black specks moving about.

"Condors," said Mr. Titus, when his attention was called to them. "Some of them are powerful birds, and they sometimes pick up a sheep and make off with it, though usually their food consists of carrion."

They went into camp before the sun went down, for it grew dark soon after sunset, and they wanted to be prepared. Supper was made ready by the Indian helpers, and when this was over, and they sat about a camp fire, Tom said:

"Now, Professor Bumper, perhaps you'll explain about the lost city."

"I wish I could explain about it," began the scientist. "For years I have dreamed of finding it, but always I have been disappointed. Now, perhaps, my luck may change."

"Do you think it may be near here?" asked Mr. Titus, motioning toward the dark and frowning peaks all about them.

"It may be. The signs are most encouraging. In brief, the story of the lost city of Pelone is this. Thousands of years ago—in fact I do not know how many—there existed somewhere in Peru an ancient city that was the centre of civilization for this region. Older it was than the civilization of the Mexicans—the Montezumas—older and more cultured.

"It is many years since I became interested in Peruvian antiquities, and then I had no idea of the lost city. But some of the antiques I picked up contained in their inscriptions references to Pelone. At first I conceived this to be a sort of god, a deity, or perhaps a powerful ruler. But as I went on in my work of gathering ancient things from Peru, I saw that the name Pelone referred to a city—a seat of government, whence everything had its origin.

"Then I got on the track more closely. I examined ancient documents. I found traces of an ancient language and writings, different from anything else in the world. I managed to construct an alphabet and to read some of the documents. From them I learned that Pelone was a city situated in some fertile valley of the Andes. It had existed for thousands of years; it was the seat of learning and culture. Much light would be thrown on the lives of the people who lived in Peru before the present races inhabited it, if I could but locate Pelone.

"Then I came across two golden tablets on which were graven the information that Pelone had utterly vanished."

"How?" asked Tom.

"The golden tablets did not say. They simply stated the fact that Pelone was lost, and one sentence read: 'He who shall find it again shall be richly rewarded.' But it is not for that that I seek. It is that I may give to the world the treasures it must contain—the treasures of an ancient civilization."

"And how do you think the city disappeared?" asked Mr. Titus.

"I do not know. Whether it was destroyed by enemies, whether it was buried under the ashes of a volcano, whether it still exists, deserted and solitary in some valley amid the mountain fastnesses of the Andes, I do not know. But I am certain the city once existed, and it may exist yet, though it may be in dust-covered ruins. That is what I seek to find. See! Here are the tablets telling about it. I got them from an old Peruvian grave."

He took from a box two thin sheets of yellow metal. They were covered with curious marks, but Tom and the others could make nothing of them. Only Professor Bumper was able to decipher them.

"And that is the story of the lost city of Pelone—as much as I know," he said. "For years I have sought it. If I can find it I shall be famous, for I shall have added to human knowledge."

"If the people of that city wrote on golden tablets, the yellow metal must have been plentiful," commented Mr. Titus. "You might strike a rich mine."

"I have no use for riches," said the professor.

"Well, I have," the contractor said, with a laugh. "That's why I'm putting through this tunnel. And if my brother and I don't do it we'll be in a bad way financially. We have struck traces of gold, but not in paying quantities. I should like to see this lost city of yours, Professor Bumper. It may contain gold."

"You may have all the gold, if I am allowed to keep the antiquities we find," stipulated the scientist. "Then you will help me in my search?"

"As much as we can spare time for from the tunnel work," promised Mr. Titus. "I'll instruct my men to keep their eyes open for any sign of ancient writings on the rocks we blast out."

"Thank you," said the professor.

The night passed uneventfully enough, if one excepts the mosquitoes which seemed to get through the nets, making life miserable for all. And once Tom thought he heard gruntings in the bush back of the tent, which noises might, he imagined, have been caused by a bear. Toward morning he heard an unearthly screech in the woods, and one of the Indians, tending the fire, grunted out a word which meant pumas.

"I can see it isn't going to be dull here," Tom mused, as he turned over and tried to sleep.

Breakfast made them all feel better, and they set off on the final stage of their journey.

"If all goes well we'll be at the tunnel entrance and camp tonight," said the contractor. "This second half of the trip is the roughest."

There was no need of saying that, for it was perfectly evident. The trail was a most precarious one, and only a mule or llama could have traveled it. The mules were most sure-footed, but, as it was, one slipped, and came near falling over a cliff.

But no real accident occurred, and finally, about an hour before sunset, the cavalcade turned down the slope and emerged on a level plain, which ended against the face of a great cliff.

As Tom rode nearer the cliff he could make out around it groups of rude buildings, covered with corrugated iron. There was quite a settlement it seemed.

Then, in the face of the cliff there showed something black—like a blot of ink, though more regular in outline.

"The mouth of the tunnel," said Mr. Titus to Tom. "Come on over to the office and I'll introduce you to my brother. I guess he will be glad we've arrived."

Tom dismounted from his mule, an example followed by the others. Professor Bumper gazed up at the great mountains and murmured:

"I wonder if the lost city of Pelone lies among them?"

Suddenly the silence of the evening was broken by a dull, rumbling sound.

"Bless my court plaster!" cried Mr. Damon. "What's that?"

"A blast," answered Mr. Titus. "But I never knew them to set off one so late before. I hope nothing is wrong!"

And, as he spoke, panic-stricken men began running out of the mouth of the tunnel, while those outside hastened toward them, shouting and calling.

CHAPTER XIII

TOM'S EXPLOSIVE

"Something has happened!" cried Mr. Titus as he ran forward, followed by Tom, Mr. Damon and Koku. Professor Bumper started with them, but on the way he saw a curious bit of rock which he stopped to pick up and examine.

At the entrance of the tunnel, from which came rushing dirt-stained and powder-blackened men, Mr. Titus was met by a man who seemed to be in authority.

"Hello, Job!" he cried. "Glad you're back. We're in trouble!"

"What's the matter?" was the question. "This is my brother Walter," he said. "This is Tom Swift and Mr. Damon," thus hurriedly he introduced them. "What happened, Walter?"

"Premature blast. Third one this week. Somebody is working against us!"

"Never mind that now," cried Job Titus. "We must see to the poor fellows who are hurt." "I guess there aren't many," his brother said. "They were on their way out when the charge went off. Some more of Blakeson & Grinder's work, I'll wager!"

They were rushing in to the smoke-filled tunnel now, followed by Tom, Mr. Damon and Koku, who would follow his young master anywhere. Tom saw that the tunnel was lighted with incandescent lamps, suspended here and there from the rocky roof or sides. The electric lights were supplied with current from a dynamo run by a gasoline engine.

"Where is it, Serato? Where was the blast?" asked Walter Titus, of a tall Indian, who seemed to be in some authority.

"Back at second turn," was the answer, in fairly good English. "I go get beds."

"He means stretchers," translated Job. "That's our Peruvian foreman. A good fellow, but easily scared."

They ran on into the tunnel, Tom and Mr. Damon noticing that a small narrow-gage railroad was laid on the floor, mules being the motive power to bring out the small dump cars loaded with rock and dirt, excavated from the big hole.

"Mind the turn!" called Job Titus, who was ahead of Tom and Mr. Damon. "It's rough here."

Tom found it so, for he slipped over some pieces of rock, and would have fallen had not Koku held him up.

"Thanks," gasped Tom, as on he ran.

A little later he came to a place where a cluster of electric lights gave better illumination, and he could see it was there that the damage had been done.

A number of men were lying on the dirt and rock floor of the tunnel, and some of them were bleeding. Others were staggering about as though shocked or stunned.

"We must get the injured ones out of here!" cried Walter Titus. "Where are the men with stretchers?"

"I sint that Spalapeen Serato for thim!" broke in a voice, rich in Irish brogue. "But he's thot stupid he might think I was after sindin' him fer wather!"

"No, Tim. Serato is after the stretchers all right," said Walter. "We passed him on the way."

"That's Tim Sullivan, our Irish foreman, though he has only a few of his own kind to boss," explained Job Titus in a whisper.

Some of the workmen (all of whom save the few Irish referred to were Peruvian Indians) had now recovered from their shock, or fright, and began to help the Titus brothers, Tom, Mr. Damon and Koku in looking after the injured. Of these there were five, only two of whom were, seemingly, seriously hurt.

"Me take them out," said Koku, and placing one gently over his left shoulder, and the other over his right, out of the tunnel he stalked with them, not waiting for the stretchers.

And it was well he did so, for one man was in need of an immediate operation, which was performed at the rude hospital the contractors maintained at the tunnel mouth. The other man died as Koku was carrying him out, but the giant had saved one life.

Serato, the Indian foreman, with some of his men now came in, and the other injured were carried out on stretchers, being attended to by the two doctors who formed part of the tunnel force. Among a large body of men some were always falling ill or getting hurt, and in that wild country a doctor had to be kept near at hand.

When the excitement had died down, and it was found that one death would be the total toll of the accident and that the premature blast had done no damage to the tunnel, the two Titus brothers began to consider matters.

Tom, Mr. Damon and the two contractors sat in the main office and talked things over. Koku was eating supper, though the others had finished, but, naturally, it took Koku twice as long as any one else. Professor Bumper was busy transcribing material in his note-book.

"Well, I'm glad you've come back, Job," said his brother. "Things have been going at sixes and sevens here since you went to get some new kind of blasting powder. By the way, I hope you got it, for we are practically at a standstill."

"Oh, I got it all right—some of Tom Swift's best—specially made for us. And, better still, I've brought Tom back with me."

"So I see. Well, I'm glad he's here."

"Now what about this accident today?" went on Job.

"Well, as I said, it's the third this week. All of them seemed to be premature blasts. But I've sent for some of the fuses used. I'm going to get at the bottom of this. Here is Sullivan with them now. Come in, Tim," he called, as the Irishman knocked at the door.

"Are they the fuses used in the blasts?" Walter asked.

"They are, sor. An' they mostly burn five minutes, which is plenty of time fer all th' min t' git out of danger. Only this time th' fuse didn't seem to burn more than a minute, an' I lit it meself."

"Let's see how long they burn now," suggested Job.

One of the longer fuses was lighted. It spluttered and smoked, while the contractors timed it with their watches.

"Four minutes!" exclaimed Job. "That's queer, and they're the regular ten minute length. I wonder what this means."

He took up another fuse, and examined it closely.

"Why!" he cried. "These aren't our fuses at all. They're another make, and much more rapid in burning. No wonder you've been having premature blasts. They go off in about half the time they should."

"I can't understhand thot!" said Tim, thoughtfully. "I keep all the fuses locked up, and only take thim out when I need thim."

"Then somebody has been at your box, Tim, and they took out our regular fuses and put in these quicker ones. It's a game to make trouble for us among our men, and to damage the tunnel."

"Bless my rubber boots!" cried Mr. Damon. "Who would do a thing like that?"

"Our rivals, perhaps, though I do not like to accuse any man on such small evidence," said Walter. "But we must adopt new measures."

"And be very careful of the fuses," said Job.

"Thot's what I will!" declared Tim. "I'll put th' supply in a new place. No wonder there was blasts before th' min could git out th' way! Bad cess t' th' imps thot did this!" and he banged his big fist down on the table.

Since the trouble began a guard had been always posted around the tunnel entrance and surrounding buildings, and this night the patrol was doubled. Tom, Mr. Damon and the two Titus brothers sat up quite late, talking over plans and ideas.

Professor Bumper went to bed early, as he said he was going to set off before sunrise to make a search for the lost city.

"I regard him as more or less of a visionary," said Mr. Job Titus; "but he seems a harmless gentleman, and we'll do all we can to help him."

"Surely," agreed his brother.

The night was not marked by any disturbance, and after breakfast, Tom, under the guidance of the Titus brothers, looked over the tunnel with a view to making his first experiment with the new explosive.

The tunnel was being driven straight into the face of one of the smaller ranges of the Andes Mountains. It was to be four miles in length, and when it emerged on the other side it would enable trains to make connections between the two railroads, thus tapping a rich and fertile country.

On the site of the tunnel, which was two days' mule travel east from Rimac, the Titus brothers had assembled their heavy machinery. They had brought some of their own men, including Tim Sullivan, with them, but the other labor was that of Peruvian Indians, with a native foreman, Serato, over them.

There were engines, boilers, dynamos, motors, diamond drills, steam shovels and a miniature railway, with mules as the motive power. A small village had sprung up at the tunnel mouth, and there was a general store, besides many buildings for the sleeping and eating quarters of the laborers, as well as places where the white men could live. Their quarters were some distance from the native section.

Powder, supplies, in fact everything save what game could be obtained in the forest, or what grains or fruits were brought in by natives living near by, had to be brought over the rough trail. But Titus Brothers had a large experience in engineering matters in wild and desolate countries, and they knew how to be as comfortable as possible.

Mr. Damon learned that one of the districts whence his company had been in the habit of getting quinine was distant a day's journey over the mountain, so he decided to make the trip, with a native guide, and see if he could get at the bottom of the difficulty in forwarding shipments.

This was a few days after the arrival of our friends. Meanwhile, Tom had been shown all through the tunnel by the Titus Brothers and had had his first sight of the hard cliff of rock which seemed to be a veritable stone wall in the way of progress—or at least such progress as was satisfactory to the contractors.

"Well, we'll try what some of my explosive will do," said Tom, when he had finished the examination. "I don't claim it will be as successful as the sample blast we set off at Shopton, but we'll do our best."

Holes were drilled in the face of the rock, and several charges of the new explosive tamped in. Wires were attached to the fuses, which were of a new kind, and warning was given to clear the tunnel. The wires ran out to the mouth of the horizontal shaft and Tom, holding the switch in his hand made ready to set off the blast.

"Are they all out?" he asked Tim Sullivan, who had emerged, herding the Indian laborers before him. Tim insisted on being the last man to seek safety when an explosion was to take place.

"All ready, sor," answered the foreman.

"Here she goes!" cried Tom, as his fingers closed the circuit.

CHAPTER XIV

MYSTERIOUS DISAPPEARANCES

There was a dull, muffled report, a sort of rumbling that seemed to extend away down under the earth and then echo back again until the ground near the mouth of the tunnel, where the party was standing, appeared to rock and heave. There followed a cloud of yellow, heavy smoke which made one choke and gasp, and Tom, seeing it, cried:

"Down! Down, everybody! There's a back draft, and if you breathe any of that powder vapor you'll have a fearful headache! Get down, until the smoke rises!"

The tunnel contractors and their men understood the danger, for they had handled explosives before. It is a well-known fact that the fumes of dynamite and other giant powders will often produce severe headaches, and even illness. Tom's explosive contained a certain percentage of dynamite, and he knew its ill effects. Stretched prone, or crouching on the ground, there was little danger, as the fumes, being lighter than air, rose. The yellow haze soon drifted away, and it was safe to rise.

"Well, I wonder how much rock your explosive tore loose for us, Tom," observed Job Titus, as he looked at the thin, yellowish cloud of smoke that was still lazily drifting from the tunnel.

"Can't tell until we go in and take a look," replied the young inventor. "It won't be safe to go in for a while yet, though. That smoke will hang in there a long time. I didn't think there'd be a back draft."

"There is, for we've often had the same trouble with our shots," Walter Titus said. "I can't account for it unless there is some opening in the shaft, connecting with the outer air, which admits a wind that drives the smoke out of the mouth, instead of forward into the blast hole. It's a queer thing and we haven't been able to get at the bottom of it."

"That's right," agreed his brother. "We've looked for some opening, or natural shaft, but haven't been able to find it. Sometimes we shoot off a charge and everything goes well, the smoke disappears in a few minutes. Again it will all blow out this way and we lose half a day waiting for the air to clear. There's a hidden shaft, or natural chimney, I'm sure, but we can't find it."

"Thot blast didn't make much racket," commented Tim Sullivan. "I doubt thot much rock come down. An' thot's not sayin' anythin' ag'in yer powder, lad," he went on to Tom.

"Oh, that's all right," Tom Swift replied, with a laugh. "My explosive doesn't work by sound. It has lots of power, but it doesn't produce much concussion."

"We've often made more noise with our blasts," confirmed Job Titus, "but I can't say much for our results."

They were all anxious, Tom included, to hurry into the tunnel to see how much rock had been loosened by the blast, but it was not safe to venture in until the fumes had been allowed to disperse. In about an hour, however, Tim Sullivan, venturing part way in, sniffed the air and called:

"It's all right, byes! Air's clear. Now come on!"

They all hurried eagerly into the shaft, Mr. Damon stumbling along at Tom's side, as anxious as the lad himself. Before they reached the face of the cliff against which the bore had been driven, and which was as a solid wall of rock to further progress, they began to tread on fragments of stone.

"Well, it blew some as far back as here," said Walter Titus. "That's a good sign."

"I hope so," Tom remarked.

There were still some fumes noticeable in the tunnel, and Mr. Damon complained of a slight feeling of illness, while Koku, who kept at Tom's side, murmured that it made his eyes smart. But the sensations soon passed.

They came to a stop as the face of the cliff loomed into view in the glare of a searchlight which Job Titus switched on. Then a murmur of wonder came from every one, save from Tom Swift. He, modestly, kept silent.

"Bless my breakfast orange!" cried Mr. Damon. "What a big hole!"

There was a great gash blown in the hard rock which had acted as a bar to the further progress of the tunnel. A great heap of rock, broken into small fragments, was on the floor of the shaft, and there was a big hole filled with debris which would have to be removed before the extent of the blast could be seen.

"That's doing the work!" cried Job Titus.

"It beats any two blasts we ever set off," declared his brother.

"Much fine!" muttered the Peruvian foreman, Serato.

"It's a lalapaloosa, lad! Thot's what it is!" enthusiastically exclaimed Tim Sullivan. "Now the black beggars will have some rock to shovel! Come on there, Serato, git yer lazy imps t' work cartin' this stuff away.

We've got a man on th' job now in this new powder of Tom Swift's. Git busy!"

"Um!" grunted the Indian, and he called to his men who were soon busy with picks and shovels, loading the loosened rock and earth into the mule-hauled dump cars which took it to the mouth of the tunnel, whence it was shunted off on another small railroad to fill in a big gulch to save bridging it.

Tom's first blast was very successful, and enough rock was loosed to keep the laborers busy for a week. The contractors were more than satisfied.

"At this rate we'll finish ahead of time, and earn a premium," said Job to his brother.

"That's right. You didn't make any mistake in appealing to Tom Swift. But I wonder if Blakeson & Grinder have given up trying to get the job away from us?"

"I don't know. I'd never trust them. We must watch out for Waddington. That bomb on the vessel had a funny look, even if it was not meant to kill Tom or me. I won't relax any."

"No, I guess it wouldn't be safe."

But a week went by without any manifestation having been made by the rival tunnel contractors. During that week more of Tom's explosive arrived, and he busied himself getting ready another blast which could be set off as soon as the debris from the first should have been cleared away.

Meanwhile, Professor Bumper, with his Indian guides and helpers, had made several trips into the mountain regions about Rimac, but each time that he returned to the tunnel camp to renew his supplies, he had only a story of failure to recite.

"But I am positive that somewhere in this vicinity is the lost Peruvian city of Pelone," he said. "Every indication points to this as the region, and the more I study the plates of gold, and read their message, the more I am convinced that this is the place spoken of.

"But we have been over many mountains, and in more valleys, without finding a trace of the ancient civilization I feel sure once flourished here. There are no relics of a lost race—not so much as an arrow or spear head. But, somehow or other, I feel that I shall find the lost city. And when I do I shall be famous!"

"Mr. Damon and I will help you all we can," Tom said. "As soon as I get ready the next blast I'll have a little time to myself, and we will go with you on a trip or two."

"I shall be very glad to have you," the bald-headed scientist remarked.

Tom's second blast was even more successful than the first, and enough of the hard rock was loosed and pulverized to give the Indian laborers ten days' work in removing it from the tunnel.

Then, as the services of the young inventor would not be needed for a week or more, he decided to go on a little trip with Professor Bumper.

"I'll come too," said Mr. Damon. "One of the sub-contractors whose men are gathering the cinchona bark for our firm has his headquarters in the region where you are going, and I can go over there and see why he isn't up to the mark."

Accordingly, preparations having been made to spend a week in camp in the forests of the Andes, Tom and his party set off one morning. Professor Bumper's Indian helpers would do the hard work, and, of course, Koku, who went wherever Tom went, would be on hand in case some feat of strength were needed.

It was a blind search, this hunt for a lost city, and as much luck might be expected going in one direction as in another; so the party had no fixed point toward which to travel. Only Mr. Damon stipulated that he wanted to reach a certain village, and they planned to include that on their route.

Tom Swift took his electric rifle with him, and with it he was able to bring down a couple of deer which formed a welcome addition to the camp fare.

The rifle was a source of great wonder to the Peruvians. They were familiar with ordinary firearms, and some of them possessed old-fashioned guns. But Tom's electric weapon, which made not a sound, but killed with the swiftness of light, was awesome to them. The interpreter accompanying Professor Bumper confided privately to Tom that the other Indians regarded the young inventor as a devil who could, if he wished, slay by the mere winking of an eye.

Mr. Damon located the quinine-gathering force he was anxious to see, and, through the interpreter, told the chief that more bark must be brought in to keep up to the terms of the contract.

But something seemed to be the matter. The Indian chief was indifferent to the interpreted demands of Mr. Damon, and that gentleman, though he blessed any number of animate and inanimate objects, seemed to make no impression.

"No got men to gather bark, him say," translated the interpreter.

"Hasn't got any men!" exclaimed Mr. Damon. "Why, look at all the lazy beggars around the village."

This was true enough, for there were any number of able-bodied Indians lolling in the shade.

"Him say him no got," repeated the translator, doggedly.

At that moment screams arose back of one the grass huts, and a child ran out into the open, followed by a savage dog which was snapping at the little one's bare legs.

"Bless my rat trap!" gasped Mr. Damon. "A mad dog!"

Shouts and cries arose from among the Indians. Women screamed, and those who had children gathered them up in their arms to run to shelter. The men threw all sorts of missiles at the infuriated animal, but seemed afraid to approach it to knock it over with a club, or to go to the relief of the frightened child which was now only a few feet ahead of the animal, running in a circle.

"Me git him!" cried Koku, jumping forward.

"No, Wait!" exclaimed Tom Swift. "You can kill the dog all right, Koku," he said, "but a scratch from his tooth might be fatal. I'll fix him!"

Snatching his electric rifle from the Indian bearer who carried it, Tom took quick aim. There was no flash, no report and no puff of smoke, but the dog suddenly crumpled up in a heap, and, with a dying yelp, rolled to one side. The child was saved.

The little one, aware that something had happened, turned and saw the stretched out form of its enemy. Then, sobbing and crying, it ran toward its mother who had just heard the news.

While the mothers gathered about the child, and while the older boys and girls made a ring at a respectful distance from the dog, there was activity noticed among the men of the village. They began hurrying out along the forest paths.

"Where are they going?" asked Tom. "Is there some trouble? Was that a sacred dog, and did I get in bad by killing it?"

The interpreter and the native chief conversed rapidly for a moment and then the former, turning to Tom, said:

"Men go git cinchona bark now. Plenty get for him," and he pointed to Mr. Damon. "They no like stay in village. T'ink yo' got lightning in yo' pocket," and he pointed to the electric rifle.

"Oh, I see!" laughed Tom. "They think I'm a sort of wizard. Well, so I am. Tell them if they don't get lots of quinine bark I'll have to stay here until all the mad dogs are shot."

The interpreter translated, and when the chief had ceased replying, Tom and the others were told:

"Plenty bark git. Plenty much. Yo' go away with yo' lightning. All right now."

"Well, it's a good thing I keeled over that dog," Tom said. "It was the best object lesson I could give them."

And from then on there was no more trouble in this district about getting a supply of the medicinal bark.

A week passed and Professor Bumper was no nearer finding the lost city than he had been at first. Reluctantly, he returned to the tunnel camp to get more provisions.

"And then I'll start out again," he said.

"We'll go with you some other time," promised Tom. "But now I expect I'll have to get another blast ready."

He found the debris brought down by the second one all removed, and in a few days, preparations for exploding more of the powder were under way.

Many holes had been drilled in the face of the cliff of hard rock, and the charges tamped in. Electric wires connected them, and they were run out to the tunnel mouth where the switch was located.

This was done late one afternoon, and it was planned to set off the blast at the close of the working day, to allow all night for the fumes to be blown away by the current of air in the tunnel.

"Get the men out, Tim," said Tom, when all was ready.

"All right, sor," was the answer, and the Irish foreman went back toward the far end of the bore to tell the last shift of laborers to come out so the blast could be set off.

But in a little while Tim came running back with a queer look on his face.

"What's the matter?" asked Tom. "Why didn't you bring the men with you?"

"Because, sor, they're not there!"

"Not in the tunnel? Why, they were working there a little while ago, when I made the last connection!"

"I know they were, but they've disappeared."

"Disappeared?"

"Yis sir. There's no way out except at this end an' you didn't see thim come out: did you?"

"Then they've disappeared! That's all there is to it! Bad goin's on, thot's what it is, sor! Bad!" and Tim shook his head mournfully.

CHAPTER XV

FRIGHTENED INDIANS

"There must be some mistake," said Tom, wondering if the Irish foreman were given to joking. Yet he did not seem that kind of man.

"Mistake? How can there be a mistake, sor? I wint in there to tell th' black imps t' come out, but they're not there to tell!"

"What's the trouble?" asked Job Titus, coming out of the office near the tunnel mouth. "What's wrong, Tom?"

"Why, I sent Tim in to tell the men to come out, as I was going to set off a blast, but he says the men aren't in there. And I'm sure the last shift hasn't come out."

By this time Koku, Mr. Damon and Walter Titus had come up to find out what the trouble was.

"The min have disappeared—that's all there is to it!" Tim said.

"Perhaps they have missed their way—the lights may have gone out, and they might have wandered into some abandoned cutting," suggested Tom.

"There aren't any abandoned cuttin's," declared Tim. "It's a straight bore, not a shaft of any kind. I've looked everywhere, and th' min aren't there I tell ye!"

"Are the lights going?" asked Job. "You might have missed them in the dark, Tim."

"The lights are going all right, Mr. Titus," said the young man in charge of the electrical arrangements. "The dynamo hasn't been stopped today."

"Come on, we'll have a look," proposed Walter Titus. "There must be some mistake. Hold back the blast, Tom."

"All right," and the young inventor disconnected the electrical detonating switch. "I'll come along and have a look too," he added. "Don't let anybody meddle with the wires, Jack," he said to the young Englishman who was in charge of the dynamo.

Into the dimly-lit tunnel advanced the party of investigators, with Tim Sullivan in the lead.

"Not a man could I find!" he said, murmuring to himself. "Not a man! An' I mind th' time in Oireland whin th' little people made vanish a whole village like this, jist bekase ould Mike Maguire uprooted a bed of shamrocks."

"That's enough of your superstitions, Tim," warned Job Titus. "If some of the other Indians hear you go on this way they'll desert as they did once before."

"Did they do that?" asked Tom.

"Yes, we had trouble that way when we first began the work. The place here was a howling wilderness then, and there were lots of pumas around.

"A puma is a small sized lion, you know, not specially dangerous unless cornered. Well, some of the men had their families here with them, and a couple of children disappeared. The story got started that there was a big puma—the king of them all—carrying off the little ones, and my brother and I awoke one morning to find every laborer missing. They departed bag and baggage. Afraid of the pumas."

"What did you do?"

"Well, we organized ourselves and our white helpers into a hunting party and killed a lot of the beasts. There wasn't any big one though."

"And what had become of the children?"

"They weren't eaten at all. They had wandered off into the woods, and some natives found them and took care of them. Eventually, they got back home. But it was a long while before we could persuade the Indians to come back. Since then we haven't had any trouble, and I don't want Tim, with his superstitious fancies, to start any."

"But the min are gone!" insisted the Irish foreman, who had listened to this story as he and the others walked along.

"We'll find them," declared Mr. Titus.

But though they looked all along the big shaft, and though the place was well lighted by extra lamps that were turned on when the investigation started, no trace could be found of the workmen, who had been left in the tunnel to finish tamping the blast charges. The party reached the rocky heading, in the face of which the powerful explosive had been placed, and not an Indian was in sight. Nor, as far as could be told, was there any side niche, or blind shaft, in which they could be hiding.

Sometimes, when small blasts were set off, the men would go behind a projecting shoulder of rock to wait until the charge had been fired, but now none was in such a refuge.

"It is queer," admitted Walter Titus. "Where can the men have gone?"

"That's what I want to know!" exclaimed Tim.

"Are you sure they didn't come out the mouth of the tunnel?" asked Job Titus.

"Positive," asserted Tom. I was there all the while, rigging up the fires."

"We'll call the roll, and check up," decided Job Titus. "Get Serato to help."

The Indian foreman had not been in the tunnel with the last shift of men, having left them to Tim Sullivan to get out in time. The Indian foreman was called from his supper in the shack where he had his headquarters, and the roll of workmen was called.

Ten men were missing, and when this fact became known there were uneasy looks among the others.

"Well," said Mr. Titus, after a pause. "The men are either in the tunnel or out of it. If they're in we don't dare set off the blast, and if they're out they'll show up, sooner or later, for supper. I never knew any of 'em to miss a meal."

"If such a thing were possible," said Walter Titus, "I would say that our rivals had a hand in this, and had induced our men to bolt in order to cripple our force. But we haven't seen any of Blakeson & Grinder's emissaries about, and, if they were, how could they get the ten men out of the tunnel without our Seeing them? It's impossible!"

"Well, what did happen then?" asked Tom.

"I'm inclined to think that the men came out and neither you, nor any one else, saw them. They ran away for reasons of their own. We'll take another look in the morning, and then set off the blast."

And this was done. There being no trace of the men in the tunnel it was deemed safe to explode the charges. This was done, a great amount of rock being loosened.

The laborers hung back when the orders were given to go in and clean up. There were mutterings among them.

"What's the matter?" asked Job Titus.

"Them afraid," answered Serato. "Them say devil in tunnel eat um up! No go in."

"They won't go in, eh?" cried Tim Sullivan. "Well, they will thot! If there's a divil inside there's a worse one outside, an' thot's me! Git in there now, ye black-livered spalapeens!" and catching up a big club the Irishman made a rush for the hesitating laborers. With a howl they rushed into the tunnel, and were soon loading rock into the dump cars.

CHAPTER XVI

ON THE WATCH

The mystery of the disappearance of the ten men—for mystery it was—remained, and as no side opening or passage could be found within the tunnel, it came to be the generally accepted explanation that the laborers had come out unobserved, and, for reasons of their own, had run away.

This habit on the part of the Peruvian workers was not unusual. In fact, the Titus brothers had to maintain a sort of permanent employment agency in Lima to replace the deserters. But they were used to this. The difference was that the Indians used to vanish from camp at night, and invariably after pay-day.

"And that's the only reason I have a slight doubt that they walked out of the tunnel," said Job Titus. "There was money due em."

"They never came out of the front entrance of the tunnel," said Tom. "Of that I'm positive."

But there was no way of proving his assertion.

The third blast, while not as successful as the second in the amount of rock loosened, was better than the first, and made a big advance in the tunnel progress. Tom was beginning to understand the nature of the mountain into which the big shaft was being driven and he learned how better to apply the force of his explosive.

That was the work which he had charge of—the placing of the giant powder so it would do the most effective work. Then, when the fumes from the blast had cleared away, in would surge the workmen to clear away the debris.

Under the direction of Mr. Swift, left at Shopton to oversee the manufacture of the explosive, new shipments came on promptly to Lima, and were brought out to the tunnel on the backs of mules, or in the case of small quantities, on the llamas. But the latter brutes will not carry a heavy load, lying down and refusing to get up if they are overburdened, whereas one has yet to find a mule's limit.

After his first success in getting the natives to take a more active interest in the gathering of the cinchona bark, Mr. Damon found it rather easy, for the story of Tom's electric rifle and how it had killed the mad dog spread among the tribes, and Mr. Damon had but to announce that the "lightning shooter," as Tom was called, was a friend of the drug concern to bring about the desired results. Mr. Damon, by paying a sort of bribe, disguised under the name "tax," secured the help of Peruvian officials so he had no trouble on that score.

Koku was in his element. He liked a wild life and Peru was much more like the country of giants where Tom had found him, than any place the big man had since visited. Koku had great strength and wanted to use it, and after a week or so of idleness he persuaded Tom to let him go in the tunnel to work.

The giant was made a sort of foreman under Tim, and the two became great friends. The only trouble with Koku was that he would do a thing himself instead of letting his men do it, as, of course, all proper foremen should do. If the giant saw two or three of the Indians trying to lift a big rock into the little dump cars, and failing because of its great weight, he would good-naturedly thrust them aside, pick up the big stone in his mighty arms, and deposit it in its place.

And once when an unusually big load had been put in a car, and the mule attached found it impossible to pull it out to the tunnel mouth,

Koku unhitched the creature and, slipping the harness around his waist, walked out, dragging the load as easily as if pulling a child on a sled.

Professor Bumper kept on with his search for the lost city of Pelone. Back and forth he wandered among the wild Andes Mountains, now hopeful that he was on the right trail, and again in despair. Tom and Mr. Damon went with him once more for a week, and though they enjoyed the trip, for the professor was a delightful companion, there were no results. But the scientist would not give up.

Tom Swift was kept busy looking after the shipments of the explosive, and arranging for the blasts. He had letters from Ned Newton in which news of Shopton was given, and Mr. Swift wrote occasionally. But the mails in the wilderness of the Andes were few and far between.

Tom wrote a letter of explanation to Mr. Nestor, in addition to the wireless he had sent regarding the box labeled dynamite, but he got no answer. Nor were his letters to Mary answered.

"I wonder what's wrong?" Tom mused. "It can't be that they think I did that on purpose. And even if Mr. Nestor is angry at me for something that wasn't my fault, Mary ought to write."

But she did not, and Tom grew a bit despondent as the days went by and no word came.

"I suppose they might be offended because I left Rad to do up that package instead of attending to it myself," thought Tom. "Well, I did make a mistake there, but I didn't mean to. I never thought about Eradicate's not reading. I'll make him go to night school as soon as I get back. But maybe I'll never get another chance to send Mary anything. If I do, I'll not let Rad deliver it—that's sure."

The feeling of alarm engendered among the Indians by the disappearance of their ten fellow-workers seemed to have disappeared. There were rumors that some of the mysterious ten had been seen in distant villages and settlements, but the Titus brothers could not confirm this.

"I don't think anything serious happened to them, anyhow," said Job Titus one day. "And I should hate to think our work was responsible for harm to any one."

"Your rivals don't seem to be doing much to hamper you," observed Tom. "I guess Waddington gave up.

"I won't be too sure of that," said Mr. Titus.

"Why, what has happened?" Tom asked.

"Well, nothing down here—that is, directly—but we are meeting with trouble on the financial end. The Peruvian government is holding back payments."

"Why is that?"

"They claim we are not as far advanced as we ought to be."

"Aren't you?"

"Practically, yes. There was no set limit of work to be done for the intermediate payments. We bonded ourselves to have the tunnel done at a certain date.

"If we fail, we lose a large sum, and if we get it done ahead of time we get a big premium. There was no question as to completing a certain amount of footage before we received certain payments. But Senor Belasdo, the government representative, claims that we will not be done in time, and therefore he is holding back money due us. I'm sure the rival contractors have set him up to this, because he was always decent to us before.

"Another matter, too, makes me suspicious. We have tried to raise money in New York to tide us over while the government is holding up our funds here. But our New York office is meeting with difficulties. They report there is a story current to the effect that we are going to fail, and while that isn't so, you know how hard it is to borrow money in the face of such rumors. We are doing all we can to fight them, of course, and maybe we'll beat out our rivals yet.

"But that isn't all. I'm sure some one is on the ground here trying to make trouble among our workers. I never knew so many men to leave, one after another. It's keeping the employment agency in Lima busy supplying us with new workers. And so many of them are unskilled. They aren't able to do half the work of the old men, and poor Tim Sullivan is in despair."

"You think some one here is causing dissensions and desertions among your men?"

"I'm sure of it! I've tried to ferret out who it is, but the spy, for such he must be, keeps his identity well hidden."

Tom thought for a moment. Then he said:

"Mr. Titus, with your permission, I'll see if I can find out about this for you."

"Find out what, Tom?"

"What is causing the men to leave. I don't believe it's the scare about the ten missing ones."

"Nor do I. That's past and gone. But how are you going to get at the bottom of it?"

"By keeping watch. I've got nothing to do now for the next week. We've just set off a big blast, and I've got the powder for the following one all ready. The men will be busy for some time getting out the broken rock. Now what I propose to do is to go in the tunnel and work among them until I can learn something.

"I can understand the language pretty well now, though I can't speak much of it. I'll go in the tunnel every day and find out what's going on."

"But you'll be known, and if one of our men, or one who we suppose is one, turns out to be a spy, he'll be very cautious while you're in there."

"He won't know me," Tom said. "This is how I'll work it. I'll go off with Professor Bumper the next time he starts on one of his weekly expeditions into the woods. But I won't go far until I turn around and come back. I'll adopt some sort of disguise, and I'll apply to you for work. You can tell Tim to put me on. You might let him into the secret, but no one else."

A few days later Tom was seen departing with Professor Bumper into the interior, presumably to help look for the lost city. Mr. Damon was away from camp on business connected with the drug concern, and Koku, to his delight, had been given charge of a stationary hoisting engine outside the tunnel, so he would not come in contact with Tom. It was not thought wise to take the giant into the secret.

Then one day, shortly after Professor Bumper and Tom had disappeared into the forest, a ragged and unkempt white man applied at the tunnel camp for work. There was just the barest wink as he accosted Mr. Titus, who winked in turn, and then the new man was handed over to Tim Sullivan, as a sort of helper.

And so Tom Swift began his watch.

CHAPTER XVII

THE CONDOR

Left to himself, with only the rather silent gang of Peruvian Indians as company, Tom Swift looked about him. There was not much active work to be done, only to see that the Indians filled the dump cars evenly full, so none of the broken rock would spill over the side and litter the tramway. Then, too, he had to keep the Indians up to the mark working, for these men were no different from any other, and they were just as inclined to "loaf on the job" when the eye of the "boss" was turned away.

They did not talk much, murmuring among themselves now and then, and little of what they said was intelligible to Tom. But he knew enough of the language to give them orders, the main one of which was:

"Hurry up!"

Now, having seen to it that the gang of which he was in temporary charge was busily engaged, Tom had a chance to look about him. The tunnel was not new to him. Much of his time in the past month had been spent in its black depths, illuminated, more or less, by the string of incandescent lights.

"What I want to find," mused Tom, as he walked to and fro, "is the place where those Indians disappeared. For I'm positive they got away through some hole in this tunnel. They never came out the main entrance."

Tom held to this view in spite of the fact that nearly every one else believed the contrary—that the men had left by the tunnel mouth, near which Tom happened to be alone at the time.

Now, left to himself, with merely nominal duties, and so disguised that none of the workmen would know him for the trim young inventor who oversaw the preparing of the blast charges, Tom Swift walked to and fro, looking for some carefully hidden passage or shaft by means of which the men had got away.

"For it must be well hidden to have escaped observation so long," Tom decided. "And it must be a natural shaft, or hole, for we are boring into native rock, and it isn't likely that these Indians ever tried to make a tunnel here. There must be some natural fissure communicating with the outside of the mountain, in a place where no one would see the men coming out."

But though Tom believed this it was another matter to demonstrate his belief. In the intervals of seeing that the natives properly loaded the dump cars, and removed as much of the debris as possible, Tom looked carefully along the walls and roof of the tunnel thus far excavated.

There were cracks and fissures, it is true, but they were all superficial ones, as Tom ascertained by poking a long pole up into them.

"No getting out that way," he said, as he met with failure after failure.

Once, while thus engaged, he saw Serato, the Indian foreman looking narrowly at him, and Serato said something in his own language which Tom could not understand. But just then along came Tim Sullivan, who, grasping the situation, exclaimed:

"Thot's all roight, now, Serri, me lad!" for thus he contracted the Indian's name. "Thot's a new helper I have, a broth of a bye, an' yez kin kape yer hands off him. He's takin' orders from me!"

"Um!" grunted the Indian. "Wha for he fish in tunnel roof?" for Tom's pole was one like those the Indians used when, on off days, they emulated Izaak Walton.

"Fishin' is it!" exclaimed Tim. "Begorra 'tis flyin' fish he's after I'm thinkin'. Lave him alone though, Serri! I'm his boss!"

"Um!" grunted the Indian again, as he moved off into the farther darkness.

"Be careful, Tom," whispered the Irishman, when the native had gone. "These black imps is mighty suspicious. Maybe thot fellah had a hand in th' disappearances hisself."

"Maybe," admitted Tom. "He may get a percentage on all new hands that are hired."

Tom kept on with his search, always hoping he might find some hidden means of getting out of the tunnel. But as the days went by, and he discovered nothing, he began to despair.

"The queer thing about it," mused Tom, "is what has become of the ten men. Even if they did find some secret means of leaving, what has become of them? They couldn't completely disappear, and they have families and relatives that would make some sort of fuss if they were out of sight completely this long. I wonder if any inquiries have been made about them?"

When Tom came off duty he asked the Titus brothers whether or not any of the relatives of the missing men had come to seek news about them. None had.

"Then," said Tom, "you can depend on it the men are all right, and their relatives know it. I wonder how it would do to make inquiries at that end? Question some of the relatives."

"Bless my hat hand!" exclaimed Mr. Damon, who was at the conference. "I never thought of that. I'll do it for you."

The odd man had gotten his quinine gathering business well under way now, and he had some spare time. So, with an interpreter who could be trusted, he went to the native village whence had come nearly all of the ten missing men. But though Mr. Damon found some of their relatives, the latter, with shrugs of their shoulders, declared they had seen nothing of the ones sought.

"And they didn't seem to worry much, either," reported Mr. Damon.

"Then we can depend on it," remarked Tom, "that the men are all right and their relatives know it. There's some conspiracy here."

So it seemed. But who was at the bottom of it?

"I can't figure out where Blakeson & Grinder come in," said Job Titus. "They would have an object in crippling us, but they seem to be working from the financial end, trying to make us fail there. I haven't seen any of their sneaking agents around here lately, and as for Waddington he seems to have stayed up North."

Tom resumed his vigil in the tunnel, poking here and there, but with little success. His week was about up, and he would soon have to resume his character as powder expert, for the debris was nearly all cleaned up, and another blast would have to be fired shortly.

"Well, I'm stumped!" Tom admitted, the day when he was to come on duty for the last time as a pretended foreman. "I've hunted all over, and I can't find any secret passage."

It was warm in the tunnel, and Tom, having seen one train of the dump cars loaded, sat down to rest on an elevated ledge of rock, where he had made a sort of easy chair for himself, with empty cement bags for cushions.

The heat, his weariness and the monotonous clank-clank of a water pump near by, and the equally monotonous thump of the lumps of rocks in the cars made Tom drowsy. Almost before he knew it he was asleep.

What suddenly awakened him he could not tell. Perhaps it was some influence on the brain cells, as when a vivid dream causes us to start up from slumber, or it may have been a voice. For certainly Tom heard a voice, he declared afterward.

As he roused up he found himself staring at the rocky wall of the tunnel. And yet the wall seemed to have an opening in it and in the opening, as if it were in the frame of a picture, appeared the face Tom had seen at his library the day Job Titus called on him—the face of Waddington!

Tom sat up so quickly that he hit his head sharply on a projecting rock spur, and, for the moment he "saw stars." And with the appearance of these twinkling points of light the face of Waddington seemed to fade away, as might a vision in a dream.

"Bless my salt mackerel, as Mr. Damon would say!" cried Tom. "What have I discovered?"

He rubbed his head where he had struck it, and then passed his hand before his eyes, to make sure he was awake. But the vision, if vision it was, had vanished, and he saw only the bare rock wall. However, the echo of the voice remained in his ears, and, looking down toward the tunnel floor Tom saw Serato, the Indian foreman.

"Were you speaking to me?" asked Tom, for the man understood and spoke English fairly well.

"No, sar. I not know you there!" and the fore man seemed startled at seeing Tom. Clearly he was in a fright.

"You were speaking!" insisted Tom.

"No, sar!" The man shook his head.

"To some one up there!" went on the young inventor, waving his hand toward the spot where he had seen the face in the rock.

"Me speak to roof? No, sar!" Serato laughed.

Tom did not know what to believe.

"You hear me tell um lazy man to much hurry," the Indian went on. "Me not know you sleep there, sar!"

"Oh, all right," Tom said, recollecting that he must keep up his disguise. "Maybe I was dreaming."

"Yes, sar," and the foreman hurried on, with a backward glance over his shoulder.

"Now was I dreaming or not?" thought Tom. "I'm going to have a look at that place though, where I saw Waddington's face. Or did I imagine it?"

He got a long pole and a powerful flash lamp, and when he had a chance, unobserved, he poked around in the vicinity where he had seen the face.

But there was only solid rock.

"It must have been a dream," Tom concluded. "I've been thinking too much about this business. I'll have to give up. I can't solve the mystery of the missing men."

The next day, much disappointed, he resumed his own character as explosive expert, and prepared for another blast. The net result of his watch was that he became suspicious of Serato, and so informed the Titus Brothers.

"Oh, but you're mistaken," said Job "We have had him for years, on other contracts in Peru, and we trust him."

"Well, I don't," Tom said, but he had to let it go at that.

Another blast was set off, but it was not very successful.

"The rock seems to be getting harder the farther in we go," commented Walter Titus. "We're not up to where we ought to be."

"I'll have to look into it," answered Tom. "I may have to change the powder mixture. Guess I'll go up the mountain a way, and see if there are any outcroppings of rock there that would give me an idea of what lies underneath."

Accordingly, while the men in the tunnel were clearing away the rock loosened by the blast, Tom, one day, taking his electric rifle with him, went up the mountain under which the big bore ran.

He located, by computation, the spot beneath which the end of the tunnel then was, and began collecting samples of the outcropping ledge. He wanted to analyze these pieces of stone later. Koku was with him, and, giving the giant a bag of stones to carry, Tom walked on rather idly.

It was a wild and desolate region in which he found himself on the side of the mountain. Beyond him stretched towering and snow-clad peaks, and high in the air were small specks, which he knew to be condors, watching with their eager eyes for their offal food.

As Tom and Koku made their way along the mountain trail they came unexpectedly upon an Indian workman who was gathering herbs and bark, an industry by which many of the natives added to their scanty livelihood. The woman was familiar with the appearance of the white men, and nodded in friendly fashion.

Tom passed on, thinking of many things, when he was suddenly startled by a scream from the woman. It was a scream of such terror and agony that, for the moment, Tom was stunned into inactivity. Then, as he turned, he saw a great condor sweeping down out of the air, the wind fairly whistling through the big, outstretched wings.

"Jove!" ejaculated Tom. "Can the bird be going to attack the woman?"

But this was not the object of the condor. It was aiming to strike, with its fierce talons, at a point some paces distant from where the woman stood, and in the intervals between her screams Tom heard her cry, in her native tongue:

"My baby! My baby! The beast-bird will carry off my baby!"

Then Tom understood. The woman herb-gatherer had brought her infant with her on her quest, and had laid it down on a bed of soft grass while she worked. And it was this infant, wrapped as Tom afterward saw in a piece of deer-skin, at which the condor was aiming.

"Master shoot!" cried Koku, pointing to the down-sweeping bird.

"You bet I'll shoot!" cried Tom.

Throwing his electric rifle to his shoulder, Tom pressed the switch trigger. The unseen but powerful force shot straight at the condor.

The outstretched wings fell limp, the great body seemed to shrivel up, and, with a crash, the bird fell into the underbrush, breaking the twigs and branches with its weight. The electric rifle, a full account of which was given in the volume entitled "Tom Swift and His Electric Rifle," had done its work well.

With a scream, in which was mingled a cry of thanks, the woman threw herself on the sleeping child. The condor had fallen dead not three paces from it.

Tom Swift had shot just in time.

CHAPTER XVIII

THE INDIAN STRIKE

Snatching up in her arms the now awakened child, the woman gazed for a moment into its face, which she covered with kisses. Then the herb-gatherer looked over to the dead, limp body of the great condor, and from thence to Tom.

In another moment the woman had rushed forward, and knelt at the feet of the young inventor. Holding the baby in one arm, in her other hand the woman seized Toms and kissed it fervently, at the same time pouring forth a torrent of impassioned language, of which Tom could only make out a word now and then. But he gathered that the woman was thanking him for having saved the child.

"Oh, that's all right," Tom said, rather embarrassed by the hand-kissing. "It was an easy shot."

An Indian came bursting through the bushes, evidently the woman's husband by the manner in which she greeted him, and Tom recognized the newcomer as one of the tunnel workers. There was some quick conversation between the husband and wife, in which the latter made all sorts of motions, including in their scope Tom, his rifle, the dead condor and the now smiling baby.

The man took off his hat and approached Tom, genuflecting as he might have done in church.

"She say you save baby from condor," the man said in his halting English. "She t'ank you—me, I t'ank you. Bird see babe in deer skin—t'ink um dead animal. Maybe so bird carry baby off, drop um on sharp stone, baby smile no more. You have our lives, senor! We do anyt'ing we can for you."

"Thanks," said Tom, easily. "I'm glad I happened to be around. I supposed condors only went for things dead, but I reckon, as you say, it mistook the baby in the deer skin for a dead animal. And I guess it might have carried your little one off, or at least lifted it up, and then it might have dropped it far enough to have killed it. It sure is a big bird," and Tom strolled over to look at what he had bagged.

The condor of the Andes is the largest bird of prey in existence. One in the Bronx Zoo, in New York, with his wings spread out, measured a little short of ten feet from tip to tip. Measure ten feet out on the ground and then imagine a bird with that wing stretch.

This same condor in the park was made angry by a boy throwing a feather boa up into the air outside the cage. The condor raised himself from the ground, and hurled himself against the heavy wire netting so that the whole, big cage shook. And the breeze caused by the flapping wings blew off the hats of several spectators. So powerful was the air force from the condor's wings that it reminded one of the current caused when standing behind the propellers of an aeroplane in motion.

The condor rarely attacks living persons or animals, though it has been known to carry off big sheep when driven by hunger.

It was one of these animals Tom Swift had shot with his electric rifle.

"We do anyt'ing you want," the man gratefully repeated.

"Well, I've got about all I want," Tom said. "But if you could tell me where those ten missing men are, and how they got out of the tunnel, I'd be obliged to you."

The woman did not seem to comprehend Tom's talk, but the man did. He started, and fear seemed to come over him.

"Me—I—I can not tell," he murmured.

"No, I don't suppose you can," said Tom, musingly. "Well, it doesn't matter, I guess I'll have to cross it off my books. I'll never find out."

Again the Indian and his wife expressed their gratitude, and Tom, after letting the little brown baby cling to his finger, and patting its chubby cheek, went on his way with Koku.

"Well, that was some excitement," mused Tom, who made little of the shot itself, for the condor was such a mark that he would have had to aim very badly indeed to miss it. And perhaps only the electric rifle could have killed quickly enough to prevent the baby's being injured in some way by the big bird, even though it was dying.

"Master heap good shot!" exclaimed Koku, admiringly.

The tunnel work went on, though not so well as when Tom's explosive was first used. The rock was indeed getting harder and was not so easily shattered. Tom made tests of the pieces he had obtained from the outcropping ledge on the mountain where he had shot the condor, and decided to make a change in the powder.

Shipments were regularly received from Shopton, Mr. Swift keeping things in progress there. Mr. Damon's business was going on satisfactorily, and he lent what aid he could to Tom. As for Professor Bumper he kept on with his search for the lost city of Pelone, but with no success.

The scientist wanted Tom and Mr. Damon to go on another trip with him, this time to a distant sierra, or fertile valley, where it was reported a race of Indians lived, different from others in that region.

"It may be that they are descendants from the Pelonians," suggested the professor. Tom was too busy to go, but Mr. Damon went. The expedition had all sorts of trouble, losing its way and getting into a swamp from which escape was not easy. Then, too, the strange Indians proved hostile, and the professor and his party could not get nearer than the boundaries of the valley.

"But the difficulties and the hostile attitude of these natives only makes me surer that I am on the right track," said Mr. Bumper. "I shall try again."

Tom was busy over a problem in explosives one day when he saw Tim Sullivan hurrying into the office of the two brothers. The Irishman seemed excited.

"I hope there hasn't been another premature blast," mused Tom. "But if there had been I think I'd have heard it."

He hastened out to see Job and Walter Titus in excited conversation with Tim.

"They didn't come out, an' thot's all there is to it," the foreman was saying. "I sint thim in mesilf, and they worked until it was time t' set off th' blast. I wint t' get th' fuse, an' I was goin' t' send th' black imps out of danger, whin—whist—they was gone whin I got back—fifteen of 'em this time!"

"Do you mean that fifteen more of our men have vanished as the first ten did?" asked Job Titus.

"That's what I mean," asserted the Irishman.

"It can't be!" declared Walter.

"Look for yersilf!" returned Tim. "They're not in th' tunnel!"

"And they didn't come out?"

"Ask th' time-keeper," and Tim motioned to a young Englishman who, since the other disappearance, had been stationed at the mouth of the tunnel to keep a record of who went in and came out.

"No, sir! Nobody kime hout, sir!" the Englishman declared. "Hi 'aven't been away frim 'ere, sir, not since hi wint on duty, sir. An' no one kime out, no, sir!"

"We've got to stop this!" declared Job Titus.

"I should say so!" agreed his brother.

With Tom and Tim the Titus brothers went into the tunnel. It was deserted, and not a trace of the men could be found. Their tools were where they had been dropped, but of the men not a sign.

"There must be some secret way out," declared Tom.

"Then we'll find it," asserted the brothers.

Work on the tunnel was stopped for a day, and, keeping out all natives, the contractors, with Tom and such white men as they had in their employ, went over every foot of roof, sides and floor in the big shaft. But not a crack or fissure, large enough to permit the passage of a child, much less a man, could be found.

"Well, I give up!" cried Walter Titus in despair. "There must be witchcraft at work here!"

"Nonsense!" exclaimed his brother. "It's more likely the craft of Blakeson & Grinder, with Waddington helping them."

"Well, if a human agency made these twenty-five men disappear, prove it!" insisted Walter.

His brother did not know what to say.

"Well, go on with the work," was Job's final conclusion. "We'll have one of the white men constantly in the tunnel after this whenever a gang is working. We won't leave the natives alone even long enough to go to get a fuse. They'll be under constant supervision."

The tunnel was opened for work, but there were no workers. The morning after the investigation, when the starting whistle blew there was no line of Indians ready to file into the big, black hole. The huts where they slept were deserted. A strange silence brooded over the tunnel camp.

"Where are the men, Serato?" asked Tom of the Indian foreman.

"Men um gone. No work any more. What you call a hit."

"You mean a strike?" asked Tom.

"Sure—strike—hit—all um same. No more work—um 'fraid!"

CHAPTER XIX

A WOMAN TELLS

"Well, if this isn't the limit!" cried Torn Swift. "As if we didn't have trouble enough without a strike on our hands!"

"I should say yes!" chimed in Job Titus.

"Do you mean that the men won't work any more?" asked his brother of the native foreman.

"Sure, no more work—um much 'fraid big devil in tunnel carry um off an' eat um."

"Well, I don't know that I blame 'em for being a bit frightened," commented Job. "It is a queer proceeding how twenty-five men can disappear like that. Where have the men gone, Serato?"

"Gone home. No more work. Go on hit—strike—same like white men."

"They waited until pay day to go on strike," commented the book-keeper, a youth about Tom's age.

This was true. The men had been paid off the day before, and usually on such occasions many of them remained away, celebrating in the nearest village. But this time all had left, and evidently did not intend to come back.

"We'll have to get a new gang," said Job. "And it's going to delay us just at the wrong time. Well, there's no help for it. Get busy, Serato. You and Tim go and see how many men you can gather. Tell them we'll give them a sol a week more if they do good work. (A sol is the standard silver coin of Peru, and is worth in United States gold about fifty cents.)

"Half a dollar a day more will look mighty big to them," went on the contractor. "Get the men, Serato, and we'll raise your wages two sols a week."

The eyes of the Indian gleamed, and he went off, saying.

"Um try, but men much 'fraid."

Whether Serato used his best arguments could not, of course, be learned, but he came back at the close of the day, unaccompanied by any workers, and he shook his head despondently.

"Indians no come for one sol, mebby not for two," he said. "I no can git."

"Then I'll try!" cried Job. "I'll get the workers. I'll make our old ones come back, for they'll be the best."

Accompanied by his brother and Tom he went to the various Indian villages, including the one whence most of the men now on strike had come. The fifteen missing ones were not found, though, as before, their relatives, and, in some cases, their families, did not seem alarmed. But the men who had gone on strike were found lolling about their cabins and huts, smoking and taking their ease, and no amount of persuasion could induce them to return.

Some of them said they had worked long enough and were tired, needing a rest. Others declared they had money enough and did not want more. Even two more sols a week would not induce them to return.

And many were frankly afraid. They said so, declaring that if they went back to the tunnel some unknown devil might carry them off under the earth.

Job Titus and his brother, who could speak the language fairly well, tried to argue against this. They declared the tunnel was perfectly safe. But one native worker, who had been the best in the gang, asked:

"Where um men go?"

The contractors could not answer.

"It's a trick," declared Walter. "Our rivals have induced the men to go on strike in order to hamper us with the work so they'll get the job."

But the closest inquiry failed to prove this statement. If Blakeson & Grinder, or any of their agents, had a hand in the strike they covered their operations well. Though diligent inquiry was made, no trace of Waddington, or any other tool, could be found.

Tom, who had some sort of suspicion of the bearded man on the steamer, tried to find him, even taking a trip in to Lima, but without avail.

The tunnel work was at a standstill, for there was little use in setting off blasts if there were no men to remove the resulting piles of debris.

So, though Tom was ready with some specially powerful explosive, he could not use it.

Efforts were made to get laborers from another section of the country, but without effect. The contractors heard of a big force of Italians who had finished work on a railroad about a hundred miles away, and they were offered places in the tunnel. But they would not come.

"Well, we may as well give up," said Walter, despondently, to his brother one day. "We'll never get the tunnel done on time now."

"We still have a margin of safety," declared Job. "If we could get the men inside of a couple of weeks, and if Tom's new powder rips out more rock, we'll finish in time."

"Yes, but there are too many ifs. We may as well admit we've failed."

"I'll never do that!"

"What will you do?"

But Job did not know.

"If we could git a gang of min from the ould sod—th' kind I used t' work wit in N'Yark," said Tim Sullivan, "I'd show yez whot could be done! We'd make th' rock fly!"

But that efficient labor was out of the question now. The tunnel camp was a deserted place.

"Come on, Koku, we'll go hunting," said Tom one day. "There's no use hanging around here, and some venison wouldn't go bad on the table."

"I'll come, too," said Mr. Damon. "I haven't anything to do."

The Titus brothers had gone to a distant village, on the forlorn hope of getting laborers, so Tom was left to his own devices, and he decided to go hunting with his electric rifle.

The taruco, or native deer, had been plentiful in the vicinity of the tunnel until the presence of so many men and the frequent blasts had driven them farther off, and it was not until after a tramp of several miles that Tom saw one. Then, after stalking it a little way, he managed to kill it with the electric rifle.

Koku hoisted the animal to his big shoulders, and, as this would provide meat enough for some time, Tom started back for camp.

As he and Mr. Damon, with Koku in the rear, passed through a little clearing, they saw, on the far side, a native hut. And from it rushed a woman, who approached Tom, casting herself on her knees, while she pressed his free hand to her head.

"Bless my scarf pin!" exclaimed Mr. Damon. "What does this mean, Tom?"

"Oh, this is the mother of the child I saved from the condor," said Tom. "Every time she sees me she thanks me all over again. How is the baby?" he asked in the Indian tongue, for he was a fair master of it by now.

"The baby is well. Will the mighty hunter permit himself to enter my miserable hovel and partake of some milk and cakes?"

"What do you say, Mr. Damon?" Tom asked. "She's clean and neat, and she makes a drink of goat's milk that isn't bad. She bakes some kind of meal cakes that are good, too. I'm hungry."

"All right, Tom, I'll do as you say."

A little later they were partaking of a rude, but none the less welcome, lunch in the woman's hut, while the baby whose life Tom had saved cooed in the rough log cradle.

"Say, Masni," asked Tom, addressing the woman by name, "don't you know where we can get some men to work the tunnel?" Of course Tom spoke the Indian language, and he had to adapt himself to the comprehension of Masni.

"Men no work tunnel?" she inquired.

"No, they've all skipped out—vamoosed. Afraid of some spirit."

The woman looked around, as though in fear. Then she approached Tom closely and whispered:

"No spirit in tunnel—bad man!"

"What!" cried Tom, almost jumping off his stool. "What do you mean, Masni?"

"Me tell mighty hunter," she went on, lowering her voice still more. "My man he no want to tell, he 'fraid, but I tell. Mighty hunter save Vashni," and she looked toward the baby. "Me help friends of mighty hunter. Bad man in tunnel—no spirit!

"Men go. Spirit no take um—bad man take um."

"Where are they now?" asked Tom. "Jove, if I could find them the secret would be solved!"

The woman looked fearfully around the hut and then whispered:

"You come—me show!"

"Bless my toothbrush!" cried Mr. Damon. "What is going to happen, Tom Swift?"

"I don't know," was the answer, "but something sure is in the wind. I guess I shot better than I knew when I killed that condor."

CHAPTER XX

DESPAIR

Calling to a girl of about thirteen years to look after her baby, Masni slipped along up a rough mountain trail, motioning to Tom, Mr. Damon and Koku to follow. Or rather, the woman gave the sign to Tom, ignoring the others, who, naturally, would not be left behind. Masni seemed to have eyes for no one but the young inventor, and the manner in which she looked at him showed the deep gratitude she felt toward him for having saved her baby from the great condor.

"Come," she said, in her strange Indian tongue, which Tom could interpret well enough for himself now.

"But where are we going, Masni?" he asked. "This isn't the way to the tunnel."

"Me know. Not go to tunnel now," was her answer. "Me show you men."

"But which men do you mean, Masni?" inquired Tom. "The lost men, or the bad ones, who are making trouble for us? Which men do you mean?"

Masni only shook her head, and murmured: "Me show."

Probably Tom's attempt to talk her language was not sufficiently clear to her.

"My man—he good man," she said, coming to a pause on the rough trail after a climb which was not easy.

"Yes, I know he is," Tom said. "But he went on a strike with the others, Masni. He no work. He go on a 'hit,' as Serato calls it," and Tom laughed.

"My man he good man—but he 'fraid," said the wife. "He want to tell you of bad mans, but he 'fraid. You save my baby, I no 'fraid. I tell."

"Oh, I see," said Tom. "Your husband would have given away the secret, only he's afraid of the bad men. He likes me, too?"

"Sure!" Masni exclaimed. "He want tell, but 'fraid. He go 'way, I tell."

Tom was not quite sure what it all meant, but it seemed that after his slaying of the condor both parents were so filled with gratitude that they wanted to reveal some secret about the tunnel, only Masni's husband was afraid. She, however, had been braver.

"Something is going to happen," said Tom Swift. "I feel it in my bones!"

"Bless my porous plaster!" cried Mr. Damon. "I hope it isn't anything serious."

"We'll see," Tom went on.

They resumed their journey up the mountain trail. It wound in and out in a region none of them had before visited. Though it could not be far from the tunnel, it was almost a strange country to Tom.

Suddenly Masni stopped in a narrow gorge where the walls of rock rose high on either hand. She seemed looking for something. Her sharp, black eyes scanned the cliff and then with an exclamation of satisfaction she approached a certain place. With a quick motion she pulled aside a mass of tangled vines, and disclosed a path leading down through a V shaped crack in the cliff.

"Mans down there," she said. "You go look."

For a moment Tom hesitated. Was this a trap? If he and his friends entered this narrow and dark opening might not the Indian woman roll down some rock back of them, cutting off forever the way of escape?

Tom turned and looked at Masni. Then he was ashamed of his suspicion, for the honest black face, smiling at him, showed no trace of guile.

"You go—you see lost men," the woman urged.

"Come on!" cried Tom. "I believe we're on the track of the mystery!"

He led the way, followed by Mr. Damon, while Koku came next and then Masni. It could be no trap since she entered it herself.

The path widened, but not much. There was only room for one to walk at a time. The trail twisted and turned, and Tom was wondering how far it led, when, from behind him, came the cry of the woman:

"Watch now—no fall down."

Tom halted around a sharp turn, and stood transfixed at the sight which met his gaze. He found himself looking out through a crack in the face of a sheer stone cliff that went straight down for a hundred feet or more to a green-carpeted valley.

Tom was standing in a narrow cleft of rock—the same rock through which they had made their way. And at the foot of the cliff was a little encampment of Indians. There were a dozen huts, and wandering about them, or sitting in the shade, were a score or more of Indians.

"There men from tunnel," said Masni, and, as he looked, wondering, Tom saw some of the workers he knew. One especially, was a laborer who walked with a peculiar limp.

"The missing men!" gasped the young inventor.

"Bless my almanac!" cried Mr. Damon. "Where?"

"Here," answered Tom. "If you squeeze past me you can see them." Mr. Damon did so.

"How did they get here?" asked the odd man, as he looked down in the little valley where the missing ones were sequestered.

"That's what we've got to find out," Tom said. "At any rate here they are, and they seem to be enjoying life while we've been worrying as to what had become of them. How did they get here, Masni?"

"Me show you. Come."

"Wait until I take another look," said Tom.

"Be careful they don't see you," cautioned Mr. Damon.

"They can't very well. The cleft is screened by bushes."

Tom looked down once more on the group of men who had so mysteriously disappeared. The little valley stretched out away from the face of the cliff, through which, by means of the crack, or cleft in it, Tom and the others had come. Tom looked down the wall of rock. It was as smooth as the side of a building, and offered no means of getting down or up. Doubtless there was an easier entrance to the valley on the other side. It was like looking down into some vast hall through an upper window or from a balcony.

"And those men have been in hiding, or been hidden here, ever since they disappeared from the tunnel," said Mr. Damon.

"It doesn't look as though they were detained by force," Tom remarked. "I think they are being paid to stay away. How did they get here, Masni?"

"Me show you. Come!"

They went back along the trail that led through the split in the rock, until they had come to the place where the natural curtain of vines concealed the entrance. Tom took particular notice of this place so he would know it again.

Then Masni led them over the mountain, and this time Tom saw that they were approaching the tunnel. He recognized some places where he had taken samples of rock from the outcropping to test the strength of his explosive.

Reaching a certain wild and desolate place, Masni made a signal of caution. She seemed to be listening intently. Then, as if satisfied there was no danger, she parted some bushes and glided in, motioning the others to follow.

"Now I wonder what's up," Tom mused.

He and the others were soon informed.

Masni stopped in front of a pile of brush. With a few vigorous motions of her arms she swept it aside and revealed a smooth slab of rock. In the centre was what seemed to be a block of metal Masni placed her foot on this and pressed heavily.

And those watching saw a strange thing.

The slab of rock tilted to one side, as if on a pivot, revealing a square opening which seemed to lead through solid stone. And at the far end of the opening Tom Swift saw a glimmer of light.

Stooping down, he looked through the hole thus strangely opened and what he saw caused him to cry out in wonder.

"It's the tunnel!" he cried. "I can look right down into the tunnel. It's the incandescent lights I see. I can look right at the ledge of rock where

I kept watch that day, and where I saw—where I saw the face of Waddington!" he cried. "It wasn't a dream after all. This is a shaft connecting with the tunnel. We didn't discover it because this rock fits right in the opening in the roof. It must have been there all the while, and some blast brought it to light. Is this how the men got out, or were taken out of the tunnel, Masni?" Tom asked.

"This how," said the Indian woman. "See, here rope!"

She pawed aside a mound of earth, and disclosed a rope buried there, a rope knotted at intervals. This, let down through the hole in the roof of the tunnel, provided a means of escape, and in such a manner that the disappearance of the men was most mysterious.

"I see how it is!" cried Tom. "Some one interested, Waddington probably, who knew about this old secret shaft going down into the earth, used it as soon as our blasting was opened that far. They got the men out this way, and hid them in the secret valley."

"But what for?" cried Mr. Damon.

"To cripple us! To cause the strike by making our other workers afraid of some evil spirit! The men were taken away secretly, and, doubtless, have been kept in idleness ever since—paid to stay away so the mystery would be all the deeper. Our rivals finding they couldn't stop us in any other way have taken our laborers away from us."

"Bless my meal ticket! It does look like that!" cried Mr. Damon.

"Of course that's the secret!" cried Tom. "Blakeson & Grinder, or some of their tools—probably the bearded man or Waddington—found out about this shaft which led down into our tunnel. They induced the first ten men to quit, and when Tim went to get the fuse the rope was let down, and the men climbed up here, one after the other. Those Indians can climb like cats. Once the ten were out the shaft was closed with the rock, and the ten men taken off to the valley to be secreted there.

"The same was done with the next fifteen, and, I suppose, if the strike hadn't come, more of our workers would have been induced to leave in this way. They're probably being better paid than when earning their wages; and their relatives must know where they are, and also be given a bonus to keep still. No wonder they didn't make a fuss.

"And no wonder we couldn't find any opening in the tunnel roof. This rock must fit in as smoothly as a secret drawer in the kind of old desk where missing wills are found in stories."

"You say you saw Waddington, or the bearded man?" asked Mr. Damon.

"At the time," replied Tom, "I thought it was a dream. Now I know it wasn't. He must have opened the shaft just as I awakened from a doze. He saw me and closed it again. He may have been getting ready then to take off more of our men, so as to scare the others. Well, we've found out the trick."

"And what are you going to do next?" asked Mr. Damon.

"Get those missing men back. That will break the hoodoo, and the others will come back to work. Then we'll get on the trail of Waddington, or Blakeson & Grinder, and put a stop to this business. We know their secret now."

"You mean to get the men out of the secret valley, Tom?"

"Yes. There must be some other way into it than down the rock where we were. How about it, Masni?" and he inquired as to the valley. The Indian woman gave Tom to understand that there was another entrance.

"Well, close up this shaft now before some one sees us at it—the bearded man, for example," Tom suggested. He took another look down into the tunnel, which was now deserted on account of the strike, and then Masni pressed on the mechanism that worked the stone. She showed Tom how to do it.

"Just a counter-balanced rock operating on the same principle as does a window," Tom explained, after a brief examination. "Probably some of the old Indian tribes made this shaft for ceremonial purposes. They never dreamed we would drive a tunnel along at the bottom of it. The shaft probably opened into a cave, and one of our blasts made it part of the tunnel. Well, this is part of the secret, anyhow. Much obliged to you, Masni!"

The Indian woman had indeed revealed valuable information. They covered the secret rock with brush, as it had been, hid the rope and came away. But Tom knew how to find the place again.

Events moved rapidly from then on. The Titus brothers were more than astonished when Tom told them what he had learned. Masni had told him how to get into the secret valley by a round about, but easy trail, and thither Tom, the contractors, Mr. Damon and some of the white tunnel workers went the next day.

The sequestered men, taken completely by surprise, tried to bolt when they saw that they were discovered, and then, shamefacedly enough, admitted their part in the trick.

They would not, however, reveal who had helped them escape from the tunnel. Threats and promises of rewards were alike unavailing, but Tom and his employers knew well enough who it was. The tunnel workers seemed rather tired of living in comparative luxury and idleness, and agreed to come back to their labors.

They packed up their few belongings, mostly cooking pots and pans, and marched out of the valley to the village at Rimac.

And so the strike was broken.

The reappearance of the missing men, in better health and spirits than when they went away, acted like magic. The other men, who had missed their wages, crowded back into the shaft, and the sounds of picks and shovels were heard again in the tunnel.

Whether the missing ones told the real story, or whether they made up some tale to account for their absence, Tom and his friends could not learn. Nor did the bearded man (if he it were who had helped in the plot), nor any representative of Blakeson & Grinder appear. The work on the tunnel was resumed as if nothing had happened. But Tom arranged a bright light so it would reflect on the spot in the roof where the moving rock was, so that if the evil face of the bearded man, or of Waddington, appeared there again, it would quickly be seen. A search of the neighborhood, and diligent inquiries, failed to disclose the presence of any of the plotters.

And then, as if Fate was not making it hard enough for the tunnel contractors, they encountered more trouble. It was after Tom had set off a big blast that Tim Sullivan, after inspecting what had happened, came out to ask.

"I soy, Mr. Swift, why didn't yez use more powder?"

"More powder!" cried Tom. "Why, this is the most I have ever set off."

"Then somethin's wrong, sor. Fer there's only a little rock down. Come an' see fer yersilf."

Tom hastened in. As the foreman had said, the effect of the blast was small indeed. Only a little rock had been shaled off. Tom picked up some of this and took it outside for examination.

"Why, it's harder than the hardest flint we've found yet," he said. "The powder didn't make any impression on it at all. I'll have to use terrific charges."

This was done, but with little better effect. The explosive, powerful as it was, ate only a little way into the rock. Blast after blast had the same poor effect.

"This won't do," said Job Titus, despairingly, one day. "We aren't making any progress at all. There's a half mile of this rock, according to my calculations, and at this rate we'll be six months getting through it. By that time our limit will be up, and we'll be forced to give up the contract What can we do, Tom Swift?"

CHAPTER XXI

A NEW EXPLOSIVE

The young inventor was idly handling some pieces of the very hard rock that had cropped out in the tunnel cut Tom had tested it, he had pulverized it (as well as he was able), he had examined it under the microscope, and he had taken great slabs of it and set off under it, or on top of it, charges of explosive of various power to note the effect. But the results had not been at all what he had hoped for.

"What's to be done, Tom?" repeated the contractor.

"Well, Mr. Titus," was the answer, "the only thing I see to do is to make a new explosive."

"Can you do it, Tom?"

The reply was characteristic.

"I can try."

And in the days that followed, Tom began work on a new line. He had brought from Shopton with him much of the needful apparatus, and he found he could obtain in Lima what he lacked.

A message to his father brought the reply that the new ingredients Tom needed would be shipped.

"The kind of explosive we need to rend that very hard rock," the young inventor explained to the Titus brothers, "is one that works slowly."

"I thought all explosions had to be as quick as a flash," said Walter.

"Well, in a sense, they do. Yet we have quick burning and slow-burning powders, the same as we have fuses. A quick-burning explosive is all right in soft rock, or in soil with rock and earth mingled. But in rock that is harder than flint if you use a quick explosive, only the outer surface of the rock will be scaled off.

"If you take a hammer and bring it down with all your force on a hard rock you may chip off a lot of little pieces, or you may crack the rock, but you won't, under ordinary circumstances, pulverize it as we want to do in the tunnel.

"On the other hand, if you take a smaller hammer, and keep tapping the rock with comparatively gentle blows, you will set up a series of vibrations, that, in time, will cause the hard rock to break up into any number of small pieces.

"Now that is the kind of explosive I want one that will deal a succession of constant blows at the hard rock instead of one great big blast."

"Can you make it, Tom?"

"Well, I don't know. I'll do the best I can."

From then on Tom was busy with his experiments.

Work on the tunnel did not cease while he was searching for a new explosive. There was plenty of the old explosive left and charges of this were set off as fast as holes could be drilled to receive it. But comparatively little was accomplished. Sometimes more rock would be loosed than at others, and the native laborers, now seemingly perfectly contented, would be kept busy. Again, when a heavy blast would be set off hardly a dozen dump cars could be filled.

But the work must go on. Already the time limit was getting perilously close, and the contractors did not doubt that their rivals were only waiting for a chance to step in and take their places.

Nothing more had been seen or heard of the bearded man, Waddington, or Blakeson & Grinder. But that the rival firm had not given up was evidenced by the efforts made in New York to cripple, financially, the firm in which Tom was interested. In fact, at one time the Titus brothers were so tied up that they could not get money enough to pay their men. But Tom cabled his father, who was quite wealthy, and Mr. Swift loaned the contractors enough to proceed with until they could dispose of some securities.

It might be mentioned that Tom was to get a large sum if the tunnel were completed on time, so it was to his interest and his father's, to bring this about if he could.

Tom kept on with his powder experiments. Mr. Damon helped him, for that gentleman had succeeded in putting the affairs of the wholesale drug business on a firm foundation, and there was no more trouble about getting the supplies of cinchona bark to market. The natives seemed to have taken kindly to the eccentric man, or perhaps it was the reputation of Tom Swift and his electric rifle that induced them to work hard.

It must not be supposed that Professor Bumper was idle all this while.

He came and went at odd times, accompanied by his little retinue of Indians, a guide and a native cook. He would come back to the tunnel camp, where he made his headquarters, travel stained, worn and weary, with disappointment showing on his face.

"No luck," he would report. "The hidden city of Pelone is still lost."

Then he would retire to his tent, to pour over his note-books, and make a new translation of the inscription on the golden plates. In a day or so, refreshed and rested, he would prepare for another start.

"I'll find it this time, surely!" he would exclaim, as he marched off up the mountain trail. "I have heard of a new valley, never before visited by a white man, in which there are some old ruins. I'm sure they must be those of Pelone."

But in a week or so he would come back, worn out and discouraged again.

"The ruins were only those of a native village," he would say. "No trace of an ancient civilization there."

The professor took little or no interest in the tunnel, though he expressed the hope that Tom and his friends would be successful. But industrial pursuits had no charm for the scientist. He only lived to find the hidden city which was to make him famous.

He heard the story of the queer shaft leading down into the bore under the mountain, and, for a time, hoped that might be some clue to the lost Pelone. But, after an examination, he decided it was but the shaft to some ancient mine which had not panned out, and so had been abandoned after having been fitted with a balanced rocky door, perhaps for some heathen religious rite.

There seemed to be no further trouble among the Indian tunnel workers. Those who had disappeared—who had, seemingly, gone willingly up the knotted rope to hide themselves in the valley—kept on with their work. If they told their fellows why and where they had gone, the others gave no sign. The evil spirits of the tunnel had been exorcised, and there was now peace, save for the blasts that were set off every so often.

Tom tried combination after combination, testing them inside and outside the tunnel, always seeking for an explosive that would give a slow, rending effect instead of a quick blow, the power of which was soon lost. And at last he announced:

"I think I have it!"

"Have you? Good!" cried Job Titus.

"Yes," Tom went on, "I've got a mixture here that seems to give just the effect I want. I tried it on some small pieces of rock, and now I want to test it on some large chunks. Have you brought any down lately?"

"Yes, we have some big slabs in there."

Some large pieces of the hard rock, which had been brought down in a recent blast, were taken outside the tunnel, and in them one afternoon Tom placed, in holes drilled to receive it, some of his new explosive. The rocks were set some distance away from the tunnel camp, and Tom attached the electric wires that were to detonate the charge.

"Well, I guess we're ready," announced the young inventor, as he looked about him.

The tunnel workers had been allowed to go for the day, and in a log shack, where they would be safe from flying pieces of rock, were Tom, Mr. Damon and the two Titus brothers.

Tom held the electric switch in his hand, and was about to press it.

"This explosive works differently from any other," he explained. "When the charge is fired there is not instantly a detonation and a bursting. The powder burns slowly and generates an immense amount of gas. It is this gas, accumulating in the cracks and crevices of the rock, that I hope will burst and disintegrate it. Of course, an explosion eventually follows, as you will see. Here she goes!"

Tom pressed the switch and, as he did so, there was a cry of alarm from Mr. Damon.

"Bless my safety match, Tom!" cried the old man. "Look! Koku!"

For, as the charge was fired, the giant emerged from the woods and calmly took a seat on the rock that was about to be broken up into fragments by Tom's new explosive.

CHAPTER XXII

THE FIGHT

"Get off there, Koku!"

"Stand up!"

"Run!"

"Get out uf the way! That's going up!"

Thus cried Tom and his friends to the big, good-natured, but somewhat stupid, giant who had sat down in the dangerous spot. Koku looked toward the hut, in front of which the young inventor and the others stood, waving their hands to him and shouting.

"Get up! Get up!" cried Tom, frantically. The powder is going off, Koku!"

"Can't you stop it?" asked Job Titus.

"No!" answered Tom. "The electric current has already ignited the charge. Only that it's slow-burning it would have been fired long ago. Get up, Koku!"

But the giant did not seem to understand. He waved his hand in friendly greeting to Tom and the others, who dared not approach closer to warn him, for the explosion would occur any second now.

Then Mr. Damon had an inspiration.

"Call him to come to you, Tom!" shouted the odd man. "He always comes to you in a hurry, you know. Call him!"

Tom acted on the suggestion at once.

"Here, Koku!" he cried. "Come here, I want you! Kelos!"

This last was a word in the giant's own language, meaning "hurry." And Koku knew when Tom used that word that there was need of haste. So, though he had sat down, evidently to take his ease after a long tramp through the woods, Koku sprang up to obey his master's bidding.

And, as he did so, something happened. The first spark from the fuse, ignited by the electric current, had reached the slow-burning powder. There was a crackle of flame, and a dull rumble. Koku sprang up from the big stone as though shot. What he saw and heard must have alarmed him, for he gave a mighty jump and started to run, at the same time shouting:

"Me come, Master!"

"You'd better!" cried the young inventor.

Koku got away only just in time, for when he was half way between the group of his friends and the big rock, the utmost force of the explosion was felt. It was not so very loud, but the power of it made the earth tremble.

The rock seemed to heave itself into the air, and when it settled back it was seen to be broken up into many pieces. Koku looked back over his shoulder and gave another tremendous leap, which carried him out of the way of the flying fragments, some of which rattled on the roof of the log hut.

"There!" cried Tom. "I guess something happened that time! The rock is broken up finer than any like it we tried to shatter before. I think I've got the mixture just right!"

"Bless my handkerchief!" cried Mr. Damon. "Think of what might have happened to Koku if he had been sitting there."

"Well," said Tom, "he might not have been killed, for he would probably have been tossed well out of the way at the first slow explosion, but afterward—well, he might have been pretty well shaken up. He got away just in time."

The giant looked thoughtfully back toward the place of the experimental blast.

"Master, him do that?" he asked.

"I did," Tom replied. "But I didn't think you'd walk out of the woods, just at the wrong time, and sit down on that rock."

"Um," murmured the giant. "Koku—he—he—Oh, by golly!" he yelled. And then, as if realizing what he had escaped, and being incapable of expressing it, the giant with a yell ran into the tunnel and stayed there for some time.

The experiment was pronounced a great success and, now that Tom had discovered the right kind of explosive to rend the very hard rock, he proceeded to have it made in sufficiently large quantities to be used in the tunnel.

"We'll have to hustle," said Job Titus. "We haven't much of our contract time left, and I have reason to believe the Peruvian government will not give any extension. It is to their interest to have us fail, for they will profit by all the work we have done, even if they have to pay our rivals a higher price than we contracted for. It is our firm that will pocket the loss."

"Well, we'll try not to have that happen," said Tom, with a smile.

"If you're going to use bigger charges of this new explosive, Tom, won't more rock be brought down?" asked Walter Titus.

"That's what I hope."

"Then we'll need more laborers to bring it out of the tunnel."

"Yes, we could use more I guess. The faster the blasted rock is removed, the quicker I can put in new charges."

"I'll get more men," decided the contractor. "There won't be any trouble now that the hoodoo of the missing workers is solved. I'll tell Serato to scare up all his dusky brethren he can find, and we'll offer a bonus for good work."

The Indian foreman readily agreed to get more laborers.

"And get some big ones, Serato," urged Job Titus. "Get some fellows like Koku," for the giant did the work of three men in the tunnel, not because he was obliged to, but because his enormous strength must find an outlet in action.

"Um want mans like him?" asked the Indian, nodding toward the giant. He and Koku were not on good terms, for once, when Koku was a hurry, he had picked up the Indian (no mean sized man himself) and had calmly set him to one side. Serato never forgave that.

"Sure, get all the giants you can," Tom said. "But I guess there aren't any in Peru."

Where Serato found his man, no one knew, and the foreman would not tell; but a day or so later he appeared at the tunnel camp with an Indian so large in size that he made the others look like pygmies, and many of them were above the average in height, too.

"Say, he's a whopper all right!" exclaimed Tom. "But he isn't as big or as strong as Koku."

"He comes pretty near it," said Job Titus. "With a dozen like him we'd finish the tunnel on time, thanks to your explosive."

Lamos, the Indian giant, was not quite as large as Koku. That is, he was not as tall, but he was broader of shoulder. And as to the strength of the two, well, it was destined to be tried out in a startling fashion.

In about a week Tom was ready with his first charges of the new explosive. The extra Indians were on hand, including Lamos, and great hopes of fast progress were held by the contractors.

The charge was fired and a great mass of broken rock brought down inside the tunnel.

"That's tearing it up!" cried Job Titus, when the fumes had blown away, the secret shaft having been opened to facilitate this. "A few more shots like that and we'll be through the strata of hard rock."

The Indians, Koku and Lamos doing their share of the work, were rushed in to clear away the debris, so another charge might be fired as soon as possible. This would be in a day or so. The contract time was getting uncomfortably close.

Blast after blast was set off, and good progress was made. But instead of half a mile of the extra hard rock the contractors found it would be nearer three quarters.

"It's going to be touch and go, whether or not we finish on time," said Mr. Job Titus one afternoon, when a clearance had been made and the men had filed out to give the drillers a chance to make holes for a new blast.

Tom was about to make a remark when Tim Sullivan came running out of the tunnel, his face showing fright and wonder.

"What's up now, I wonder," said Mr. Titus. "More men missing?"

"Quick! Come quick!" cried the Irishman. "Thim two giants is fightin' in there, an' they'll tear th' tunnel apart if we don't stop 'em. It's an awful fight! Awful!"

CHAPTER XXIII

A GREAT BLAST

Hardly comprehending what the Irish foreman had said, Tom Swift, the Titus brothers and Mr. Damon followed Tim Sullivan back into the tunnel. They had not gone far before they heard the murmur of many voices, and mingled with that were roarings like those of wild beasts.

"That's thim!" cried Tim. "They're chawin' each other up!"

"Koku and that Indian giant fighting!" cried Tom. "What's it all about?"

"Don't ask me!" shouted Tim. "They've been on bad terms iver since they met." This was true enough, for one giant was jealous of the other's power, and they were continually trying feats of strength against one another. Probably this had culminated in a fight, Tom concluded.

"And it will be some fight!" mused the young inventor.

Hurrying on, Tom and his companions came upon a strange and not altogether pleasant sight. In an open place in the tunnel, where the lights were brightest, and in front of the rocky wall which offered a bar to further progress and which was soon to be blasted away, struggled the two giants.

With their arms locked about one another, they swayed this way and that—a struggle between two Titans. Of nearly the same height and big-ness, it was a wrestling match such as had never been seen before. Had it been merely a friendly test of strength it would have been good to look upon. But it needed only a glance into the faces of either giant to show that it was a struggle in deadly earnest.

Back and forth they reeled over the rocky floor of the tunnel, bones and sinews cracking. One sought to throw the other, and first, as Koku would gain a slight advantage, his friends would call encouragement, while, when Lamos seemed about to triumph, the Indians favoring him would let out a yell of triumph.

For a few minutes Tom and his friends watched, fascinated. Then they saw Koku slip, while Lamos bent him farther toward the earth. The Indian giant raised his big fist, and Tom saw in it a rock, which the big man was about to bring down on Koku's head.

"Look out, Koku!" yelled Tom.

Tom's giant slid to one side only just in time, for the blow descended, catching him on his muscular shoulder where it only raised a bruise. And then Koku gathered himself for a mighty effort. His face flamed with rage at the unfair trick.

"Bless my bath sponge!" cried Mr. Damon. "This is awful!"

"They must stop!" said Job Titus. "We can't have them fighting like this. It is bad for the others. If it were in fun it would be all right, but they are in deadly earnest. They must stop!"

"Koku, stop!" called Tom. "You must not fight any more!"

"No fight more!" gasped the giant, through his clenched teeth. "This end fight!"

With a mighty effort he broke the hold of Lamos' arms. Then stooping suddenly he seized his rival about the middle, and with a tremendous heave, in which his muscles stood out in great bunches while his very bones seemed to crack, Koku raised Lamos high in the air. Up over his head he raised that mass of muscle, bone and flesh, squirming and wriggling, trying in vain to save itself.

Up and up Koku raised Lamos as the murmur of those watching grew to a shout of amazement and terror. Never had the like been seen in that land for generations. Up and up one giant raised the other. Then calling out something in his native tongue Koku hurled the other from him, clear across the tunnel and up against the opposite rocky wall. The murmuring died to frightened whispers as Lamos fell in a shapeless heap on the floor.

"Ah!" breathed Koku, stretching himself, and extending his brawny arms. "Fight all over, Master."

"Yes, so it seems, Koku," said Tom, solemnly, "but you have killed him. Shame on you!" and he spoke bitterly.

Job Titus had hurried over to the fallen giant.

"He isn't dead," he called, "but I guess he won't wrestle or fight any more. He's badly crippled."

"And him no more try to blow up tunnel, either," said Koku in his hoarse voice. "Me fix: him! No more him take powder, and make tunnel all bust."

"What do you mean, Koku?" asked Tom. "Is that why you fought him? Did he try to wreck the tunnel?"

"So him done, Master. But Koku see—Koku stop. Then um fight."

"Be jabbers an' I wouldn't wonder but what he was right!" cried Tim Sullivan, excitedly. "I did see that beggar." and he pointed to Lamos, who was slowly crawling away, "at the chist where I kape th' powder, but I thought nothin' of it at th' time. What did he try t' do, Koku?"

Then the giant explained in his own language, Tom Swift translating, for Koku spoke English but indifferently well.

"Koku says," rendered Torn, "that he saw Lamos trying to put a big charge of powder up in the place where the balanced rock fits in the secret opening of the tunnel roof. The charge was all ready to fire, and if the giant had set it off he might have brought down the roof of the tunnel and so choked it up that we'd have been months cleaning it out. Koku saw him and stopped him, and then the fight began. We only saw the end."

"Bless my shoe string!" gasped Mr. Damon. "And a terrible end it was. Will Lamos die?"

"I don't think so," answered Job Titus. "But he will be a cripple for life. Not only would he have wrecked the tunnel, but he would have killed many of our men had he set off that blast. Koku saved them, though it seems too bad he had to fight to do it."

An investigation showed that Koku spoke truly. The charge, all ready to set off, was found where he had knocked it from the hand of Lamos. And so Tom's giant saved the day. Lamos was sent back to his own village, a broken and humbled giant. And to this day, in that part of Peru, the great struggle between Koku and Lamos is spoken of with awe where Indians gather about their council fires, and they tell their children of the Titanic fight.

"It was part of the plot," said Job Titus when the usual blast had been set off that day, with not very good results. "This giant was sent to us by our rivals. They wanted him to hamper our work, for they see we have a chance to finish on time. I think that foreman, Serato, is in the plot. He brought Lamos here. We'll fire him!"

This was done, though the Indian protested his innocence. But he could not be trusted.

"We can't take any chances," said Job Titus. "Our time is too nearly up. In fact I'm afraid we won't finish on time as it is. There is too much of that hard rock to cut through."

"There's only one thing to do," said Tom, after an investigation. "As you say, there is more of that hard rock than we calculated on. To try to blast and take it out in the ordinary way will be useless. We must try desperate means."

"What is that?" asked Walter Titus.

"We must set off the biggest blast we can with safety. We'll bore a lot of extra holes, and put in double charges of the explosive. I'll add some ingredients to it that will make it stronger. It's our last chance. Either we'll blow the tunnel all to pieces, or we'll loosen enough rock to make sufficient progress so we can finish on time. What do you say? Shall we take the chance?"

The Titus brothers looked at one another. Failure stared them in the face. Unless they completed the tunnel very soon they would lose all the money they had sunk in it.

"Take the chance!" exclaimed Job. "It's sink or swim anyhow. Set off the big blast, Tom."

"All right. We'll get ready for it as soon as we can."

That day preparations were made for setting off a great charge of the powerful explosive. The work was hurried as fast as was consistent with safety, but even then progress was rather slow. Precautions had to be taken, and the guards about the tunnel were doubled. For it was feared that some word of what was about to be done would reach the rival firm, who might try desperate means to prevent the completion of the work.

There was plenty of the explosive on hand, for Mr. Swift had sent Tom a large shipment. All this while no word had come from Mr. Nestor, and Tom was beginning to think that his prospective father-in-law was very angry with him. Nor had Mary written.

Professor Bumper came and went as he pleased, but his quest was regarded as hopeless now. Tom and his friends had little time for the bald-headed scientist, for they were too much interested in the success of the big blast.

"Well, we'll set her off tomorrow," Tom said one night, after a hard day's work. "The rocky wall is honeycombed with explosive. If all goes well we ought to bring down enough rock to keep the gangs busy night and day."

Everything was in readiness. What would the morrow bring—success or failure?

CHAPTER XXIV

THE HIDDEN CITY

Gathered beyond the mouth of the tunnel, far enough away so that the wind of the great blast would not bowl them over like ten pins, stood Tom Swift and his friends. In his hand Tom held the battery box, the setting of the switch in which would complete the electrical circuit and set off the hundreds of pounds of explosive buried deep in the hard rock.

"Are all the men out?" asked the young inventor of Tim Sullivan, who had charge of this important matter. Tim was in sole charge as foreman now, having picked up enough of the Indian language to get along without an interpreter.

"All out, sor," Tim responded. "Yez kin fire whin ready, Mr. Swift."

It was a portentous moment. No wonder Tom Swift hesitated. In a sense he and his friends, the contractors, had staked their all on a single throw. If this blast failed it was not likely that another would succeed, even if there should be time to prepare one.

The time limit had almost expired, and there was still a half mile of hard rock between the last heading and the farther end of the big tunnel. If the blast succeeded enough rock might be brought down to enable the work to go on, by using a night and day shift of men. Then, too, there was the chance that the hard strata of rock would come to an end and softer stone, or easily-dug dirt, be encountered.

"Well, we may as well have it over with," said Tom in a low voice. Every one was very quiet—tensely quiet.

The young inventor looked up to see Professor Bumper observing him.

"Why, Professor!" Tom exclaimed, "I thought you had gone off to the mountains again, looking for the lost city."

"I am going, Tom, very soon. I thought I would stop and see the effect of your big blast. This is my last trip. If I do not find the hidden city of Pelone this time, I am going to give up."

"Give up!" cried Mr. Damon. "Bless my fountain pen!"

"Oh, not altogether," went on the bald-headed scientist. "I mean I will give up searching in this part of Peru, and go elsewhere. But I will never completely give up the search, for I am sure the hidden city exists somewhere under these mountains," and he looked off toward the snow-covered peaks of the Andes.

Tom looked at the battery box. He drew a long breath, and said:

"Here she goes!"

There was a contraction of his hand as he pressed the switch over, and then, for perhaps a half second, nothing happened. Just for an instant Tom feared something had gone wrong that the electric current had failed, or that the wires had become disconnected—perhaps through some action of the plotting rivals.

And then, gently at first, but with increasing intensity, the solid ground on which they were all standing seemed to rock and sway, to heave itself up, and then sink down.

"Bless my—" began Mr. Damon, but he got no further, for a mighty gust of wind swept out of the tunnel, and blew off his hat. That gust was but a gentle breeze, though, compared to what followed. For there came such a rush of air that it almost blew over those standing near the opening of the great shaft driven under the mountain. There was a roar as of Niagara, a howling as in the Cave of the Winds, and they all bent to the blast.

Then followed a dull, rumbling roar, not as loud as might have been expected, but awful in its intensity. Deep down under the very foundations of the earth it seemed to rumble.

"Run! Run back!" cried Tom Swift. "There's a back-draft and the powder gas is poisonous. Stoop down and run back!"

They understood what he meant. The vapor from the powder was deadly if breathed in a confined space. Even in the open it gave one a terrible headache. And Tom could see floating out of the tunnel the first wisps of smoke from the fired explosive. It was lighter than air, and would rise. Hence the necessity, as in a smoke-filled room, of keeping low down where the air is purer.

They all rushed back, stooping low. Mr. Damon stumbled and fell, but Koku picked him up and, tucking him under one arm, as he might have done a child, the giant followed Tom to a place of safety.

"Well, Tom, it went off all right," said Mr. Job Titus, as they stood among the shacks of the workmen and watched the smoke pouring out of the tunnel mouth.

"Yes, it went off. But did it do the work? That's what we've got to find out."

They waited impatiently for the deadly vapor to clear out of the tunnel. It was more than an hour before they dared venture in, and then it was with smarting eyes and puckered throats. But the atmosphere was quickly clearing.

"Switch on the lights," cried Tom to Tim, for the illuminating current had been cut off when the blast was fired. "Let's see what we've brought down."

Following the eager young inventor came the contractors, some of the white workers, Mr. Damon and Professor Bumper. The little scientist said he would like to see the effect of the big blast.

Along they stumbled over pieces of rock, large and small.

"Some force to it," observed Job Titus, as he observed pieces of rock close to the mouth of the tunnel. "If it only exerted the force the other way, against the face of the rock, as well as back this way, we'll be all right."

"The greater force was in the opposite direction," Tom said.

A big search-light had been got ready to flash on the place where the blast had been set off. This was to enable them to see how much rock had been torn away. And, as they reached the place where the flint-like wall had been, they saw a strange sight.

"Bless my strawberry short-cake!" gasped Mr. Damon. "What a hole!"

"It is a hole," admitted Tom, in a low voice. "A bigger hole than I dared hope for."

For a great cave, seemingly, had been blown in the face of the rock wall that had hindered the progress of the tunnel. A great black void confronted them.

"Shift the light over this way," called Tom to Walter Titus, who was operating it. "I can't see anything."

The great beam of light flashed into the void, and then a murmur of awe came from every throat.

For there, revealed in the powerful electrical rays, was what seemed to be a long tunnel, high and wide, as smooth as a paved street. And on either side of it were what appeared to be buildings, some low, others taller. And, branching off from the main tunnel, or street, were other passages, also lined with buildings, some of which had crumbled to ruins.

"Bless my dictionary!" cried Mr. Damon. "What is it?"

Professor Bumper had crawled forward over the mass of broken rock. He gazed as if fascinated at what the searchlight showed, and then he cried:

"I have found it! I have found it! The hidden city of Pelone!"

CHAPTER XXV

SUCCESS

Had it not been for Tom Swift, the excited professor would have rushed pellmell over the jagged pile of rocks into the great cave which had been opened by the blast, the cave in which the scientist declared was the lost city for which he had been searching. But the young inventor grasped Mr. Bumper by the arm.

"Better wait a bit," Tom suggested. "There may be powder gas in there. Some of it must have blown forward."

"I don't care!" cried the professor. "That is the hidden city! I'm sure of it! I have found it at last! I must go in and examine it!"

"There'll be plenty of time," said Tom. "It isn't going to run away. Wait until I make a test Tim, hand me one of those torches."

Some torches of a very inflammable wood were used to test for the presence of the deadly smoke-gas. Lighting one of these, Tom tossed it into the big excavation.

It fell to the stone floor—to the stone street to be more exact—and, flaring up brightly, further revealed the rows of houses as they stood, silent and uninhabited.

"It's all right," Tom announced. "There's no danger so long as the torch burns. You can go on, Professor."

And Professor Bumper rushed forward, scrambling over the pile of blasted rock, followed by Tom and the others. Some of the debris from the explosion had fallen into the cave, and was scattered for some distance along the main street of what had been Pelone. But beyond that the way was clear.

"Yes, it is Pelone," cried Professor Bumper. "See!"

He pointed to inscriptions in queer characters over the doorway of some of the houses, but he alone could read them.

"I have found Pelone!" he kept repeating over and over again.

And that is just what had happened. That last great blast Tom Swift had set off had broken down the rock wall that hid the lost city from view. There it was, buried deep down under the mountain, where it had been covered from sight ages ago by some mighty earthquake or landslide; perhaps both. And the earth and rocks had fallen over the main portion of the city of Pelone in such a way—in such an arch formation—that the greater part of it was preserved from the pressure of the mountain above it.

The outlying portions were crushed into dust by the awful pressure of the mountain—millions of tons of stone—but where the natural arch had formed the weight was kept off the buildings, most of which were as perfect as they had been before the cataclysm came.

The buildings were of stone block construction, mostly only one story in height, though some were two. They were simply made, somewhat after the fashion of the Aztecs. A look into some of them by the light of portable electric lamps showed that the houses were furnished with some degree of taste and luxury. There were traces of an ancient civilization.

But of the inhabitants, there was not a trace: either they had fled before the earthquake or the volcanic eruption had engulfed the city, or the countless centuries had turned their very bones to dust.

"Oh, what a find! What a find!" murmured Professor Bumper. "I shall be famous! And so will you, Tom Swift. For it was your blast that revealed the lost city of Pelone. Your name will be honored by every archeological society in the world, and all will be eager to make you an honorary member."

"That's all very nice," said Tom, "but what pleases me better is that this tunnel is a success."

"Success!" cried Mr. Damon. "I should call it a failure, Tom Swift. Why, you've run smack into an old city, and you'll have either to curve the tunnel to one side, or start a new one."

"Nothing of the sort!" laughed Tom. "Don't you see? The tunnel comes right up to the main street of Pelone. And the street is as straight as a die, and just the width and height of the tunnel. All we will have to do will be to keep on blasting away, where the main street comes to an end, and our tunnel will be finished. The street is over half a mile long, I should judge, and we'll save all that blasting. The tunnel will be finished in time!"

"So it will!" cried Job Titus. "We can use the main street of the hidden city as part of the tunnel."

"Use the street all you like," said Mr. Bumper, "but leave the houses to me. They are a perfect mine of ancient lore and information. At last I have found it! The ancient, hidden city of Pelone, spoken of on the Peruvian tablets, of gold."

The story of the discoveries the scientist made in Pelone is an enthralling one. But this is a story of Tom Swift and his big tunnel, and no place for telling of the archeological discoveries.

Suffice it to say that Professor Bumper, though he found no gold, for which the contractors hoped, made many curious finds in the ancient houses. He came upon traces of a strange civilization, though he could find no record of what had caused the burial of Pelone beneath the mountains. He wrote many books about his discovery, giving Tom Swift due credit for uncovering the place with the mighty blast. Other scientists came in flocks, and for a time Pelone was almost as busy a place as it had been originally.

Even when the tunnel was completed and trains ran through it, the scientists kept on with their work of classifying what they found. An underground station was built on the main street of the old city, and visitors often wandered through the ancient houses, wherein was the bone-dust of the dead and gone people.

But to go back to the story of Tom Swift. Tom's surmise was right. He and the contractors were able to use the main street of Pelone as part of their tunnel, and a good half mile of blasting through solid rock was saved. The flint came to an end at the extremity of Pelone, and the last part of the tunnel had only to be dug through sand-stone and soft dirt, an easy undertaking.

So the big bore was finished on time—ahead of time in fact, and Titus Brothers received from Senor Belasdo, the Peruvian representative, a large bonus of money, in which Tom Swift shared.

"So our rivals didn't balk us after all," said Walter Titus, "though they tried mighty hard."

The big tunnel was finished—at least Tom Swift's work on it. All that remained to do was to clear away the debris and lay the connecting rails. Tom and Mr. Damon prepared to go back home. The latter's work was done. As for Professor Bumper, nothing could take him from Pelone. He said he was going to live there, and, practically, he did.

Tom, Koku and Mr. Damon returned to Lima, thence to go to Callao to take the steamer for San Francisco. One day the manager of the hotel spoke to them.

"You are Americans, are you not?" he asked.

"Yes," answered Tom. "Why?"

"Because there is another American here. He is friendless and alone, and he is dying. He has no friends, he says. Perhaps—"

"Of course we'll do what we can for him," said Tom, impulsively. "Where is he?"

With Mr. Damon he entered the room where the dying man lay. He had caught a fever, the hotel manager said, and could not recover. Tom, catching sight of the sufferer, cried:

"The bearded man! Waddington!"

He had recognized the mysterious person who had been on the Bellaconda, and the man whose face had stared at him through the secret shaft of the tunnel.

"Yes, the 'bearded man' now," said the sufferer in a hoarse voice, "and some one else too. You are right. I am Waddington!"

And so it proved. He had grown a beard to disguise himself so he might better follow Tom Swift and Mr. Titus. And he had followed them, seeking to prevent the completion of the tunnel. But he had not been successful.

Waddington it was who had thrown the bomb, though he declared he only hoped to disable Tom and Mr. Titus, and not to injure them. He was fighting for delay. And it was Waddington, working in conjunction with the rascally foreman Serato, who had induced the tunnel workers to desert so mysteriously, hoping to scare the other Indians away. He nearly succeeded too, had it not been for the gratitude of the woman whose baby Tom had saved from the condor.

Waddington had been an actor before he became involved with the rival contractors. He was smooth shaven when first he went to Shopton, to spy on Mr. Titus, whose movements he had been commanded to follow by Blakeson & Grinder. Then he disappeared after Mr. Titus chased him, only to reappear, in disguise, on board the Bellaconda, as Senor Pinto.

Waddington, meanwhile, had grown a beard and this, with his knowledge of theatrical makeup, enabled him to deceive even Mr. Titus. Of course it was comparatively easy to deceive Tom, who had not known him. Waddington had really been ill when he called for help on the ship, and he had not noticed that it was Tom and Mr. Titus who came into his stateroom to his aid. When he did recognize them, he relied on his disguise to screen him from recognition, and he was successful. He had only pretended to be ill, though, the time he slipped out and threw the bomb.

Reaching Peru he at once began his plotting. Serato told him about the secret shaft leading into the tunnel, and with the knotted rope, and with the aid of the faithless foreman, the men were got out of the tunnel and paid to hide away. Waddington was planning further disappearances when Tom saw him, but thought it a dream.

Masni, the Indian woman, out herb-hunting one day, had seen Waddington, 'the bearded man' as he then was—working the secret stone. Hidden, she observed him and told her husband, who was afraid to reveal what he knew. But when Tom saved the baby the woman rewarded him in the only way possible. And it was Serato, who, at Waddington's suggestion, caused the "hit" among the men by working on their superstitious fears.

Waddington, knowing that he was dying, confessed everything, and begged forgiveness from Tom and his friends, which was granted, in as much as no real harm had been done. Waddington was but a tool in the hands of the rival contractors, who deserted him in his hour of need. His last hours, however, were made as comfortable as possible by the generosity of Tom and Mr. Damon.

No effort was made to bring Blakeson & Grinder to justice, as there was no evidence against them after Waddington died. And, as the tunnel was finished, the Titus brothers had no further cause for worry.

"But if it had not been for Tom's big blast, and the discovery of the hidden city of Pelone just in the right place, we might be digging at that tunnel yet," said Job Titus.

The day before the steamer was to sail, Tom Swift received a cable message. Its receipt seemed to fill him with delight, so that Mr. Damon asked:

"Is it from your father, Tom?"

"No it's from Mary Nestor. She says her father has forgiven me. They have been away, and Mary has been ill, which accounts for no letters up to now. But everything is all right now, and they feel that the dynamite trick wasn't my fault. But, all the same, I'm going to teach Eradicate to read," concluded Tom.

"I think it would be a good idea," agreed Mr. Damon.

Tom, Mr. Damon and Koku, bidding farewell to the friends they had made in Peru, went aboard the steamer, Job Titus and his brother coming to see them off.

"Give us an option on all that explosive you make, Tom Swift!" begged Walter Titus. "We were so successful with this tunnel, thanks to you, that the government is going to have us dig another. Will you come down and help?"

"Maybe," said Tom, with a smile. "But I'm going home first," and once more he read the message from Mary Nestor.

And as Tom, on the deck of the steamer, waved his hands to Professor Bumper and his other friends whom he was leaving in Peru, we also, will say farewell.

TOM SWIFT IN THE LAND OF WONDERS

Or, THE UNDERGROUND SEARCH FOR THE IDOL OF GOLD

CHAPTER I

A WONDERFUL STORY

Tom Swift, who had been slowly looking through the pages of a magazine, in the contents of which he seemed to be deeply interested, turned the final folio, ruffled the sheets back again to look at a certain map and drawing, and then, slapping the book down on a table before him, with a noise not unlike that of a shot, exclaimed:

"Well, that is certainly one wonderful story!"

"What's it about, Tom?" asked his chum, Ned Newton. "Something about inside baseball, or a new submarine that can be converted into an airship on short notice?"

"Neither one, you—you unscientific heathen," answered Tom, with a laugh at Ned. "Though that isn't saying such a machine couldn't be invented."

"I believe you—that is if you got on its trail," returned Ned, and there was warm admiration in his voice.

"As for inside baseball, or outside, for that matter, I hardly believe I'd be able to tell third base from the second base, it's so long since I went to a game," proceeded Tom. "I've been too busy on that new airship stabilizer dad gave me an idea for. I've been working too hard, that's a fact. I need a vacation, and maybe a good baseball game—"

He stopped and looked at the magazine he had so hastily slapped down. Something he had read in it seemed to fascinate him.

"I wonder if it can possibly be true," he went on. "It sounds like the wildest dream of a professional sleep-walker; and yet, when I stop to think, it isn't much worse than some of the things we've gone through with, Ned."

"Say, for the love of rice-pudding! will you get down to brass tacks and strike a trial balance? What are you talking of, anyhow? Is it a joke?"

"A joke?"

"Yes. What you just read in that magazine which seems to cause you so much excitement."

"Well, it may be a joke; and yet the professor seems very much in earnest about it," replied Tom. "It certainly is one wonderful story!"

"So you said before. Come on—the 'fillium' is busted. Splice it, or else put in a new reel and on with the show. I'd like to know what's doing. What professor are you talking of?"

"Professor Swyington Bumper."

"Swyington Bumper?" and Ned's voice showed that his memory was a bit hazy.

"Yes. You ought to remember him. He was on the steamer when I went down to Peru to help the Titus Brothers dig the big tunnel. That plotter Waddington, or some of his tools, dropped a bomb where it might have done us some injury, but Professor Bumper, who was a fellow passenger, on his way to South America to look for the lost city of Pelone, calmly picked up the bomb, plucked out the fuse, and saved us from bad injuries, if not death. And he was as cool about it as an ice-cream cone. Surely you remember!"

"Swyington Bumper! Oh, yes, now I remember him," said Ned Newton. "But what has he got to do with a wonderful story? Has he written more about the lost city of Pelone? If he has I don't see anything so very wonderful in that."

"There isn't," agreed Tom. "But this isn't that," and Tom picked up the magazine and leafed it to find the article he had been reading.

"Let's have a look at it," suggested Ned. "You act as though you might be vitally interested in it. Maybe you're thinking of joining forces with the professor again, as you did when you dug the big tunnel."

"Oh, no. I haven't any such idea," Tom said. "I've got enough work laid out now to keep me in Shopton for the next year. I have no notion of going anywhere with Professor Bumper. Yet I can't help being impressed by this," and, having found the article in the magazine to which he referred, he handed it to his chum.

"Why, it's by Bumper himself!" exclaimed Ned.

"Yes. Though there's nothing remarkable in that, seeing that he is constantly contributing articles to various publications or writing books. It's the story itself that's so wonderful. To save you the trouble of wading through a lot of scientific detail, which I know you don't care about, I'll tell you that the story is about a queer idol of solid gold, weighing many pounds, and, in consequence, of great value."

"Of solid gold you say?" asked Ned eagerly.

"That's it. Got on your banking air already," Tom laughed. "To sum it up for you—notice I use the word 'sum,' which is very appropriate for a bank—the professor has got on the track of another lost or hidden city. This one, the name of which doesn't appear, is in the Copan valley of Honduras, and—"

"Copan," interrupted Ned. "It sounds like the name of some new floor varnish."

"Well, it isn't, though it might be," laughed Tom. "Copan is a city, in the Department of Copan, near the boundary between Honduras and Guatemala. A fact I learned from the article and not because I remembered my geography."

"I was going to say," remarked Ned with a smile, "that you were coming it rather strong on the school-book stuff."

"Oh, it's all plainly written down there," and Tom waved toward the magazine at which Ned was looking. "As you'll see, if you take the trouble to go through it, as I did, Copan is, or maybe was, for all I know, one of the most important centers of the Mayan civilization."

"What's Mayan?" asked Ned. "You see I'm going to imbibe my information by the deductive rather than the excavative process," he added with a laugh.

"I see," laughed Tom. "Well, Mayan refers to the Mayas, an aboriginal people of Yucatan. The Mayas had a peculiar civilization of their own, thousands of years ago, and their calendar system was so involved—"

"Never mind about dates," again interrupted Ned. "Get down to brass tacks. I'm willing to take your word for it that there's a Copan valley in Honduras. But what has your friend Professor Bumper to do with it?"

"This. He has come across some old manuscripts, or ancient document records, referring to this valley, and they state, according to this article he has written for the magazine, that somewhere in the valley is a wonderful city, traces of which have been found twenty to forty feet below the surface, on which great trees are growing, showing that the city was covered hundreds, if not thousands, of years ago."

"But where does the idol of gold come in?"

"I'm coming to that," said Tom. "Though, if Professor Bumper has his way, the idol will be coming out instead of coming in."

"You mean he wants to get it and take it away from the Copan valley, Tom?"

"That's it, Ned. It has great value not only from the amount of pure gold that is in it, but as an antique. I fancy the professor is more interested in that aspect of it. But he's written a wonderful story, telling how he happened to come across the ancient manuscripts in the tomb of some old Indian whose mummy he unearthed on a trip to Central America.

"Then he tells of the trouble he had in discovering how to solve the key to the translation code; but when he did, he found a great story unfolded to him.

"This story has to do with the hidden city, and tells of the ancient civilization of those who lived in the Copan valley thousands of years ago. The people held this idol of gold to be their greatest treasure, and they put to death many of other tribes who sought to steal it."

"Whew!" whistled Ned. "That IS some yarn. But what is Professor Bumper going to do about it?"

"I don't know. The article seems to be written with an idea of interesting scientists and research societies, so that they will raise money to conduct a searching expedition.

"Perhaps by this time the party may be organized—this magazine is several months old. I have been so busy on my stabilizer patent that I haven't kept up with current literature. Take it home and read it! Ned. That is if you're through telling me about my affairs," for Ned, who had formerly worked in the Shopton bank, had recently been made general financial manager of the interests of Tom and his father. The two were inventors and proverbially poor business men, though they had amassed a fortune.

"Your financial affairs are all right, Tom," said Ned. "I have just been going over the books, and I'll submit a detailed report later."

The telephone bell rang and Tom picked up the instrument from the desk. As he answered in the usual way and then listened a moment, a strange look came over his face.

"Well, this certainly is wonderful!" he exclaimed, in much the same manner as when he had finished reading the article about the idol. "It certainly is a strange coincidence," he added, speaking in an aside to Ned while he himself still listened to what was being told to him over the telephone wire.

CHAPTER II

PROFESSOR BUMPER ARRIVES

"What's the matter, Tom? What is it?" asked Ned Newton, attracted by the strange manner of his chum at the telephone. "Has anything happened?"

But the young inventor was too busy listening to the unseen speaker to answer his chum, even if he heard what Ned remarked, which is doubtful.

"Well, I might as well wait until he is through," mused Ned, as he started to leave the room. Then as Tom motioned to him to remain, he murmured: "He may have something to say to me later. But I wonder who is talking to him."

There was no way of finding out, however, until Tom had a chance to talk to Ned, and at present the young scientist was eagerly listening to what came over the wire. Occasionally Ned could hear him say:

"You don't tell me! That is surprising! Yes—yes! Of course if it's true it means a big thing, I can understand that. What's that? No, I couldn't make a promise like that. I'm sorry, but—"

Then the person at the other end of the wire must have plunged into something very interesting and absorbing, for Tom did not again interrupt by interjected remarks.

Tom Swift, as has been said, was an inventor, as was his father. Mr. Swift was now rather old and feeble, taking only a nominal part in the activities of the firm made up of himself and his son. But his inventions were still used, many of them being vital to the business and trade of this country.

Tom and his father lived in the village of Shopton, New York, and their factories covered many acres of ground. Those who wish to read of the earliest activities of Tom in the inventive line are referred to the initial volume, "Tom Swift and His Motor Cycle." From then on he and his father had many and exciting adventures. In a motor boat, an airship, and a submarine respectively the young inventor had gone through many perils. On some of the trips his chum, Ned Newton, accompanied him, and very often in the party was a Mr. Wakefield Damon, who had a curious habit of "blessing" everything that happened to strike his fancy.

Besides Tom and his father, the Swift household was made up of Eradicate Sampson, a colored man-of-all-work, who, with his mule Boomerang, did what he could to keep the grounds around the house in order. There was also Mrs. Baggert, the housekeeper, Tom's mother being dead. Mr. Damon, living in a neighboring town, was a frequent visitor in the Swift home.

Mary Nestor, a girl of Shopton, might also be mentioned. She and Tom were more than just good friends. Tom had an idea that some day—. But there, I promised not to tell that part, at least until the young people themselves were ready to have a certain fact announced.

From one activity to another had Tom Swift gone, now constructing some important invention for himself, as among others, when he made the photo-telephone, or developed a great searchlight which he presented to the Government for use in detecting smugglers on the border.

The book immediately preceding this is called "Tom Swift and His Big, Tunnel," and deals with the efforts of the young inventor to help a firm of contractors penetrate a mountain in Peru. How this was done and how, incidentally, the lost city of Pelone was discovered, bringing joy to the heart of Professor Swyington Bumper, will be found fully set forth in the book.

Tom had been back from the Peru trip for some months, when we again find him interested in some of the work of Professor Bumper, as set forth in the magazine mentioned.

"Well, he certainly is having some conversation," reflected Ned, as, after more than five minutes, Tom's ear was still at the receiver of the instrument, into the transmitter of which he had said only a few words.

"All right," Tom finally answered, as he hung the receiver up, "I'll be here," and then he turned to Ned, whose curiosity had been growing with the telephone talk, and remarked:

"That certainly was wonderful!"

"What was?" asked Ned. "Do you think I'm a mind reader to be able to guess?"

"No, indeed! I beg your pardon. I'll tell you at once. But I couldn't break away. It was too important. To whom do you think I was talking just then?"

"I can imagine almost any one, seeing I know something of what you have done. It might be almost anybody from some person you met up in the caves of ice to a red pygmy from the wilds of Africa."

"I'm afraid neither of them would be quite up to telephone talk yet," laughed Tom. "No, this was the gentleman who wrote that interesting article about the idol of gold," and he motioned to the magazine Ned held in his hand.

"You don't mean Professor Bumper!"

"That's just whom I do mean."

"What did he want? Where did he call from?"

"He wants me to help organize an expedition to go to Central America—to the Copan valley, to be exact—to look for this somewhat mythical idol of gold. Incidentally the professor will gather in any other antiques of more or less value, if he can find any, and he hopes, even if he doesn't find the idol, to get enough historical material for half a dozen books, to say nothing of magazine articles."

"Where did he call from; did you say?"

"I didn't say. But it was a long-distance call from New York. The Professor stopped off there on his way from Boston, where he has been lecturing before some society. And now he's coming here to see me," finished Tom.

"What! Is he going to lecture here?" cried Ned. "If he is, and spouts a whole lot of that bone-dry stuff about the ancient Mayan civilization and their antiquities, with side lights on how the old-time Indians used to scalp their enemies, I'm going to the moving pictures! I'm willing to be your financial manager, Tom Swift, but please don't ask me to be a high-brow. I wasn't built for that."

"Nor I, Ned. The professor isn't going to lecture. He's only going to talk, he says."

"What about?"

"He's going to try to induce me to join his expedition to the Copan valley."

"Do you feel inclined to go?"

"No, Ned, I do not. I've got too many other irons in the fire. I shall have to give the professor a polite but firm refusal."

"Well, maybe you're right, Tom; and yet that idol of gold—GOLD—weighing how many pounds did you say?"

"Oh, you're thinking of its money value, Ned, old man!"

"Yes, I'd like to see what a big chunk of gold like that would bring. It must be quite a nugget. But I'm not likely to get a glimpse of it if you don't go with the professor."

"I don't see how I can go, Ned. But come over and meet the delightful gentleman when he arrives. I expect him day after tomorrow."

"I'll be here," promised Ned; and then he went downtown to attend to some matters connected with his new duties, which were much less irksome than those he had had when he had been in the bank.

"Well, Tom, have you heard any more about your friend?" asked Ned, two days later, as he came to the Swift home with some papers needing the signature of the young inventor and his father.

"You mean—?"

"Professor Bumper."

"No, I haven't heard from him since he telephoned. But I guess he'll be here all right. He's very punctual. Did you see anything of my giant Koku as you came in?"

"Yes, he and Eradicate were having an argument about who should move a heavy casting from one of the shops. Rad wanted to do it all alone, but Koku said he was like a baby now."

"Poor Rad is getting old," said Tom with a sigh. "But he has been very faithful. He and Koku never seem to get along well together."

Koku was an immense man, a veritable giant, one of two whom Tom had brought back with him after an exciting trip to a strange land. The giant's strength was very useful to the young inventor.

"Now Tom, about this business of leasing to the English Government the right to manufacture that new explosive of yours," began Ned, plunging into the business at hand. "I think if you stick out a little you can get a better royalty price."

"But I don't want to gouge 'em, Ned. I'm satisfied with a fair profit. The trouble with you is you think too much of money. Now—"

At that moment a voice was heard in the hall of the house saying:

"Now, my dear lady, don't trouble yourself. I can find my way in to Tom Swift perfectly well by myself, and while I appreciate your courtesy I do not want to trouble you."

"No, don't come, Mrs. Baggert," added another voice. "Bless my hat band, I think I know my way about the house by this time!"

"Mr. Damon!" ejaculated Ned.

"And Professor Bumper is with him," added Tom. "Come in!" he cried, opening the hall door, to confront a bald-headed man who stood peering at our hero with bright snapping eyes, like those of some big bird spying out the land from afar. "Come in, Professor Bumper; and you too, Mr. Damon!"

CHAPTER III

BLESSINGS AND ENTHUSIASM

Greetings and inquiries as to health having been passed, not without numerous blessings on the part of Mr. Damon, the little party gathered in the library of the home of Tom Swift sat down and looked at one another.

On Professor Bumper's face there was, plainly to be seen, a look of expectation, and it seemed to be shared by Mr. Damon, who seemed eager to burst into enthusiastic talk. On the other hand Tom Swift appeared a bit indifferent.

Ned himself admitted that he was frankly curious. The story of the big idol of gold had occupied his thoughts for many hours.

"Well, I'm glad to see you both," said Tom again. "You got here all right, I see, Professor Bumper. But I didn't expect you to meet and bring Mr. Damon with you."

"I met him on the train," explained the author of the book on the lost city of Pelone, as well as books on other antiquities. "I had no expectation of seeing him, and we were both surprised when we met on the express."

"It stopped at Waterfield, Tom," explained Mr. Damon, "which it doesn't usually do, being an aristocratic sort of train, not given even to hesitating at our humble little town. There were some passengers to get off, which caused the flier to stop, I suppose. And, as I wanted to come over to see you, I got aboard."

"Glad you did," voiced Tom.

"Then I happened to see Professor Bumper a few seats ahead of me," went on Mr. Damon, "and, bless my scarfpin! he was coming to see you also."

"Well, I'm doubly glad," answered Tom.

"So here we are," went on Mr. Damon, "and you've simply got to come, Tom Swift. You must go with us!" and Mr. Damon, in his enthusiasm, banged his fist down on the table with such force that he knocked some books to the floor.

Koku, the giant, who was in the hall, opened the door and in his imperfect English asked:

"Master Tom knock for him bigs man?"

"No," answered Tom with a smile, "I didn't knock or call you, Koku. Some books fell, that is all."

"Massa Tom done called fo' me, dat's what he done!" broke in the petulant voice of Eradicate.

"No, Rad, I don't need anything," Tom said. "Though you might make a pitcher of lemonade. It's rather warm."

"Right away, Massa Tom! Right away!" cried the old colored man, eager to be of service.

"Me help, too!" rumbled Koku, in his deep voice. "Me punch de lemons!" and away he hurried after Eradicate, fearful lest the old servant do all the honors.

"Same old Rad and Koku," observed Mr. Damon with a smile. "But now, Tom, while they're making the lemonade, let's get down to business. You're going with us, of course!"

"Where?" asked Tom, more from habit than because he did not know.

"Where? Why to Honduras, of course! After the idol of gold! Why, bless my fountain pen, it's the most wonderful story I ever heard of! You've read Professor Bumper's article, of course. He told me you had. I read it on the train coming over. He also told me about it, and— Well, I'm going with him, Tom Swift.

"And think of all the adventures that may befall us! We'll get lost in buried cities, ride down raging torrents on a raft, fall over a cliff maybe and be rescued. Why, it makes me feel quite young again!" and Mr. Damon arose, to pace excitedly up and down the room.

Up to this time Professor Bumper had said very little. He had sat still in his chair listening to Mr. Damon. But now that the latter had ceased, at least for a time, Tom and Ned looked toward the scientist.

"I understand, Tom," he said, "that you read my article in the magazine, about the possibility of locating some of the lost and buried cities of Honduras?"

"Yes, Ned and I each read it. It was quite wonderful."

"And yet there are more wonders to tell," went on the professor. "I did not give all the details in that article. I will tell you some of them. I have brought copies of the documents with me," and he opened a small valise and took out several bundles tied with pink tape.

"As Mr. Damon said," he went on while arranging his papers, "he met me on the train, and he was so taken by the story of the idol of gold that he agreed to accompany me to Central America."

"On one condition!" put in the eccentric man.

"What's that? You didn't make any conditions while we were talking," said the scientist.

"Yes, I said I'd go if Tom Swift did."

"Oh, yes. You did say that. But I don't call that a condition, for of course Tom Swift will go. Now let me tell you something more than I could impart over the telephone.

"Soon after I called you up, Tom—and it was quite a coincidence that it should have been at a time when you had just finished my magazine article. Soon after that, as I was saying, I arranged to come on to Shopton. And now I'm glad we're all here together."

"But how comes it, Ned Newton, that you are not in the bank?"

"I've left there," explained Ned.

"He's now general financial man for the Swift Company," Tom explained. "My father and I found that we could not look after the inventing and experimental end, and money matters, too, and as Ned had had considerable experience this way we made him take over those worries," and Tom laughed genially.

"No worries at all, as far as the Swift Company is concerned," returned Ned.

"Well, I guess you earn your salary," laughed Tom. "But now, Professor Bumper, let's hear from you. Is there anything more about this idol of gold that you can tell us?"

"Plenty, Tom, plenty. I could talk all day, and not get to the end of the story. But a lot of it would be scientific detail that might be too dry for you in spite of this excellent lemonade."

Between them Koku and Eradicate had managed to make a pitcher of the beverage, though Mrs. Baggert, the housekeeper, told Tom afterward that the two had a quarrel in the kitchen as to who should squeeze the lemons, the giant insisting that he had the better right to "punch" them.

"So, not to go into too many details," went on the professor, "I'll just give you a brief outline of this story of the idol of gold.

"Honduras, as you of course know, is a republic of Central America, and it gets its name from something that happened on the fourth voyage of Columbus. He and his men had had days of weary sailing and had sought in vain for shallow water in which they might come to an anchorage. Finally they reached the point now known as Cape Gracias-a-Dios, and when they let the anchor go, and found that in a short time it came to rest on the floor of the ocean, some one of the sailors—perhaps Columbus himself—is said to have remarked:

"'Thank the Lord, we have left the deep waters (honduras)' that being the Spanish word for unfathomable depths. So Honduras it was called, and has been to this day.

"It is a queer land with many traces of an ancient civilization, a civilization which I believe dates back farther than some in the far East. On the sculptured stones in the Copan valley there are characters which seem to resemble very ancient writing, but this pictographic writing is largely untranslatable.

"Honduras, I might add, is about the size of our state of Ohio. It is rather an elevated tableland, though there are stretches of tropical forest, but it is not so tropical a country as many suppose it to be. There is much gold scattered throughout Honduras, though of late it has not been found in large quantities.

"In the old days, however, before the Spaniards came, it was plentiful, so much, so that the natives made idols of it. And it is one of the largest of these idols—by name Quitzel—that I am going to seek."

"Do you know where it is?" asked Ned.

"Well, it isn't locked up in a safe deposit box, of that I'm sure," laughed the professor. "No, I don't know exactly where it is, except that it is somewhere in an ancient and buried city known as Kurzon. If I knew exactly where it was there wouldn't be much fun in going after it. And if it was known to others it would have been taken away long ago.

"No, we've got to hunt for the idol of gold in this land of wonders where I hope soon to be. Later on I'll show you the documents that put me on the track of this idol. Enough now to show you an old map I found, or, rather, a copy of it, and some of the papers that tell of the idol," and he spread out his packet of papers on the table in front of him, his eyes shining with excitement and pleasure. Mr. Damon, too, leaned eagerly forward.

"So, Tom Swift," went on the professor, "I come to you for help in this matter. I want you to aid me in organizing an expedition to go to Honduras after the idol of gold. Will you?"

"I'll help you, of course," said Tom. "You may use any of my inventions you choose—my airships, my motor boats and submarines, even my giant cannon if you think you can take it with you. And as for the money part, Ned will arrange that for you. But as for going with you myself, it is out of the question. I can't. No Honduras for me!"

CHAPTER IV

FENIMORE BEECHER

Had Tom Swift's giant cannon been discharged somewhere in the vicinity of his home it could have caused but little more astonishment to Mr. Damon and Professor Bumper than did the simple announcement of the young inventor. The professor seemed to shrink back in his chair, collapsing like an automobile tire when the air is let out. As for Mr. Damon he jumped up and cried:

"Bless my—!"

But that is as far as he got—at least just then. He did not seem to know what to bless, but he looked as though he would have liked to include most of the universe.

"Surely you don't mean it, Tom Swift," gasped Professor Bumper at length. "Won't you come with us?"

"No," said Tom, slowly. "Really I can't go. I'm working on an invention of a new aeroplane stabilizer, and if I go now it will be just at a time when I am within striking distance of success. And the stabilizer is very much needed."

"If it's a question of making a profit on it, Tom," began Mr. Damon, "I can let you have some money until—"

"Oh, no! It isn't the money!" cried Tom. "Don't think that for a moment. You see the European war has called for the use of a large number of aeroplanes, and as the pilots of them frequently have to fight, and so can not give their whole attention to the machines, some form of automatic stabilizer is needed to prevent them turning turtle, or going off at a wrong tangent.

"So I have been working out a sort of modified gyroscope, and it seems to answer the purpose. I have already received advance orders for a number of my devices from abroad, and as they are destined to save lives I feel that I ought to keep on with my work.

"I'd like to go, don't misunderstand me, but I can't go at this time. It is out of the question. If you wait a year, or maybe six months—"

"No, it is impossible to wait, Tom," declared Professor Bumper.

"Is it so important then to hurry?" asked Mr. Damon. "You did not mention that to me, Professor Bumper."

"No, I did not have time. There are so many ends to my concerns. But, Tom Swift, you simply must go!"

"I can't, my dear professor, much as I should like to."

"But, Tom, think of it!" cried Mr. Damon, who was as much excited as was the little bald-headed scientist. "You never saw such an idol of gold as this. What's its name?" and he looked questioningly at the professor.

"Quitzel the idol is called," supplied Professor Bumper. "And it is supposed to be in a buried city named Kurzon, somewhere in the Sierra de Merendon range of mountains, in the vicinity of the Copan valley. Copan is a city, or maybe we'll find it only a town when we get there, and it is not far from the borders of Guatemala.

"Tom, if I could show you the translations I have made of the ancient documents, referring to this idol and the wonderful city over which it kept guard, I'm sure you'd come with us."

"Please don't tempt me," Tom said with a laugh. "I'm only too anxious to go, and if it wasn't for the stabilizer I'd be with you in a minute. But— Well, you'll have to get along without me. Maybe I can join you later."

"What's this about the idol keeping guard over the ancient city?" asked Ned, for he was interested in strange stories.

"It seems," explained the professor, "that in the early days there was a strange race of people, inhabiting Central America, with a somewhat high civilization, only traces of which remained when the Spaniards came.

"But these traces, and such hieroglyphics, or, to be more exact pictographs, as I have been able to decipher from the old documents, tell of one country, or perhaps it was only a city, over which this great golden idol of Quitzel presided.

"There is in some of these papers a description of the idol, which is not exactly a beauty, judged from modern standards. But the main fact is that it is made of solid gold, and may weigh anywhere from one to two tons."

"Two tons of gold!" cried New Newton. "Why, if that's the case it would be worth—" and he fell to doing a sum in mental arithmetic.

"I am not so concerned about the monetary value of the statue as I am about its antiquity," went on Professor Bumper. "There are other statues in this buried city of Kurzon, and though they may not be so valuable they will give me a wealth of material for my research work."

"How do you know there are other statues?" asked Mr. Damon.

"Because my documents tell me so. It was because the people made other idols, in opposition, as it were, to Quitzel, that their city or country was destroyed. At least that is the legend. Quitzel, so the story goes, wanted to be the chief god, and when the image of a rival was set up in the temple near him, he toppled over in anger, and part of the temple went with him, the whole place being buried in ruins. All the inhabitants were killed, and trace of the ancient city was lost forever. No, I hope not forever, for I expect to find it."

"If all the people were killed, and the city buried, how did the story of Quitzel become known?" asked Mr. Damon.

"One only of the priests in the temple of Quitzel escaped and set down part of the tale," said the professor. "It is his narrative, or one based on it, that I have given you."

"And now, what I want to do, is to go and make a search for this buried city. I have fairly good directions as to how it may be reached. We will have little difficulty in getting to Honduras, as there are fruit steamers frequently sailing. Of course going into the interior—to the Copan valley—is going to be harder. But an expedition from a large college was recently there and succeeded, after much labor, in excavating part of a buried city. Whether or not it was Kurzon I am unable to say.

"But if there was one ancient city there must be more. So I want to make an attempt. And I counted on you, Tom. You have had considerable experience in strange quarters of the earth, and you're just the one to help me. I don't need money, for I have interested a certain millionaire, and my own college will put up part of the funds."

"Oh, it isn't a question of money," said Tom. "It's time."

"That's just what it is with me!" exclaimed Professor Bumper. "I haven't any time to lose. My rivals may, even now, be on their way to Honduras!"

"Your rivals!" cried Tom. "You didn't say anything about them!"

"No, I believe I didn't. There were so many other things to talk about. But there is a rival archaeologist who would ask nothing better than to get ahead of me in this matter. He is younger than I am, and youth is a big asset nowadays."

"Pooh! You're not old!" cried Mr. Damon. "You're no older than I am, and I'm still young. I'm a lot younger than some of these boys who are afraid to tackle a trip through a tropical wilderness," and he playfully nudged Tom in the ribs.

"I'm not a bit afraid!" retorted the young inventor.

"No, I know you're not," laughed Mr. Damon. "But I've got to say something, Tom, to stir you up. Ned, how about you? Would you go?"

"I can't, unless Tom does. You see I'm his financial man now."

"There you are, Tom Swift!" cried Mr. Damon. "You see you are holding back a number of persons just because you don't want to go."

"I certainly wouldn't like to go without Tom," said the professor slowly. "I really need his help. You know, Tom, we would never have found the city of Pelone if it had not been for you and your marvelous powder. The conditions in the Copan valley are likely to be still more difficult to overcome, and I feel that I risk failure without your young energy and your inventive mind to aid in the work and to suggest possible means of attaining our object. Come, Tom, reconsider, and decide to make the trip."

"And my promise to go was dependent on Tom's agreement to accompany us," said Mr. Damon.

"Come on!" urged the professor, much as one boy might urge another to take part in a ball game. "Don't let my rival get ahead of me."

"I wouldn't like to see that," Tom said slowly. "Who is he—any one I know?"

"I don't believe so, Tom. He's connected with a large, new college that has plenty of money to spend on explorations and research work. Beecher is his name—Fenimore Beecher."

"Beecher!" exclaimed Tom, and there was such a change in his manner that his friends could not help noticing it. He jumped to his feet, his eyes snapping, and he looked eagerly and anxiously at Professor Bumper.

"Did you say his name was Fenimore Beecher?" Tom asked in a tense voice.

"That's what it is—Professor Fenimore Beecher. He is really a learned young man, and thoroughly in earnest, though I do not like his manner. But he is trying to get ahead of me, which may account for my feeling."

Tom Swift did not answer. Instead he hurried from the room with a murmured apology.

"I'll be back in about five minutes," he said, as he went out.

"Well, what's up now?" asked Mr. Damon of Ned, as the young inventor departed. "What set him off that way?"

"The mention of Beecher's name, evidently. Though I never heard him mention such a person before."

"Nor did I ever hear Professor Beecher speak of Tom," said the bald-headed scientist. "Well, we'll just have to wait until—"

At that moment Tom came back into the room.

"Gentlemen," he said, "I have reconsidered my refusal to go to the Copan valley after the idol of gold. I'm going with you!"

"Good!" cried Professor Bumper.

"Fine!" ejaculated Mr. Damon. "Bless my time-table! I thought you'd come around, Tom Swift."

"But what about your stabilizer?" asked Ned.

"I was just talking to my father about it," the young inventor replied. "He will be able to put the finishing touches on it. So I'll leave it with him. As soon as I can get ready I'll go, since you say haste is necessary, Professor Bumper."

"It is, if we are to get ahead of Beecher."

"Then we'll get ahead of him!" cried Tom. "I'm with you now from the start to the finish. I'll show him what I can do!" he added, while Ned and the others wondered at the sudden change in their friend's manner.

CHAPTER V

THE LITTLE GREEN GOD

"Tom how soon can we go?" asked Professor Bumper, as he began arranging his papers, maps and documents ready to place them back in the valise.

"Within a week, if you want to start that soon."

"The sooner the better. A week will suit me. I don't know just what Beecher's plans are, but, he may try to get on the ground first. Though, without boasting, I may say that he has not had as much experience as I have had, thanks to you, Tom, when you helped me find the lost city of Pelone."

"Well, I hope we'll be as successful this time," murmured Tom. "I don't want to see Beecher beat you."

"I didn't know you knew him, Tom," said the professor.

"Oh, yes, I have met him, once," and there was something in Tom's manner, though he tried to speak indifferently, that made Ned believe there was more behind his chum's sudden change of determination than had yet appeared.

"He never mentioned you," went on Professor Bumper; "yet the last time I saw him I said I was coming to see you, though I did not tell him why."

"No, he wouldn't be likely to speak of me," said Tom significantly.

"Well, if that's all settled, I guess I'll go back home and pack up," said Mr. Damon, making a move to depart.

"There's no special rush," Tom said. "We won't leave for a week. I can't get ready in much less time than that."

"Bless my socks! I know that," ejaculated Mr. Damon. "But if I get my things packed I can go to a hotel to stay while my wife is away. She might take a notion to come home unexpectedly, and, though she is a dear, good soul, she doesn't altogether approve of my going off on these wild trips with you, Tom Swift. But if I get all packed, and clear out, she can't find me and she can't hold me back. She is visiting her mother now. I can send her a wire from Kurzon after I get there."

"I don't believe the telegraph there is working," laughed Professor Bumper. "But suit yourself. I must go back to New York to arrange for the goods we'll have to take with us. In a week, Tom, we'll start."

"You must stay to dinner," Tom said. "You can't get a train now any-how, and father wants to meet you again. He's pretty well, considering his age. And he's much better I verily believe since I said I'd turn over to him the task of finishing the stabilizer. He likes to work."

"We'll stay and take the night train back," agreed Mr. Damon. "It will be like old times, Tom," he went on, "traveling off together into the wilds. Central America is pretty wild, isn't it?" he asked, as if in fear of being disappointed! on that score.

"Oh, it's wild enough to suit any one," answered Professor Bumper.

"Well, now to settle a few details," observed Tom. "Ned, what is the situation as regards the financial affairs of my father and myself? Nothing will come to grief if we go away, will there?"

"I guess not, Tom. But are you going to take your father with you?"

"No, of course not."

"But you spoke of 'we.'"

"I meant you and I are going."

"Me, Tom?"

"Sure, you! I wouldn't think of leaving you behind. You want Ned along, don't you, Professor?"

"Of course. It will be an ideal party—we four. We'll have to take natives when we get to Honduras, and make up a mule pack-train for the interior. I had some thoughts of asking you to take an airship along, but it might frighten the Indians, and I shall have to depend on them for guides, as well as for porters. So it will be an old-fashioned expedition, in a way."

Mr. Swift came in at this point to meet his old friends.

"The boy needs a little excitement," he said. "He's been puttering over that stabilizer invention too long. I can finish the model for him in a very short time."

Professor Bumper told Mr. Swift something about the proposed trip, while Mr. Damon went out with Tom and Ned to one of the shops to look at a new model aeroplane the young inventor had designed.

There was a merry party around the table at dinner, though now and then Ned noticed that Tom had an abstracted and preoccupied air.

"Thinking about the idol of gold?" asked Ned in a whisper to his chum, when they were about to leave the table.

"The idol of gold? Oh, yes! Of course! It will be great if we can bring that back with us." But the manner in which he said this made Ned feel sure that Tom had had other thoughts, and that he had used a little subterfuge in his answer.

Ned was right, as he proved for himself a little later, when, Mr. Damon and the professor having gone home, the young financial secretary took his friend to a quiet corner and asked:

"What's the matter, Tom?"

"Matter? What do you mean?"

"I mean what made you make up your mind so quickly to go on this expedition when you heard Beecher was going?"

"Oh—er—well, you wouldn't want to see our old friend Professor Bumper left, would you, after he had worked out the secret of the idol of gold? You wouldn't want some young whipper-snapper to beat him in the race, would you, Ned?"

"No, of course not."

"Neither would I. That's why I changed my mind. This Beecher isn't going to get that idol if I can stop him!"

"You seem rather bitter against him."

"Bitter? Oh, not at all. I simply don't want to see my friends disappointed."

"Then Beecher isn't a friend of yours?"

"Oh, I've met him, that is all," and Tom tried to speak indifferently.

"Humph!" mused Ned, "there's more here than I dreamed of. I'm going to get at the bottom of it."

But though Ned tried to pump Tom, he was not successful. The young inventor admitted knowing the youthful scientist, but that was all, Tom reiterating his determination not to let Professor Bumper be beaten in the race for the idol of gold.

"Let me see," mused Ned, as he went home that evening. "Tom did not change his mind until he heard Beecher's name mentioned. Now this shows that Beecher had something to do with it. The only reason Tom doesn't want Beecher to get this idol or find the buried city is because Professor Bumper is after it. And yet the professor is not an old or close friend of Tom's. They met only when Tom went to dig his big tunnel. There must be some other reason."

Ned did some more thinking. Then he clapped his hands together, and a smile spread over his face.

"I believe I have it!" he cried. "The little green god as compared to the idol of gold! That's it. I'm going to make a call on my way home."

This he did, stopping at the home of Mary Nestor, a pretty girl, who, rumor had it, was tacitly engaged to Tom. Mary was not at home, but Mr. Nestor was, and for Ned's purpose this answered.

"Well, well, glad to see you!" exclaimed Mary's father. "Isn't Tom with you?" he asked a moment later, seeing that Ned was alone.

"No, Tom isn't with me this evening," Ned answered. "The fact is, he's getting ready to go off on another expedition, and I'm going with him."

"You young men are always going somewhere," remarked Mrs. Nestor. "Where is it to this time?"

"Some place in Central America," Ned answered, not wishing to be too particular. He was wondering how he could find out what he wanted to know, when Mary's mother unexpectedly gave him just the information he was after.

"Central America!" she exclaimed. "Why, Father," and she looked at her husband, "that's where Professor Beecher is going, isn't it?"

"Yes, I believe he did mention something about that."

"Professor Beecher, the man who is an authority on Aztec ruins?" asked Ned, taking a shot in the dark.

"Yes," said Mr. Nestor. "And a mighty fine young man he is, too. I knew his father well. He was here on a visit not long ago, young Beecher was, and he talked most entertainingly about his discoveries. You remember how interested Mary was, Mother?"

"Yes, she seemed to be," said Mrs. Nestor. "Tom Swift dropped in during the course of the evening," she added to Ned, "and Mary introduced him to Professor Beecher. But I can't say that Tom was much interested in the professor's talk."

"No?" questioned Ned.

"No, not at all. But Tom did not stay long. He left just as Mary and the professor were drawing a map so the professor could indicate where he had once made a big discovery."

"I see," murmured Ned. "Well, I suppose Tom must have been thinking of something else at the time."

"Very likely," agreed Mr. Nestor. "But Tom missed a very profitable talk. I was very much interested myself in what the professor told us, and so was Mary. She invited Mr. Beecher to come again. He takes after his father in being very thorough in what he does.

"Sometimes I think," went on Mr. Nestor, "that Tom isn't quite steady enough. He's thinking of so many things, perhaps, that he can't get his mind down to the commonplace. I remember he once sent something here in a box labeled 'dynamite.' Though there was no explosive in it, it gave us a great fright. But Tom is a boy, in spite of his years. Professor Beecher seems much older. We all like him very much."

"That's nice," said Ned, as he took his departure. He had found out what he had come to learn.

"I knew it!" Ned exclaimed as he walked home. "I knew something was in the wind. The little green god of jealousy has Tom in his clutches. That's why my inventive friend was so anxious to go on this expedition when he learned Beecher was to go. He wants to beat him. I guess the professor has plainly shown that he wouldn't like anything better than to cut Tom out with Mary. Whew! that's something to think about!"

CHAPTER VI

UNPLEASANT NEWS

Ned Newton decided to keep to himself what he had heard at the Nestor home. Not for the world would he let Tom Swift know of the situation.

"That is, I won't let him know that I know," said Ned to himself, "though he is probably as well aware of the situation as I am. But it sure is queer that this Professor Beecher should have taken such a fancy to Mary, and that her father should regard him so well. That is natural, I suppose. But I wonder how Mary herself feels about it. That is the part Tom would be most interested in.

"No wonder Tom wants to get ahead of this young college chap, who probably thinks he's the whole show. If he can find the buried city, and get the idol of gold, it would be a big feather in his cap.

"He'd have no end of honors heaped on him, and I suppose his hat wouldn't come within three sizes of fitting him. Then he'd stand in better than ever with Mr. Nestor. And, maybe, with Mary, too, though I think she is loyal to Tom. But one never can tell.

"However, I'm glad I know about it. I'll do all I can to help Tom, without letting him know that I know. And if I can do anything to help in finding that idol of gold for Professor Bumper, and, incidentally, Tom, I'll do it," and he spoke aloud in his enthusiasm.

Ned, who was walking along in the darkness, clapped his open hand down on Tom's magazine he was carrying home to read again, and the resultant noise was a sharp crack. As it sounded a figure jumped from behind a tree and called tensely:

"Hold on there!"

Ned stopped short, thinking he was to be the victim of a holdup, but his fears were allayed when he beheld one of the police force of Shopton confronting him.

"I heard what you said about gettin' the gold," went on the officer. "I was walkin' along and I heard you talkin'. Where's your pal?"

"I haven't any, Mr. Newbold," answered Ned with a laugh, as he recognized the man.

"Oh, pshaw! It's Ned Newton!" exclaimed the disappointed officer. "I thought you was talkin' to a confederate about gold, and figured maybe you was goin' to rob the bank."

"No, nothing like that," answered Ned, still much amused. "I was talking to myself about a trip Tom Swift and I are going to take and—"

"Oh, that's all right," responded the policeman. "I can understand it, if it had anything to do with Tom. He's a great boy."

"Indeed he is," agreed Ned, making a mental resolve not to be so public with his thoughts in the future. He chatted for a moment with the officer, and then, bidding him good-night, walked on to his home, his mind in a whirl with conglomerate visions of buried cities, great grinning idols of gold, and rival professors seeking to be first at the goal.

The next few days were busy ones for Tom, Ned and, in fact, the whole Swift household. Tom and his father had several consultations and conducted several experiments in regard to the new stabilizer, the completion of which was so earnestly desired. Mr. Swift was sure he could carry the invention to a successful conclusion.

Ned was engaged in putting the financial affairs of the Swift Company in shape, so they would practically run themselves during his absence. Then, too, there was the packing of their baggage which must be seen to.

Of course, the main details of the trip were left to Professor Bumper, who knew just what to do. He had told Tom and Ned that all they and Mr. Damon would have to do would be to meet him at the pier in New York, where they would find all arrangements made.

One day, near the end of the week (the beginning of the next being set for the start) Eradicate came shuffling into the room where Tom was sorting out the possessions he desired to take with him, Ned assisting him in the task.

"Well, Rad, what is it?" asked Tom, with businesslike energy.

"I done heah, Massa Tom, dat yo' all's gwine off on a long trip once mo'. Am dat so?"

"Yes, that's so, Rad."

"Well, den, I'se come to ast yo' whut I'd bettah take wif me. Shall I took warm clothes or cool clothes?"

"Well, if you were going, Rad," answered Tom with a smile, "you'd need cool clothes, for we're going to a sort of jungle-land. But I'm sorry to say you're not going this trip."

"I— I ain't gwine? Does yo' mean dat yo' all ain't gwine to take me, Massa Tom?"

"That's it, Rad. It isn't any trip for you."

"In certain not!" broke in the voice of Koku, the giant, who entered with a big trunk Tom had sent him for. "Master want strong man like a bull. He take Koku!"

"Look heah!" spluttered Eradicate, and his eyes flashed. "Yo'—yo' giant yo'—yo' may be strong laik a bull, but ya' ain't got as much sense as mah mule, Boomerang! Massa Tom don't want no sich pusson wif him. He's gwine to take me."

"He take me!" cried Koku, and his voice was a roar while he beat on his mighty chest with his huge fists.

Tom, seeing that the dispute was likely to be bothersome, winked at Ned and began to speak.

"I don't believe you'd like it there, Rad—not where we're going. It's a bad country. Why the mosquitoes there bite holes in you—raise bumps on you as big as eggs."

"Oh, good land!" ejaculated the old colored man. "Am dat so Massa Tom?"

"It sure is. Then there's another kind of bug that burrows under your fingernails, and if you don't get 'em out, your fingers drop off."

"Oh, good land, Massa Tom! Am dat a fact?"

"It sure is. I don't want to see those things happen to you, Rad."

Slowly the old colored man shook his head.

"I don't mahse'f," he said. "I— I guess I won't go."

Eradicate did not stop to ask how Tom and Ned proposed to combat these two species of insects.

But there remained Koku to dispose of, and he stood smiling broadly as Eradicate shuffled of.

"Me no 'fraid bugs," said the giant.

"No," said Tom, with a look at Ned, for he did not want to take the big man on the trip for various reasons. "No, maybe not, Koku. Your skin is pretty tough. But I understand there are deep pools of water in the land where we are going, and in them lives a fish that has a hide like an alligator and a jaw like a shark. If you fall in it's all up with you."

"Dat true, Master Tom?" and Koku's voice trembled.

"Well, I've never seen such a fish, I'm sure, but the natives tell about it."

Koku seemed to be considering the matter. Strange as it may seem, the giant, though afraid of nothing human and brave when it came to a hand-to-claw argument with a wild animal, had a very great fear of the water and the unseen life within it. Even a little fresh-water crab in a brook was enough to send him shrieking to shore. So when Tom told of this curious fish, which many natives of Central America firmly believe in, the giant took thought with himself. Finally, he gave a sigh and said:

"Me stay home and keep bad mans out of master's shop."

"Yes, I guess that's the best thing for you," assented Tom with an air of relief. He and Ned had talked the matter over, and they had agreed that the presence of such a big man as Koku, in an expedition going on a more or less secret mission, would attract too much attention.

"Well, I guess that clears matters up," said Tom, as he looked over a collection of rifles and small arms, to decide which to take. "We won't have them to worry about."

"No, only Professor Beecher," remarked Ned, with a sharp look at his chum.

"Oh, we'll dispose of him all right!" asserted Tom boldly. "He hasn't had any experience in business of this sort, and with what you and Professor Bumper and Mr. Damon know we ought to have little trouble in getting ahead of the young man."

"Not to speak of your own aid," added Ned.

"Oh, I'll do what I can, of course," said Tom, with an air of indifference. But Ned knew his chum would work ceaselessly to help get the idol of gold.

Tom gave no sign that there was any complication in his affair with Mary Nestor, and of course Ned did not tell anything of what he knew about it.

That night saw the preparations of Ned and Tom about completed. There were one or two matters yet to finish on Tom's part in relation to his business, but these offered no difficulties.

The two chums were in the Swift home, talking over the prospective trip, when Mrs. Baggert, answering a ring at the front door, announced that Mr. Damon was outside.

"Tell him to come in," ordered Tom.

"Bless my baggage check!" exclaimed the excitable man, as he shook hands with Tom and Ned and noted the packing evidences all about. "You're ready to go to the land of wonders."

"The land of wonders?" repeated Ned.

"Yes, that's what Professor Bumper calls the part of Honduras we're going to. And it must be wonderful, Tom. Think of whole cities, some of them containing idols and temples of gold, buried thirty and forty feet under the surface! Wonderful is hardly the name for it!"

"It'll be great!" cried Ned. "I suppose you're ready, Mr. Damon—you and the professor?"

"Yes. But, Tom, I have a bit of unpleasant news for you."

"Unpleasant news?"

"Yes. You know Professor Bumper spoke of a rival—a man named Beecher who is a member of the faculty of a new and wealthy college."

"I heard him speak of him—yes," and the way Tom said it no one would have suspected that he had any personal interest in the matter.

"He isn't going to give his secret away," thought Ned.

"Well, this Professor Beecher, you know," went on Mr. Damon, "also knows about the idol of gold, and is trying to get ahead of Professor Bumper in the search."

"He did say something of it, but nothing was certain," remarked Tom.

"But it is certain!" exclaimed Mr. Damon. "Bless my toothpick, it's altogether too certain!"

"How is that?" asked Tom. "Is Beecher certainly going to Honduras?"

"Yes, of course. But what is worse, he and his party will leave New York on the same steamer with us!"

CHAPTER VII

TOM HEARS SOMETHING

On hearing Mr. Damon's rather startling announcement, Tom and Ned looked at one another. There seemed to be something back of the simple statement—an ominous and portending "something."

"On the same steamer with us, is he?" mused Tom.

"How did you learn this?" asked Ned.

"Just got a wire from Professor Bumper telling me. He asked me to telephone to you about it, as he was too busy to call up on the long distance from New York. But instead of 'phoning I decided to come over myself."

"Glad you did," said Tom, heartily. "Did Professor Bumper want us to do anything special, now that it is certain his rival will be so close on his trail?"

"Yes, he asked me to warn you to be careful what you did and said in reference to the expedition."

"Then does he fear something?" asked Ned.

"Yes, in a way. I think he is very much afraid this young Beecher will not only be first on the site of the underground city, but that he may be the first to discover the idol of gold. It would be a great thing for a young archaeologist like Beecher to accomplish a mission of this sort, and beat Professor Bumper in the race."

"Do you think that's why Beecher decided to go on the same steamer we are to take?" asked Ned.

"Yes, I do," said Mr. Damon. "Though from what Professor Bumper said I know he regards Professor Beecher as a perfectly honorable man, as well as a brilliant student. I do not believe Beecher or his party would stoop to anything dishonorable or underhand, though they would not hesitate, nor would we, to take advantage of every fair chance to win in the race."

"No, I suppose that's right," observed Tom; but there was a queer gleam in his eye, and his chum wondered if Tom did not have in mind the prospective race between himself and Fenimore Beecher for the regard of Mary Nestor. "We'll do our best to win, and any one is at liberty to travel on the same steamer we are to take," added the young inventor, and his tone became more incisive.

"It will be all the livelier with two expeditions after the same golden idol," remarked Ned.

"Yes, I think we're in for some excitement," observed Tom grimly. But even he did not realize all that lay before them ere they would reach Kurzon.

Mr. Damon, having delivered his message, and remarking that his preparations for leaving were nearly completed, went back to Waterfield, from there to proceed to New York in a few days with Tom and Ned, to meet Professor Bumper.

"Well, I guess we have everything in pretty good shape," remarked Tom to his chum a day or so after the visit of Mr. Damon. "Everything is packed, and as I have a few personal matters to attend to I think I'll take the afternoon off."

"Go to it!" laughed Ned, guessing a thing of two. "I've got a raft of stuff myself to look after, but don't let that keep you."

"If there is anything I can do," began Tom, "don't hesitate to—"

"Nonsense!" exclaimed Ned. "I can do it all alone. It's some of the company's business, anyhow, and I'm paid for looking after that."

"All right, then I'll cut along," Tom said, and he wore a relieved air.

"He's going to see Mary," observed Ned with a grin, as he observed Tom hop into his trim little roadster, which under his orders, Koku had polished and cleaned until it looked as though it had just come from the factory.

A little later the trim and speedy car drew up in front of the Nestor home, and Tom bounded up on the front porch, his heart not altogether as light as his feet.

"No, I'm sorry, but Mary isn't in," said Mrs. Nestor, answering his inquiry after greeting him.

"Not at home?"

"No, she went on a little visit to her cousin's at Fayetteville. She said something about letting you know she was going."

"She did drop me a card," answered Tom, and, somehow he did not feel at all cheerful. "But I thought it wasn't until next week she was going."

"That was her plan, Tom. But she changed it. Her cousin wired, asking her to advance the date, and this Mary did. There was something about a former school chum who was also to be at Myra's house—Myra is Mary's cousin you know."

"Yes, I know," assented the young inventor. "And so Mary is gone. How long is she going to stay?"

"Oh, about two weeks. She wasn't quite certain. It depends on the kind of a time she has, I suppose."

"Yes, I suppose so," agreed Tom. "Well, if you write before I do you might say I called, Mrs. Nestor."

"I will, Tom. And I know Mary will be sorry she wasn't here to take a ride with you; it's such a nice day," and the lady smiled as she looked at the speedy roadster.

"Maybe—maybe you'd like to come for a spin?" asked Tom, half desperately.

"No, thank you. I'm too old to be jounced around in one of those small cars."

"Nonsense! She rides as easily as a Pullman sleeper."

"Well, I have to go to a Red Cross meeting, anyhow, so I can't come, Tom. Thank you, just the same."

Tom did not drive back immediately to his home. He wanted to do a bit of thinking, and he believed he could do it best by himself. So it was late afternoon when he again greeted Ned, who, meanwhile, had been kept very busy.

"Well?" called Tom's chum.

"Um!" was the only answer, and Tom called Koku to put the car away in the garage.

"Something wrong," mused Ned.

The next three days were crowded with events and with work. Mr. Damon came over frequently to consult with Tom and Ned, and finally the last of their baggage had been packed, certain of Tom's inventions and implements sent on by express to New York to be taken to Honduras, and then our friends themselves followed to the metropolis.

"Good-bye, Tom," said his father. "Good-bye, and good luck! If you don't get the idol of gold I'm sure you'll have experiences that will be valuable to you."

"We're going to get the idol of gold!" said Tom determinedly.

"Look out for the bad bugs," suggested Eradicate.

"We will," promised Ned.

Tom's last act was to send a message to Mary Nestor, and then he, with Ned and Mr. Damon, who blessed everything in sight from the gasoline in the automobile to the blue sky overhead, started for the station.

New York was reached without incident. The trio put up at the hotel where Professor Bumper was to meet them.

"He hasn't arrived yet," said Tom, after glancing over the names on the hotel register and not seeing Professor Bumper's among them.

"Oh, he'll be here all right," asserted Mr. Damon. "Bless my galvanic battery! he sent me a telegram at one o'clock this morning saying he'd be sure to meet us in New York. No fear of him not starting for the land of wonders."

"There are some other professors registered, though," observed Ned, as he glanced at the book, noting the names of several scientists of whom he and Tom had read.

"Yes. I wonder what they're doing in New York," replied Tom. "They are from New England. Maybe there's a convention going on. Well, we'll have to wait, that's all, until Professor Bumper comes."

And during that wait Tom heard something that surprised him and caused him no little worry. It was when Ned came back to his room, which adjoined Tom's, that the young treasurer gave his chum the news.

"I say, Tom!" Ned exclaimed. "Who do you think those professors are, whose names we saw on the register?"

"I haven't the least idea."

"Why, they're of Beecher's party!"

"You don't mean it!"

"I surely do."

"How do you know?"

"I happened to overhear two of them talking down in the lobby a while ago. They didn't make any secret of it. They spoke freely of going with Beecher to some ancient city in Honduras, to look for an idol of gold."

"They did? But where is Beecher?"

"He hasn't joined them yet. Their plans have been changed. Instead of leaving on the same steamer we are to take in the morning they are to come on a later one. The professors here are waiting for Beecher to come."

"Why isn't he here now?"

"Well, I heard one of the other scientists say that he had gone to a place called Fayetteville, and will come on from there."

"Fayetteville!" ejaculated Tom. "Yes. That isn't far from Shopton."

"I know," assented Tom. "I wonder—I wonder why he is going there?"

"I can tell you that, too."

"You can? You're a regular detective."

"No, I just happened to overhear it. Beecher is going to call on Mary Nestor in Fayetteville, so his friends here said he told them, and his call has to do with an important matter—to him!" and Ned gazed curiously at his chum.

CHAPTER VIII

OFF FOR HONDURAS

Just what Tom's thoughts were, Ned, of course, could not guess. But by the flush that showed under the tan of his chum's cheeks the young financial secretary felt pretty certain that Tom was a bit apprehensive of the outcome of Professor Beecher's call on Mary Nestor.

"So he is going to see her about 'something important,' Ned?"

"That's what some members of his party called it."

"And they're waiting here for him to join them?"

"Yes. And it means waiting a week for another steamer. It must be something pretty important, don't you think, to cause Beecher to risk that delay in starting after the idol of gold?"

"Important? Yes, I suppose so," assented Tom. "And yet even if he waits for the next steamer he will get to Honduras nearly as soon as we do."

"How is that?"

"The next boat is a faster one."

"Then why don't we take that? I hate dawdling along on a slow freighter."

"Well, for one thing it would hardly do to change now, when all our goods are on board. And besides, the captain of the _Relstab_, on which we are going to sail, is a friend of Professor Bumper's."

"Well, I'm just as glad Beecher and his party aren't going with us," resumed Ned, after a pause. "It might make trouble."

"Oh, I'm ready for any trouble HE might make!" quickly exclaimed Tom.

He meant trouble that might be developed in going to Honduras, and starting the search for the lost city and the idol of gold. This kind of trouble Tom and his friends had experienced before, on other trips where rivals had sought to frustrate their ends.

But, in his heart, though he said nothing to Ned about it, Tom was worried. Much as he disliked to admit it to himself, he feared the visit of Professor Beecher to Mary Nestor in Fayetteville had but one meaning.

"I wonder if he's going to propose to her," thought Tom. "He has the field all to himself now, and her father likes him. That's in his favor. I guess Mr. Nestor has never quite forgiven me for that mistake about the dynamite box, and that wasn't my fault. Then, too, the Beecher and Nestor families have been friends for years. Yes, he surely has the inside edge on me, and if he gets her to throw me over— Well, I won't give up without a fight!" and Tom mentally girded himself for a battle of wits.

"He's relying on the prestige he'll get out of this idol of gold if his party finds it," thought on the young inventor. "But I'll help find it first. I'm glad to have a little start of him, anyhow, even if it isn't more than two days. Though if our vessel is held back much by storms he may get on the ground first. However, that can't be helped. I'll do the best I can."

These thoughts shot through Tom's mind even as Ned was asking his questions and making comments. Then the young inventor, shaking his shoulders as though to rid them of some weight, remarked:

"Well, come on out and see the sights. It will be long before we look on Broadway again."

When the chums returned from their sightseeing excursion, they found that Professor Bumper had arrived.

"Where's Professor Bumper?" asked Ned, the next day.

"In his room, going over books, papers and maps to make sure he has everything."

"And Mr. Damon?"

Tom did not have to answer that last question. Into the apartment came bursting the excited individual himself.

"Bless my overshoes!" he cried, "I've been looking everywhere for you! Come on, there's no time to lose!"

"What's the matter now?" asked Ned. "Is the hotel on fire?"

"Has anything happened to Professor Bumper?" Tom demanded, a wild idea forming in his head that perhaps some one of the Beecher party had tried to kidnap the discoverer of the lost city of Pelone.

"Oh, everything is all right," answered Mr. Damon. "But it's nearly time for the show to start, and we don't want to be late. I have tickets."

"For what?" asked Tom and Ned together.

"The movies," was the laughing reply. "Bless my loose ribs! but I wouldn't miss him for anything. He's in a new play called 'Up in a Balloon Boys.' It's great!" and Mr. Damon named a certain comic moving picture star in whose horse-play Mr. Damon took a curious interest. Tom and Ned were glad enough to go, Tom that he might have a chance to do a certain amount of thinking, and Ned because he was still boy enough to like moving pictures.

"I wonder, Tom," said Mr. Damon, as they came out of the theater two hours later, all three chuckling at the remembrance of what they had seen, "I wonder you never turned your inventive mind to the movies."

"Maybe I will, some day," said Tom.

He spoke rather uncertainly. The truth of the matter was that he was still thinking deeply of the visit of Professor Beecher to Mary Nestor, and wondering what it portended.

But if Tom's sleep was troubled that night he said nothing of it to his friends. He was up early the next morning, for they were to leave that day, and there was still considerable to be done in seeing that their baggage and supplies were safely loaded, and in attending to the last details of some business matters.

While at the hotel they had several glimpses of the members of the Beecher party who were awaiting the arrival of the young professor who was to lead them into the wilds of Honduras. But our friends did not seek the acquaintance of their rivals. The latter, likewise, remained by themselves, though they knew doubtless that there was likely to be a strenuous race for the possession of the idol of gold, then, it was presumed, buried deep in some forest-covered city.

Professor Bumper had made his arrangements carefully. As he explained to his friends, they would take the steamer from New York to Puerto Cortes, one of the principal seaports of Honduras. This is a town of about three thousand inhabitants, with an excellent harbor and a big pier along which vessels can tie up and discharge their cargoes directly into waiting cars.

The preparations were finally completed. The party went aboard the steamer, which was a large freight vessel, carrying a limited number of passengers, and late one afternoon swung down New York Bay.

"Off for Honduras!" cried Ned gaily, as they passed the Statue of Liberty. "I wonder what will happen before we see that little lady again."

"Who knows?" asked Tom, shrugging his shoulders, Spanish fashion. And there came before him the vision of a certain "little lady," about whom he had been thinking deeply of late.

CHAPTER IX

VAL JACINTO

"Rather tame, isn't it, Tom?"

"Well, Ned, it isn't exactly like going up in an airship," and Tom Swift who was gazing over the rail down into the deep blue water of the Caribbean Sea, over which their vessel was then steaming, looked at his chum beside him.

"No, and your submarine voyage had it all over this one for excitement," went on Ned. "When I think of that—"

"Bless my sea legs!" interrupted Mr. Damon, overhearing the conversation. "Don't speak of THAT trip. My wife never forgave me for going on it. But I had a fine time," he added with a twinkle of his eyes.

"Yes, that was quite a trip," observed Tom, as his mind went back to it. "But this one isn't over yet remember. And I shouldn't be surprised if we had a little excitement very soon."

"What do you mean?" asked Ned.

Up to this time the voyage from New York down into the tropical seas had been anything but exciting. There were not many passengers besides themselves, and the weather had been fine.

At first, used as they were to the actions of unscrupulous rivals in trying to thwart their efforts, Tom and Ned had been on the alert for any signs of hidden enemies on board the steamer. But aside from a little curiosity when it became known that they were going to explore little-known portions of Honduras, the other passengers took hardly any interest in our travelers.

It was thought best to keep secret the fact that they were going to search for a wonderful idol of gold. Not even the mule and ox-cart drivers, whom they would hire to take them into the wilds of the interior would be told of the real object of the search. It would be given out that they were looking for interesting ruins of ancient cities, with a view to getting such antiquities as might be there.

"What do you mean?" asked Ned again, when Tom did not answer him immediately. "What's the excitement?"

"I think we're in for a storm," was the reply. "The barometer is falling and I see the crew going about making everything snug. So we may have a little trouble toward this end of our trip."

"Let it come!" exclaimed Mr. Damon. "We're not afraid of trouble, Tom. Swift, are we?"

"No, to be sure we're not. And yet it looks as though the storm would be a bad one."

"Then I am going to see if my books and papers are ready, so I can get them together in a hurry in case we have to take to the life-boats," said Professor Bumper, coming on deck at that moment. "It won't do to lose them. If we didn't have the map we might not be able to find—"

"Ahem!" exclaimed Tom, with unnecessary emphasis it seemed. "I'll help you go over your papers, Professor," he added, and with a wink and a motion of his hand, he enjoined silence on his friend. Ned looked around for a reason for this, and observed a man, evidently of Spanish extraction, passing them as he paced up and down the deck.

"What's the matter?" asked the scientist in a whisper, as the man went on. "Do you know him? Is he a—?"

"I don't know anything about him," said Tom; "but it is best not to speak of our trip before strangers."

"You are right, Tom," said Professor Bumper. "I'll be more careful."

A storm was brewing, that was certain. A dull, sickly yellow began to obscure the sky, and the water, from a beautiful blue, turned a slate color and ran along the sides of the vessel with a hissing sound as though the sullen waves would ask nothing better than to suck the craft down into their depths. The wind, which had been freshening, now sang in louder tones as it hummed through the rigging and the funnel stays and bowled over the receiving conductors of the wireless.

Sharp commands from the ship's officers hastened the work of the crew in making things snug, and life lines were strung along deck for the safety of such of the passengers as might venture up when the blow began.

The storm was not long in coming. The howling of the wind grew louder, flecks of foam began to separate themselves from the crests of the waves, and the vessel pitched, rolled and tossed more violently. At first Tom and his friends thought they were in for no more than an ordinary blow, but as the storm progressed, and the passengers became aware of the anxiety on the part of the officers and crew, the alarm spread among them.

It really was a violent storm, approaching a hurricane in force, and at one time it seemed as though the craft, having been heeled far over under a staggering wave that swept her decks, would not come back to an even keel.

There was a panic among some of the passengers, and a few excited men behaved in a way that caused prompt action on the part of the first officer, who drove them back to the main cabin under threat of a revolver. For the men were determined to get to the lifeboats, and a small craft would not have had a minute to live in such seas as were running.

But the vessel proved herself sturdier than the timid ones had dared to hope, and she was soon running before the blast, going out of her course, it is true, but avoiding the danger among the many cays, or small islands, that dot the Caribbean Sea.

There was nothing to do but to let the storm blow itself out, which it did in two days. Then came a period of delightful weather. The cargo had shifted somewhat, which gave the steamer a rather undignified list.

This, as well as the loss of a deckhand overboard, was the effect of the hurricane, and though the end of the trip came amid sunshine and sweet-scented tropical breezes, many could not forget the dangers through which they had passed.

In due time Tom and his party found themselves safely housed in the small hotel at Puerto Cortes, their belongings stored in a convenient warehouse and themselves, rather weary by reason of the stress of weather, ready for the start into the interior wilds of Honduras.

"How are we going to make the trip?" asked Ned, as they sat at supper, the first night after their arrival, eating of several dishes, the red-pepper condiments of which caused frequent trips to the water pitcher.

"We can go in two ways, and perhaps we shall find it to our advantage to use both means," said Professor Bumper. "To get to this city of Kurzon," he proceeded in a low voice, so that none of the others in the dining-room would hear them, "we will have to go either by mule back or boat to a point near Copan. As near as I can tell by the ancient maps, Kurzon is in the Copan valley.

"Now the Chamelecon river seems to run to within a short distance of there, but there is no telling how far up it may be navigable. If we can go by boat it will be much more comfortable. Travel by mules and ox-carts is slow and sure, but the roads are very bad, as I have heard from friends who have made explorations in Honduras.

"And, as I said, we may have to use both land and water travel to get us where we want to go. We can proceed as far as possible up the river, and then take to the mules."

"What about arranging for boats and animals?" asked Tom. "I should think—"

He suddenly ceased talking and reached for the water, taking several large swallows.

"Whew!" he exclaimed, when he could catch his breath. "That was a hot one."

"What did you do?" asked Ned.

"Bit into a nest of red pepper. Guess I'll have to tell that cook to scatter his hits. He's bunching 'em too much in my direction," and Tom wiped the tears from his eyes.

"To answer your question," said Professor Bumper, "I will say that I have made partial arrangements for men and animals, and boats if it is found feasible to use them. I've been in correspondence with one of the merchants here, and he promised to make arrangements for us."

"When do we leave?" asked Mr. Damon.

"As soon as possible. I am not going to risk anything by delay," and it was evident the professor referred to his young rival whose arrival might be expected almost any time.

As the party was about to leave the table, they were approached by a tall, dignified Spaniard who bowed low, rather exaggeratedly low, Ned thought, and addressed them in fairly good English.

"Your pardons, Senors," he began, "but if it will please you to avail yourself of the humble services of myself, I shall have great pleasure in guiding you into the interior. I have at my command both mules and boats."

"How do you know we are going into the interior?" asked Tom, a bit sharply, for he did not like the assurance of the man.

"Pardon, Senor. I saw that you are from the States. And those from the States do not come to Honduras except for two reasons. To travel and make explorations or to start trade, and professors do not usually engage in trade," and he bowed to Professor Bumper.

"I saw your name on the register," he proceeded, "and it was not difficult to guess your mission," and he flashed a smile on the party, his white teeth showing brilliantly beneath his small, black moustache.

"I make it my business to outfit traveling parties, either for business, pleasure or scientific matters. I am, at your service, Val Jacinto," and he introduced himself with another low bow.

For a moment Tom and his friends hardly knew how to accept this offer. It might be, as the man had said, that he was a professional tour conductor, like those who have charge of Egyptian donkey-boys and guides. Or might he not be a spy?

This occurred to Tom no less than to Professor Bumper. They looked at one another while Val Jacinto bowed again and murmured:

"At your service!"

"Can you provide means for taking us to the Copan valley?" asked the professor. "You are right in one respect. I am a scientist and I purpose doing some exploring near Copan. Can you get us there?"

"Most expensively—I mean, most expeditionlessly," said Val Jacinto eagerly. "Pardon my unhappy English. I forget at times. The charges will be most moderate. I can send you by boat as far as the river travel is good, and then have mules and ox-carts in waiting."

"How far is it?" asked Tom.

"A hundred miles as the vulture flies, Senor, but much farther by river and road. We shall be a week going."

"A hundred miles in a week!" groaned Ned. "Say, Tom, if you had your aeroplane we'd be there in an hour."

"Yes, but we haven't it. However, we're in no great rush."

"But we must not lose time," said Professor Bumper. "I shall consider your offer," he added to Val Jacinto.

"Very good, Senor. I am sure you will be pleased with the humble service I may offer you, and my charges will be small. Adios," and he bowed himself away.

"What do you think of him?" asked Ned, as they went up to their rooms in the hotel, or rather one large room, containing several beds.

"He's a pretty slick article," said Mr. Damon. "Bless my check-book! but he spotted us at once, in spite of our secrecy."

"I guess these guide purveyors are trained for that sort of thing," observed the scientist. "I know my friends have often spoken of having had the same experience. However, I shall ask my friend, who is in business here, about this Val Jacinto, and if I find him all right we may engage him."

Inquiries next morning brought the information, from the head of a rubber exporting firm with whom the professor was acquainted, that the Spaniard was regularly engaged in transporting parties into the interior, and was considered efficient, careful and as honest as possible, considering the men he engaged as workers.

"So we have decided to engage you," Professor Bumper informed Val Jacinto the afternoon following the meeting.

"I am more than pleased, Senor. I shall take you into the wilds of Honduras. At your service!" and he bowed low.

"Humph! I don't just like the way our friend Val says that," observed Tom to Ned a little later. "I'd have been better pleased if he had said he'd guide us into the wilds and out again."

If Tom could have seen the crafty smile on the face of the Spaniard as the man left the hotel, the young inventor might have felt even less confidence in the guide.

CHAPTER X

IN THE WILDS

"All aboard! Step lively now! This boat makes no stops this side of Boston!" cried Ned Newton gaily, as he got into one of the several tree canoes provided for the transportation of the party up the Chamelecon river, for the first stage of their journey into the wilds of Honduras. "All aboard! This reminds me of my old camping days, Tom."

It brought those days back, in a measure, to Tom also. For there were a number of canoes filled with the goods of the party, while the members themselves occupied a larger one with their personal baggage. Strong, half-naked Indian paddlers were in charge of the canoes which were of sturdy construction and light draft, since the river, like most tropical streams, was of uncertain depths, choked here and there with sand bars or tropical growths.

Finding that Val Jacinto was regularly engaged in the business of taking explorers and mine prospectors into the interior, Professor Bumper had engaged the man. He seemed to be efficient. At the promised time he had the canoes and paddlers on hand and the goods safely stowed away while one big craft was fitted up as comfortably as possible for the men of the party.

As Ned remarked, it did look like a camping party, for in the canoes were tents, cooking utensils and, most important, mosquito canopies of heavy netting.

The insect pests of Honduras, as in all tropical countries, are annoying and dangerous. Therefore it was imperative to sleep under mosquito netting.

On the advice of Val Jacinto, who was to accompany them, the travelers were to go up the river about fifty miles. This was as far as it would be convenient to use the canoes, the guide told Tom and his friends, and from there on the trip to the Copan valley would be made on the backs of mules, which would carry most of the baggage and equipment. The heavier portions would be transported in ox-carts.

As Professor Bumper expected to do considerable excavating in order to locate the buried city, or cities, as the case might be, he had to contract for a number of Indian diggers and laborers. These could be hired in Copan, it was said.

The plan, therefore, was to travel by canoes during the less heated parts of the day, and tie up at night, making camp on shore in the net-protected tents. As for the Indians, they did not seem to mind the bites of the insects. They sometimes made a smudge fire, Val Jacinto had said, but that was all.

"Well, we haven't seen anything of Beecher and his friends," remarked the young inventor as they were about to start.

"No, he doesn't seem to have arrived," agreed Professor Bumper. "We'll get ahead of him, and so much the better.

"Well, are we all ready to start?" he continued, as he looked over the little flotilla which carried his party and his goods.

"The sooner the better!" cried Tom, and Ned fancied his chum was unusually eager.

"I guess he wants to make good before Beecher gets the chance to show Mary Nestor what he can do," thought Ned. "Tom sure is after that idol of gold."

"You may start, Senor Jacinto," said the professor, and the guide called something in Indian dialect to the rowers. Lines were cast off and the boats moved out into the stream under the influence of the sturdy paddlers.

"Well, this isn't so bad," observed Ned, as he made himself comfortable in his canoe. "How about it, Tom?"

"Oh, no. But this is only the beginning."

A canopy had been arranged over their boat to keep off the scorching rays of the sun. The boat containing the exploring party and Val Jacinto took the lead, the baggage craft following. At the place where it flowed into the bay on which Puerto Cortes was built, the stream was wide and deep.

The guide called something to the Indians, who increased their stroke.

"I tell them to pull hard and that at the end of the day's journey they will have much rest and refreshment," he translated to Professor Bumper and the others.

"Bless my ham sandwich, but they'll need plenty of some sort of refreshment," said Mr. Damon, with a sigh. "I never knew it to be so hot."

"Don't complain yet," advised Tom, with a laugh. "The worst is yet to come."

It really was not unpleasant traveling, aside from the heat. And they had expected that, coming as they had to a tropical land. But, as Tom said, what lay before them might be worse.

In a little while they had left behind them all signs of civilization. The river narrowed and flowed sluggishly between the banks which were luxuriant with tropical growth. Now and then some lonely Indian hut could be seen, and occasionally a craft propelled by a man who was trying to gain a meager living from the rubber forest which hemmed in the stream on either side.

As the canoe containing the men was paddled along, there floated down beside it what seemed to be a big, rough log.

"I wonder if that is mahogany," remarked Mr. Damon, reaching over to touch it. "Mahogany is one of the most valuable woods of Honduras, and if this is a log of that nature—

"Bless my watch chain!" he suddenly cried. "It's alive!"

And the "log" was indeed so, for there was a sudden flash of white teeth, a long red opening showed, and then came a click as an immense alligator, having opened and closed his mouth, sank out of sight in a swirl of water.

Mr. Damon drew back so suddenly that he tilted the canoe, and the black paddlers looked around wonderingly.

"Alligator," explained Jacinto succinctly, in their tongue.

"Ugh!" they grunted.

"Bless my—bless my—" hesitated Mr. Damon, and for one of the very few times in his life his language failed him.

"Are there many of them hereabouts?" asked Ned, looking back at the swirl left by the saurian.

"Plenty," said the guide, with a shrug of his shoulders. He seemed to do as much talking that way, and with his hands, as he did in speech. "The river is full of them."

"Dangerous?" queried Tom.

"Don't go in swimming," was the significant advice. "Wait, I'll show you," and he called up the canoe just behind.

In this canoe was a quantity of provisions. There was a chunk of meat among other things, a gristly piece, seeing which Mr. Damon had objected to its being brought along, but the guide had said it would do for fish bait. With a quick motion of his hand, as he sat in the awning-covered stern with Tom, Ned and the others, Jacinto sent the chunk of meat out into the muddy stream.

Hardly a second later there was a rushing in the water as though a submarine were about to come up. An ugly snout was raised, two rows of keen teeth snapped shut as a scissors-like jaw opened, and the meat was gone.

"See!" was the guide's remark, and something like a cold shiver of fear passed over the white members of the party. "This water is not made in which to swim. Be careful!"

"We certainly shall," agreed Tom. "They're fierce."

"And always hungry," observed Jacinto grimly.

"And to think that I—that I nearly had my hand on it," murmured Mr. Damon. "Ugh! Bless my eyeglasses!"

"The alligator nearly had your hand," said the guide. "They can turn in the water like a flash, wherefore it is not wise to pat one on the tail lest it present its mouth instead."

They paddled on up the river, the dusky Indians now and then breaking out into a chant that seemed to give their muscles new energy. The song, if song it was, passed from one boat to the other, and as the chant boomed forth the craft shot ahead more swiftly.

They made a landing about noon, and lunch was served. Tom and his friends were hungry in spite of the heat. Moreover, they were experienced travelers and had learned not to fret over inconveniences and discomforts. The Indians ate by themselves, two acting as servants to Jacinto and the professor's party.

As is usual in traveling in the tropics, a halt was made during the heated middle of the day. Then, as the afternoon shadows were waning, the party again took to the canoes and paddled on up the river.

"Do you know of a good place to stop during the night?" asked Professor Bumper of Jacinto.

"Oh, yes; a most excellent place. It is where I always bring scientific parties I am guiding. You may rely on me."

It was within an hour of dusk—none too much time to allow in which to pitch camp in the tropics, where night follows day suddenly—when a halt was called, as a turn of the river showed a little clearing on the edge of the forest-bound river.

"We stay here for the night," said Jacinto. "It is a good place."

"It looks picturesque enough," observed Mr. Damon. "But it is rather wild."

"We are a good distance from a settlement," agreed the guide. "But one can not explore—and find treasure in cities," and he shrugged his shoulders again.

"Find treasure? What do you mean?" asked Tom quickly. "Do you think that we—?"

"Pardon, Senor," replied Jacinto softly. "I meant no offense. I think that all you scientific parties will take treasure if you can find it."

"We are looking for traces of the old Honduras civilization," put in Professor Bumper.

"And doubtless you will find it," was the somewhat too courteous answer of the guide. "Make camp quickly!" he called to the Indians in their tongue. "You must soon get under the nets or you will be eaten alive!" he told Tom. "There are many mosquitoes here."

The tents were set up, smudge fires built and supper quickly prepared. Dusk fell rapidly, and as Tom and Ned walked a little way down toward the river before turning in under the mosquito canopies, the young financial man said:

"Sort of lonesome and gloomy, isn't it, Tom?"

"Yes. But you didn't expect to find a moving picture show in the wilds of Honduras, did you?"

"No, and yet— Look out! What's that?" suddenly cried Ned, as a great soft, black shadow seemed to sweep out of a clump of trees toward him. Involuntarily he clutched Tom's arm and pointed, his face showing fear in the fast-gathering darkness.

CHAPTER XI

THE VAMPIRES

Tom Swift looked deliberately around. It was characteristic of him that, though by nature he was prompt in action, he never acted so hurriedly as to obscure his judgment. So, though now Ned showed a trace of strange excitement, Tom was cool.

"What is it?" asked the young inventor. "What's the matter? What did you think you saw, Ned; another alligator?"

"Alligator? Nonsense! Up on shore? I saw a black shadow, and I didn't THINK I saw it, either. I really did."

Tom laughed quietly.

"A shadow!" he exclaimed. "Since when were you afraid of shadows, Ned?"

"I'm not afraid of ordinary shadows," answered Ned, and in his voice there was an uncertain tone. "I'm not afraid of my shadow or yours, Tom, or anybody's that I can see. But this wasn't any human shadow. It was as if a great big blob of wet darkness had been waved over your head."

"That's a queer explanation," Tom said in a low voice. "A great big blob of wet darkness!"

"But that just describes it," went on Ned, looking up and around. "It was just as if you were in some dark room, and some one waved a wet velvet cloak over your head—spooky like! It didn't make a sound, but there was a smell as if a den of some wild beast was near here. I remember that odor from the time we went hunting with your electric rifle in the jungle, and got near the den in the rocks where the tigers lived."

"Well, there is a wild beast smell all around here," admitted Tom, sniffing the air. "It's the alligators in the river I guess. You know they have an odor of musk."

"Do you mean to say you didn't feel that shadow flying over us just now?" asked Ned.

"Well, I felt something sail through the air, but I took it to be a big bird. I didn't pay much attention. To tell you the truth I was thinking about Beecher—wondering when he would get here," added Tom quickly as if to forestall any question as to whether or not his thoughts had to do with Beecher in connection with Tom's affair of the heart.

"Well it wasn't a bird—at least not a regular bird," said Ned in a low voice, as once more he looked at the dark and gloomy jungle that stretched back from the river and behind the little clearing where the camp had been made.

"Come on!" cried Tom, in what he tried to make a cheerful voice. "This is getting on your nerves, Ned, and I didn't know you had any. Let's go back and turn in. I'm dog-tired and the mosquitoes are beginning to find that we're here. Let's get under the nets. Then the black shadows won't get you."

Not at all unwilling to leave so gloomy a scene, Ned, after a brief glance up and down the dark river, followed his chum. They found Professor Bumper and Mr. Damon in their tent, a separate one having been set up for the two men adjoining that of the youths.

"Bless my fountain pen!" exclaimed Mr. Damon, as he caught sight of Tom and Ned in the flickering light of the smudge fire between the two canvas shelters. "We were just wondering what had become of you."

"We were chasing shadows!" laughed Tom. "At least Ned was. But you look cozy enough in there."

It did, indeed, look cheerful in contrast to the damp and dark jungle all about. Professor Bumper, being an experienced traveler, knew how to provide for such comforts as were possible. Folding cots had been opened for himself, Mr. Damon and the guide to sleep on, others, similar, being set up in the tent where Tom and Ned were to sleep. In the middle of the tent the professor had made a table of his own and Mr. Damon's suit cases, and on this placed a small dry battery electric light. He was making some notes, doubtless for a future book. Jacinto was going about the camp, seeing that the Indians were at their duties, though most of them had gone directly to sleep after supper.

"Better get inside and under the nets," advised Professor Bumper to Tom and Ned. "The mosquitoes here are the worst I ever saw."

"We're beginning to believe that," returned Ned, who was unusually quiet. "Come on, Tom. I can't stand it any longer. I'm itching in a dozen places now from their bites."

As Tom and Ned had no wish for a light, which would be sure to attract insects, they entered their tent in the dark, and were soon stretched out in comparative comfort. Tom was just on the edge of a deep sleep when he heard Ned murmur:

"I can't understand it!"

"What's that?" asked the young inventor.

"I say I can't understand it."

"Understand what?"

"That shadow. It was real and yet—"

"Oh, go to sleep!" advised Tom, and, turning over, he was soon breathing heavily and regularly, indicating that he, at least, had taken his own advice.

Ned, too, finally succumbed to the overpowering weariness of the first day of travel, and he, too, slept, though it was an uneasy slumber, disturbed by a feeling as though some one were holding a heavy black quilt over his head, preventing him from breathing.

The feeling, sensation or dream—whatever it was—perhaps a nightmare—became at last so real to Ned that he struggled himself into wakefulness. With an effort he sat up, uttering an inarticulate cry. To his surprise he was answered. Some one asked:

"What is the matter?"

"Who—who are you?" asked Ned quickly, trying to peer through the darkness.

"This is Jacinto—your guide," was the soft answer. "I was walking about camp and, hearing you murmuring, I came to your tent. Is anything wrong?"

For a moment Ned did not answer. He listened and could tell by the continued heavy and regular breathing of his chum that Tom was still asleep.

"Are you in our tent?" asked Ned, at length:

"Yes," answered Jacinto. "I came in to see what was the matter with you. Are you ill?"

"No, of course not," said Ned, a bit shortly. "I—I had a bad dream, that was all. All right now."

"For that I am glad. Try to get all the sleep you can, for we must start early to avoid the heat of the day," and there was the sound of the guide leaving and arranging the folds of the mosquito net behind him to keep out the night-flying insects.

Once more Ned composed himself to sleep, and this time successfully, for he did not have any more unpleasant dreams. The quiet of the jungle settled down over the camp, at least the comparative quiet of the jungle, for there were always noises of some sort going on, from the fall of some rotten tree limb to the scream or growl of a wild beast, while, now and again, from the river came the pig-like grunts of the alligators.

It was about two o'clock in the morning, as they ascertained later, when the whole camp—white travelers and all—was suddenly awakened by a wild scream. It seemed to come from one of the natives, who called out a certain word ever and over again. To Tom and Ned it sounded like:

"Oshtoo! Oshtoo! Oshtoo!"

"What's the matter?" cried Professor Bumper.

"The vampires!" came the answering voice of Jacinto. "One of the Indians has been attacked by a big vampire bat! Look out, every one! It may be a raid by the dangerous creatures! Be careful!"

Notwithstanding this warning Ned stuck his head out of the tent. The same instant he was aware of a dark enfolding shadow passing over him, and, with a shudder of fear, he jumped back.

CHAPTER XII

A FALSE FRIEND

"What is it? What's the matter?" cried Tom springing from his cot and hastening to the side of his chum in the tent. "What has happened, Ned?"

"I don't know, but Jacinto is yelling something about vampires!"

"Vampires?"

"Yes. Big bats. And he's warning us to be careful. I stuck my head out just now and I felt that same sort of shadow I felt this evening when we were down near the river."

"Nonsense!"

"I tell you I did!"

At that instant Tom flashed a pocket electric lamp he had taken from beneath his pillow and in the gleam of it he and Ned saw fluttering about the tent some dark, shadow-like form, at the sight of which Tom's chum cried:

"There it is! That's the shadow! Look out!" and he held up his hands instinctively to shield his face.

"Shadow!" yelled Tom, unconsciously adding to the din that seemed to pervade every part of the camp. "That isn't a shadow. It's substance. It's a monster bat, and here goes for a strike at it!"

He caught up his camera tripod which was near his cot, and made a swing with it at the creature that had flown into the tent through an opening it had made for itself.

"Look out!" yelled Ned. "If it's a vampire it'll—"

"It won't do anything to me!" shouted Tom, as he struck the creature, knocking it into the corner of the tent with a thud that told it must be completely stunned, if not killed. "But what's it all about, anyhow?" Tom asked. "What's the row?"

From without the tent came the Indian cries of:

"Oshtoo! Oshtoo!"

Mingled with them were calls of Jacinto, partly in Spanish, partly in the Indian tongue and partly in English.

"It is a raid by vampire bats!" was all Tom and Ned could distinguish. "We shall have to light fires to keep them away, if we can succeed. Every one grab up a club and strike hard!"

"Come on!" cried Tom, getting on some clothes by the light of his gleaming electric light which he had set on his cot.

"You're not going out there, are you?" asked Ned.

"I certainly am! If there's a fight I want to be in it, bats or anything else. Here, you have a light like mine. Flash it on, and hang it somewhere on yourself. Then get a club and come on. The lights will blind the bats, and we can see to hit 'em!"

Tom's plan seemed to be a good one. His lamp and Ned's had small hooks on them, so they could be carried in the upper coat pocket, showing a gleam of light and leaving the hands free for use.

Out of the tents rushed the young men to find Professor Bumper and Mr. Damon before them. The two men had clubs and were striking about in the half darkness, for now the Indians had set several fires aglow. And in the gleams, constantly growing brighter as more fuel was piled on, the young inventor and his chum saw a weird sight.

Circling and wheeling about in the camp clearing were many of the black shadowy forms that had caused Ned such alarm. Great bats they were, and a dangerous species, if Jacinto was to be believed.

The uncanny creatures flew in and out among the trees and tents, now swooping low near the Indians or the travelers. At such times clubs would be used, often with the effect of killing or stunning the flying pests. For a time it seemed as if the bats would fairly overwhelm the camp, so many of them were there. But the increasing lights, and the attacks made by the Indians and the white travelers turned the tide of battle, and, with silent flappings of their soft, velvety wings, the bats flew back to the jungle whence they had emerged.

"We are safe—for the present!" exclaimed Jacinto with a sigh of relief.

"Do you think they will come back?" asked Tom.

"They may—there is no telling."

"Bless my speedometer!" cried Mr. Damon, "If those beasts or birds—whatever they are—come back I'll go and hide in the river and take my chances with the alligators!"

"The alligators aren't much worse," asserted Jacinto with a visible shiver. "These vampire bats sometimes depopulate a whole village."

"Bless my shoe laces!" cried Mr. Damon. "You don't mean to say that the creatures can eat up a whole village?"

"Not quite. Though they might if they got the chance," was the answer of the Spanish guide. "These vampire bats fly from place to place in great swarms, and they are so large and blood-thirsty that a few of them can kill a horse or an ox in a short time by sucking its blood. So when the villagers find they are visited by a colony of these vampires they get out, taking their live stock with them, and stay in caves or in densely wooded places until the bats fly on. Then the villagers come back.

"It was only a small colony that visited us tonight or we would have had more trouble. I do not think this lot will come back. We have killed too many of them," and he looked about on the ground where many of the uncanny creatures were still twitching in the death struggle.

"Come back again!" cried Mr. Damon. "Bless my skin! I hope not! I've had enough of bats—and mosquitoes," he added, as he slapped at his face and neck.

Indeed the party of whites were set upon by the night insects to such an extent that it was necessary to hurry back to the protection of the nets.

Tom and Ned kicked outside the bat the former had killed in their tent, and then both went back to their cots. But it was some little time before they fell asleep. And they did not have much time to rest, for an early start must be made to avoid the terrible heat of the middle of the day.

"Whew!" whistled Ned, as he and Tom arose in the gray dawn of the morning when Jacinto announced the breakfast which the Indian cook had prepared. "That was some night! If this is a sample of the wilds of Honduras, give me the tameness of Shopton."

"Oh, we've gone through with worse than this," laughed Tom. "It's all in the day's work. We've only got started. I guess we're a bit soft, Ned, though we had hard enough work in that tunnel-digging."

After breakfast, while the Indians were making ready the canoes, Professor Bumper, who, in a previous visit to Central America, had become interested in the subject, made a brief examination of some of the dead bats. They were exceptionally large, some almost as big as hawks, and were of the sub-family _Desmodidae_, the scientist said.

"This is a true blood-sucking bat," went on the professor. "This," and he pointed to the nose-leaves, "is the sucking apparatus. The bat makes an opening in the skin with its sharp teeth and proceeds to extract the blood. I can well believe two or three of them, attacking a steer or mule at once, could soon weaken it so the animal would die."

"And a man, too?" asked Ned.

"Well a man has hands with which to use weapons, but a helpless quadruped has not. Though if a sufficient number of these bats attacked a man at the same time, he would have small chance to escape alive. Their bites, too, may be poisonous for all I know."

The Indians seemed glad to leave the "place of the bats," as they called the camp site. Jacinto explained that the Indians believed a vampire could kill them while they slept, and they were very much afraid of the blood-sucking bats. There were many other species in the tropics, Professor Bumper explained, most of which lived on fruit or on insects they caught. The blood-sucking bats were comparatively few, and the migratory sort fewer still.

"Well, we're on our way once more," remarked Tom as again they were in the canoes being paddled up the river. "How much longer does your water trip take, Professor?"

"I hardly know," and Professor Bumper looked to Jacinto to answer.

"We go two more days in the canoes," the guide answered, "and then we shall find the mules waiting for us at a place called Hidjio. From then on we travel by land until—well until you get to the place where you are going.

"I suppose you know where it is?" he added, nodding toward the professor. "I am leaving that part to you."

"Oh, I have a map, showing where I want to begin some excavations," was the answer. "We must first go to Copan and see what arrangements we can make for laborers. After that—well, we shall trust to luck for what we shall find."

"There are said to be many curious things," went on Jacinto, speaking as though he had no interest. "You have mentioned buried cities. Have you thought what may be in them—great heathen temples, idols, perhaps?"

For a moment none of the professor's companions spoke. It was as though Jacinto had tried to get some information. Finally the scientist said:

"Oh, yes, we may find an idol. I understand the ancient people, who were here long before the Spaniards came, worshiped idols. But we shall take whatever antiquities we find."

"Huh!" grunted Jacinto, and then he called to the paddlers to increase their strokes.

The journey up the river was not very eventful. Many alligators were seen, and Tom and Ned shot several with the electric rifle. Toward the close of the third day's travel there was a cry from one of the rear boats, and an alarm of a man having fallen overboard was given.

Tom turned in time to see the poor fellow's struggles, and at the same time there was a swirl in the water and a black object shot forward.

"An alligator is after him!" yelled Ned.

"I see," observed Tom calmly. "Hand me the rifle, Ned."

Tom took quick aim and pulled the trigger. The explosive electric bullet went true to its mark, and the great animal turned over in a death struggle. But the river was filled with them, and no sooner had the one nearest the unfortunate Indian been disposed of than another made a dash for the man.

There was a wild scream of agony and then a dark arm shot up above the red foam. The waters seethed and bubbled as the alligators fought under it for possession of the paddler. Tom fired bullet after bullet from his wonderful rifle into the spot, but though he killed some of the alligators this did not save the man's life. His body was not seen again, though search was made for it.

The accident cast a little damper over the party, and there was a feeling of gloom among the Indians. Professor Bumper announced that he would see to it that the man's family did not want, and this seemed to give general satisfaction, especially to a brother who was with the party.

Aside from being caught in a drenching storm and one or two minor accidents, nothing else of moment marked the remainder of the river journey, and at the end of the third day the canoes pulled to shore and a night camp was made.

"But where are the mules we are to use in traveling tomorrow?" asked the professor of Jacinto.

"In the next village. We shall march there in the morning. No use to go there at night when all is dark."

"I suppose that is so."

The Indians made camp as usual, the goods being brought from the canoes and piled up near the tents. Then night settled down.

"Hello!" cried Tom, awakening the next morning to find the sun streaming into his tent. "We must have overslept, Ned. We were to start before old Sol got in his heavy work, but we haven't had breakfast yet."

"I didn't hear any one call us," remarked Ned.

"Nor I. Wonder if we're the only lazy birds." He looked from the tent in time to see Mr. Damon and the professor emerging. Then Tom noticed something queer. The canoes were not on the river bank. There was not an Indian in sight, and no evidence of Jacinto.

"What's the matter?" asked the young inventor. "Have the others gone on ahead?"

"I rather think they've gone back," was the professor's dry comment.

"Gone back?"

"Yes. The Indians seem to have deserted us at the ending of this stage of our journey."

"Bless my time-table!" cried Mr. Damon. "You don't say so! What does it mean? What has becomes of our friend Jacinto?"

"I'm afraid he was rather a false friend," was the professor's answer. "This is the note he left. He has gone and taken the canoes and all the Indians with him," and he held out a paper on which was some scribbled writing.

CHAPTER XIII

FORWARD AGAIN

"What does it all mean?" asked Tom, seeing that the note was written in Spanish, a tongue which he could speak slightly but read indifferently.

"This is some of Beecher's work," was Professor Bumper's grim comment. "It seems that Jacinto was in his pay."

"In his pay!" cried Mr. Damon. "Do you mean that Beecher deliberately hired Jacinto to betray us?"

"Well, no. Not that exactly. Here, I'll translate this note for you," and the professor proceeded to read:

"Senors: I greatly regret the step I have to take, but I am a gentleman, and, having given my word, I must keep it. No harm shall come to you, I swear it on my honor!"

"Queer idea of honor he has!" commented Tom, grimly.
Professor Bumper read on:

"Know then, that before I engaged myself to you I had been engaged by Professor Beecher through a friend to guide him into the Copan valley, where he wants to make some explorations, for what I know not, save maybe that it is for gold. I agreed, in case any rival expeditions came to lead them astray if I could.

"So, knowing from what you said that you were going to this place, I engaged myself to you, planning to do what I have done. I greatly regret it, as I have come to like you, but I had given my promise to Professor Beecher's friend, that I would first lead him to the Copan valley, and would keep others away until he had had a chance to do his exploration.

"So I have led you to this wilderness. It is far from the Copan, but you are near an Indian village, and you will be able to get help in a week or so. In the meanwhile you will not starve, as you have plenty of supplies. If you will travel northeast you will come again to Puerto Cortes in due season. As for the money I had from you, I deposit it to your credit, Professor Beecher having made me an allowance for steering rival parties on the wrong trail. So I lose nothing, and I save my honor.

"I write this note as I am leaving in the night with the Indians. I put some harmless sedative in your tea that you might sleep soundly, and not awaken until we were well on our way. Do not try to follow us, as the river will carry us swiftly away. And, let me add, there is no personal animosity on the part of Professor Beecher against you. I should have done to any rival expedition the same as I have done with you.

JACINTO."

For a moment there was silence, and then Tom Swift burst out with:

"Well, of all the mean, contemptible tricks of a human skunk this is the limit!"

"Bless my hairbrush, but he is a scoundrel!" ejaculated Mr. Damon, with great warmth.

"I'd like to start after him the biggest alligator in the river," was Ned's comment.

Professor Bumper said nothing for several seconds. There was a strange look on his face, and then he laughed shortly, as though the humor of the situation appealed to him.

"Professor Beecher has more gumption than I gave him credit for," he said. "It was a clever trick!"

"Trick!" cried Tom.

"Yes. I can't exactly agree that it was the right thing to do, but he, or some friend acting for him, seems to have taken precautions that we are not to suffer or lose money. Beecher goes on the theory that all is fair in love and war, I suppose, and he may call this a sort of scientific war."

Ned wondered, as he looked at his chum, how much love there was in it. Clearly Beecher was determined to get that idol of gold.

"Well, it can't be helped, and we must make the best of it," said Tom, after a pause.

"True. But now, boys, let's have breakfast, and then we'll make what goods we can't take with us as snug as possible, until we can send the mule drivers after them," went on Professor Bumper.

"Send the mule drivers after them?" questioned Ned. "What do you mean to do?"

"Do? Why keep on, of course. You don't suppose I'm going to let a little thing like this stand between me and the discovery of Kurzon and the idol of gold, do you?"

"But," began Mr. Damon, "I don't see how—"

"Oh, we'll find a way," interrupted Tom. "It isn't the first time I've been pretty well stranded on an expedition of this kind, and sometimes from the same cause—the actions of a rival. Now we'll turn the tables on the other fellows and see how they like it. The professor's right—let's have breakfast. Jacinto seems to have told the truth. Nothing of ours is missing."

Tom and Ned got the meal, and then a consultation was held as to what was best to be done.

"We can't go on any further by water, that's sure," said Tom. "In the first place the river is too shallow, and secondly we have no canoes. So the only thing is to go on foot through the jungle."

"But how can we, and carry all this stuff?" asked Ned.

"We needn't carry it!" cried Professor Bumper. "We'll leave it here, where it will be safe enough, and tramp on to the nearest Indian village. There we'll hire bearers to take our stuff on until we can get mules. I'm not going to turn back!"

"Good!" cried Mr. Damon. "Bless my rubber boots! but that's what I say—keep on!"

"Oh, no! we'll never turn back," agreed Tom.

"But how can we manage it?" asked Ned.

"We've just got to! And when you have to do a thing, it's a whole lot easier to do than if you just feel as though you ought to. So, lively is the word!" cried Tom, in answer.

"We'll pack up what we can carry and leave the rest," added the scientist.

Being an experienced traveler Professor Bumper had arranged his baggage so that it could be carried by porters if necessary. Everything could be put into small packages, including the tents and food supply.

"There are four of us," remarked Tom, "and if we can not pack enough along with us to enable us to get to the nearest village, we had better go back to civilization. I'm not afraid to try."

"Nor I!" cried Mr. Damon.

The baggage, stores and supplies that were to be left behind were made as snug as possible, and so piled up that wild beasts could do the least harm. Then a pack was made up for each one to carry.

They would take weapons, of course, Tom Swift's electric rifle being the one he choose for himself. They expected to be able to shoot game on their way, and this would provide them food in addition to the concentrated supply they carried. Small tents, in sections, were carried, there being two, one for Tom and Ned and one for Mr. Damon and the professor.

As far as could be learned from a casual inspection, Jacinto and his deserting Indians had taken back with them only a small quantity of food. They were traveling light and down stream, and could reach the town much more quickly than they had come away from it.

"That Beecher certainly was slick," commented Professor Bumper when they were ready to start. "He must have known about what time I would arrive, and he had Jacinto waiting for us. I thought it was too good to be true, to get an experienced guide like him so easily. But it was all planned, and I was so engrossed in thinking of the ancient treasures I hope to find that I never thought of a possible trick. Well, let's start!" and he led the way into the jungle, carrying his heavy pack as lightly as did Tom.

Professor Bumper had a general idea in which direction lay a number of native villages, and it was determined to head for them, blazing a path through the wilderness, so that the Indians could follow it back to the goods left behind.

It was with rather heavy hearts that the party set off, but Tom's spirits could not long stay clouded, and the scientist was so good-natured about the affair and seemed so eager to do the utmost to render Beecher's trick void, that the others fell into a lighter mood, and went on more cheerfully, though the way was rough and the packs heavy.

They stopped at noon under a bower they made of palms, and, spreading the nets over them, got a little rest after a lunch. Then, when the sun was less hot, they started off again.

"Forward is the word!" cried Ned cheerfully. "Forward!"

They had not gone more than an hour on the second stage of their tramp when Tom, who was in the lead, following the direction laid out by the compass, suddenly stopped, and reached around for his electric rifle, which he was carrying at his back.

"What is it?" asked Ned in a whisper.

"I don't know, but it's some big animal there in the bushes," was Tom's low-voiced answer. "I'm ready for it."

The rustling increased, and a form could be seen indistinctly. Tom aimed the deadly gun and stood ready to pull the trigger.

Ned, who had a side view into the underbrush, gave a sudden cry.

"Don't shoot, Tom!" he yelled. "It's a man!"

CHAPTER XIV

A NEW GUIDE

In spite of Ned Newton's cry, Tom's finger pressed the switch-trigger of the electric rifle, for previous experience had taught him that it was sometimes the best thing to awe the natives in out-of-the-way corners of the earth. But the young inventor quickly elevated the muzzle, and the deadly missile went hissing through the air over the head of a native Indian who, at that moment, stepped from the bush.

The man, startled and alarmed, shrank back and was about to run into the jungle whence he had emerged. Small wonder if he had, considering the reception he so unwittingly met with. But Tom, aware of the necessity for making inquiries of one who knew that part of the jungle, quickly called to him.

"Hold on!" he shouted. "Wait a minute. I didn't mean that. I thought at first you were a tapir or a tiger. No harm intended. I say, Professor," Tom called back to the savant, "you'd better speak to him in his lingo, I can't manage it. He may be useful in guiding us to that Indian village Jacinto told us of."

This Professor Bumper did, being able to make himself understood in the queer part-Spanish dialect used by the native Hondurians, though he could not, of course, speak it as fluently as had Jacinto.

Professor Bumper had made only a few remarks to the man who had so unexpectedly appeared out of the jungle when the scientist gave an exclamation of surprise at some of the answers made.

"Bless my moving picture!" cried Mr. Damon.

"What's the matter now? Is anything wrong? Does he refuse to help us?"

"No, it isn't that," was the answer. "In fact he came here to help us. Tom, this is the brother of the Indian who fell overboard and who was eaten by the alligators. He says you were very kind to try to save his brother with your rifle, and for that reason he has come back to help us."

"Come back?" queried Tom.

"Yes, he went off with the rest of the Indians when Jacinto deserted us, but he could not stand being a traitor, after you had tried to save his brother's life. These Indians are queer people. They don't show much emotion, but they have deep feelings. This one says he will devote himself to your service from now on. I believe we can count on him. He is deeply grateful to you, Tom."

"I'm glad of that for all our sakes. But what does he say about Jacinto?"

The professor asked some more questions, receiving answers, and then translated them.

"This Indian, whose name is Tolpec, says Jacinto is a fraud," exclaimed Professor Bumper. "He made all the Indians leave us in the night, though many of them were willing to stay and fill the contract they had made. But Jacinto would not let them, making them desert. Tolpec went away with the others, but because of what Tom had done he planned to come back at the first chance and be our guide. Accordingly he jumped ashore from one of the canoes, and made his way to our camp. He got there, found it deserted and followed us, coming up just now."

"Well I'm glad I didn't frighten him off with my gun," remarked Tom grimly. "So he agrees with us that Jacinto is a scoundrel, does he? I guess he might as well classify Professor Beecher in the same way."

"I am not quite so sure of that," said Professor Bumper slowly. "I can not believe Beecher would play such a trick as this, though some over-zealous friend of his might."

"Oh, of course Beecher did it!" cried Tom. "He heard we were coming here, figured out that we'd start ahead of him, and he wanted to side-track us. Well, he did it all right," and Tom's voice was bitter.

"He has only side-tracked us for a while," announced Professor Bumper in cheerful tones.

"What do you mean?" asked Mr. Damon.

"I mean that this Indian comes just in the nick of time. He is well acquainted with this part of the jungle, having lived here all his life, and he offers to guide us to a place where we can get mules to transport ourselves and our baggage to Copan."

"Fine!" cried Ned. "When can we start?"

Once more the professor and the native conversed in the strange tongue, and then Professor Bumper announced:

"He says it will be better for us to go back where we left our things and camp there. He will stay with us tonight and in the morning go on to the nearest Indian town and come back with porters and helpers."

"I think that is good advice to follow," put in Tom, "for we do need our goods; and if we reached the settlement ourselves, we would have to send back for our things, with the uncertainty of getting them all."

So it was agreed that they would make a forced march back through the jungle to where they had been deserted by Jacinto. There they would make camp for the night, and until such time as Tolpec could return with a force of porters.

It was not easy, that backward tramp through the jungle, especially as night had fallen. But the new Indian guide could see like a cat, and led the party along paths they never could have found by themselves. The use of their pocket electric lights was a great help, and possibly served to ward off the attacks of jungle beasts, for as they tramped along they could hear stealthy sounds in the underbush on either side of the path, as though tigers were stalking them. For there was in the woods an animal of the leopard family, called tiger or "tigre" by the natives, that was exceedingly fierce and dangerous. But watchfulness prevented any accident, and eventually the party reached the place where they had left their goods. Nothing had been disturbed, and finally a fire was made, the tents set up and a light meal, with hot tea served.

"We'll get ahead of Beecher yet," said Tom.

"You seem as anxious as Professor Bumper," observed Mr. Damon.

"I guess I am," admitted Tom. "I want to see that idol of gold in the possession of our party."

The night passed without incident, and then, telling his new friends that he would return as soon as possible with help, Tolpec, taking a small supply of food with him, set out through the jungle again.

As the green vines and creepers closed after him, and the explorers were left alone with their possessions piled around them, Ned remarked:

"After all, I wonder if it was wise to let him go?"

"Why not?" asked Tom.

"Well, maybe he only wanted to get us back here, and then he'll desert, too. Maybe that's what he's done now, making us lose two or three days by inducing us to return, waiting for what will never happen—his return with other natives."

A silence followed Ned's intimation.

CHAPTER XV

IN THE COILS

"Ned, do you really think Tolpec is going to desert us?" asked Tom.

"Well, I don't know," was the slowly given reply. "It's a possibility, isn't it?"

"Yes, it is," broke in Professor Bumper. "But what if it is? We might as well trust him, and if he proves true, as I believe he will, we'll be so much better off. If he proves a traitor we'll only have lost a few days, for if he doesn't come back we can go on again in the way we started."

"But that's just it!" complained Tom. "We don't want to lose any time with that Beecher chap on our trail."

"I am not so very much concerned about him," remarked Professor Bumper, dryly.

"Why not?" snapped out Mr. Damon.

"Well, because I think he'll have just about as hard work locating the hidden city, and finding the idol of gold, as we'll have. In other words it will be an even thing, unless he gets too far ahead of us, or keeps us back, and I don't believe he can do that now.

"So I thought it best to take a chance with this Indian. He would hardly have taken the trouble to come all the way back, and run the risks he did, just to delay us a few days. However, we'll soon know. Meanwhile, we'll take it easy and wait for the return of Tolpec and his friends."

Though none of them liked to admit it, Ned's words had caused his three friends some anxiety, and though they busied themselves about the camp there was an air of waiting impatiently for something to occur. And waiting is about the hardest work there is.

But there was nothing for it but to wait, and it might be at least a week, Professor Bumper said, before the Indian could return with a party of porters and mules to move their baggage.

"Yes, Tolpec has not only to locate the settlement," Tom admitted, "but he must persuade the natives to come back with him. He may have trouble in that, especially if it is known that he has left Jacinto, who, I imagine, is a power among the tribes here."

But there were only two things left to do—wait and hope. The travelers did both. Four days passed and there was no sign of Tolpec. Eagerly, and not a little anxiously, they watched the jungle path along which he had disappeared.

"Oh, come on!" exclaimed Tom one morning, when the day seemed a bit cooler than its predecessor. "Let's go for a hunt, or something! I'm tired of sitting around camp."

"Bless my watch hands! So am I!" cried Mr. Damon. "Let's all go for a trip. It will do us good."

"And perhaps I can get some specimens of interest," added Professor Bumper, who, in addition to being an archaeologist, was something of a naturalist.

Accordingly, having made everything snug in camp, the party, Tom and Ned equipped with electric rifles, and the professor with a butterfly net and specimen boxes, set forth. Mr. Damon said he would carry a stout club as his weapon.

The jungle, as usual, was teeming with life, but as Ned and Tom did not wish to kill wantonly they refrained from shooting until later in the day. For once it was dead, game did not keep well in that hot climate, and needed to be cooked almost immediately.

"We'll try some shots on our back trip," said the young inventor.

Professor Bumper found plenty of his own particular kind of "game" which he caught in the net, transferring the specimens to the boxes he carried. There were beautiful butterflies, moths and strange bugs in the securing of which the scientist evinced great delight, though when one beetle nipped him firmly and painfully on his thumb his involuntary cry of pain was as real as that of any other person.

"But I didn't let him get away," he said in triumph when he had dropped the clawing insect into the cyanide bottle where death came painlessly. "It is well worth a sore thumb."

They wandered on through the jungle, taking care not to get too far from their camp, for they did not want to lose their way, nor did they want to be absent too long in case Tolpec and his native friends should return.

"Well, it's about time we shot something, I think," remarked Ned, when they had been out about two hours. "Let's try for some of these wild turkeys. They ought to go well roasted even if it isn't Thanksgiving."

"I'm with you," agreed Tom. "Let's see who has the best luck. But tone down the charge in your rifle and use a smaller projectile, or you'll have nothing but a bunch of feathers to show for your shot. The guns are loaded for deer."

The change was made, and once more the two young men started off, a little ahead of Professor Bumper and Mr. Damon. Tom and Ned had not gone far, however, before they heard a strange cry from Mr. Damon.

"Tom! Ned!" shouted the eccentric man, "Here's a monster after me! Come quick!"

"A tiger!" ejaculated Tom, as he began once more to change the charge in his rifle to a larger one, running back, meanwhile, in the direction of the sound of the voice.

There were really no tigers in Honduras, the jaguar being called a tiger by the natives, while the cougar is called a lion. The presence of these animals, often dangerous to man, had been indicated around camp, and it was possible that one had been bold enough to attack Mr. Damon, not through hunger, but because of being cornered.

"Come on, Ned!" cried Tom. "He's in some sort of trouble!"

But when, a moment later, the young inventor burst through a fringe of bushes and saw Mr. Damon standing in a little clearing, with upraised club, Tom could not repress a laugh.

"Kill it, Tom! Kill it!" begged the eccentric man. "Bless my insurance policy, but it's a terrible beast!"

And so it was, at first glance. For it was a giant iguana, one of the most repulsive-looking of the lizards. Not unlike an alligator in shape, with spikes on its head and tail, with a warty, squatty ridge-encrusted body, a big pouch beneath its chin, and long-toed claws, it was enough to strike terror into the heart of almost any one. Even the smaller ones look dangerous, and this one, which was about five feet long, looked capable of attacking a man and injuring him. As a matter of fact the iguanas are harmless, their shape and coloring being designed to protect them.

"Don't be afraid, Mr. Damon," called Tom, still laughing. "It won't hurt you!"

"I'm not so positive of that. It won't let me pass."

"Just take your club and poke it out of the way," the young inventor advised. "It's only waiting to be shoved."

"Then you do it, Tom. Bless my looking glass, but I don't want to go near it! If my wife could see me now she'd say it served me just right."

Mr. Damon was not a coward, but the giant iguana was not pleasant to look at. Tom, with the butt of his rifle, gave it a gentle shove, whereupon the creature scurried off through the brush as though glad to make its escape unscathed.

"I thought it was a new kind of alligator," said Mr. Damon with a sigh of relief.

"Where is it?" asked Professor Bumper, coming up at this juncture. "A new species of alligator? Let me see it!"

"It's too horrible," said Mr. Damon. "I never want to see one again. It was worse than a vampire bat!"

Notwithstanding this, when he heard that it was one of the largest sized iguanas ever seen, the professor started through the jungle after it.

"We can't take it with us if we get it," Tom called after his friend.

"We might take the skin," answered the professor. "I have a standing order for such things from one of the museums I represent. I'd like to get it. Then they are often eaten. We can have a change of diet, you see."

"We'd better follow him," said Tom to Ned. "We'll have to let the turkeys go for a while. He may get into trouble. Come on."

Off they started through the jungle, trailing after the impetuous professor who was intent on capturing the iguana. The giant lizard's progress could be traced by the disturbance of the leaves and underbrush, and the professor was following as closely as possible.

So fast did he go that Ned, Tom and Mr. Damon, following, lost sight of him several times, and Tom finally called:

"Wait a minute. We'll all be lost if you keep this up."

"I'll have him in another minute," answered the professor. "I can almost reach him now. Then— Oh!"

His voice ended in a scream that seemed to be one of terror. So sudden was the change that Tom and Ned, who were together, ahead of Mr. Damon, looked at one another in fear.

"What has happened?" whispered Ned, pausing.

"Don't stop to ask—come on!" shouted Tom.

At that instant again came the voice of the savant.

"Tom! Ned!" he gasped, rather than cried.

"I'm caught in the coils! Quick—quick if you would save me!"

"In the coils!" repeated Ned. "What does he mean? Can the giant iguana—"

Tom Swift did not stop to answer. With his electric rifle in readiness, he leaped forward through the jungle.

CHAPTER XVI

A MEETING IN THE JUNGLE

Before Tom and Ned reached the place whence Professor Bumper had called, they heard strange noises, other than the imploring voice of their friend. It seemed as though some great body was threshing about in the jungle, lashing the trees, bushes and leaves about, and when the two young men, followed by Mr. Damon, reached the scene they saw that, in a measure, this really accounted for what they heard.

Something like a great whip was beating about close to two trees that grew near together. And then, when the storm of twigs, leaves and dirt, caused by the leaping, threshing thing ceased for a moment, the onlookers saw something that filled them with terror.

Between the two trees, and seemingly bound to them by a great coiled rope, spotted and banded, was the body of Professor Bumper. His arms were pinioned to his sides and there was horror and terror on his face, that looked imploringly at the youths from above the topmost coil of those encircling him.

"What is it?" cried Mr. Damon, as he ran pantingly up. "What has caught him? Is it the giant iguana?"

"It's a snake—a great boa!" gasped Tom. "It has him in its coils. But it is wound around the trees, too. That alone prevents it from crushing the professor to death.

"Ned, be ready with your rifle. Put in the heaviest charge, and watch your chance to fire!"

The great, ugly head of the boa reared itself up from the coils which it had, with the quickness of thought, thrown about the man between the two trees. This species of snake is not poisonous, and kills its prey by crushing it to death, making it into a pulpy mass, with scarcely a bone left unbroken, after which it swallows its meal. The crushing power of one of these boas, some of which reach a length of thirty feet, with a body as large around as that of a full-grown man, is enormous.

"I'm going to fire!" suddenly cried Tom. He had seen his chance and he took it. There was the faint report—the crack of the electric rifle—and the folds of the serpent seemed to relax.

"I see a good chance now," added Ned, who had taken the small charge from his weapon, replacing it with a heavier one.

His rifle was also discharged in the direction of the snake, and Tom saw that the hit was a good one, right through the ugly head of the reptile.

"One other will be enough to make him loosen his coils!" cried Tom, as he fired again, and such was the killing power of the electric bullets that the snake, though an immense one, and one that short of decapitation could have received many injuries without losing power, seemed to shrivel up.

Its folds relaxed, and the coils of the great body fell in a heap at the roots of the two trees, between which the scientist had been standing.

Professor Bumper seemed to fall backward as the grip of the serpent relaxed, but Tom, dropping his rifle, and calling to Ned to keep an eye on the snake, leaped forward and caught his friend.

"Are you hurt?" asked Tom, carrying the limp form over to a grassy place. There was no answer, the savant's eyes were closed and he breathed but faintly.

Ned Newton fired two more electric bullets into the still writhing body of the boa.

"I guess he's all in," he called to Tom.

"Bless my horseradish! And so our friend seems to be," commented Mr. Damon. "Have you anything with which to revive him, Tom?"

"Yes. Some ammonia. See if you can find a little water."

"I have some in my flask."

Tom mixed a dose of the spirits which he carried with him, and this, forced between the pallid lips of the scientist, revived him.

"What happened?" he asked faintly as he opened his eyes. "Oh, yes, I remember," he added slowly. "The boa—"

"Don't try to talk," urged Tom. "You're all right. The snake is dead, or dying. Are you much hurt?"

Professor Bumper appeared to be considering. He moved first one limb, then another. He seemed to have the power over all his muscles.

"I see how it happened," he said, as he sat up, after taking a little more of the ammonia. "I was following the iguana, and when the big lizard came to a stop, in a little hollow place in the ground, at the foot of those two trees, I leaned over to slip a noose of rope about its neck. Then I felt myself caught, as if in the hands of a giant, and bound fast between the two trees."

"It was the big boa that whipped itself around you, as you leaned over," explained Tom, as Ned came up to announce that the snake was no longer dangerous. "But when it coiled around you it also coiled around the two trees, you, fortunately slipping between them. Had it not been that their trunks took off some of the pressure of the coils you wouldn't have lasted a minute."

"Well, I was pretty badly squeezed as it was," remarked the professor. "I hardly had breath enough left to call to you. I tried to fight off the serpent, but it was of no use."

"I should say not!" cried Mr. Damon. "Bless my circus ring! one might as well try to combat an elephant! But, my dear professor, are you all right now?"

"I think so—yes. Though I shall be lame and stiff for a few days, I fear. I can hardly walk."

Professor Bumper was indeed unable to go about much for a few days after his encounter with the great serpent. He stretched out in a hammock under trees in the camp clearing, and with his friends waited for the possible return of Tolpec and the porters.

Ned and Tom made one or two short hunting trips, and on these occasions they kept a lookout in the direction the Indian had taken when he went away.

"For he's sure to come back that way—if he comes at all," declared Ned; "which I am beginning to doubt."

"Well, he may not come," agreed Tom, who was beginning to lose some of his first hope. "But he won't necessarily come from the same direction he took. He may have had to go in an entirely different way to get help. We'll hope for the best."

A week passed. Professor Bumper was able to be about, and Tom and Ned noticed that there was an anxious look on his face. Was he, too, beginning to despair?

"Well, this isn't hunting for golden idols very fast," said Mr. Damon, the morning of the eighth day after their desertion by the faithless Jacinto. "What do you say, Professor Bumper; ought we not to start off on our own account?"

"We had better if Tolpec does not return today," was the answer.

They had eaten breakfast, had put their camp in order, and were about to have a consultation on what was best to do, when Tom suddenly called to Ned, who was whistling:

"Hark!"

Through the jungle came a faint sound of singing—not a harmonious air, but the somewhat barbaric chant of the natives.

"It is Tolpec coming back!" cried Mr. Damon. "Hurray! Now our troubles are over! Bless my meal ticket! Now we can start!"

"It may be Jacinto," suggested Ned.

"Nonsense! you old cold-water pitcher!" cried Tom. "It's Tolpec! I can see him! He's a good scout all right!"

And then, walking at the head of a band of Indians who were weirdly chanting while behind them came a train of mules, was Tolpec, a cheerful grin covering his honest, if homely, dark face.

"Me come back!" he exclaimed in gutteral English, using about half of his foreign vocabulary.

"I see you did," answered Professor Bumper in the man's own tongue. "Glad to see you. Is everything all right?"

"All right," was the answer. "These Indians will take you where you want to go, and will not leave you as Jacinto did."

"We'll start in the morning!" exclaimed the savant his own cheerful self again, now that there was a prospect of going further into the interior. "Tell the men to get something to eat, Tolpec. There is plenty for all."

"Good!" grunted the new guide and soon the hungry Indians, who had come far, were satisfying their hunger.

As they ate Tolpec explained to Professor Bumper, who repeated it to the youths and Mr. Damon, that it had been necessary to go farther than he had intended to get the porters and mules. But the Indians were a friendly tribe, of which he was a member, and could be depended on.

There was a feast and a sort of celebration in camp that night. Tom and Ned shot two deer, and these formed the main part of the feast and the Indians made merry about the fire until nearly midnight. They did not seem to mind in the least the swarms of mosquitoes and other bugs that flew about, attracted by the light. As for Tom Swift and his friends, their nets protected them.

An early start was made the following morning. Such packages of goods and supplies as could not well be carried by the Indians in their head straps, were loaded on the backs of the pack-mules. Tolpec explained that on reaching the Indian village, where he had secured the porters, they could get some ox-carts which would be a convenience in traveling into the interior toward the Copan valley.

The march onward for the next two days was tiresome; but the Indians Tolpec had secured were as faithful and efficient as he had described them, and good progress was made.

There were a few accidents. One native fell into a swiftly running stream as they were fording it and lost a box containing some much-needed things. But as the man's life was saved Professor Bumper said it made up for the other loss. Another accident did not end so auspiciously. One of the bearers was bitten by a poisonous snake, and though prompt measures were taken, the poison spread so rapidly that the man died.

In due season the Indian village was reached, where, after a day spent in holding funeral services over the dead bearer, preparations were made for proceeding farther.

This time some of the bearers were left behind, and ox-carts were substituted for them, as it was possible to carry more goods this way.

"And now we're really off for Copan!" exclaimed Professor Bumper one morning, when the cavalcade, led by Tolpec in the capacity of head guide, started off. "I hope we have no more delays."

"I hope not, either," agreed Tom. "That Beecher may be there ahead of us."

Weary marches fell to their portion. There were mountains to climb, streams to ford or swim, sending the carts over on rudely made rafts. There were storms to endure, and the eternal heat to fight.

But finally the party emerged from the lowlands of the coast and went up in among the hills, where though the going was harder, the climate was better. It was not so hot and moist.

Not wishing to attract attention in Copan itself, Professor Bumper and his party made a detour, and finally, after much consultation with Tom over the ancient maps, the scientist announced that he thought they were in the vicinity of the buried city.

"We will begin test excavations in the morning," he said.

The party was in camp, and preparations were made for spending the night in the forest, when from among the trees there floated to the ears of our friends a queer Indian chant.

"Some one is coming," said Tom to Ned.

Almost as he spoke there filed into the clearing where the camp had been set up, a cavalcade of white men, followed by Indians. And at the sight of one of the white men Tom Swift uttered a cry.

"Professor Beecher!" gasped the young inventor.

CHAPTER XVII

THE LOST MAP

The on-marching company of white men, with their Indian attendants, came to a halt on the edge of the clearing as they caught sight of the tents already set up there. The barbaric chant of the native bearers ceased abruptly, and there was a look of surprise shown on the face of Professor Fenimore Beecher. For Professor Beecher it was, in the lead of the rival expedition.

"Bless my shoe laces!" exclaimed Mr. Damon.

"Is it really Beecher?" asked Ned, though he knew as well as Tom that it was the young archaeologist.

"It certainly is!" declared Tom. "And he has nerve to follow us so closely!"

"Maybe he thinks we have nerve to get here ahead of him," suggested Ned, smiling grimly.

"Probably," agreed Tom, with a short laugh. "Well, it evidently surprises him to find us here at all, after the mean trick he played on us to get Jacinto to lead us into the jungle and desert us."

"That's right," assented Ned. "Well, what's the next move?"

There seemed to be some doubt about this on the part of both expeditions. At the sight of Professor Beecher, Professor Bumper, who had come out of his tent, hurriedly turned to Tom and asked him what he thought it best to do.

"Do!" exclaimed the eccentric Mr. Damon, not giving Tom time to reply. "Why, stand your ground, of course! Bless my house and lot! but we're here first! For the matter of that, I suppose the jungle is free and we can no more object to his coming: here than he can to our coming. First come, first served, I suppose is the law of the forest."

Meanwhile the surprise occasioned by the unexpected meeting of their rivals seemed to have spread something like consternation among the white members of the Beecher party. As for the natives they evidently did not care one way or the other.

There was a hasty consultation among the professors accompanying Mr. Beecher, and then the latter himself advanced toward the tents of Tom and his friends and asked:

"How long have you been here?"

"I don't see that we are called upon to answer that question," replied Professor Bumper stiffly.

"Perhaps not, and yet—"

"There is no perhaps about it!" said Professor Bumper quickly. "I know what your object is, as I presume you do mine. And, after what I may term your disgraceful and unsportsmanlike conduct toward me and my friends, I prefer not to have anything further to do with you. We must meet as strangers hereafter."

"Very well," and Professor Beecher's voice was as cold and uncompromising as was his rival's. "Let it be as your wish. But I must say I don't know what you mean by unsportsmanlike conduct."

"An explanation would be wasted on you," said Professor Bumper stiffly. "But in order that you may know I fully understand what you did I will say that your efforts to thwart us through your tool Jacinto came to nothing. We are here ahead of you."

"Jacinto!" cried Professor Beecher in real or simulated surprise. "Why, he was not my 'tool,' as you term it."

"Your denial is useless in the light of his confession," asserted Professor Bumper.

"Confession?"

"Now look here!" exclaimed the older professor, "I do not propose to lower myself by quarreling with you. I know certainly what you and your party tried to do to prevent us from getting here. But we got out of the trap you set for us, and we are on the ground first. I recognize your right to make explorations as well as ourselves, and I presume you have not fallen so low that you will not recognize the unwritten law in a case of this kind—the law which says the right of discovery belongs to the one who first makes it."

"I shall certainly abide by such conduct as is usual under the circumstances," said Professor Beecher more stiffly than before. "At the same time I must deny having set a trap. And as for Jacinto—"

"It will be useless to discuss it further!" broke in Professor Bumper.

"Then no more need be said," retorted the younger man. "I shall give orders to my friends, as well as to the natives, to keep away from your camp, and I shall expect you to do the same regarding mine."

"I should have suggested the same thing myself," came from Tom's friend, and the two rival scientists fairly glared at one another, the others of both parties looking on with interest.

Professor Bumper turned and walked defiantly back to his tent. Professor Beecher did the same thing. Then, after a short consultation among the white members of the latter's organization, their tents were set up in another clearing, removed and separated by a screen of trees and bushes from those of Tom Swift's friends. The natives of the Beecher party also withdrew a little way from those of Professor Bumper's organization, and then preparations for spending the night in the jungle went on in the rival headquarters.

"Well, he certainly had nerve, to deny, practically, that he had set Jacinto up to do what he did," commented Tom.

"I should say so!" agreed Ned.

"How do you imagine he got here nearly as soon as we did, when he did not start until later?" asked Mr. Damon.

"He did not have the unfortunate experience of being deserted in the jungle," replied Tom. "He probably had Jacinto, or some of that unprincipled scoundrel's friends, show him a short route to Copan and he came on from there."

"Well, I did hope we might have the ground to ourselves, at least for the preliminary explorations and excavations. But it is not to be. My rival is here," sighed Professor Bumper.

"Don't let that discourage you!" exclaimed Tom. "We can fight all the better now the foe is in the open, and we know where he is."

"Yes, Tom Swift, that is true," agreed the scientist. "I am not going to give up, but I shall have to change my plans a little. Perhaps you will come into the tent with me," and he nodded to Tom and Ned. "I want to talk over certain matters with you and Mr. Damon."

"Pleased to," assented the young inventor, and his financial secretary nodded.

A little later, supper having been eaten, the camp made shipshape and the natives settled down, Tom, Ned, Mr. Damon and Professor Bumper assembled in the tent of the scientist, where a dry battery lamp gave sufficient illumination to show a number of maps and papers scattered over an improvised table.

"Now, gentlemen," said the professor, "I have called you here to go over my plans more in detail than I have hitherto done, now we are on the ground. You know in a general way what I hope to accomplish, but the time has come when I must be specific.

"Aside from being on the spot, below which, or below the vicinity where, I believe, lies the lost city of Kurzon and, I hope, the idol of gold, a situation has arisen—an unexpected situation, I may say—which calls for different action from that I had counted on.

"I refer to the presence of my rival, Professor Beecher. I will not dwell now on what he has done. It is better to consider what he may do."

"That's right," agreed Ned. "He may get up in the night, dig up this city and skip with that golden image before we know it."

"Hardly," grinned Tom.

"No," said Professor Bumper. "Excavating buried cities in the jungle of Honduras is not as simple as that. There is much work to be done. But accidents may happen, and in case one should occur to me, and I be unable to prosecute the search, I want one of you to do it. For that reason I am going to show you the maps and ancient documents and point out to you where I believe the lost city lies. Now, if you will give me your attention, I'll proceed."

The professor went over in detail the story of how he had found the old documents relating to the lost city of Kurzon, and of how, after much labor and research, he had located the city in the Copan valley. The great idol of gold was one of the chief possessions of Kurzon, and it was often referred to in the old papers; copies and translations of which the professor had with him.

"But this is the most valuable of all," he said, as he opened an oiled-silk packet. "And before I show it to you, suppose you two young men take a look outside the tent."

"What for?" asked Mr. Damon.

"To make sure that no emissaries from the Beecher crowd are sneaking around to overhear what we say," was the somewhat bitter answer of the scientist. "I do not trust him, in spite of his attempted denial."

Tom and Ned took a quick but thorough observation outside the tent. The blackness of the jungle night was in strange contrast to the light they had just left.

"Doesn't seem to be any one around here," remarked Ned, after waiting a minute or two.

"No. All's quiet along the Potomac. Those Beecher natives are having some sort of a song-fest, though."

In the distance, and from the direction of their rivals' camp, came the weird chant.

"Well, as long as they stay there we'll be all right," said Tom. "Come on in. I'm anxious to hear what the professor has to say."

"Everything's quiet," reported Ned.

"Then give me your attention," begged the scientist.

Carefully, as though about to exhibit some, precious jewel, he loosened the oiled-silk wrappings and showed a large map, on thin but tough paper.

"This is drawn from the old charts," the professor explained. "I worked on it many months, and it is the only copy in the world. If it were to be destroyed I should have to go all the way back to New York to make another copy. I have the original there in a safe deposit vault."

"Wouldn't it have been wise to make two copies?" asked Tom.

"It would have only increased the risk. With one copy, and that constantly in my possession, I can be sure of my ground. Otherwise not. That is why I am so careful of this. Now I will show you why I believe we are about over the ancient city of Kurzon."

"Over it!" cried Mr. Damon. "Bless my gunpowder! What do you mean?" and he looked down at the earthen floor of the tent as though expecting it to open and swallow him.

"I mean that the city, like many others of Central and South America, is buried below the refuse of centuries," went on the professor. "Very soon, if we are fortunate, we shall be looking on the civilization of hundreds of years ago—how long no one knows.

"Considerable excavation has been done in Central America," went on Professor Bumper, "and certain ruins have been brought to light. Near us are those of Copan, while toward the frontier are those of Quirigua, which are even better preserved than the former. We may visit them if we have time. But I have reason to believe that in this section of Copan is a large city, the existence of which has not been made certain of by any one save myself—and, perhaps, Professor Beecher.

"Certainly no part of it has seen the light of day for many centuries. It shall be our pleasure to uncover it, if possible, and secure the idol of gold."

"How long ago do you think the city was buried?" asked Tom.

"It would be hard to say. From the carvings and hieroglyphics I have studied it would seem that the Mayan civilization lasted about five hundred years, and that it began perhaps in the year A. D. five hundred."

"That would mean," said Mr. Damon, "that the ancient cities were in ruins, buried, perhaps, long before Columbus discovered the new world."

"Yes," assented the professor. "Probably Kurzon, which we now seek, was buried deep for nearly five hundred years before Columbus landed at San Salvadore. The specimens of writing and architecture heretofore disclosed indicate that. But, as a matter of fact, it is very hard to decipher the Mayan pictographs. So far, little but the ability to read their calendars and numerical system is possessed by us, though we are gradually making headway.

"Now this is the map of the district, and by the markings you can see where I hope to find what I seek. We shall begin digging here," and he made a small mark with a pencil on the map.

"Of course," the professor explained, "I may be wrong, and it will take some time to discover the error if we make one. When a city is buried thirty or forty feet deep beneath earth and great trees have grown over it, it is not easy to dig down to it."

"How do you ever expect to find it?" asked Ned.

"Well, we will sink shafts here and there. If we find carved stones, the remains of ancient pottery and weapons, parts of buildings or building stones, we shall know we are on the right track," was the answer. "And now that I have shown you the map, and explained how valuable it is, I will put it away again. We shall begin our excavations in the morning."

"At what point?" asked Tom.

"At a point I shall indicate after a further consultation of the map. I must see the configuration of the country by daylight to decide. And now let's get some rest. We have had a hard day."

The two tents housing the four white members of the Bumper party were close together, and it was decided that the night would be divided into four watches, to guard against possible treachery on the part of the Beecher crowd.

"It seems an unkind precaution to take against a fellow scientist," said Professor Bumper, "but I can not afford to take chances after what has occurred."

The others agreed with him, and though standing guard was not pleasant it was done. However the night passed without incident, and then came morning and the excitement of getting breakfast, over which the Indians made merry. They did not like the cold and darkness, and always welcomed the sun, no matter how hot.

"And now," cried Tom, when the meal was over, "let us begin the work that has brought us here."

"Yes," agreed Professor Bumper, "I will consult the map, and start the diggers where I think the city lies, far below the surface. Now, gentlemen, if you will give me your attention—"

He was seeking through his outer coat pockets, after an ineffectual search in the inner one. A strange look came over his face.

"What's the matter?" asked Tom.

"The map—the map!" gasped the professor. "The map I was showing you last night! The map that tells where we are to dig for the idol of gold! It's gone!"

"The map gone?" gasped Mr. Damon.

"I—I'm afraid so," faltered the professor. "I put it away carefully, but now—"

He ceased speaking to make a further search in all his pockets.

"Maybe you left it in another coat," suggested Ned.

"Or maybe some of the Beecher crowd took it!" snapped Tom.

CHAPTER XVIII

"EL TIGRE!"

The four men gazed at one another. Consternation showed on the face of Professor Bumper, and was reflected, more or less, on the countenances of his companions.

"Are you sure the map is gone?" asked Tom. "I know how easy it is to mislay anything in a camp of this sort. I couldn't at first find my safety razor this morning, and when I did locate it the hoe was in one of my shoes. I'm sure a rat or some jungle animal must have dragged it there. Now maybe they took your map, Professor. That oiled silk in which it was wrapped might have appealed to the taste of a rat or a snake."

"It is no joking matter," said Professor Bumper. "But I know you appreciate the seriousness of it as much as I do, Tom. But I had the map in the pocket of this coat, and now it is gone!"

"When did you put it there?" asked Ned.

"This morning, just before I came to breakfast."

"Oh, then you have had it since last night!" Tom ejaculated.

"Yes, I slept with it under my clothes that I rolled up for a pillow, and when it was my turn to stand guard I took it with me. Then I put it back again and went to sleep. When I awoke and dressed I put the packet in my pocket and ate breakfast. Now when I look for it—why, it's gone!"

"The map or the oiled-silk package?" asked Mr. Damon, who, once having been a businessman, was sometimes a stickler for small points.

"Both," answered the professor. "I opened the silk to tie it more smoothly, so it would not be such a lump in my pocket, and I made sure the map was inside."

"Then the whole thing has been taken—or you have lost it," suggested Ned.

"I am not in the habit of losing valuable maps," retorted the scientist. "And the pocket of my coat I had made deep, for the purpose of carrying the long map. It could not drop out."

"Well, we mustn't overlook any possible chances," suggested Tom. "Come on now, we'll search every inch of the ground over which you traveled this morning, Professor."

"It MUST be found," murmured the scientist. "Without it all our work will go for naught."

They all went into the tent where the professor and Mr. Damon had slept when they were not on guard. The camp was a busy place, with the Indians finishing their morning meal, and getting ready for the work of the day. For word had been given out that there would be no more long periods of travel.

In consequence, efforts were being directed by the head men of the bearers to making a more permanent camp in the wilderness. Shelters of palm-thatched huts were being built, a site for cooking fires made, and, at the direction of Mr. Damon, to whom this part was entrusted, some sanitary regulations were insisted on.

Leaving this busy scene, the four, with solemn faces, proceeded to the tent where it was hoped the map would be found. But though they went through everything, and traced and retraced every place the professor could remember having traversed about the canvas shelter, no signs of the important document could be found.

"I don't believe I dropped it out of my pocket," said the scientist, for perhaps the twentieth time.

"Then it was taken," declared Tom.

"That's what I say!" chimed in Ned. "And by some of Beecher's party!"

"Easy, my boy," cautioned Mr. Damon. "We don't want to make accusations we can't prove."

"That is true," agreed Professor Bumper. "But, though I am sorry to say it of a fellow archaelogist, I can not help thinking Beecher had something to do with the taking of my map."

"But how could any of them get it?" asked Mr. Damon. "You say you had the map this morning, and certainly none of them has been in our camp since dawn, though of course it is possible that some of them sneaked in during the night."

"It does seem a mystery how it could have been taken in open daylight, while we were about camp together," said Tom. "But is the loss such a grave one, Professor Bumper?"

"Very grave. In fact I may say it is impossible to proceed with the excavating without the map."

"Then what are we to do?" asked Ned.

"We must get it back!" declared Tom.

"Yes," agreed the scientist, "we can not work without it. As soon as I make a little further search, to make sure it could not have dropped in some out-of-the-way place, I shall go over to Professor Beecher's camp and demand that he give me back my property."

"Suppose he says he hasn't taken it?" asked Tom.

"Well, I'm sure he either took it personally, or one of his party did. And yet I can't understand how they could have come here without our seeing them," and the professor shook his head in puzzled despair.

A more detailed search did not reveal the missing map, and Mr. Damon and his friend the scientist were on the point of departing for the camp of their rivals, less than a mile away, when Tom had what really amounted to an inspiration.

"Look here, Professor!" he cried. "Can you remember any of the details of your map—say, for instance, where we ought to begin excavating to get at the wonders of the underground city?"

"Well, Tom, I did intend to compare my map with the configuration of the country about here. There is a certain mountain which serves as a landmark and a guide for a starting point. I think that is it over there," and the scientist pointed to a distant snow-capped peak.

The party had left the low and marshy land of the true jungle, and were among the foothills, though all about them was dense forest and underbush, which, in reality, was as much a jungle as the lower plains, but was less wet.

"The point where I believe we should start to dig," said the professor, "is near the spot where the top of the mountain casts a shadow when the sun is one hour high. At least that is the direction given in the old manuscripts. So, though we can do little without the map, we might make a start by digging there."

"No, not there!" exclaimed Tom.

"Why not?"

"Because we don't want to let Beecher's crowd know that we are on the track of the idol of gold."

"But they know anyhow, for they have the map," commented Ned, puzzled by his chum's words.

"Maybe not," said Tom slowly. "I think this is a time for a big bluff. It may work and it may not. Beecher's crowd either has the map or they have not. If they have it they will lose no time in trying to find the right place to start digging and then they'll begin excavating.

"Very good! If they do that we have a right to dig near the same place. But if they have not the map, which is possible, and if we start to dig where the professor's memory tells him is the right spot, we'll only give them the tip, and they'll dig there also."

"I'm sure they have the map," the professor said. "But I believe your plan is a good one, Tom."

"Just what do you propose doing?" asked Ned.

"Fooling 'em!" exclaimed Tom quickly. "We'll dig in some place remote from the spot where the mountain casts its shadow. They will think, if they haven't the map, that we are proceeding by it, and they'll dig, too. When they find nothing, as will also happen to us, they may go away.

"If, on the other hand, they have the map, and see us digging at a spot not indicated on it, they will be puzzled, knowing we must have some idea of where the buried city lies. They will think the map is at fault, perhaps, and not make use of it. Then we can get it back."

"Bless my hatband!" cried Mr. Damon. "I believe you're right, Tom. We'll dig in the wrong place to fool 'em."

And this was done. Search for the precious map was given up for the time being, and the professor and his friends set the natives to work digging shafts in the ground, as though sinking them down to the level of the buried city.

But though this false work was prosecuted with vigor for several days, there was a feeling of despair among the Bumper party over the loss of the map.

"If we could only get it back!" exclaimed the professor, again and again.

Meanwhile the Beecher party seemed inactive. True, some members of it did come over to look on from a respectful distance at what the diggers were doing. Some of the rival helpers, under the direction of the head of the expedition, also began sinking shafts. But they were not in the locality remembered by Professor Bumper as being correct.

"I can't imagine what they're up to," he said. "If they have my map they would act differently, I should think."

"Whatever they're up to," answered Tom, "the time has come when we can dig at the place where we can hope for results." And the following day shafts were started in the shadow of the mountain.

Until some evidence should have been obtained by digging, as to the location beneath the surface of a buried city, there was nothing for the travelers to do but wait. Turns were taken in directing the efforts of the diggers, and an occasional inspection was made of the shafts.

"What do you expect to find first?" asked Tom of Professor Bumper one day, when the latter was at the top of a shaft waiting for a bucket load of dirt to be hoisted up.

"Potsherds and artifacts," was the answer.

"What sort of bugs are they?" asked Ned with a laugh. He and Tom were about to go hunting with their electric rifles.

"Artifacts are things made by the Indians—or whatever members of the race who built the ancient cities were called—such as household articles, vases, ornaments, tools and so on. Anything made by artificial means is called an artifact."

"And potsherds are things with those Chinese laundry ticket scratches on them," added Tom.

"Exactly," said the professor, laughing. "Though some of the strange-appearing inscriptions give much valuable information. As soon as we find some of them—say a broken bit of pottery with hieroglyphics on—I will know I am on the right track."

And while the scientist and Mr. Damon kept watch at the top of the shaft, Tom and Ned went out into the jungle to hunt. They had killed some game, and were stalking a fine big deer, which would provide a feast for the natives, when suddenly the silence of the lonely forest was broken by a piercing scream, followed by an agonized cry of "El tigre! El tigre!"

CHAPTER XIX

POISONED ARROWS

"Did you hear that, Tom?" asked Ned, in a hoarse whisper.

"Surely," was the cautious answer. "Keep still, and I'll try for a shot."

"Better be quick," advised Ned in a tense voice. "The chap who did that yelling seems to be in trouble!"

And as Ned's voice trailed off into a whisper, again came the cry, this time in frenzied pain.

"El tigre! El tigre!" Then there was a jumble of words.

"It's over this way!" and this time Ned shouted, seeing no need for low voices since the other was so loud.

Tom looked to where Ned had parted the bushes alongside a jungle path. Through the opening the young inventor saw, in a little glade, that which caused him to take a firmer grip on his electric rifle, and also a firmer grip on his nerves.

Directly in front of him and Ned, and not more than a hundred yards away, was a great tawny and spotted jaguar—the "tigre" or tiger of Central America. The beast, with lashing tail, stood over an Indian upon whom it seemed to have sprung from some lair, beating the unfortunate man to the ground. Nor had he fallen scatheless, for there was blood on the green leaves about him, and it was not the blood of the spotted beast.

"Oh, Tom, can you—can you—" and Ned faltered.

The young inventor understood the unspoken question.

"I think I can make a shot of it without hitting the man," he answered, never turning his head. "It's a question, though, if the beast won't claw him in the death struggle. It won't last long, however, if the electric bullet goes to the right place, and I've got to take the chance."

Cautiously Tom brought his weapon to bear. Quiet as Ned and he had been after the discovery, the jaguar seemed to feel that something was wrong. Intent on his prey, for a time he had stood over it, gloating. Now the brute glanced uneasily from side to side, its tail nervously twitching, and it seemed trying to gain, by a sniffing of the air, some information as to the direction in which danger lay, for Tom and Ned had stooped low, concealing themselves by a screen of leaves.

The Indian, after his first frenzied outburst of fear, now lay quiet, as though fearing to move, moaning in pain.

Suddenly the jaguar, attracted either by some slight movement on the part of Ned or Tom, or perhaps by having winded them, turned his head quickly and gazed with cruel eyes straight at the spot where the two young men stood behind the bushes.

"He's seen us," whispered Ned.

"Yes," assented Tom. "And it's a perfect shot. Hope I don't miss!"

It was not like Tom Swift to miss, nor did he on this occasion. There was a slight report from the electric rifle—a report not unlike the crackle of the wireless—and the powerful projectile sped true to its mark.

Straight through the throat and chest under the uplifted jaw of the jaguar it went—through heart and lungs. Then with a great coughing, sighing snarl the beast reared up, gave a convulsive leap forward toward its newly discovered enemies, and fell dead in a limp heap, just beyond the native over which it had been crouching before it delivered the death stroke, now never to fall.

"You did it, Tom! You did it!" cried Ned, springing up from where he had been kneeling to give his chum a better chance to shoot. "You did it, and saved the man's life!" And Ned would have rushed out toward the still twitching body.

"Just a minute!" interposed Tom. "Those beasts sometimes have as many lives as a cat. I'll give it one more for luck." Another electric projectile through the head of the jaguar produced no further effect than to move the body slightly, and this proved conclusively that there was no life left. It was safe to approach, which Tom and Ned did.

Their first thought, after a glance at the jaguar, was for the Indian. It needed but a brief examination to show that he was not badly hurt. The jaguar had leaped on him from a low tree as he passed under it, as the boys learned afterward, and had crushed the man to earth by the weight of the spotted body more than by a stroke of the paw.

The American jaguar is not so formidable a beast as the native name of tiger would cause one to suppose, though they are sufficiently dangerous, and this one had rather badly clawed the Indian. Fortunately the scratches were on the fleshy parts of the arms and shoulders, where, though painful, they were not necessarily serious.

"But if you hadn't shot just when you did, Tom, it would have been all up with him," commented Ned.

"Oh, well, I guess you'd have hit him if I hadn't," returned the young inventor. "But let's see what we can do for this chap."

The man sat up wonderingly—hardly able to believe that he had been saved from the dreaded "tigre." His wounds were bleeding rather freely, and as Tom and Ned carried with them a first-aid kit they now brought it into use. The wounds were bound up, the man was given water to drink and then, as he was able to walk, Tom and Ned offered to help him wherever he wanted to go.

"Blessed if I can tell whether he's one of our Indians or whether he belongs to the Beecher crowd," remarked Tom.

"Senor Beecher," said the Indian, adding, in Spanish, that he lived in the vicinity and had only lately been engaged by the young professor who hoped to discover the idol of gold before Tom's scientific friend could do so.

Tom and Ned knew a little Spanish, and with that, and simple but expressive signs on the part of the Indian, they learned his story. He had his palm-thatched hut not far from the Beecher camp, in a small Indian village, and he, with others, had been hired on the arrival of the Beecher party to help with the excavations. These, for some reason, were delayed.

"Delayed because they daren't use the map they stole from us," commented Ned.

"Maybe," agreed Tom.

The Indian, whose name, it developed, was Tal, as nearly as Tom and Ned could master it, had left camp to go to visit his wife and child in the jungle hut, intending to return to the Beecher camp at night. But as he passed through the forest the jaguar had dropped on him, bearing him to earth.

"But you saved my life, Senor," he said to Tom, dropping on one knee and trying to kiss Tom's hand, which our hero avoided. "And now my life is yours," added the Indian.

"Well, you'd better get home with it and take care of it," said Tom. "I'll have Professor Bumper come over and dress your scratches in a better and more careful way. The bandages we put on are only temporary."

"My wife she make a poultice of leaves—they cure me," said the Indian.

"I guess that will be the best way," observed Ned. "These natives can doctor themselves for some things, better than we can."

"Well, we'll take him home," suggested Tom. "He might keel over from loss of blood. Come on," he added to Tal, indicating his object.

It was not far to the native's hut from the place where the jaguar had been killed, and there Tom and Ned underwent another demonstration of affection as soon as those of Tal's immediate family and the other natives understood what had happened.

"I hate this business!" complained Tom, after having been knelt to by the Indian's wife and child, who called him the "preserver" and other endearing titles of the same kind. "Come on, let's hike back."

But Indian hospitality, especially after a life has been saved, is not so simple as all that.

"My life—my house—all that I own is yours," said Tal in deep gratitude. "Take everything," and he waved his hand to indicate all the possessions in his humble hut.

"Thanks," answered Tom, "but I guess you need all you have. That's a fine specimen of blow gun though," he added, seeing one hanging on the wall. "I wouldn't mind having one like that. If you get well enough to make me one, Tal, and some arrows to go with it, I'd like it for a curiosity to hang in my room at home."

"The Senor shall have a dozen," promised the Indian.

"Look, Ned," went on Tom, pointing to the native weapon. "I never saw one just like this. They use small arrows or darts, tipped with wild cotton, instead of feathers."

"These the arrows," explained Tal's wife, bringing a bundle from a corner of the one-room hut. As she held them out her husband gave a cry of fear.

"Poisoned arrows! Poisoned arrows!" he exclaimed. "One scratch and the senors are dead men. Put them away!"

In fear the Indian wife prepared to obey, but as she did so Tom Swift caught sight of the package and uttered a strange cry.

"Thundering hoptoads, Ned!" he exclaimed. "The poisoned arrows are wrapped in the piece of oiled silk that was around the professor's missing map!"

CHAPTER XX

AN OLD LEGEND

Fascinated, Tom and Ned gazed at the package the Indian woman held out to them. Undoubtedly it was oiled silk on the outside, and through the almost transparent covering could be seen the small arrows, or darts, used in the blow gun.

"Where did you get that?" asked Tom, pointing to the bundle and gazing sternly at Tal.

"What is the matter, Senor?" asked the Indian in turn. "Is it that you are afraid of the poisoned arrows? Be assured they will not harm you unless you are scratched by them."

Tom and Ned found it difficult to comprehend all the rapid Spanish spoken by their host, but they managed to understand some, and his eloquent gestures made up the rest.

"We're not afraid," Tom said, noting that the oiled skin well covered the dangerous darts. "But where did you get that?"

"I picked it up, after another Indian had thrown it away. He got it in your camp, Senor. I will not lie to you. I did not steal. Valdez went to your camp to steal—he is a bad Indian—and he brought back this wrapping. It contained something he thought was gold, but it was not, so he—"

"Quick! Yes! Tell us!" demanded Tom eagerly. "What did he do with the professor's map that was in the oiled silk? Where is it?"

"Oh, Senors!" exclaimed the Indian woman, thinking perhaps her husband was about to be dealt harshly with when she heard Tom's excited voice. "Tal do no harm!"

"No, he did no harm," went on Tom, in a reassuring tone. "But he can do a whole lot of good if he tells us what became of the map that was in this oiled silk. Where is it?" he asked again.

"Valdez burn it up," answered Tal.

"What, burned the professor's map?" cried Ned.

"If that was in this yellow cloth—yes," answered the injured man. "Valdez he is bad. He say to me he is going to your camp to see what he can take. How he got this I know not, but he come back one morning with the yellow package. I see him, but he make me promise not to tell. But you save my life I tell you everything.

"Valdez open the package; but it is not gold, though he think so because it is yellow, and the man with no hair on his head keep it in his pocket close, so close," and Tal hugged himself to indicate what he meant.

"That's Professor Bumper," explained Ned.

"How did Valdez get the map out of the professor's coat?" asked Tom.

"Valdez he very much smart. When man with no hair on his head take coat off for a minute to eat breakfast Valdez take yellow thing out of pocket."

"The Indian must have sneaked into camp when we were eating," said Tom. "Those from Beecher's party and our workers look all alike to us. We wouldn't know one from the other, and one of our rival's might slip in."

"One evidently did, if this is really the piece of oiled silk that was around the professor's map," said Ned.

"It certainly is the same," declared the young inventor. "See, there is his name," and he stretched out his hand to point.

"Don't touch!" cried Tal. "Poisoned arrows snake poison—very dead-like and quick."

"Don't worry, I won't touch," said Tom grimly. "But go on. You say Valdez sneaked into our camp, took the oiled-silk package from the coat pocket of Professor Bumper and went back to his own camp with it, thinking it was gold."

"Yes," answered Tal, though it is doubtful if he understood all that Tom said, as it was half Spanish and half English. But the Indian knew a little English, too. "Valdez, when he find no gold is very mad. Only papers in the yellow silk-papers with queer marks on. Valdez think it maybe a charm to work evil, so he burn them up—all up!"

"Burned that rare map!" gasped Tom.

"All in fire," went on Tal, indicating by his hands the play of flames. "Valdez throw away yellow silk, and I take for my arrows so rain not wash off poison. I give to you, if you like, with blow gun."

"No, thank you," answered Tom, in disappointed tones. "The oiled silk is of no use without the map, and that's gone. Whew! but this is tough!" he said to his chum. "As long as it was only stolen there was a chance to get it back, but if it's burned, the jig is up."

"It looks so," agreed Ned. "We'd better get back and tell the professor. It he can't get along without the map it's time he started a movement toward getting another. So it wasn't Beecher, after all, who got it."

"Evidently not," assented Tom. "But I believe him capable of it."

"You haven't much use for him," remarked Ned.

"Huh!" was all the answer given by his chum.

"I am sorry, Senors," went on Tal, "but I could not stop Valdez, and the burning of the papers—"

"No, you could not help it," interrupted the young inventor. "But it just happens that it brings bad luck to us. You see, Tal, the papers in this yellow covering, told of an old buried city that the bald-headed professor—the-man-with-no-hair-on-his-head—is very anxious to discover. It is somewhere under the ground," and he waved to the jungle all about them, pointing earthwards.

"Paper Valdez burn tell of lost city?" asked Tal, his face lighting up.

"Yes. But now, of course, we can't tell where to dig for it."

The Indian turned to his wife and talked rapidly with her in their own dialect. She, too, seemed greatly excited, making quick gestures. Finally she ran out of the hut.

"Where is she going?" asked Tom suspiciously.

"To get her grandfather. He very old Indian. He know story of buried cities under trees. Very old story—what you call legend, maybe. But Goosal know. He tell same as his grandfather told him. You wait. Goosal come, and you listen."

"Good, Ned!" suddenly cried Tom. "Maybe, we'll get on the track of lost Kurzon after all, through some ancient Indian legend. Maybe we won't need the map!"

"It hardly seems possible," said Ned slowly. "What can these Indians know of buried cities that were out of existence before Columbus came here? Why, they haven't any written history."

"No, and that may be just the reason they are more likely to be right," returned Tom. "Legends handed down from one grandfather to another go back a good many hundred years. If they were written they might be destroyed as the professor's map was. Somehow or other, though I can't tell why, I begin to see daylight ahead of us."

"I wish I did," remarked Ned.

"Here comes Goosal I think," murmured Tom, and he pointed to an Indian, bent with the weight of years, who, led by Tal's wife, was slowly approaching the hut.

CHAPTER XXI

THE CAVERN

"Now Goosal can tell you," said Tal, evidently pleased that he had, in a measure, solved the problem caused by the burning of the professor's map. "Goosal very old Indian. He know old stories—legends—very old."

"Well, if he can tell us how to find the buried city of Kurzon and the—the things in it," said Tom, "he's all right!"

The aged Indian proceeded slowly toward the hut where the impatient youths awaited him.

"I know what you seek in the buried city," remarked Tal.

"Do you?" cried Tom, wondering if some one had indiscreetly spoken of the idol of gold.

"Yes you want pieces of rock, with strange writings on them, old weapons, broken pots. I know. I have helped white men before."

"Yes, those are the things we want," agreed Tom, with a glance at his chum. "That is—some of them. But does your wife's grandfather talk our language?"

"No, but I can tell you what he says."

By this time the old man, led by "Mrs. Tal"—as the young men called the wife of the Indian they had helped—entered the hut. He seemed nervous and shy, and glanced from Tom and Ned to his grandson-in-law, as the latter talked rapidly in the Indian dialect. Then Goosal made answer, but what it was all about the boys could not tell.

"Goosal say," translated Tal, "that he know a story of a very old city away down under ground."

"Tell us about it!" urged Tom eagerly.

But a difficulty very soon developed. Tal's intentions were good, but he was not equal to the task of translating. Nor was the understanding of Tom and Ned of Spanish quite up to the mark.

"Say, this is too much for me!" exclaimed Tom. "We are losing the most valuable part of this by not understanding what Goosal says, and what Tal translates."

"What can we do?" asked Ned.

"Get the professor here as soon as possible. He can manage this dialect, and he'll get the information at first hand. If Goosal can tell where to begin excavating for the city he ought to tell the professor, not us."

"That's right," agreed Ned. "We'll bring the professor here as soon as we can."

Accordingly they stopped the somewhat difficult task of listening to the translated story and told Tal, as well as they could, that they would bring the "man-with-no-hair-on-his-head" to listen to the tale.

This seemed to suit the Indians, all of whom in the small colony appeared to be very grateful to Tom and Ned for having saved the life of Tal.

"That was a good shot you made when you bowled over the jaguar," said Ned, as the two young explorers started back to their camp.

"Better than I realized, if it leads to the discovery of Kurzon and the idol of gold," remarked Tom.

"And to think we should come across the oiled-silk holding the poisoned arrows!" went on Ned. "That's the strangest part of the whole affair. If it hadn't been that you shot the jaguar this never would have come about."

That Professor Bumper was astonished, and Mr. Damon likewise, when they heard the story of Tom and Ned, is stating it mildly.

"Come on!" exclaimed the scientist, as Tom finished, "we must see this Goosal at once. If my map is destroyed, and it seems to be, this old Indian may be our only hope. Where did he say the buried city was, Tom?"

"Oh, somewhere in this vicinity, as nearly as I could make out. But you'd better talk with him yourself. We didn't say anything about the idol of gold."

"That's right. It's just as well to let the natives think we are only after ordinary relics."

"Bless my insurance policy!" gasped Mr. Damon. "It does not seem possible that we are on the right track."

"Well, I think we are, from what little information Goosal gave us," remarked Tom. "This buried city of his must be a wonderful place."

"It is, if it is what I take it to be," agreed the professor. "I told you I would bring you to a land of wonders, Tom Swift, and they have hardly begun yet. Come, I am anxious to talk to Goosal."

In order that the Indians in the Bumper camp might not hear rumors of the new plan to locate the hidden city, and, at the same time, to keep rumors from spreading to the camp of the rivals, the scientist and his friends started a new shaft, and put a shift of men at work on it.

"We'll pretend we are on the right track, and very busy," said Tom. "That will fool Beecher."

"Are you glad to know he did not take your map Professor Bumper?" asked Mr. Damon.

"Well, yes. It is hard to believe such things of a fellow scientist."

"If he didn't take it he wanted to," said Tom. "And he has done, or will do, things as unsportsmanlike."

"Oh, you are hardly fair, perhaps, Tom," commented Ned.

"Um!" was all the answer he received.

With the Indians in camp busy on the excavation work, and having ascertained that similar work was going on in the Beecher outfit, Professor Bumper, with Mr. Damon and the young men, set off to visit the Indian village and listen to Goosal's story. They passed the place where Tom had slain the jaguar, but nothing was left but the bones; the ants, vultures and jungle animals having picked them clean in the night.

On the arrival of Tom and his friends at the Indian's hut, Goosal told, in language which Professor Bumper could understand, the ancient legend of the buried city as he had had it from his grandfather.

"But is that all you know about it, Goosal?" asked the savant.

"No, Learned One. It is true most of what I have told you was told to me by my father and his father's father. But I—I myself—with these eyes, have looked upon the lost city."

"You have!" cried the professor, this time in English. "Where? When? Take us to it! How do you get here?"

"Through the cavern of the dead," was the answer when the questions were modified.

"Bless my diamond ring!" exclaimed Mr. Damon, when Professor Bumper translated the reply. "What does he mean?"

And then, after some talk, this information came out. Years before, when Goosal was a young man, he had been taken by his grandfather on a journey through the jungle. They stopped one day at the foot of a high mountain, and, clearing away the brush and stones at a certain place, an entrance to a great cavern was revealed. This, it appeared, was the Indian burial ground, and had been used for generations.

Goosal, though in fear and trembling, was lead through it, and came to another cavern, vaster than the first. And there he saw strange and wonderful sights, for it was the remains of a buried city, that had once been the home of a great and powerful tribe unlike the Indians—the ancient Mayas it would seem.

"Can you take us to this cavern?" asked the professor.

"Yes," answered Goosal. "I will lead to it those who saved the life of Tal—them and their friends. I will take you to the lost city!"

"Good!" cried Mr. Damon, when this had been translated. "Now let Beecher try to play any more tricks on us! Ho! for the cavern and the lost city of Kurzon."

"And the idol of gold," said Tom Swift to himself. "I hope we can get it ahead of Beecher. Perhaps if I can help in that—Oh, well, here's hoping, that's all!" and a little smile curved his lips.

Greatly excited by the strange news, but maintaining as calm an air outwardly as possible, so as not to excite the Indians, Tom and his friends returned to camp to prepare for their trip. Goosal had said the cavern lay distant more than a two-days' journey into the jungle.

CHAPTER XXII

THE STORM

"Now," remarked Tom, once they were back again in their camp, "we must go about this trip to the cavern in a way that will cause no suspicion over there as to what our object is," and he nodded in the direction of the quarters of his rival.

"Do you mean to go off quietly?" asked Ned.

"Yes. And to keep the work going on here, at these shafts," put in the scientist, "so that if any of their spies happen to come here they will think we still believe the buried city to be just below us. To that end we must keep the Indians digging, though I am convinced now that it is useless."

Accordingly preparations were made for an expedition into the jungle under the leadership of Goosal. Tal had not sufficiently recovered from the jaguar wounds to go with the party, but the old man, in spite of his years, was hale and hearty and capable of withstanding hardships.

One of the most intelligent of the Indians was put in charge of the digging gangs as foreman, and told to keep them at work, and not to let them stray. Tolpec, whose brother Tom had tried to save, proved a treasure. He agreed to remain behind and look after the interests of his friends, and see that none of their baggage or stores were taken.

"Well, I guess we're as ready as we ever shall be," remarked Tom, as the cavalcade made ready to start. Mules carried the supplies that were to be taken into the jungle, and others of the sturdy animals were to be ridden by the travelers. The trail was not an easy one, Goosal warned them.

Tom and his friends found it even worse than they had expected, for all their experience in jungle and mountain traveling. In places it was necessary to dismount and lead the mules along, sometimes pushing and dragging them. More than once the trail fairly hung on the edge of some almost bottomless gorge, and again it wound its way between great walls of rock, so poised that they appeared about to topple over and crush the travelers. But they kept on with dogged patience, through many hardships.

To add to their troubles they seemed to have entered the abode of the fiercest mosquitoes encountered since coming to Honduras. At times it was necessary to ride along with hats covered with mosquito netting, and hands encased in gloves.

They had taken plenty of condensed food with them, and they did not suffer in this respect. Game, too, was plentiful and the electric rifles of Tom and Ned added to the larder.

One night, after a somewhat sound sleep induced by hard travel on the trail that day, Tom awoke to hear some one or something moving about among their goods, which included their provisions.

"Who's there?" asked the young inventor sharply, as he reached for his electric rifle.

There was no answer, but a rattling of the pans.

"Speak, or I'll fire!" Tom warned, adding this in such Spanish as he could muster, for he thought it might be one of the Indians. No reply came, and then, seeing by the light of the stars a dark form moving in front of the tent occupied by himself and Ned, Tom fired.

There was a combined grunt and squeal of pain, then a savage growl, and Ned yelled:

"What's the matter, Tom?" for he had been awakened, and heard the crackle of the electrical discharge.

"I don't know," Tom answered. "But I shot something—or somebody!"

"Maybe some of Beecher's crowd," ventured his chum. But when they got their electric torches, and focused them on the inert, black object, it was found to be a bear which had come to nose about the camp for dainty morsels.

Bruin was quite dead, and as he was in prime condition there was a feast of bear meat at the following dinner. The white travelers found it rather too strong for their palates, but the Indians reveled in it.

It was shortly after noon the next day, when Goosal, after remarking that a storm seemed brewing, announced that they would be at the entrance to the cavern in another hour.

"Good!" cried Professor Bumper. "At last we are near the buried city."

"Don't be too sure," advised Mr. Damon, "We may be disappointed. Though I hope not for your sake, my dear Professor."

Goosal now took the lead, and the old Indian, traveling on foot, for he said he could better look for the old landmark that way than on the back of a mule, walked slowly along a rough cliff.

"Here, somewhere, is the entrance to the cavern," said the aged man. "It was many years ago that I was here—many years. But it seems as though yesterday. It is little changed."

Indeed little did change in that land of wonders. Only nature caused what alterations there were. The hand of man had long been absent.

Slowly Goosal walked along the rocky trail, on one side a sheer rock, towering a hundred feet or more toward the sky. On the other side a deep gash leading to a great fertile valley below.

Suddenly the old man paused, and looked about him as though uncertain. Then, more slowly still, he put out his hand and pulled at some bushes that grew on a ledge of the rock. They came away, having no depth of earth, and a small opening was disclosed.

"It is here," said Goosal quietly. "The entrance to the cavern that leads to the burial place of the dead, and the city that is dead also. It is here."

He stood aside while the others hurried forward. It took but a few minutes to prove that he was right—at least as to the existence of the cavern—for the four men were soon peering into the opening.

"Come on!" cried Tom, impetuously.

"Wait a moment," suggested the professor, "Sometimes the air in these places is foul. We must test it." But a torch one of the Indians threw in burned with a steady glow. That test was conclusive at least. They made ready to enter.

Torches of a light bark, that glowed with a steady flame and little smoke, had been provided, as well as a good supply of electric dry-battery lamps, and the way into the cavern was thus well lighted. At first the Indians were afraid to enter, but a word or two from Goosal reassured them, and they followed Professor Bumper, Tom, and the others into the cavern.

For several hundred feet there was nothing remarkable about the cave. It was like any other cavern of the mountains, though wonderful for the number of crystal formations on the root and walls—formations that sparkled like a million diamonds in the flickering lights.

"Talk about a wonderland!" cried Tom. "This is fairyland!"

A moment later, as Goosal walked on beside the professor and Tom, the aged Indian came to a pause, and, pointing ahead, murmured:

"The city of the dead!"

They saw the niches cut in the rock walls, niches that held the countless bones of those who had died many, many years before. It was a vast Indian grave.

"Doubtless a wealth of material of historic interest here," said Professor Bumper, flashing his torch on the skeletons. "But it will keep. Where is the city you spoke of, Goosal?"

"Farther on, Senor. Follow me."

Past the stone graves they went, deeper and deeper into the great cave. Their footsteps echoed and re-echoed. Suddenly Tom, who with Ned had gone a little ahead, came to a sudden halt and said:

"Well, this may be a burial place sure enough, but I think I see something alive all right—if it isn't a ghost."

He pointed ahead. Surely those were lights flickering and moving about, and, yes, there were men carrying them. The Bumper party came to a surprised halt. The other lights advanced, and then, to the great astonishment of Professor Bumper and his friends, there confronted them in the cave several scientists of Professor Beecher's party and a score or more of Indians. Professor Hylop, who was known to Professor Bumper, stepped forward and asked sharply:

"What are you doing here?"

"I might ask you the same thing," was the retort.

"You might, but you would not be answered," came sharply. "We have a right here, having discovered this cavern, and we claim it under a concession of the Honduras Government. I shall have to ask you to withdraw."

"Do you mean leave here?" asked Mr Damon.

"That is it, exactly. We first discovered this cave. We have been conducting explorations in it for several days, and we wish no outsiders."

"Are you speaking for Professor Beecher?" asked Tom.

"I am. But he is here in the cave, and will speak for himself if you desire it. But I represent him, and I order you to leave. If you do not go peaceably we will use force. We have plenty of it," and he glanced back at the Indians grouped behind him—scowling savage Indians.

"We have no wish to intrude," observed Professor Bumper, "and I fully recognize the right of prior discovery. But one member of our party (he did not say which one) was in this cave many years ago. He led us to it."

"Ours is a government concession!" exclaimed Professor Hylop harshly. "We want no intruders! Go!" and he pointed toward the direction whence Tom's party had come.

"Drive them out!" he ordered the Indians in Spanish, and with muttered threats the dark-skinned men advanced toward Tom and the others.

"You need not use force," said Professor Bumper.

He and Professor Hylop had quarreled bitterly years before on some scientific matter, and the matter was afterward found to be wrong. Perhaps this made him vindictive.

Tom stepped forward and started to protest, but Professor Bumper interposed.

"I guess there is no help for it but to go. It seems to be theirs by right of discovery and government concession," he said, in disappointed tone. "Come friends"; and dejectedly they retraced their steps.

Followed by the threatening Indians, the Bumper party made its way back to the entrance. They had hoped for great things, but if the cavern gave access to the buried city—the ancient city of Kurzon on the chief altar of which stood the golden idol, Quitzel—it looked as though they were never to enter it.

"We'll have to get our Indians and drive those fellows out!" declared Tom. "I'm not going to be beaten this way—and by Beecher!"

"It is galling," declared Professor Bumper. "Still he has right on his side, and I must give in to priority, as I would expect him to. It is the unwritten law."

"Then we've failed!" cried Tom bitterly.

"Not yet," said Professor Bumper. "If I can not unearth that buried city I may find another in this wonderland. I shall not give up."

"Hark! What's that noise?" asked Tom, as they approached the entrance to the cave.

"Sounds like a great wind blowing," commented Ned.

It was. As they stood in the entrance they looked out to find a fierce storm raging. The wind was sweeping down the rocky trail, the rain was falling in veritable bucketfuls from the overhanging cliff, and deafening thunder and blinding lightning roared and flashed.

"Surely you would not drive us out in this storm," said Professor Bumper to his former rival.

"You can not stay in the cave! You must get out!" was the answer, as a louder crash of thunder than usual seemed to shake the very mountain.

CHAPTER XXIII

ENTOMBED ALIVE

For an instant Tom and his friends paused at the entrance to the wonderful cavern, and looked at the raging storm. It seemed madness to venture out into it, yet they had been driven from the cave by those who had every right of discovery to say who, and who should not, partake of its hospitality.

"We can't go out into that blow!" cried Ned. "It's enough to loosen the very mountains!"

"Let's stay here and defy them!" murmured Tom. "If the—if what we seek—is here we have as good a right to it as they have."

"We must go out," said Professor Bumper simply. "I recognize the right of my rival to dispossess us."

"He may have the right, but it isn't human," said Mr. Damon. "Bless my overshoes! If Beecher himself were here he wouldn't have the heart to send us out in this storm."

"I would not give him the satisfaction of appealing to him," remarked Professor Bumper. "Come, we will go out. We have our ponchos, and we are not fair-weather explorers. If we can't get to the lost city one way we will another. Come my friends."

And despite the downpour, the deafening thunder and the lightning that seemed ready to sear one's eyes, he walked out of the cave entrance, followed by Tom and the others.

"Come on!" cried Tom, in a voice he tried to render confident, as they went out into the terrible storm. "We'll beat 'em yet!"

The rain fell harder than ever. Small torrents were now rushing down the trail, and it was only a question of a few minutes before the place where they stood would be a raging river, so quickly does the rain collect in the mountains and speed toward the valleys.

"We must take to the forest!" cried Tom. "There'll be some shelter there, and I don't like the way the geography of this place is behaving. There may be a landslide at any moment."

As he spoke he motioned upward through the mist of the rain to the sloping side of the mountain towering above them. Loose stones were beginning to roll down, accompanied by patches of earth loosened by the water. Some of the patches carried with them bunches of grass and small bushes.

"Yes, it will be best to move into the jungle," said the professor. "Goosal, you had better take the lead."

It was wonderful to see how well the aged Indian bore up in spite of his years, and walked on ahead. They had left their mules tethered some distance back, in a sheltering clump of trees, and they hoped the animals would be safe.

The guide found a place where they could leave the trail, though going down a dangerous slope, and take to the forest. As carefully as possible they descended this, the rain continuing to fall, the wind to blow, the lightning to sizzle all about them and the thunder to boom in their ears.

They went on until they were beneath the shelter of the thick jungle growth of trees, which kept off some of the pelting drops.

"This is better!" exclaimed Ned, shaking his poncho and getting rid of some of the water that had settled on it.

"Bless my overcoat!" cried Mr. Damon. "We seem to have gotten out of the frying pan into the fire!"

"How?" asked Tom. "We are partly sheltered here, though had we stayed in the cave in spite of—"

A deafening crash interrupted him, and following the flash one of the giant trees of the forest was seen to blaze up and then topple over.

"Struck by lightning!" yelled Ned.

"Yes; and it may happen to us!" exclaimed Mr. Damon. "We were safer from the lightning in the open. Maybe—"

Again came an interruption, but this time a different one. The very ground beneath their feet seemed to be shaking and trembling.

"What is it?" gasped Ned, while Goosal fell on his knees and began fervently to pray.

"It's an earthquake!" yelled Tom Swift.

As he spoke there came another sound—the sound of a mass of earth in motion. It came from the direction of the mountain trail they had just left. They looked toward it and their horror-stricken eyes saw the whole side of the mountain sliding down.

Slowly at first the earth slid down, but constantly gathering force and speed. In the face of this new disaster the rain seemed to have ceased and the thunder and lightning to be less severe. It was as though one force of nature gave way to the other.

"Look! Look!" gasped Ned.

In silence, which was broken now only by a low and ominous rumble, more menacing than had been the awful fury of the elements, the travelers looked.

Suddenly there was a quicker movement of seemingly one whole section of the mountain. Great rocks and trees, carried down by the appalling force of the landslide were slipping over the trail, obliterating it as though it had never existed.

"There goes the entrance to the cavern!" cried Ned, and as the others looked to where he pointed they saw the hole in the side of the mountain—the mouth of the cave that led to the lost city of Kurzon—completely covered by thousands of tons of earth and stones.

"That's the end of them!" exclaimed Tom, as the rumble of the earthquake died away.

"Of—" Ned stopped, his eyes staring.

"Of Professor Beecher's party. They're entombed alive!"

CHAPTER XXIV

THE REVOLVING STONE

Stunned, not alone by the realization of the awfulness of the fate of their rivals, but also by the terrific storm and the effect of the earthquake and the landslide, Tom and his friends remained for a moment gazing toward the mouth of the cavern, now completely out of sight, buried by a mass of broken trees, tangled bushes, rocks and earth. Somewhere, far beyond that mass, was the Beecher party, held prisoners in the cave that formed the entrance to the buried city.

Tom was the first to come to a realization of what was needed to be done.

"We must help them!" he exclaimed, and it was characteristic of him that he harbored no enmity.

"How?" asked Ned.

"We must get a force of Indians and dig them out," was the prompt answer.

At Tom's vigorous words Professor Bumper's forces were energized into action, and he stated: "Fortunately we have plenty of excavating tools. We may be in time to save them. Come on! the storm seems to have passed as suddenly as it came up, and the earthquake, which, after all did not cover a wide area, seems to be over. We must start the work of rescue at once. We must go back to camp and get all the help we can muster."

The storm, indeed, seemed to be over, but it was no easy matter to get back over the soggy, rain-soaked ground to the trail they had left to take shelter in the forest. Fortunately the earthquake had not involved that portion where they had left their mules, but most of the frightened animals had broken loose, and it was some little time before they could all be caught.

"It is no use to try to get back to camp tonight," said Tom, when the last of the pack and saddle animals had been corralled. "It is getting late and there is no telling the condition of the trail. We must stay here until morning."

"But what about them?" and Mr. Damon nodded in the direction of the entombed ones.

"We can help them best by waiting until the beginning of a new day," said the professor. "We shall need a large force, and we could not bring it up tonight. Besides, Tom is right, and if we tried to go along the trail after dark, torn and disturbed as it is bound to be by the rain, we might get into difficulties ourselves. No, we must camp here until morning and then go for help."

They all decided finally this was best. The professor, too, pointed out that their rivals were in a large and roomy cave, not likely to suffer from lack of air nor food or water, since they must have supplies with them.

"The only danger is that the cave has been crushed in," added Tom; "but in that event we would be of no service to them anyhow."

The night seemed very long, and it was a most uncomfortable one, because of the shock and exertions through which the party had passed. Added to this was the physical discomfort caused by the storm.

But in time there was the light in the east that meant morning was at hand, and with it came action. A hasty breakfast, cups of steaming coffee forming a most welcome part, put them all in better condition, and once more they were on their way, heading back to the main camp where they had left their force of Indians.

"My!" exclaimed Tom, as they made their way slowly along, "it surely was some storm! Look at those big trees uprooted over there. They're almost as big as the giant redwoods of California, and yet they were bowled over as if they were tenpins."

"I wonder if the wind did it or the earthquake," ventured Mr. Damon.

"No wind could do that," declared Ned. "It must have been the landslide caused by the earthquake."

"The wind could do it if the ground was made soft by the rain; and that was probably what did it," suggested Tom.

"There is no harm in settling the point," commented Professor Bumper. "It is not far off our trail, and will take only a few minutes to go over to the trees. I should like to get some photographs to accompany an article that perhaps I shall write on the effects of sudden and severe tropical storms. We will go to look at the overturned trees and then we'll hurry on to camp to get the rescue party."

The uprooted trees lay on one side of the mountain trail, perhaps a mile from the mouth of the cave which had been covered over, entombing the Beecher party. Leaving the mules in charge of one of the Indians, Professor Bumper and his friends, accompanied by Goosal, approached the fallen trees. As they neared them they saw that in falling the trees had lifted with their roots a large mass of earth and imbedded rocks that had clung to the twisted and gnarled fibers. This mass was as large as a house.

"Look at the hole left when the roots pulled out!" cried Ned. "Why, it's like the crater of a small volcano!" he added. And, as they stood on the edge of it looking curiously at the hole made, the others agreed with Tom's chum.

Professor Bumper was looking about, trying to ascertain if there were any evidences of the earthquake in the vicinity, when Tom, who had cautiously gone a little way down into the excavation caused by the fallen trees, uttered a cry of surprise.

"Look!" he shouted. "Isn't that some sort of tunnel or underground passage?" and he pointed to a square opening, perhaps seven feet high and nearly as broad, which extended, no one knew where, downward and onward from the side of the hole made by the uprooting of the trees.

"It's an underground passage all right," said Professor Bumper eagerly; "and not a natural one, either. That was fashioned by the hand of man, if I am any judge. It seems to go right under the mountain, too. Friends, we must explore this! It may be of the utmost importance! Come, we have our electric torches, and we shall need them, for it's very dark in there," and he peered into the passage in front of which they all stood now. It seemed to have been tunneled through the earth, the sides being lined by either slabs of stone, or walls made by a sort of concrete.

"But what about the rescue work?" asked Mr. Damon.

"I am not forgetting Professor Beecher and his friends," answered the scientist.

"Perhaps this may be a better means of rescuing them than by digging them out, which will take a week at least," observed Tom.

"This a better way?" asked Ned, pointing to the tunnel.

"That's it," confirmed the savant. "If you will notice it extends back in the direction of the cave from which we were driven. Now if there is a buried city beneath all this jungle, this mountain of earth and stones, the accumulation of centuries, it is probably on the bottom of some vast cavern. It is my opinion that we were only in one end of that cavern, and this may be the entrance to another end of it."

"Then," asked Mr. Damon, "do you mean that we can enter here, get into the cave that contains the buried city, or part of it, and find there Beecher and his friends?"

"That's it. It is possible, and if we could it would save an immense lot of work, and probably be a surer way to save their lives than by digging a tunnel through the landslide to find the mouth of the cave where we first entered."

"It's a chance worth taking," said Mr. Damon. "Of course it is a chance. But then everything connected with this expedition is; so one is no worse than another. As you say, we may find the entombed men more easily this way than any other."

"I wonder," said Tom slowly, "if, by any chance, we shall find, through this passage, the lost city we are looking for."

"And the idol of gold," added Ned.

"Goosal, do you know anything about this?" asked Professor Bumper. "Did you ever hear of another passage leading to the cave where you saw the ancient city?"

"No, Learned One, though I have heard stories about there being many cities, or parts of a big one, beneath the mountain, and when it was above ground there were many entrances to it."

"That settles it!" cried the professor in English, having talked to Goosal in Spanish. "We'll try this and see where it leads."

They entered the stone-lined passage. In spite of the fact that it had probably been buried and concealed from light and air for centuries, as evidenced by the growth of the giant trees above it, the air was fresh.

"And this is one reason," said Tom, in commenting on this fact, "why I believe it leads to some vast cavern which is connected in some fashion with the outer air. Well, perhaps we shall soon make a discovery."

Eagerly and anxiously the little party pressed forward by the light of the pocket electric lamps. They were obsessed by two thoughts—what they might find and the necessity for aiding in the rescue of their rivals.

On and on they went, the darkness illuminated only by the torches they carried. But they noticed that the air was still fresh, and that a gentle wind blew toward them. The passage was undoubtedly artificial, a tunnel made by the hands of men now long crumbled into dust. It had a slightly upward slope, and this, Professor Bumper said, indicated that it was bored upward and perhaps into the very heart of the mountain somewhere in the interior of which was the Beecher party.

Just how far they went they did not know, but it must have been more than two miles. Yet they did not tire, for the way was smooth.

Suddenly Tom, who, with Professor Bumper, was in the lead, uttered a cry, as he held his torch above his head and flashed it about in a circle.

"We're blocked!" he exclaimed. "We're up against a stone wall!"

It was but too true. Confronting them, and extending from side to side across the passage and from roof to floor, was a great rough stone. Immense and solid it seemed when they pushed on it in vain.

"Nothing short of dynamite will move that," said Ned in despair. "This is a blind lead. We'll have to go back."

"But there must be something on the other side of that stone," cried Tom. "See, it is pierced with holes, and through them comes a current of air. If we could only move the stone!"

"I believe it is an ancient door," remarked Professor Bumper.

Eagerly and frantically they tried to move it by their combined weight. The stone did not give the fraction of the breadth of a hair.

"We'll have to go back and get some of your big tunnel blasting powder, Tom," suggested Ned.

As he spoke old Goosal glided forward. He had remained behind them in the passage while they were trying to move the rock. Now he said something in Spanish.

"What does he mean?" asked Ned.

"He asks that he be allowed to try," translated Professor Bumper. "Sometimes, he says, there is a secret way of opening stone doors in these underground caves. Let him try."

Goosal seemed to be running his fingers lightly over the outer edge of the door. He was muttering to himself in his Indian tongue.

Suddenly he uttered an exclamation, and, as he did so, there was a noise from the door itself. It was a grinding, scraping sound, a rumble as though rocks were being rolled one against the other.

Then the astonished eyes of the adventurers saw the great stone door revolve on its axis and swing to one side, leaving a passage open through which they could pass. Goosal had discovered the hidden mechanism.

What lay before them?

CHAPTER XXV

THE IDOL OF GOLD

"Forward! cried Tom Swift.

"Where?" asked Mr Damon, hanging back for an instant. "Bless my compass, Tom! *Do* you know where you're going?"

"I haven't the least idea, but it must lead to something, or the ancients who made this revolving stone door wouldn't have taken such care to block the passage."

"Ask Goosal if he knows anything about it," suggested Mr. Damon to the professor.

"He says he never was here before," translated the savant, "but years ago, when he went into the hidden city by the cave we left yesterday, he saw doors like this which opened this way."

"Then we're on the right track!" cried Tom. "If this is the same kind of door, it must lead to the same place. Ho for Kurzon and the idol of gold!"

As they passed through the stone door, Tom and Professor Bumper tried to get some idea of the mechanism by which it worked. But they found this impossible, it being hidden within the stone itself or in the adjoining walls. But, in order that it might not close of itself and entomb them, the portal was blocked open with stones found in the passage.

"It's always well to have a line of retreat open," said Tom. "There's no telling what may lie beyond us."

For a time there seemed to be nothing more than the same passage along which they had come. Then the passage suddenly widened, like the large end of a square funnel. Upward and outward the stone walls swept, and they saw dimly before them, in the light of their torches, a vast cavern, seemingly formed by the falling in of mountains, which, in toppling over, had met overhead in a sort of rough arch, thus protecting, in a great measure, that which lay beneath them.

Goosal, who had brought with him some of the fiber bark torches, set a bundle of them aflame. As they flared up, a wondrous sight was revealed to Tom Swift and his friends.

Stretching out before them, as though they stood at the end of an elevated street and gazed down on it, was a city—a large city, with streets, houses, open squares, temples, statues, fountains, dry for centuries—a buried and forgotten city—a city in ruins—a city of the dead, now dry as dust, but still a city, or, rather, the strangely preserved remains of one.

"Look!" whispered Tom. A louder voice just then, would have seemed a sacrilege. "Look!"

"Is it what we are looking for?" asked Ned in a low voice.

"I believe it is," replied the professor. "It is the lost city of Kurzon, or one just like it. And now if we can find the idol of gold our search will be ended—at least the major part of it."

"Where did you expect to find the idol?" asked Tom.

"It should be in the main temple. Come, we will walk in the ancient streets—streets where no feet but ours have trod in many centuries. Come!"

In eager silence they pressed on through this newly discovered wonderland. For it was a wonderful city, or had been. Though much of it was in ruins, probably caused by an earthquake or an eruption from a volcano, the central portion, covered as it was by the overtoppling mountains that formed the arching roof, was well preserved.

There were rude but beautiful stone buildings. There were archways; temples; public squares; and images, not at all beautiful, for they seemed to be of man-monsters—doubtless ancient gods. There were smoothly paved streets; wondrously carved fountains, some in ruins, all now as dry as bone, but which must have been places of beauty where youths and maidens gathered in the ancient days.

Of the ancient population there was not a trace left. Tom and his friends penetrated some of the houses, but not so much as a bone or a heap of mouldering dust showed where the remains of the people were. Either they had fled at the approaching doom of the city and were buried elsewhere, or some strange fire or other force of nature had consumed and obliterated them.

"What a wealth of historic information I shall find here!" murmured Professor Bumper, as he caught sight of many inscriptions in strange characters on the walls and buildings. "I shall never get to the end of them."

"But what about the idol of gold?" asked Mr. Damon, "Do you think you'll find that?"

"We must hurry on to the temple over there," said the scientist, indicating a building further along.

"And then we must see about rescuing your rivals, Professor," put in Tom.

"Yes, Tom. But fortunately we are on the ground here before them," agreed the professor.

Undoubtedly it was the chief temple, or place of worship, of the long-dead race which the explorers now entered. It was a building beautiful in its barbaric style, and yet simple. There were massive walls, and a great inner court, at the end of which seemed to be some sort of altar. And then, as they lighted fresh torches, and pressed forward with them and their electric lights, they saw that which caused a cry of satisfaction to burst from all of them.

"The idol of gold!"

Yes, there it squatted, an ugly, misshapen, figure, a cross between a toad and a gila monster, half man, half beast, with big red eyes—rubies probably—that gleamed in the repulsive golden face. And the whole figure, weighing many pounds, seemed to be of SOLID GOLD!

Eagerly the others followed Professor Bumper up the altar steps to the very throne of the golden idol. The scientist touched it, tried to raise it and make sure of its solidity and material.

"This is it!" he cried. "It is the idol of gold! I have found— We have found it, for it belongs to all of us!"

"Hurray!" cried Tom Swift, and Ned and Mr. Damon joined in the cry.

There was no need for silence or caution now; and yet, as they stood about the squat and ugly figure, which, in spite of its hideousness, was worth a fortune intrinsically and as an antique, they heard from the direction of the stone passage a noise.

"What is it?" asked Tom Swift.

There was a murmur of voices.

"Indians!" cried Professor Bumper, recognizing the language—a mixture of Spanish and Indian.

The cave was illuminated by the glare of other torches which seemed to rush forward. A moment later it was seen that they were being carried by a number of Indians.

"Friends," murmured Goosal, using the Spanish term, "Amigos."

"They are our own Indians!" cried Tom Swift. "I see Tolpec!" and he pointed to the native who had deserted from Jacinto's force to help them.

"How did they get here?" asked Professor Bumper.

This was quickly told. In their camp, where, under the leadership of Tolpec they had been left to do the excavating, the natives had heard, seen and felt the effects of the storm and the earthquake, though it did little damage in their vicinity. But they became alarmed for the safety of the professor and his party and, at Tolpec's suggestion, set off in search of them.

The Indians had seen, passing along the trail, the uprooted trees, and had noted the footsteps of the explorers going down to the stone passage. It was easy for them to determine that Tom and his friends had gone in, since the marks of their boots were plainly in evidence in the soft soil.

None of the Indians was as much wrought up over the discovery of Kurzon and the idol as were the white adventurers. The gold, of course, meant something to the natives, but they were indifferent to the wonders of the underground city. Perhaps they had heard too many legends concerning such things to be impressed.

"That statue is yours—all yours," said old Goosal when he had talked with his relatives and friends among the natives. "They all say what you find you keep, and we will help you keep it."

"That's good," murmured Professor Bumper. "There was some doubt in my mind as to our right to this, but after all, the natives who live in this land are the original owners, and if they pass title to us it is clear. That settles the last difficulty."

"Except that of getting the idol out," said Mr. Damon.

"Oh, we'll accomplish that!" cried Tom.

"I can hardly believe my good luck," declared Professor Bumper. "I shall write a whole book on this idol alone and then—"

Once more came an interruption. This time it was from another direction, but it was of the same character—an approaching band of torch-bearers. They were Indians, too, but leading them were a number of whites.

And at their head was no less personage than Professor Beecher himself.

For a moment, as the three parties stood together in the ancient temple, in the glare of many torches, no one spoke. Then Professor Bumper found his voice.

"We are glad to see you," he said to his rival. "That is glad to see you alive, for we saw the landslide bury you. And we were coming to dig you out. We thought this cave—the cave of the buried city—would lead us to you easier than by digging through the slide. We have just discovered this idol," and he put his hand on the grim golden image.

"Oh, you have discovered it, have you?" asked Professor Beecher, and his voice was bitter.

"Yes, not ten minutes ago. The natives have kindly acknowledged my right to it under the law of priority. I am sorry but—"

With a look of disgust and chagrined disappointment on his face, Professor Beecher turned to the other scientists and said:

"Let us go. We are too late. He has what I came after."

"Well, it is the fortune of war—and discovery," put in Mr. Hardy, one of the party who seemed the least ill-natured. "Your luck might have been ours, Professor Bumper. I congratulate you."

"Thank you! Are you sure your party is all right—not in need of assistance? How did you get out of the place you were buried?"

"Thank you! We do not require any help. It was good of you to think of us. But we got out the way we came in. We did not enter the tunnel as you did, but came in through another entrance which was not closed by the landslide. Then we made a turn through a gateway in a tunnel connecting with ours—a gateway which seems to have been opened by the earthquake—and we came here, just now.

"Too late, I see, to claim the discovery of the idol of gold," went on Mr. Hardy. "But I trust you will be generous, and allow us to make observations of the buildings and other relics."

"As much as you please, and with the greatest pleasure in the world," was the prompt answer of Professor Bumper. "All I lay sole claim to is the golden idol. You are at liberty to take whatever else you find in Kurzon and to make what observations you like."

"That is generous of you, and quite in contrast to—er—to the conduct of our leader. I trust he may awaken to a sense of the injustice he did you."

But Professor Beecher was not there to hear this. He had stalked away in anger.

"Humph!" grunted Tom. Then he continued: "That story about a government concession was all a fake, Professor, else he'd have put up a fight now. Contemptible sneak!"

In fact the story of Tom Swift's trip to the underground land of wonders is ended, for with the discovery of the idol of gold the main object of the expedition was accomplished. But their adventures were not over by any means, though there is not room in this volume to record them.

Suffice it to say that means were at once taken to get the golden image out of the cave of the ancient city. It was not accomplished without hard work, for the gold was heavy, and Professor Bumper would not, naturally, consent to the shaving off of so much as an ear or part of the flat nose, to say nothing of one of the half dozen extra arms and legs with which the ugly idol was furnished.

Finally it was safely taken out of the cave, and along the stone passage to the opening formed by the overthrown trees, and thence on to camp.

And at the camp a surprise awaited Tom.

Some long-delayed mail had been forwarded from the nearest place of civilization and there were letters for all, including several for our hero. One in particular he picked out first and read eagerly.

"Well, is every little thing all right, Tom?" asked Ned, as he saw a cheerful grin spread itself over his chum's face.

"I should say it is, and then some! Look here, Ned. This is a letter from—"

"I know. Mary Nestor. Go on."

"How'd you guess?"

"Oh, I'm a mind-reader."

"Huh! Well, you know she was away when I went to call to say good-bye, and I was a little afraid Beecher had got an inside edge on me."

"Had he?"

"No, but he tried hard enough. He went to see Mary in Fayetteville, just as you heard, before he came on to join his party, but he didn't pay much of a visit to her."

"No?"

"No. Mary told him he'd better hurry along to Central America, or wherever it was he intended going, as she didn't care for him as much as he flattered himself she did."

"Good!" cried Ned. "Shake, old man. I'm glad!"

They shook hands.

"Well, what's the matter? Didn't you read all of her letter?" asked Ned when he saw his chum once more perusing the epistle.

"No. There's a postscript here."

> "'Sorry I couldn't see you before you left. It was a mistake, but when you come back——'"

"Oh, that part isn't any of your affair!" and, blushing under his tan, Tom thrust the letter into his pocket and strode away, while Ned laughed happily.

With the idol of gold safe in their possession, Professor Bumper's party could devote their time to making other explorations in the buried city. This they did, as is testified to by a long list of books and magazine articles since turned out by the scientist, dealing strictly with archaeological subjects, touching on the ancient Mayan race and its civilization, with particular reference to their system of computing time.

Professor Beecher, young and foolish, would not consent to delve into the riches of the ancient city, being too much chagrined over the loss of the idol. It seems he had really promised to give a part of it to Mary Nestor. But he never got the chance.

His colleagues, after their first disappointment at being beaten, joined forces with Professor Bumper in exploring the old city, and made many valuable discoveries.

In one point Professor Bumper had done his rival an injustice. That was in thinking Professor Beecher was responsible for the treachery of Jacinto. That was due to the plotter's own work. It was true that Professor Beecher had tentatively engaged Jacinto, and had sent word to him to keep other explorers away from the vicinity of the ancient city if possible; but Jacinto, who did not return Professor Bumper's money, as he had promised, had acted treacherously in order to enrich himself.

Professor Beecher had nothing to do with that, nor had he with the taking of the map, as has been seen, the loss of which, after all, was a blessing in disguise, for Kurzon would never have been located by following the directions given there, as it was very inaccurate.

In another point it was demonstrated that the old documents were at fault. This was in reference to the golden idol having been overthrown and another set up in its place, an act which had caused the destruction of Kurzon.

It is true that the city was destroyed, or rather, buried, but this catastrophe was probably brought about by an earthquake. And another great idol, one of clay, was found, perhaps a rival of Quitzel, but it was this clay image which was thrown down and broken, and not the golden one.

Perhaps an effort had been made, just before the burying of the city, to change idols and the system of worship, but Quitzel seemed to have held his own. The old manuscripts were not very reliable, it was found, except in general.

"Well, I guess this will hold Beecher for a while," said Tom, the night of the arrival of Mary's letter, and after he had written one in answer, which was dispatched by a runner to the nearest place whence mail could be forwarded.

"Yes, luck seems to favor you," replied Ned. "You've had a hand in the discovery of the idol of gold, and—"

"Yes. And I discovered something else I wasn't quite sure of," interrupted Tom, as he felt to make sure he had a certain letter safe in his pocket.

It was several weeks later that the explorations of Kurzon came to an end—a temporary end, for the rainy season set in, when the tropics are unsuitable for white men. Tom, Professor Bumper, Ned and Mr. Damon set sail for the United States, the valuable idol of gold safe on board.

And there, with their vessel plowing the blue waters of the Caribbean Sea, we will take leave of Tom Swift and his friends.

Made in the USA
Columbia, SC
03 December 2020